BOUND BY BETRAYAL

THE SEVERED SIGNET BOOK THREE
ELLE MALDONADO

Copyright © 2024 Elle Maldonado

All rights reserved. No part of this publication may be reproduced, distributed, or transmitted in any form or by any means, including photocopying, recording, or other electronic or mechanical methods, without the author's prior written permission, except in the case of brief quotations embodied in critical reviews.

This is a work of fiction. Any resemblance to actual events or persons, living or dead, is entirely coincidental.

Editing: Mackenzie Letson of Nice Girl, Naughty Edits
Cover Design: Haya In Designs
Interior Formatting: Mayonaka Designs

Bound by Betrayal is a dark romance.
It contains explicit content and depictions that
some may find triggering.

It is intended for readers 18+.

A complete list of triggers can be found here:
https://tr.ee/m-kuu-R8Rz

Or visit my social media:
https://www.instagram.com/authorellemaldonado

To the women who would drop to their knees and beg for it when he says, "My wife."

This one is for you…

Contents

Playlist	9
Amalia	11
Kai	23
Amalia	31
Kai	41
Amalia	47
Amalia	53
Kai	59
Kai	63
Amalia	71
Kai	81
Amalia	89
Amalia	97
Kai	105
Amalia	111
Kai	119
Kai	129
Amalia	139
Kai	145
Amalia	151
Kai	163
Amalia	169
Kai	177
Amalia	183
Amalia	193
Amalia	199

Kai	207
Kai	213
Amalia	221
Amalia	231
Amalia	239
Kai	245
Kai	253
Amalia	261
Amalia	269
Amalia	277
Kai	285
Amalia	295
Amalia	301
Kai	313
Kai	317
Amalia	325
About The Author	339
Acknowledgments	341

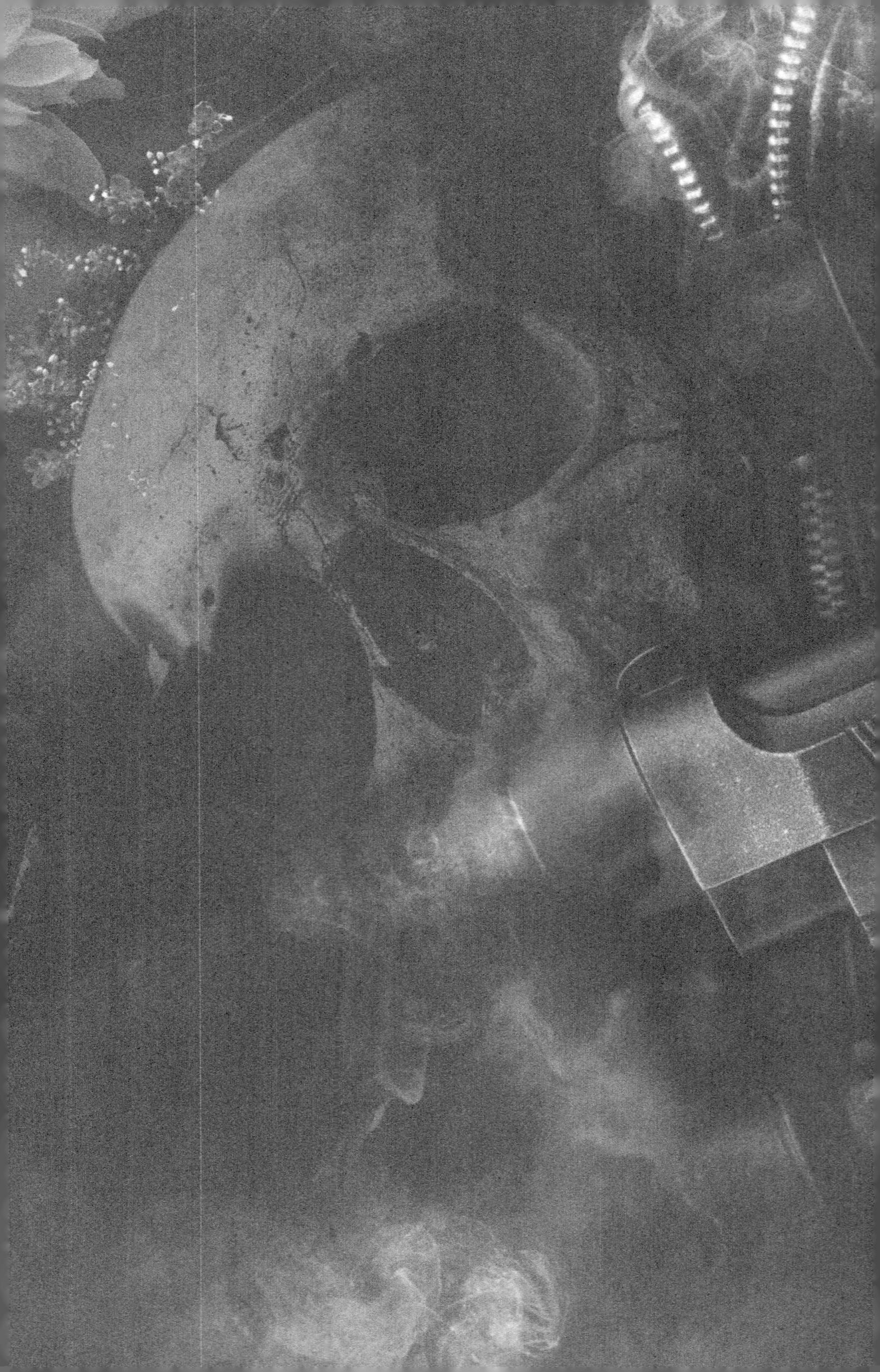

Playlist

La Llorona by Angela Aguilar
The Devil Wears Lace by Steven Rodriguez
Cold Blooded by Chris Grey
Criminal by Natti Natasha, Ozuna
Deja Tus Besos by Natti Natasha
Mala Santa by Becky G
Shackles by Steven Rodriguez
You Don't Own Me by Saygrace, G-Eazy
Please by Omido, Ex Habit
Addict by Don Louis
Greedy by 3slow2
Slow Down by Chase Atlantic
Too Sweet by Hozier
Monster by Chandler Leighton
Sin Pijama by Becky G, Natti Natasha
Us Against The World by Chris Grey
U in my head by Omido, Truu
Closer by Kings of Leon
Ride by Chris Grey

*More songs can be found on the Spotify playlist.

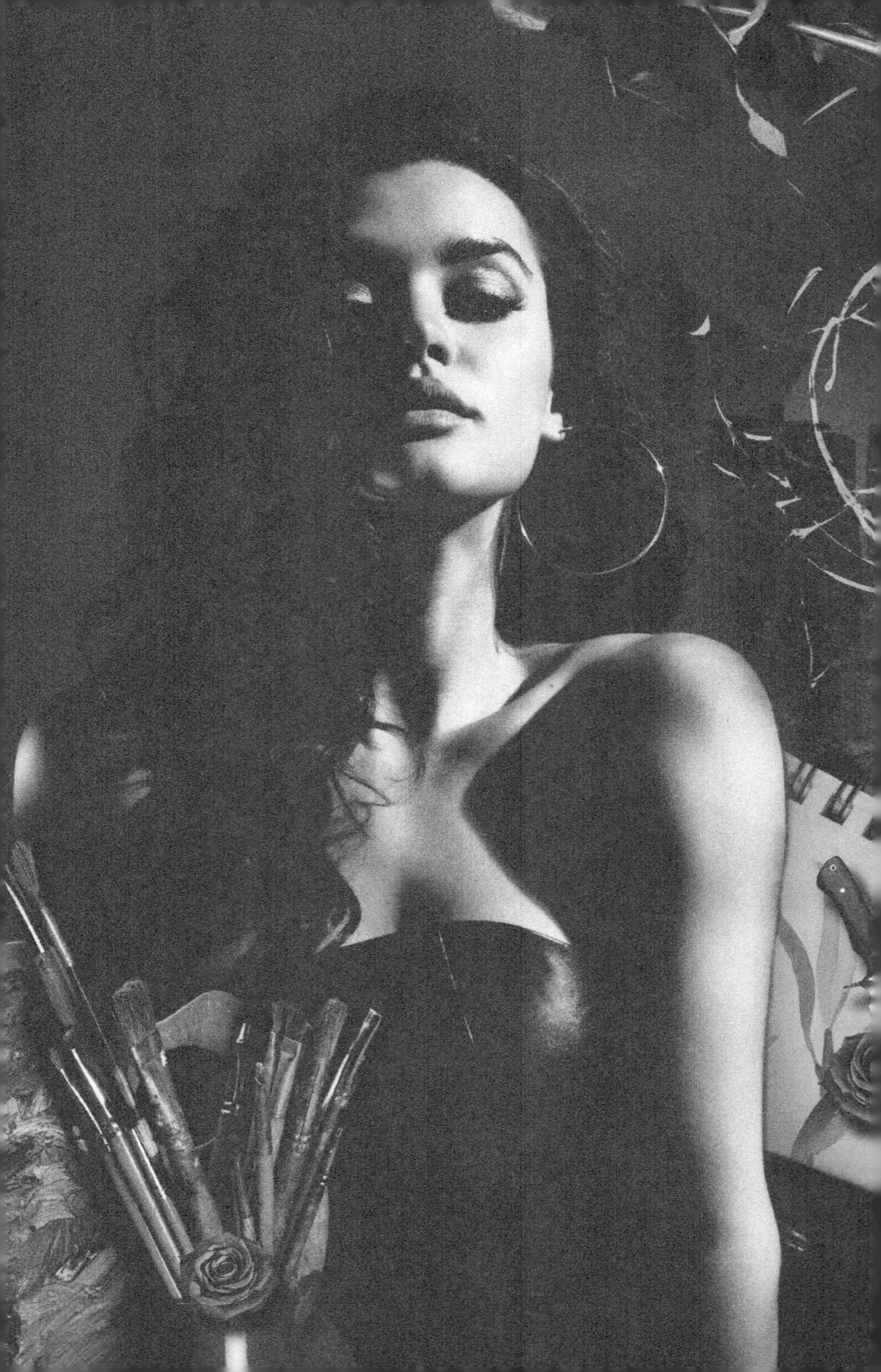

Chapter 1
Amalia

Dallas, Texas

THE heel of my boot hit the tarmac with a soft click as I stepped out of the car. Four more black SUVs lined the private runway, two on either side of mine. Their occupants were instructed to remain inside unless assistance was needed. My girls could be intimidating, and while I thoroughly enjoyed watching men squirm in their presence, it was imperative for this man to know I didn't need an entourage. That I was the woman in charge. He'd learn to fall in line and understand that our contract was merely a business transaction and nothing more.

Kai Cain.

Not my first choice. But the next best thing to his brother, nonetheless.

Marriage. The word alone was enough to make me want to spit. I didn't particularly despise the idea, but when it was forced upon me by some archaic tradition, I couldn't help feeling especially murderous.

Kai was the first to breach the exit of the private plane I'd sent, and my eyes caught the hard lines of muscle between an open collar and the tattoos branching against tanned skin. Where Derek was always polished and well-dressed, Kai had a more relaxed style, and I had to admit, it suited him.

The devil himself emerged next, a sleeping infant girl in his arms. I'd heard he'd married and had a child with the detective, yet the sight of the once ruthless assassin as a doting father and husband was still as unbelievable as the rumors. We briefly made eye contact across the distance, but he twisted around and extended a hand to his wife. The smile on his face was one I assumed he reserved only for her, though even through the softened expression, there still lived a darkness in his features. One I recognized well.

"The infamous Cain brothers," I said, with a grin and a hand on my hip as they approached. Both men barely nodded a greeting, and I couldn't have cared less. I supposed they had every reason to feel resentment toward the woman who was collecting on a debt that meant the forfeiture of freedom and choice. It was a luxury not afforded to me either, so they could fuck all the way off.

My gaze rolled to Eva, the once naked princess whose ass I'd saved. Literally. She returned my cynical smile, an arch in her brow. And I decided right then I liked her. "How was the flight?"

Wind whipped my hair, and a strand caught on red gloss between the seam of my lips. Not missing an opportunity to test the waters, I removed the errant tendril as my tongue slowly rolled across. Satisfaction warmed my chest when I noticed the slight tension in Kai's jaw as his eyes fixed on my mouth.

"It was smooth," the taller brother replied, unabashedly giving me a once-over.

The smoke behind his eyes let me know he liked what he saw. Kai and I had met in passing at the compound of that Russian bastard, Belov. At the time, there was far too much chaos, bloodshed, and adrenaline for a formal introduction, and I barely remembered what he looked like. But I'm questioning how I ever forgot in the first place.

Soft whimpers of the baby pulled my attention away from my soon-to-be husband… Even in my thoughts, those words were bitter, carrying with them the weight of resentment and impotence.

"She's beautiful," I said, my voice surprisingly tender as big brown eyes found mine from the safety of her father's arms. Valentina. She was a unique mix of Evangelina and Derek.

"Thank you," Eva said with pride.

Not surprised in the least, Derek hadn't bothered with a response.

"We should get going," I said, tilting my head toward an angry gray sky and motioning toward my waiting car. "The clouds are about to break open, and I just got my hair done."

Derek took Evangelina's hand and led them forward. Kai hung back, as if waiting for me to move as well.

"This doesn't have to be weird," I said, glancing over my shoulder as I started for the car. "It's simply a business. I get what I need, and you…"

"What do I get?" he bit back as he fell into step with me.

I stopped and turned toward him, leveling him with a cautionary glare. "You clear your brother's debt. Is that not the goal?"

Kai had a perfectly angular jaw, and I didn't miss the tension on his face behind the trimmed beard. "Most people pay their debts with currency, not in exchange for marriage."

"No one is forcing your hand, Kai Cain. As far as I know, you're here of your own will. Am I right?" I didn't take a step, not even as the heat of him neared my back or when he whispered close to my ear.

"Well, seeing as my brother is a little indisposed at the moment, what choice did I have?"

Denying the spark of electricity that sizzled across my skin at his proximity was pointless. So I allowed my eyes to close for several moments before twisting to face him, our bodies brushing, yet neither of us seemed bothered by the lack of distance.

"There's always a choice, Cain. Whether the outcome is a favorable one is irrelevant."

His gaze lifted beyond me, a subtle shake to his head. I didn't have to venture a guess as to who was on the receiving end of his silent communication. Derek would be stupid to try anything. He'd be dropped on the spot. My only regret would be the collateral damage of his wife and child caught in the crossfire. I was a bitch. True enough. But I didn't murder the innocent, let alone children.

"Well? I guess this is the point where you make that choice."

Blue eyes lowered to meet mine, the corners narrowing into suspicious slits. "That decision was made the moment you and your people came calling."

There was something alluring in those eyes and the way his mouth twitched. Even just a few minutes into our first genuine meeting, I could tell he was the more level-headed of the Cain duo, making it easy to forget that Kai's hands were just as thick with blood as his brother's. But behind his statement lived an implicit warning.

And I liked it.

"You and your brother are loyal men." I began my stride toward the car. "Or stupid."

He scoffed behind me but said nothing.

"*Señorita* Amalia." Felipe held the door as I approached. "I've gotten word that a produce truck has overturned about three miles from our exit, blocking the freeway. I've got a detour and informed the others if that's okay."

"Of course." He nodded, though his eyes were fixed behind me. "Felipe, this is Mr. Cain."

"Pleasure to meet you, sir."

Kai brushed my shoulder as he held out a hand to Felipe, and I couldn't decide if the gesture was intentional. But it made me pause all the same. I wasn't used to others invading my space or acts of disrespect…at least not by those who wished to keep all their limbs intact. Kai's eyes found mine when he addressed my driver, as if feeling my gaze.

"Pleasure is mine."

Maybe he hadn't meant for the words to roll off his tongue the way they had, but I found myself swallowing hard at the sound. I snapped my head forward and inhaled a long breath. Feeling flustered. Not even five minutes, and this man already had me slightly…confused.

I slid into the car without another word, just as fat raindrops pelted the vehicle's roof. Kai slipped in behind me, and I avoided him.

"Thank you for the car seat," Evangelina said, caressing her daughter's cheek. The baby had fallen asleep again.

"Of course." My cousin's daughter was just a few months older—which reminded me. "Derek, my cousin Sofía sends her regards."

He remained still as a statue, unfazed, though I was sure he remembered how he'd choked her out on the rooftop of that hotel in Manhattan when he'd come groveling for my help just over four years ago. Or perhaps he didn't. The man seemed to only have eyes for one woman, and I supposed that was commendable. Apart from my father, I didn't personally know of any man who remained faithful. While my mother was cherished, even then, I wouldn't vouch for him.

"Sofia?" Eva questioned, turning to her husband. He leaned in and whispered into her ear. She nodded, seemingly complacent with whatever he'd explained.

"You always travel this heavy?"

Kai looked out the car window as the other vehicles pulled out in front of and behind us.

"Do my girls make you uncomfortable, Cain? Emasculated?" The taunt fled my lips before I could stop it.

"Not in the slightest," he replied with a scoff, taking my retort in stride. The difference between the Cain brothers was glaring. Derek was a man of few words for those to whom he had no emotional ties. And Kai…

Well, I found myself taking in the sight of the man beside me again, his knee now grazing my thigh as he relaxed and did that spreading thing most men do. His long legs stretched, nearly reaching across the way. He was easily 6'4" or 6' 5".

Maybe I'd been distracted or lost in thought because his eyes were on me when I came back, saying something I couldn't process fast enough. "I'm sorry, what?"

"The cars ahead of us are stopping."

I peered through the windshield, and in that instant, the thunderous boom of an explosion stole my response and then rattled us with its aftershock. Reality seemed to slow. Derek and Kai lunged protectively toward Evangelina and the baby, and I gripped the seat, my heart staggering in my chest as another explosion shook us, only this time shattering the windows and catapulting us across the median. That was when I realized it wasn't just an explosion. Something had rammed us, sending the car into a series of rolls.

Glass and debris pierced my skin as the world seemed to collapse around us. Maybe I blacked out for a second, because the next thing I remembered was opening my eyes to a smoky cabin and the shrill ringing in my ears drowning out the chaos I knew was unfolding.

"Eva! Are you okay?" Derek's voice was the first to register, followed by the sharp cries of his daughter.

"I'm fine. Get Vali!"

I pulled a blade from my pocket and cut myself free of the seatbelt, hitting the roof of the upturned cabin with a painful thud. Shards of glass dug into my hands and knees as I crawled forward toward a broken window.

"Shit!" I cried out when I sliced my forearm with a piece of shrapnel.

"Amalia, you're bleeding. Are you okay?"

Kai pulled my hands into his, examining the wounds there. "What happened?"

He leaned in close, trying to speak over the infant's cries, surprising me when he pushed back my hair. "I think it's an ambush. Do you have more weapons? Ammo?"

I snatched my hands back and nodded, eyes lifting to the seats above our heads. "They're compartments." No sooner had the words left my lips when gunfire erupted from outside.

And everything descended into madness.

Kai and I reached for the stash beneath the seats, tossing guns and magazines to Derek and Eva.

"Take the baby and keep cover behind the cars." Derek pushed a Glock into his wife's hand and pulled her in for a brief kiss.

"Derek, please…please be careful. Don't you fucking die on me. You hear me."

He held her close by the back of her neck. "I can't make any promises, angel. I'll do whatever it takes, as long as you two are safe."

I looked away, feeling almost as if I was intruding on an intimate moment.

That's when I caught sight of an embankment just outside the driver's side window where Felipe's unconscious body lay just feet away. I didn't know if he was alive or dead or if he'd been shot or died in the crash. I couldn't afford to mourn his death, not if I wanted to get out of this car alive. At the very least, save that little girl.

"This way," I said, then finally exited the overturned vehicle. Kai followed, extending his hand to Eva and the baby.

Now, with a clear view of the freeway, I was horrified to see the extent of the carnage. Flames engulfed two SUVs, and twisted metal scattered across the pavement. Pieces of what used to be one of my girls, along with them. I looked away for a brief second, squeezing my eyes closed and sucking in a long breath before cocking my gun. Ready to spill blood.

Men in dark coveralls I didn't recognize were blasting their way toward us and dodging bullets from the remaining cars.

Charging forward, I sent relentless rounds into the group, with Kai and Derek on either side of me. Several of the men hit the ground while others dove out of our line of fire. Disregarding his safety, Derek broke away, sprinting toward two wounded men. I didn't care to see the fate that awaited those bastards. Their pained howls were enough.

"Amalia! You need to take cover." Kai snatched my wrist and tugged me behind the front end of a mangled car.

"What are you doing? Your brother is out there risking his ass, and you're hiding?"

"I'm not hiding. And Derek can take care of himself."

Ripping my arm from his grasp, I dropped my mag and reloaded, never once breaking eye contact. "So can I."

I motioned to get to my feet, and again, he reached for me, only this time, I was ready. The barrel of my Glock pushed against his forehead, yet he didn't flinch.

"You want to be a hero, Cain?" I asked, motioning toward the embankment where Eva and the baby were hiding. "Go find your fucking damsel because I'm not the one."

As if the world around us wasn't crumbling, we found ourselves in a stare-down, and I could have sworn I saw the whisper of a grin.

High-pitched screams pulled my gaze behind him, where Cassandra, one of my best, dragged herself along the pavement, her left arm visibly broken and bent into an unnatural position. I bolted toward her, stopping dead, when two bullets pierced the side of her skull.

A man in a black ski mask stood over her and unloaded two more rounds before I could stop him. By the time he noticed me, it was too late. He collapsed face first, and like Derek, I didn't think, didn't rationalize the possibility of becoming a target. All I saw was red, all-consuming rage and spilled blood on concrete. Cassandra's. Felipe's.

I stood over the man's twitching figure, making sure to put a round through the back of his head at close range.

"Fuck! Cassie!" Falling to my knees, I placed a hand on her shoulder and pushed back her blood-soaked hair. Tears blurred the vision of her lifeless body until I caught a movement in my peripheral. Kai had his gun on me. At that moment, I thought about how easy it would be for him to kill me. Blame my death on whoever had orchestrated this ambush and be rid of his brother's debt. I couldn't blame him. Maybe I would have done the same had I been in his position.

Gripping the handle of my Glock, I figured I'd get a shot in before I was dead.

But he was faster. The bullet exploded out of the chamber, and I closed my eyes, waiting for the impact…

But it never came.

The heavy thud of a body behind me had me twisting around where a bald man lay bleeding from a wound to his neck. I snapped back toward Kai, and he nodded before dashing out to join his brother.

More gunfire broke out around me, serving to fuel my fury and join my soon-to-be husband in kicking some ass.

Between the three of us and my girls, the echoes of gunfire died down quickly.

"Where is Eva?" Derek asked as I approached, panic in his voice even as he sank a blade into some poor bastard's throat.

"Exactly where you instructed her to be."

"Go to her."

"I'm not your wife's personal bodyguard. I already saved her once."

It was the second time I had a gun in my face. Only this one was aimed at me with intent. Derek Cain would drag his dick through broken glass for Evangelina. It was disturbing and maybe a little sad, but a part of me also felt envious of such an unconditional devotion. Perhaps because I knew it was something that I would never experience. But I couldn't miss something I'd never had.

So fuck him and his wife.

Kai stepped between us when I raised my gun, shielding me from his brother.

"Cut the shit, Derek. Eva is fine. No one else dies here today."

Derek lowered his weapon when his brother was in his line of fire. He watched me, even as he wrenched his knife from the dead man's body, taking one last glance before standing and heading toward his wife.

"I thought I told you I didn't need a hero."

Kai started after Derek. "Sometimes what we think we need is different from reality. And you were two seconds from joining your friend back there."

He was several steps away when I said, "It would have been easier for you that way."

"Maybe. But I already told you, I don't run. I don't hide." He'd stopped walking but didn't turn to face me.

There was something different about this man. I couldn't pinpoint it. It was just a feeling—an intuition. But I decided right then and there that I didn't like how it made me feel.

Uncomfortable.

Unsure.

Sudden rapid-fire shots rang out. Derek yelled for Evangelina when the cries of his little girl followed. I took off after him and Kai, both in a full sprint toward where Eva was emptying her magazine into the body of one of the assailants.

I ran past her, spotting the baby on her hands and knees in the brush several feet away. Tucking my gun inside the back waistband of my pants, I bent down and picked up the one-year-old, and gave her a quick once-over. Apart from some superficial scratches, she seemed okay.

"*No llores*," (Don't cry.) I whispered, holding her to my chest. But the baby was too agitated and didn't know who the hell I was. She shoved me away, attempting to claw out of my grasp. Kai reached for his niece from behind me, assessed her briefly, and then kissed her forehead before tucking her securely in his arms. Valentina settled almost immediately and fisted his shirt as she sniffled.

Our eyes connected. "Thank you."

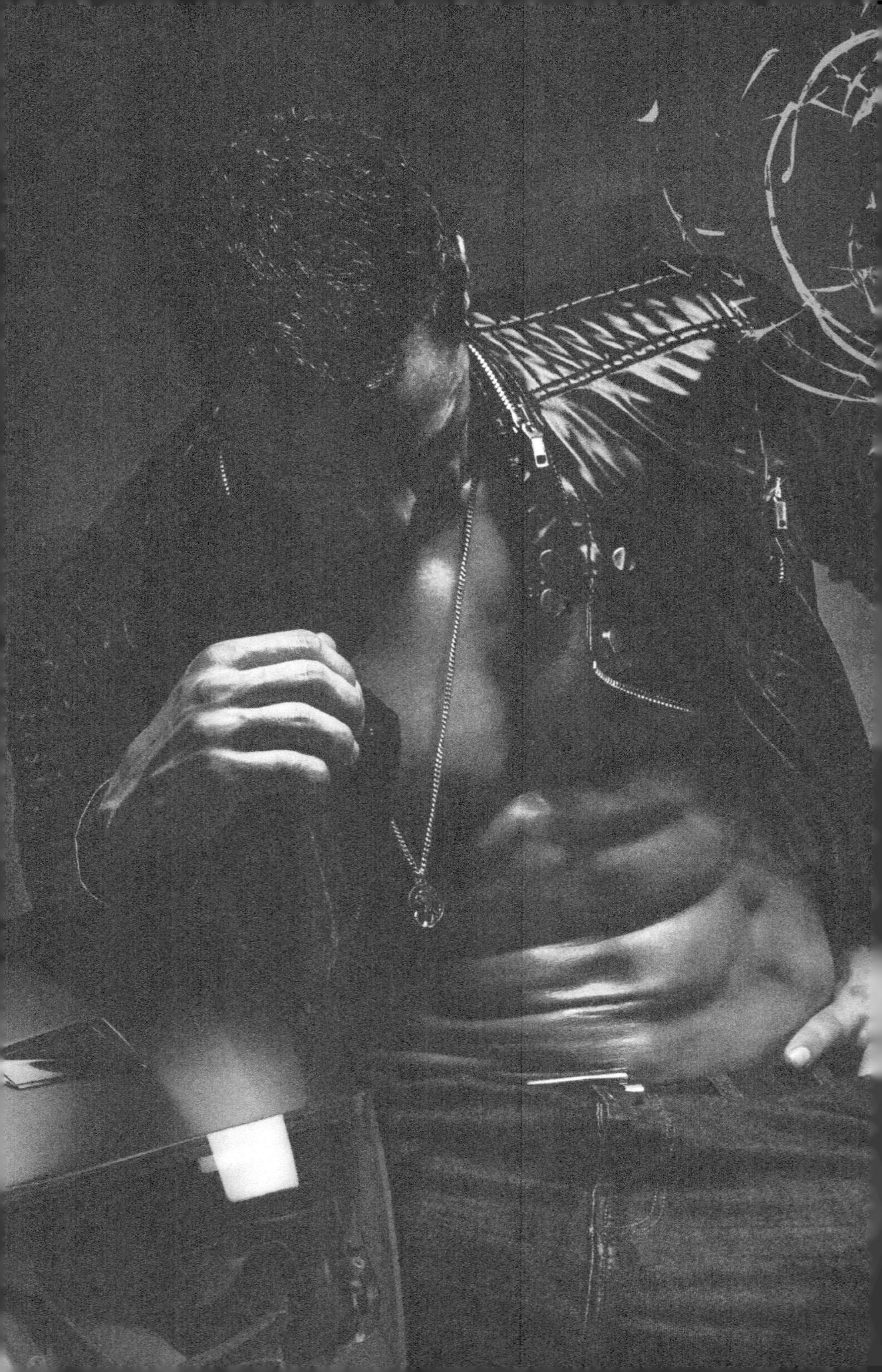

Chapter 2
Kai

Highland Park, Texas
Villa Dorada

THE clicking of her heels on the cobblestone was the only sound echoing off the walls of that courtyard. From the moment we reached the Montesinos estate, Amalia had taken off, and I gave chase. I needed answers, and she was the only one who would know what the hell had happened back there and why her driver and two of her team were dead.

"Amalia! Wait."

She didn't stop. Didn't look back. Her pace remained steady as we reached a large stone fountain. Fed up with being ignored, I caught her wrist, only to be met with a Glock to the chest. I'd been in the presence of this woman for less than twenty-four hours, and she'd already shoved a gun in my face twice.

"Let go."

"Tell me what happened back there. Who were those men? And why were they targeting you?"

Ripping her hand from my grasp, she narrowed her gaze. While she hadn't shed tears for her fallen friends, her brown eyes gleamed with emotion.

"Are you serious? What makes you think I'm the target? You and your brother have made your share of enemies, no? Not even in town ten minutes, and we get ambushed."

I put my hand on the barrel of her gun and lowered it. Amalia didn't resist, but she was on edge, the tension evident in her shoulders. As I scanned the vast courtyard, I concluded we were too deep inside the property to gauge any possible weak areas or unmanned entry points.

"Are we safe here?"

"Why? You need to hide again?"

With an eye roll, I tilted my head. I thought I saw her crack a smile for a second, but I must have imagined the gesture because her deep red lips pulled into a frown as she took two steps back and holstered her weapon.

"I can't give you a concrete answer. But to ease your nerves, yes, we're safe here."

"To ease my nerves?"

I ate the space between us. Amalia, similar to Eva in height, craned her neck to meet my eyes. She wasn't the least bit fazed by my closeness, though I wasn't surprised.

"I think you forget who I am. I don't scare easily."

She chuckled almost tauntingly. "Ah, the younger Cain brother. Cute."

Choosing to ignore her dig, I pressed for more answers.

"Are you on someone's hit list?"

"Look around you. A woman like me, like my family, we're always on someone's roster. You don't get wealthy on blood money without gaining a few enemies. If anyone knows that, it's you."

She turned away from me, and as uncalled for as it was, my eyes strayed to her ass.

I'd heard of Amalia through Leni several years ago, but it wasn't until Eva's capture that I'd seen her in person. My first impression of the woman was, of course, her striking beauty and signature red lips. But there was more to her than surface-level beauty. Amalia was a professional in every sense of the word. She carried herself as if she owned every space she occupied. I'd taken notice, though at the time, it seemed she only had eyes for Derek.

That night, she had all but taken over the operation, equipped with blueprints of the Belov compound, and had even spoken over Derek, damn near telling him to shut up and sit the fuck down. Between everything that happened, finding Eva, and Derek almost dying, Amalia's presence in my memories had become obsolete—until the day she came to collect.

"So I ask you again: Is it safe here? And this isn't about me. Eva and my niece are here. Today was too close."

She sighed and seemed to relax, her slightly accented voice softer..

"Your niece is safe. We have security and safe rooms."

Amalia still had her back to me, and I dared to reach out. "What about you? Are you okay?" My fingers brushed her elbow, and she immediately recoiled and whirled to face me. Her expression was harsh again, her smile cynical.

"There's no need to pretend. You and I both know what this is. You don't give a damn about me, just as I don't about you."

"It's a question I'd ask a random stranger on the street if they'd tripped over their own feet."

She crossed her arms. "And you'd ask said stranger this while checking out their tits?"

If she thought she'd caught me in some embarrassing situation, she was dead wrong.

"Only if they look as good as yours."

Amalia's plump lips opened as if she were about to respond, but she closed them instead, releasing a small huff of air.

The word *adorable* rolled around in my thoughts, and I didn't know what to make of it, mainly because the woman standing before me was anything but. She was feral, with claws and a sharp tongue—and like a chambered bullet, ready to tear someone's head off.

Vicious.

Again, she turned away from me. "My staff will show you to your quarters. When you're settled, you and I can discuss the terms of this arrangement."

My quarters. Not ours. Just mine.

Not that I'd arrived with the expectations of reaping the benefits of a husband, but she couldn't possibly expect me to live shackled to a woman I couldn't touch for the next three years.

Fuck that.

"So what happens now?"

Eva peered out a window, assessing the property. "How do we know we're safe here? What did Amalia say?"

"She didn't say much, and to be honest, I'm not sure she knows," I added, biting one of Valentina's chubby little feet. She squealed and kicked me in the face.

"We can't stay here if there's a threat. Not with Vali." Derek stood beside Eva, taking watch. "What if Ronan's behind this? We haven't heard shit from him in over a year. But he's still out there…just waiting for me to take his head."

Eva put a gentle hand on his back. "Not in front of the baby, Derek," she said in a hushed voice.

Ronan was still very much alive and always a presence in the back of our minds. Leni and Silas had warned us of his plans. I glanced down at my niece, who was idly playing with my watch, and shuddered at the thought of her in Ronan's custody. Over mine and Derek's cold, dead bodies.

A knock at the door had us all on alert. Eva had motioned to open it, but Derek held her back. "Who is it?" he barked harshly, so much it startled Valentina, who was serious.

"Me, of course." The sound of Amalia's voice from the other side of the door sent a strange rush through my body. It had been hours since we'd last spoken but I couldn't deny her pretty face had made a home in my thoughts, scowl and all.

"Come in," Eva finally said.

There was a pause before the knob turned, and Amalia stepped inside. The chaos from the morning had caused her makeup to smear slightly, that much I remembered, but the woman in front of us was fresh-faced, still beautiful, only there was a striking difference from the cold and impassive features from earlier. Pink tinged the rim of her eyes, and it was evident she'd been crying.

And why the hell did that make me feel…things?

"Was the crib okay for her?" she asked, eyes on Vali with a hint of a smile.

"It's perfect," Eva said. "Thank you."

Amalia turned her attention to me, and the softness in her features disappeared the moment our eyes met. "I understand it's been a strange day—"

"That's an interesting choice of words," Derek interjected.

Her eyes slid to my brother and narrowed. "Oh, would you have preferred I said *fucked*, gone to hell, a shitshow? Take your pick, Derek Cain. I wasn't aware I had to spell things out for you."

Derek eyed Vali, who looked to be enraptured by the adults in the room. He took a step toward Amalia, and she squared her shoulders and grinned.

"Enough," I said, then handed Eva the baby, taking Amalia by the wrist, and leaving the room.

"Who the fuck do you think you are?" she seethed, tearing out of my hold.

"Don't provoke him. When it comes to his family, Derek is—"

"He's what? Dangerous?"

"Something like that," I said, as I folded my arms and leaned against the wall.

She snickered and closed in on me. "Is that why you dragged me out of there?"

"Why else?" Amalia inched closer, and it was like every cell in my body was on high alert to her proximity.

Two fingers of a bandaged hand traced the front of my shirt. "I already told you. I'm not helpless. And Derek and I aren't that different."

The pricks of something hot crawled up the back of my neck.

"It's always Derek with you."

She chuckled and slowly raised a hand to my face. "Are you jealous of your big brother?"

Catching her wrist, I twisted her, slamming her back against the wall and caging her in. "Never. But I won't be toyed with."

Her eyes were on my lips, and her chest rose and fell a little faster. "That's good because I don't play games."

"Then we know where we stand."

"Feels like your cock is standing at attention as well," she said with a grin.

Despite everything, this woman was beautiful and fiery, and all I could think about was bending her over the hallway table.

But when I met her eyes again, I was reminded of what I'd seen earlier. The traces of grief. She wasn't as unbreakable as she wanted to portray. We all had our weaknesses, and it was almost tragic that she felt unable to grieve properly.

"I'm sorry," I said in a softer tone.

Her brow furrowed as she looked at me. "For what?"

"You lost people today, and I—"

With the palms of her hands against my chest, Amalia shoved me back. "Stop. That doesn't concern you. You and I don't mix business with our personal lives."

"Do you hear yourself?"

"Tomorrow. 8 a.m. My downstairs office." Turning around, she headed toward the main staircase. "My family arrives tomorrow, and we need to convince them we're in love."

Amalia had lost her goddamn mind if she thought she was going to drop that bomb and run.

"Amalia!"

"Tomorrow, Cain. Don't be late."

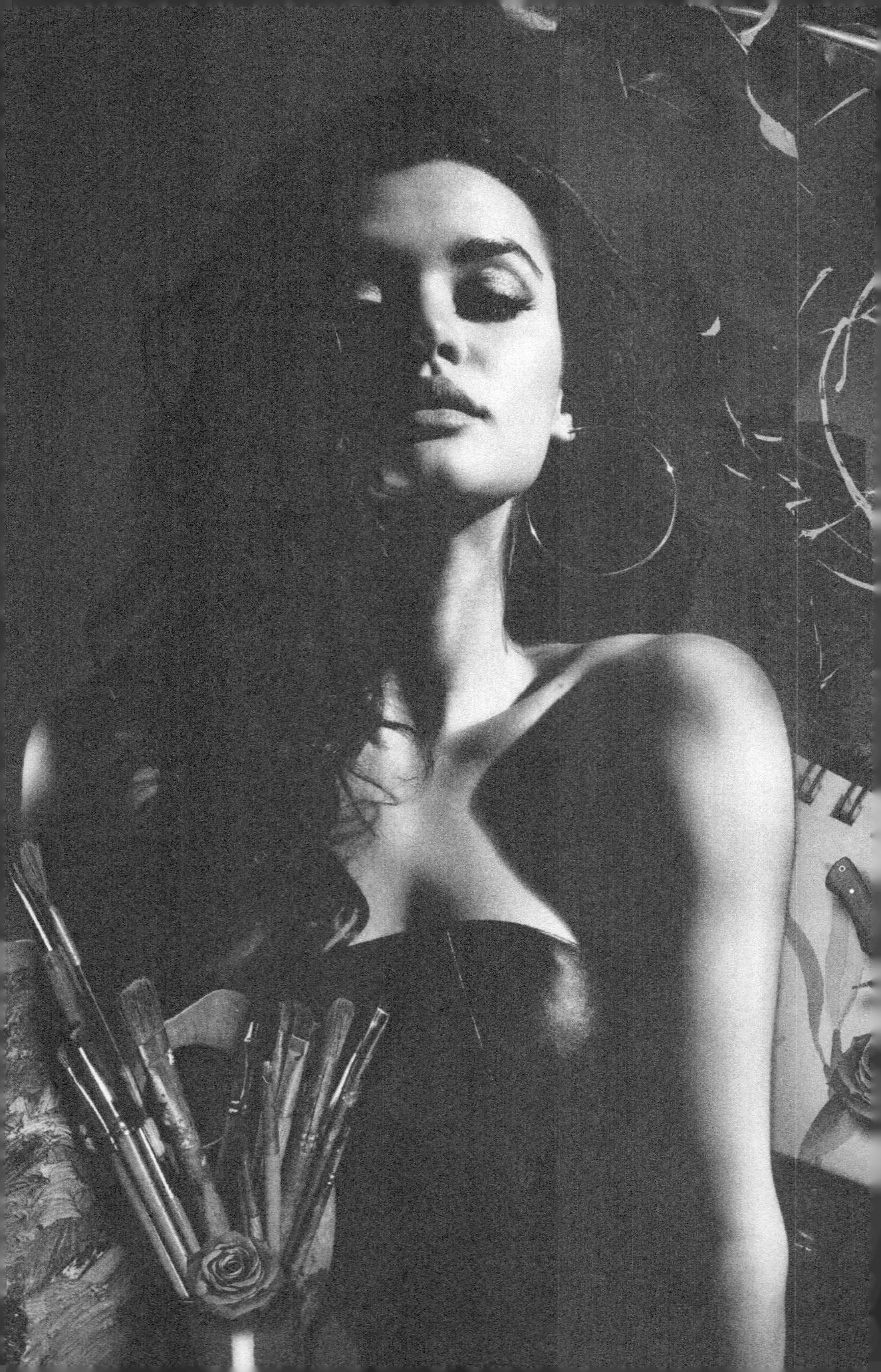

Chapter 3
Amalia

    I TOSSED an aspirin into my mouth and downed it with a swig of water. My head still pounded from the cry fest I'd allowed myself last night. Two of my girls were dead, along with Felipe. But I had to pull it together. Being a contract assassin came with its risks, and we all understood that. We gave ourselves a moment to grieve, then moved on. I still felt the distant burn of tears in the backs of my eyes, but I had no time to fall apart.

    Maybe later. At the moment, there were more pressing matters—like possibly killing my future husband for already disappointing me.

    Late.

    Thirty-five minutes late. I'd told him to be at my office at exactly 8 a.m. Last night, emotions were running high, so I postponed our talk for the morning, giving him strict instructions. I had a small window to make sure we'd ironed out details, the logistics of our relationship, and everything this contract entailed.

    It was bullshit. All of it. They could marry me off to whomever they saw fit to be the most beneficial to the family. But if it were my choice, then it had to be a genuine relationship, or the union would be invalidated. My hands were tied, and no amount of kicking and screaming, slit throats, or rolling heads would get me out of this. Not unless I forfeited the estate and a bulk of my inheritance.

I stalked forward toward Kai's room, my boots tapping violently against the polished travertine. The fact he hadn't had the decency to inform me he'd miss our appointment wasn't a good sign. How could I expect him to convince my family we were in love if he couldn't even…

The words raging in my thoughts disintegrated when I tore open the door and found him laying clothes over his bed, with nothing but a white towel tied low around his waist. Water droplets from a recent shower dotted his glistening, tanned skin. Tattoos shadowed most of his upper body, like fine art carved onto hardened muscle.

He whipped around when the doorknob slipped from my hand and subsequently slammed against the wall. Our eyes locked for a beat longer than I was comfortable with. But I found myself unsure of where else to look. While I was never one to be shy or subtle around men with whom I had every intention of taking to bed…Kai Cain, however, was a different case.

"I know this is your home and everything. But knocking is a common courtesy. And I was just about to drop this towel." The cocky tone of his voice and the grin on his face made me want to slap him. "I don't mind in the least, but I'm not sure that's something you want to get into…yet."

Like a bucket of ice water, I suddenly remembered why I found the man aggravating. Rolling my eyes, I jarred myself out of the muscles and ink stupor that had momentarily clouded my judgment.

"I thought we had an agreement. You were supposed to meet me nearly an hour ago. I don't like being stood up or kept waiting."

"I'm sorry. I didn't think it was that serious. I hit the gym this morning—nice, by the way—and was just about to head over."

Kai motioned to the clothes on his bed and turned toward me. It took every ounce of strength not to stray from his gaze down to the broadness of his chest, swollen from his recent workout.

"Would it have killed you to give me a heads up?"

"Come on, it's not like it was a business meeting."

I huffed an exasperated breath. "Everything about this is business. Might I remind you that you and I aren't friends? We sure as hell aren't lovers. There's a lot at stake here, Cain, so I expect you to hold up your end of this deal. Starting with punctuality."

Kai folded his large arms across his chest and regarded me, one eye narrowing. "Okay," he said with a sarcastic edge to his tone. "I'm listening."

"I can't speak to you like this."

"What, naked? You put a bullet through a man's head yesterday while completely disregarding your own safety. Me in a towel shouldn't faze you." Again, that maddening grin was fucking with me. Only, he didn't know who he was up against.

"You don't intimidate me."

"Oh, I know that."

His blue eyes darkened, and we found ourselves in another staredown. I wasn't sure what it was about this man, because I didn't tolerate insolence from anyone, let alone a practical stranger. But I needed the bastard, and killing him would leave me without options.

"Good. So now that we have that clear—"

"*Speak*, Amalia."

Call it a sizzle, a spark…something I hadn't quite felt before rippled deep in my belly when the command rolled off his tongue and straight to my pussy. I instinctively clenched my thighs and looked away, trying my best to act casual.

"Cain, my parents and my little brother do not know that this a sham. They wanted to marry me off to some asshole I barely know—"

"You don't know me at all."

My eyes snapped to his and that infuriating smirk reappeared. "No, but I'm in control. *I* made the choice, and to me, that's what matters. And like I said, he's an asshole."

"I can't promise that I'm not an even bigger one. In fact, I can guarantee he's a saint in comparison."

His amusement was gone, replaced by a heated gaze.

I didn't hold back this time. I let my eyes roam his torso and muscled arms, following the ripple of his abs down to the V of his hips and where I could see the outline of his cock.

"That may be true," I whispered, my eyes traveling back to his lips. "But let's just say, I like my assholes a bit prettier."

"So you think I'm pretty?"

I hadn't noticed when Kai stepped closer until he lifted my chin.

"Amalia, if you want to convince your family that what we have is real, sleeping in different rooms would probably raise some flags."

Going into this, I had no intention of sleeping with this man, but now, I wasn't so sure. I'd never denied myself in the past. A good fuck was a good fuck. As long as we both went into it on the same page as far as expectations and boundaries.

"We're Mexican, Cain. I'm not married—yet. My parents wouldn't delude themselves into thinking I'm still a virgin, but tradition is tradition. And until we say our vows, they'll be happy you're willing to respect me. Whatever that means."

"Then what? We sleep in the same room and play house?"

I slapped his hand away and put distance between us. Being close to him was growing increasingly dangerous and confusing.

"Business. There are terms to this deal, and you and I aren't anything more than two people with a mutual interest."

"The benefits here seem a little lopsided, don't you think?"

I shrugged and shuffled toward a window, parting the long white curtain. A group of men were putting together a gazebo in the east courtyard, while others tended to the landscaping, prepping the space for a ceremony. My wedding.

Our wedding.

Chills skated up my body when I realized I'd be married to the man standing just feet from me—someone with an expiration date and who I didn't love. But when had I ever expected to find such a thing?

"They'll only be here for a couple of weeks. I need you to try—"

A warm body pressed against my back, lips at the junction of my neck. Kai placed a hand on my waist and used his thumb to rub circles into my hip. He was like a damn furnace, heat emanating from him and threatening to set my skin on fire.

"I can assure you I won't have a problem pretending you're mine."

The low rasp danced across my flesh. My nipples hardened, and I closed my eyes briefly, clamping my lips closed as some traitorous noise fought to claw its way up my throat.

Mine.

That word had never evoked the feelings now buzzing through me.

And I hated it. The loss of control when it came to this stranger. Was it because he'd saved my life and also placed himself between me and his brother twice? Did my subconscious feel like it owed him something?

Whipping around in his arms, what was meant to be a grin faltered when I found myself face to face with his strong, inked body. He tipped my chin again, a gesture that proved he was already a little too comfortable touching me. I wrapped one hand around his wrist and pressed an open palm to his chest. Fortunately, he didn't resist when I shoved him back.

"Cain, don't fuck this up."

"I'm not sure I'm the one you have to worry about," he said, leaning against the bedpost. "Though I do have a question." With a sigh, I motioned for him to proceed.

"Does this contract include sex?"

Straight to the point.

"We don't fuck. Got it? *You* don't fuck—anyone."

He scoffed. "Okay, let's say I humor you. How long?"

"Three years."

Kai turned and shook his head as he made his way back to the clothes on the bed.

"That's funny."

"What? Can't keep it in your pants?"

"If you think I'm going to be celibate for three goddamn years, you might as well call this off."

"I think you're forgetting you're not here of your own will. Debt is debt. You volunteered to fill in for your brother. So, looks like you're the man for the job." I crossed the small distance between us. "Are you in or not?"

"Okay, so you and I don't sleep together. Fine." Shrugging, he tugged on his t-shirt. He didn't need to elaborate. I knew exactly what that statement implied.

"No, you're not understanding. My family is well known here. People will know who you are. That you're my husband, and you *won't* embarrass me by hooking up with random whores."

He laughed. "You're crazy if you think I'm agreeing to that."

"You will because you have no choice."

"I thought you said there was always a choice."

I flashed him a wry smile. "My words still stand." Stepping forward, I put a finger to his chest and poked him out of spite. He looked at the digit, then back to my face, his eyes simmering with anger. "You made a choice yesterday, did you not?"

"I don't follow."

"You saved my life, even though you had other options. You had the perfect opportunity to rid yourself of this obligation, but you chose to be here."

His jaw ticked.

"If you're going to be my wife, then I expect you to act like it." He traced a slow hand up the side of my cheek, cuffing a tendril of hair and tucking it behind my ear. "Maybe you're the delusional one here. You think you have me by the proverbial balls, but you couldn't be more wrong." I wanted to push him away when his lips feathered against my skin. "You need me just as much as I need you, because you're out of options and out of time."

I gripped his bicep, digging my nails into his skin. The edges of his mouth pulled into a grin. "If you dare to—"

"I don't have to coerce a damn thing out of anyone."

"Oh, of course you don't. You just flash those baby blues, and I'm supposed to fall to my knees and worship your cock."

Kai raised an eyebrow, mischief written all over his face. The towel that had once been wrapped around his waist lay on the floor between us. The urge to glance down was almost overwhelming, so I did the next best thing, thoroughly enjoying the way his eyes widened in surprise when my hand wound around his thick and rock-hard dick.

It flexed in my palm, and I gave him a squeeze.

"You think I'm intimidated by cock?"

His hand closed over mine, the other tugging me closer and settling like a branding iron over the small of my back. "Not yet." Kai's soft lips brushed the crest of my ear. "But soon you'll be on your knees begging for it."

"I like your confidence, Cain. You're going to need it."

"Sure."

If I throat-punched him, would he heal in time before my parents' arrival?

Giving him another forceful shove, I turned toward the door. "You have twenty minutes."

"Amalia," he called, his voice surprisingly tender. I stopped walking. "You're forgetting something important."

"What would that be?" I asked, returning to where he was standing.

Kai pulled a small black object from the top drawer of his nightstand. And again, he took the liberty of grabbing my wrist, turning my hand over, and placing a small object in my palm.

My heart was traitorous. It wasn't supposed to be impressed with small gestures. I wanted to kick myself for overlooking this one minor but very important detail.

The ring.

It was gorgeous. A black band with a black solitaire diamond.

Kai attempted to reach for the band again, maybe to slip it on my finger, but I jerked my hand away, refusing to give him power over me.

"Eighteen minutes," I said, my tone harsh as I walked out the door.

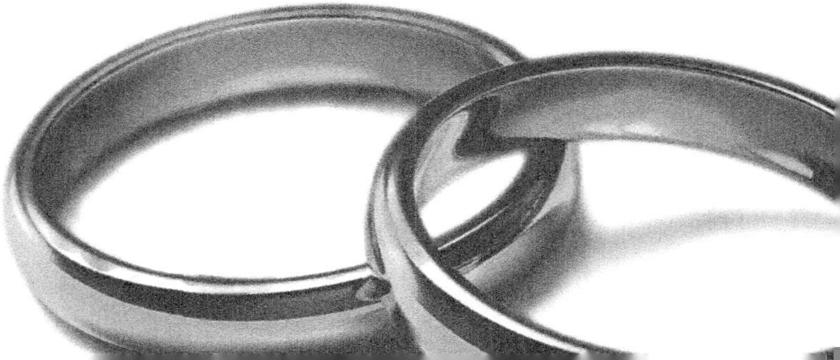

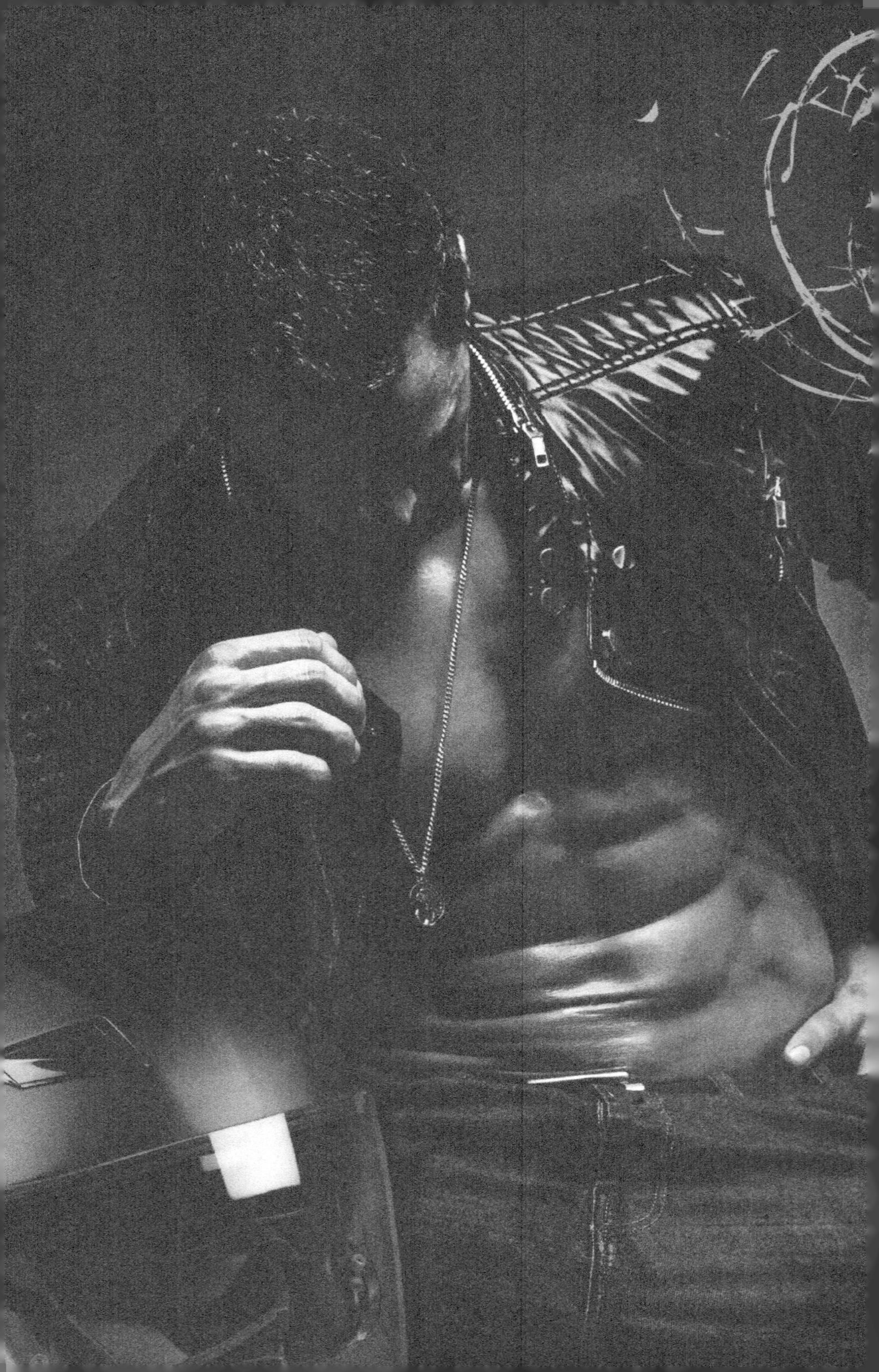

Chapter 4
Kai

    AMALIA greeted her parents warmly. I fell back, giving them space as I observed their dynamic. Having lived similar experiences in adulthood, I'd imagined her parents were people like Ronan and Maeve: cold and uninvolved. But my assumption couldn't have been more wrong.

    The love Isabel and Antonio Montesinos held for their daughter was glaringly obvious. They embraced as if it had been months rather than the two weeks she'd mentioned since their last visit. The sight starkly contrasted with the family I'd been born into and the one thrust upon me against my will. It begged the question of how, instead of shielding their daughter from a life of blood and warfare, they'd bred her into a killer.

    Isabel was the first to break from the group, her dark brown eyes regarding me almost curiously as an easy smile spread over her lips. While Amalia shared many features with her mother, both beautiful and regal, the older Montesinos wore a softer expression. Even the lines on her face seemed relaxed, but she had a good two decades on her daughter, tempering emotions and perfecting a poker face.

"You must be Kai Cain. The man who stole my daughter's heart." Her accented voice was warm and sincere as she framed cool hands on each side of my face and pulled me in for a kiss on the cheek.

"Ma'am," I said, tipping my head. "It's my pleasure."

"You *are* handsome," she gushed, as her eyes flitted to her daughter and then back to me. "I need some beautiful grandbabies, you know?"

"Oh, fuck."

Her head whipped to Amalia. "*Mija*, is that any way to speak around your fiancé?"

Surprisingly, Amalia leaned into my side and threaded her fingers into mine, squeezing my hand. As I attempted to steer my thoughts from what had occurred earlier that morning, my cock twitched at the memory of how tightly she'd held it.

"You haven't been here for more than five minutes, and you're already planning a baby shower."

Isabel chuckled and bumped my arm, sending a wink my way. "I wouldn't waste time practicing, if you know what I mean. Look at this bicep."

"¡*Mamá!*"

This time, her mother tipped her head back and laughed wholeheartedly as she returned to the vehicle's passenger side door.

Amalia sunk her nails into my hand for attention. "Whatever you do, don't entertain her."

"She seems nice. Are you sure you're related?"

"Probably not, because I'm not nice."

Yeah, she was fucking adorable, even when she tried to be a bitch.

"Where's Gio?" Amalia asked, peering inside the empty cabin.

"Oh, you know how he is. Asked to be dropped off by the stables."

"He'd rather see horses before his sister?"

Unable to resist, I dipped my head close to her ear. "I don't blame him."

She rolled her eyes and elbowed me lightly in the rib. I was borderline disappointed her reaction was so mild when she'd threatened me with death just two hours prior. When Amalia tried to pry her hand from mine, I wouldn't let up, not even as her father approached. Better she knew now than later that she wasn't in charge.

Antonio looked at me with slight suspicion and eyed the tattoo on my neck. Ink branched out from the sleeve and collar of his suit, so I knew the tattoo itself didn't bother him so much as intrigued him. Both knew I was still a member of Ares, as the Montesinos had close ties to the organization. I wasn't sure how she'd convinced them our relationship was genuine, though I felt her mother suspected otherwise.

"I always said I'd pity the poor bastard who ended up with my daughter."

"Wow," she chimed in, finally tearing her hand from mine and stalking forward onto the curved driveway. "I'm going to find the only man in this family who appreciates me."

"Amalia." Her father's tone had taken a serious note. "We need to talk about what happened yesterday. I received some intel, and we'll be sure to rain hell on everyone involved."

She nodded, and her eyes flashed to me briefly before she took off down the pathway that I could only assume led to the stables. I dismissed myself moments later and followed Amalia, taking my time to catch up while I admired how her sundress clung to her ass as if by design.

"Why are you following me?"

"We're supposed to make this believable, are we not? Meeting your brother without me raises suspicion."

Amalia stopped so abruptly that I crashed into her back, sending her tumbling forward. But before she could lose her balance, I reached out and pulled her into my chest.

Maybe it was the adrenaline of the moment, but I could swear I felt her heart pounding.

"You damn near bulldozed me over."

It was then I realized I hadn't been imagining things. Her voice was breathier, and her expression more relaxed. Lowering my mouth to her ear, I whispered, "You brake-checked me, remember?"

Amalia shoved out of my arms and turned around. "My brother, Giovanni, is the baby of the family. He just turned seventeen, and he's the sweetest soul. He's pretty good at reading people, so we need to look like we at least tolerate each other."

"What, you don't like me?"

"I like you enough to use you for my benefit. Is there anything else you want to know? Because I've got about one hundred ways to bruise your ego, Cain."

"Let's hear them," I challenged, calling her bluff.

She waved me off, but I caught a glint of amusement in her eyes.

"You held my cock today, and since you'd never pass up an opportunity, I'll take your silence on the subject as a stamp of approval."

"Kai, I said I would bruise your ego, not stroke it. And I'm not afraid to admit when a man has a pretty dick, so get over yourself."

She picked up her pace, and I followed.

"You called me Kai."

"Are you asking for a nickname?"

I laughed, my interest thoroughly piqued by this woman.

"As I said before, don't fuck this up. Gio isn't the best keeper of secrets."

I couldn't help grinning. She reminded me of a feral cat.

One word came to mind.

"Come, then, vicious. Let's impress Gio." I took her hand, feeling resistance for a split second before she let me lead her forward.

"What the fuck did you just call me?"

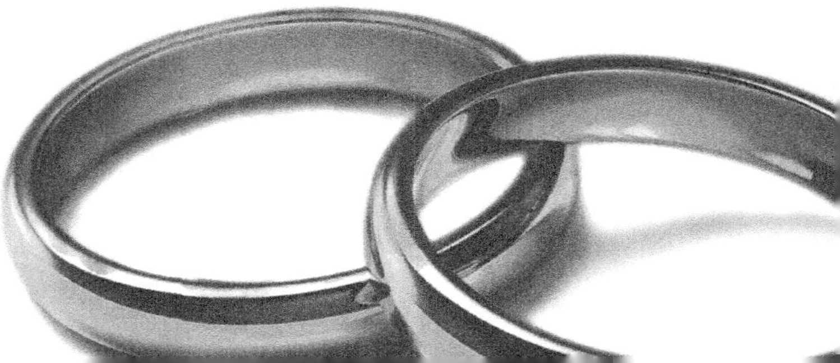

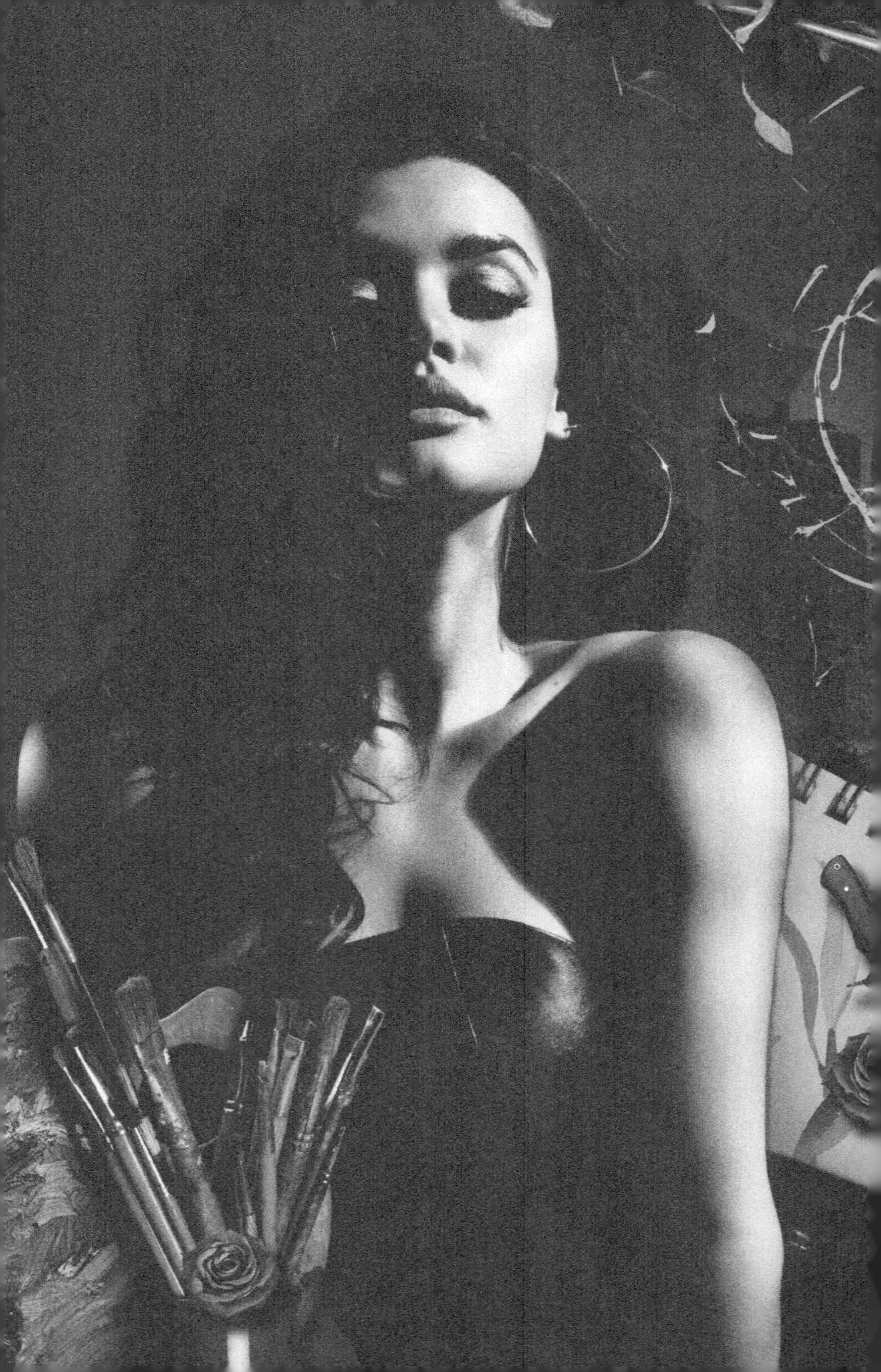

Chapter 5
Amalia

GIO'S voice was a low whisper from inside one of the stalls. I knew what he was doing, talking to and grooming his favorite mare, Mrs. Oscar. She was a gift from our grandfather on Gio's seventh birthday. He'd wanted a male horse to name him Oscar after one of his favorite TV characters, so I'd suggested Mrs. Oscar as a happy medium. Seemed like a good idea at the time.

Strangely enough, he was never interested in riding. He'd said the probability of an accident was far greater than the joy of the ride. He preferred to keep his feet on the ground and control his environment. He'd always been that way for as long as I could remember. Cautious, observant, and obsessed with statistics.

"I had the stablemen get her ready for you." The red grooming mitt in his hand stopped midair, yet he didn't turn to face us. "Gio, you can't possibly still be upset with me."

"I won first place."

"Of course you did. And I'm so proud of you."

"If you were proud, you would have been there."

His teenage dirtbag attitude aside, guilt twisted in my belly. I'd promised to attend his math championship, but as usual, business had kept me away. Throughout the years, I made it a point to be present in his life as much as possible. Not just for the bond we'd forged, but when I was with my baby brother, it was the only time I felt…normal.

I felt Kai's gaze on me and became irrationally upset, even though nothing about his demeanor or expression brokered any judgment. Call it instinct. I'd been my brother's protector his whole life. He'd unseated me as the baby of the family when I was just eight. I'd hated him. Hated the idea of my parents sharing more of their time and love. They had already spent enough energy on my oldest brother, as he managed to get into trouble often. But I knew Gio was special when I stared into his big, dark eyes from behind the glass. I thought he was the cutest thing in the world, even with all the tubes.

"Mamá sent me the video." He shrugged. "Gio, you can't be upset with me forever. Besides, I have a surprise for you. I—"

Twisting to look back at Kai, my stomach heated when I found him watching me intently, eyebrows drawn together as if he was trying to solve some puzzle. "There's someone I want you to meet. He's going to be part of our family soon. We're getting married."

My brother finally turned to face me. His handsome features contorted into a look of disgust.

"You better not be marrying that asshole, Rocco."

Gio rarely cussed, only when something upset him, and Rocco Solis was a source of his rage more often than not. The son of my father's late right-hand man and business partner and my childhood friend had been one of my parents' obvious choices for this sham of a union. Still, I'd already given in to being bound to some bastard I didn't love to fulfill my family's debt and my abuelo's dying wish. Being able to choose the man I'd be forcibly shackled to provided a sliver of solace.

With a chuckle, I touched his forearm and motioned toward Kai. "You know I'd never. This is Kai Cain."

"Hi," he said, as enthusiastic as a teenager could muster. "He has cool hair. Is that why you like him?"

"Yeah," I said with a laugh. "It's one of his better qualities."

Gio wasn't a fan of my jokes, so his lack of humor didn't surprise me, but his serious look wiped away my smile. Before I could ask, he took my bandaged hand and flipped it over twice before finding my eyes.

"Again?"

Gently pulling back from his grasp, I waved him off. "Just broken glass. A misstep in the kitchen."

"But you don't cook."

Dammit. "Gio, I was helping Milly. I'm going to be a married woman, after all. Maybe I want to learn some things."

He shook his head in disbelief. "You let this happen to her?"

Kai drew an arm around my waist.

"I would never let anything happen to her." Obviously, he was appeasing my brother and following through on his end of our deal, but his words rippled through me like a fuse, nonetheless.

Kai was far from a righteous man. His heart was as black and tainted as his brother's. He had no loyalties or ties to me other than the proverbial ball and chain I'd placed around his neck.

Not the type to care about those outside of his circle, he sure as hell wouldn't give a damn about the woman forcing him into an unwanted marriage and uprooting his life. Thinking back, not that I'd expected differently, but when our vehicle began to flip, Kai had reached for Eva and the baby. Call me irrational because while we were still practical strangers, I couldn't deny that the memory stung.

Residual annoyance had me wriggling from his grasp, but Kai lifted my hand to his lips, and the urge to slap him was suddenly stronger than the need to continue our charade for Gio's sake.

He was fucking with me.

"I'll keep her out of the kitchen from now on," he said with a chuckle.

Bastard.

Gio nodded in agreement, a smile lifting the corners of his mouth.

"Amalia," Kai called my name as I climbed the steps to my home's front entrance. Gentle fingers held my elbow, and while my initial instinct was to pull away from his touch, I stilled, waiting for him to say whatever was on his mind.

"He seems like a good kid."

"He is."

Kai tugged me until I was facing him. "You're different with him."

"Of course I am."

I didn't know why I was annoyed that my brother seemed to like Kai more than anyone I'd ever introduced him to. Once those first fifteen minutes of awkward small talk were behind them, he and Kai fell into an easy companionship. Gio talked his ear off about robotics and everything else he was into while my soon-to-be fake husband pretended to be interested, even though he seemed genuinely entertained.

That son of a bitch. I knew what he was doing, trying to get under my skin, using my brother.

"Amalia." He placed his forefinger under my chin. "We don't have to be like this."

"Oh, thank God," I said, with blatant sarcasm.

"Exactly."

Without warning, Kai tightened his grip. "If we're going to spend the next three years tolerating each other, can we at least make it bearable?"

I offered him a grin and shoved him back.

"Don't be a pussy, Cain. This is me being nice. Because men who dare to lay their hands on me without permission lose their fingers, dicks, or their lives if I'm in a particularly good mood. And seeing as you still have all three, consider yourself my *fucking* bestie."

As I pivoted toward the door, he yanked me back until I collided with his hard chest. His fist was wrapped into my hair, lips at my ear. Caught off guard, I was momentarily stunned…but worst of all, I was wet.

"We can be friends, vicious. The best goddamn friends with benefits." His other arm snaked around my belly, pulling me flush to him, his cock hard at my back. When my eyes fluttered closed, I didn't know whether I wanted to slap him or slap myself for letting him get to me. I hated the way he made me feel like I could lose control.

The thought was terrifying.

"Kai, you bastard." My nails dug into his forearm, and he hissed over the shell of my ear, causing yet another flush of wetness between my thighs.

The vibration of his chuckle against my skin forced me to clamp my lips together. I'd be damned if he knew how much he affected me. I wasn't sure what this game was between us. Worst of all, I didn't know that I entirely hated it.

"You know, from the moment I saw you, even years ago, I wondered what my fist would look like wrapped around this hair of yours." The tighter he gripped me, the more aroused I became. "Small world, isn't it?"

"You're playing with fire, Cain."

"I know. You feel it, too?"

Kai turned out to be bolder than I ever imagined he would be, but I could play that game, too.

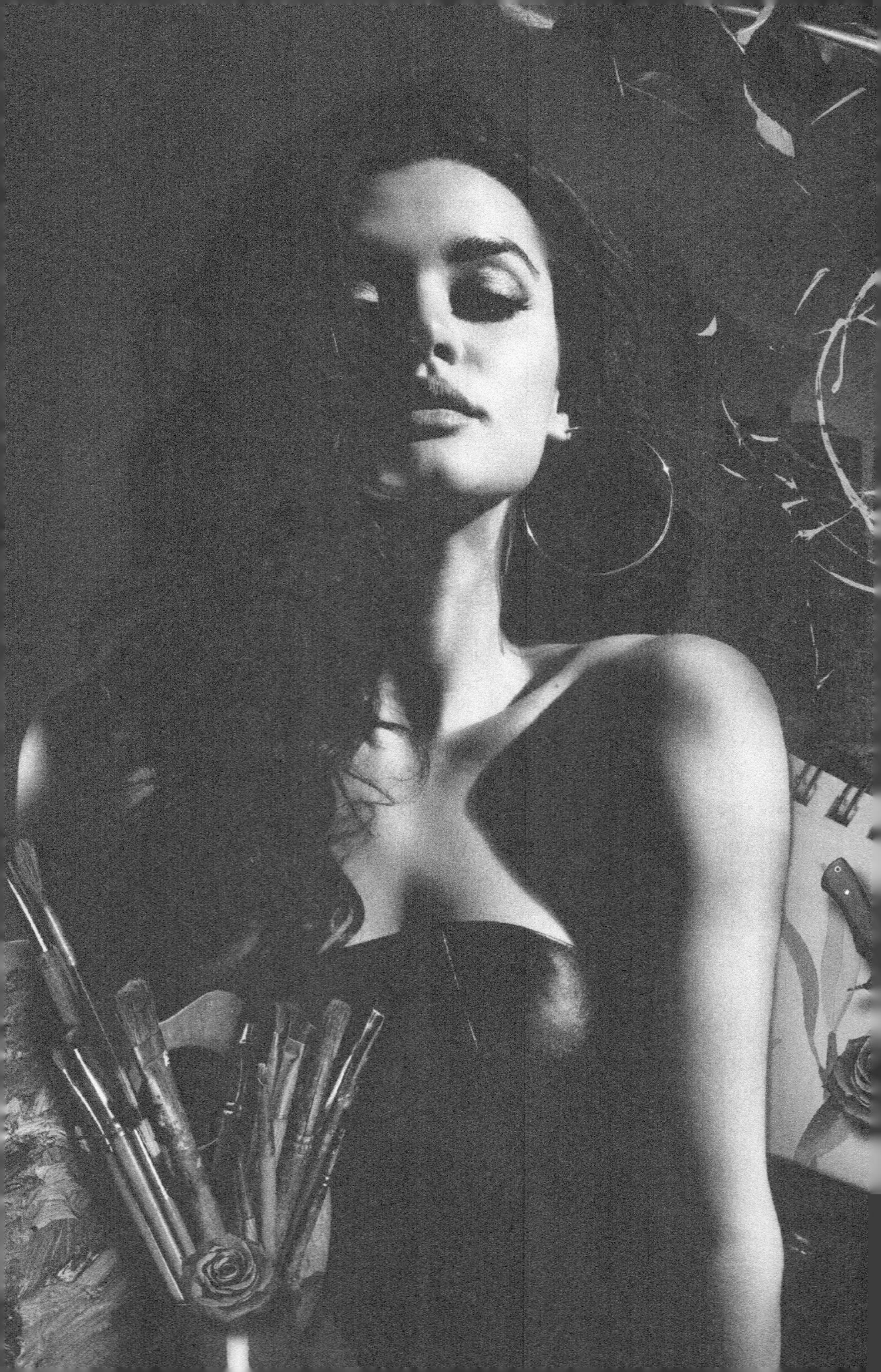

Chapter 6
Amalia

IF I stepped with more force, I would surely stab my heels straight through the tile. The long expanse of corridor did nothing to quiet my angry footfalls as I stomped in a rage toward the kitchen and away from the source of my ire and…

And…

Confusion.

Kai was infuriating. He had all the audacity to think he could touch me and get under my skin, that he could affect me and wear me down and bend me to his will. Did he not know who I was? And what was more maddening was the fact that he could and had.

What was wrong with me?

I ran my fingers through my hair, where a phantom sting still vibrated on my scalp.

Stopping abruptly, a very unladylike growl rippled between my teeth. I bent and tore off my heels, launching them across the hall.

Fuck you, Cain.

High-pitched squeals grabbed my attention from around the corner, and I followed the sweet noise, my shoes forgotten and my mood already lifting as I was met with dimpled cheeks and a mouth smeared with avocado. Eva and Valentina were in the kitchen with Milly. The older woman was at the counter flattening dough for tonight's dinner and chatting in Spanish with the infamous Mrs. Cain.

I swallowed a knot in my throat, realizing that the same last name would also belong to me soon…not that I had plans to take his name, but it was who I'd be in principle.

"*Mi niña*, you haven't touched your lunch."

Milly's soulful gaze fell on me, and her soft smile disappeared as she took in my aggravation. I must have had my default bitch face on, though I didn't need it where she was concerned. Milly could always read me, sometimes better than my own mother, who she also helped raise.

"I'm not hungry. Maybe later."

"Later is dinner. We have to put a little more meat on your bones, *mija*. Men need places to hold on to, if you know what I mean." She winked.

"Really? In front of the baby?"

Her eyes crinkled at the corners as she laughed and waved me off. "*La princesita* is too busy enjoying the lunch *you* refused."

"Not in front of our guest then," I chided playfully, pulling a stool next to Valentina.

"Oh, she doesn't mind, do you, Evangelina?" Milly pronounced her name in Spanish. "Those brothers…" She whistled, shaking her head with a dreamy look. "You two are very lucky ladies."

Her thoughts seemed to drift somewhere I had no business thinking about. I'd heard the stories of when she was in her prime.

I looked at Eva, who was smiling and spooning more avocado into her daughter's messy mouth.

Fifteen minutes later, my far too-talkative cook left us for afternoon prayer.

I suddenly realized it was the first time Evangelina and I had been alone together since the day I'd saved her ass from that long-dead bastard, Belov.

We spoke up at the same time that neither of us heard what the other had said, so I motioned for her to speak first, my curiosity piqued.

"Amalia, I know I'm over four years too late, but I wanted to thank you for what you did for me that day. You saved my life...saved me in so many ways." Her eyes misted as she caressed her daughter's brown curls. "If you hadn't gotten there when you did...I wouldn't—"

"It was nothing. Just another day at the office...*princess*," I said with a grin, recalling the nickname I'd given her. Evangelina wiped her eyes and laughed. In the next second, she was on her feet, with her arms around me, before I could stop her.

"Thank you," she whispered, her voice clogged with emotion.

While I didn't return the hug, Eva didn't seem to mind. She gave me one last squeeze before returning to her chair.

I wasn't sure what to make of what had just happened; despite our past and the soon-to-be link we'd share, she and I were still very much strangers. While Eva gave off genuine vibes and all that, at the end of the day, this woman was still a cop. One married to none other than one of Ares's most prolific and ruthless ex-members. Maybe deep down, they weren't that different. His ghosts didn't seem to haunt her, as one would assume.

"She has your eyes."

Eva nodded. "I hoped she would. As beautiful as Derek's are, these eyes were my mother's and brother's." She stared almost longingly at her child, even as the baby caked chunks of avocado into her hair. I fought a laugh. "Before she was born, and before I knew Frankie... Silas was alive; I prayed for a piece of them in her."

"You must have prayed extra hard that day."

I couldn't help the pangs of envy twisting my insides when I thought of Eva's brother and how he'd come back to her. No amount of prayer would ever bring Tony back. I was there with my father the day we'd gone to identify his body—what was left of him, anyway.

Pushing those gruesome images from my mind, and never one to hold back, I met Eva's gaze and asked, "So you're still a detective?"

She nodded in understanding, inhaling a deep breath. "I know what you're thinking. But I love him. It's just that simple. Maybe it's hypocritical. And maybe I'm just as guilty as all those people I help put away." Eva held my gaze, her resolve unwavering. "But I don't care. Not anymore."

I leaned back on the stool and crossed my arms, surprised and slightly impressed by her admission. In hindsight, this woman had run back into that compound naked, wounded, and having had the day from hell, all while the place was under siege. Her one objective: finding Derek. She was either foolishly loyal or an absolute idiot.

Me? Fuck that.

I would *never* be like Eva.

"Can I ask something of you?" she said, a hand on mine. My eyes slid to where she touched, then back up to meet hers again.

"You're going to ask anyway, so go ahead."

She smiled. "Go easy on Kai."

I couldn't help the laughter that bubbled up my throat. Even the baby stopped and turned to me, puzzled.

"Kai is a big boy. He doesn't need you taking up for him."

"That's not what I meant. He's just as much a victim here as you are. Neither of you want to go through with this, so there's no sense in making things worse than they already are."

I pushed to my feet, my chair scraping loudly against the floor. "Poor Kai, marrying a wealthy and powerful woman against his will. How ever will he survive?"

"Amalia…" she called as I exited the kitchen, no longer interested in anything she had to say.

Admittedly, there was a part of me that felt slightly insulted. Had he expressed his misery to her? I mean, sure, I wasn't happy either. But I was a *fucking* catch, and he'd have his freedom within three short years. It wasn't a death sentence—yet.

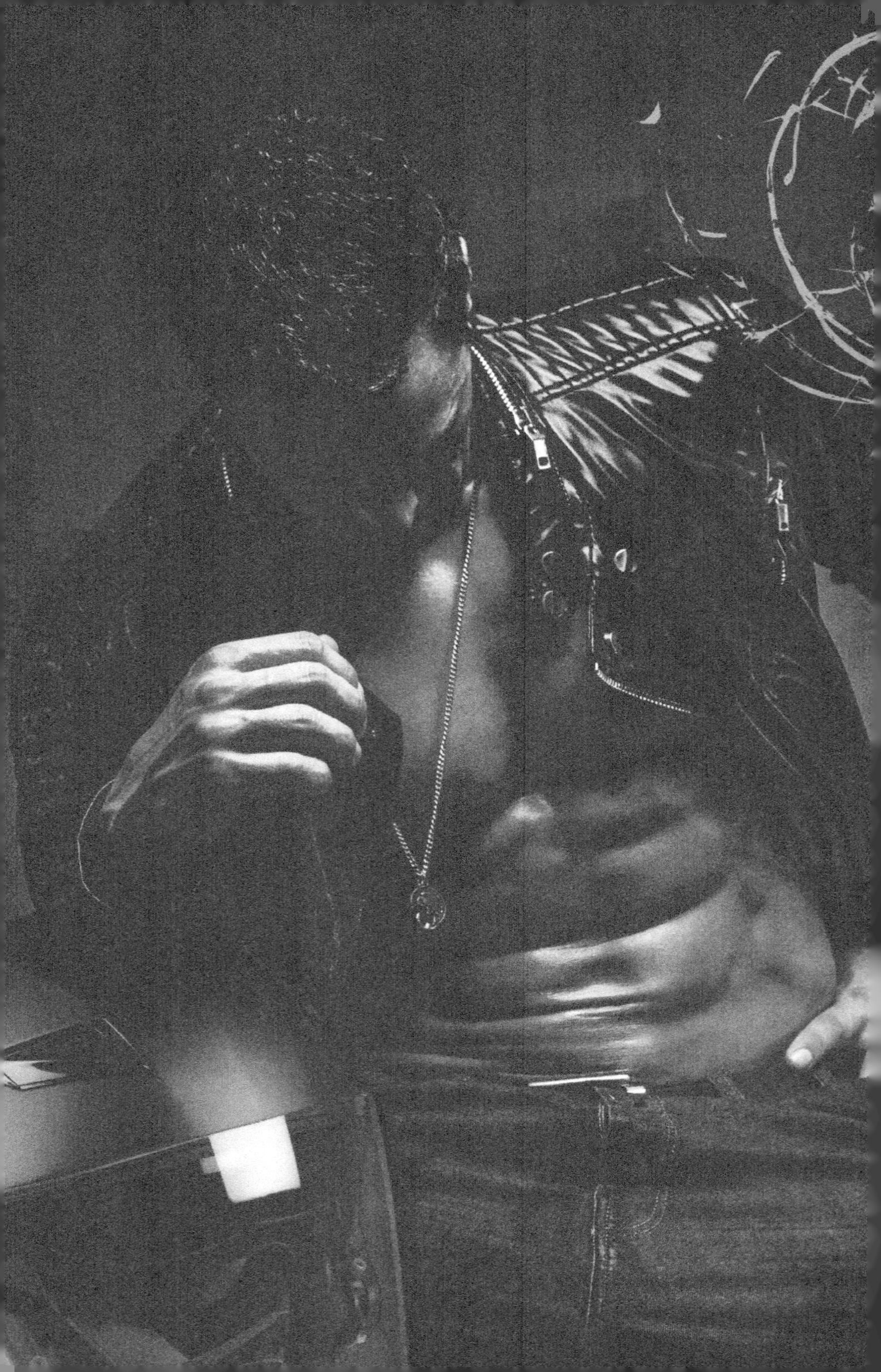

Chapter 7
Kai

  I RESTED my head on the back of a dressing chair in the guest room, my legs stretched out in front of me as I contemplated the fucked-up circumstance that was my life. Maybe I hadn't thought this all the way through. I'd jumped the gun and threw myself headfirst into a decision I regretted with every second that ticked by like a silent countdown to my demise.

  Sure, she was beautiful. I'd thought that alone would get me through whatever hell awaited me for the next three years. It was just a small sacrifice. For Derek, after all he'd done for me, I owed him my life. But now, I wasn't sure I could go through with this marriage.

  Amalia was…she was something else.

  A harsh knock at the door had me straightening and rubbing a hand down my face as I exhaled and shouted for whoever it was to come inside.

  Derek cocked a brow as he approached. I must have looked exactly the way I felt.

Like fucking hell.

"Everything good?"

I glanced up at him and raked my fingers through my hair. "Remember that time I said your little meeting with Amalia would come back to bite us in the ass? Well, yeah. Here we are."

Derek sat beside me.

"Kai, you don't have to do this." Moving closer, his voice lowered to a whisper. "We can take her out. Call Leni, Silas—some more of our people, and get you out of this mess before hers even know what happened."

I shook my head. "Derek, her family has deep connections, not only to Ares and The Six, but Cartel. We'd be putting a target on our backs—Eva, Vali. Come on."

All I had to do was mention his family. They were sacred. He put them above everyone, including me. But I understood. I'd grown to love Eva, and Vali was so special.

My thoughts drifted to Gio and Amalia's mother, and a twinge of guilt ran through me at the thought of ending their lives. But neither was as strong as when I envisioned *her* lifeless. "No," I said, shaking my head and feeling a strange sense of deja vu. "Not an option. No one touches her."

"Okay. So what's the plan?"

"Sign the marriage license and be thoroughly fucked—or not. Can you believe there's a damn no-sex clause?"

Derek put a hand on my shoulder and huffed a resigned breath. "I'm sorry, brother."

"Yeah, well, you owe me for this."

A soft knock at the door sent a small rush of blood through my veins at the possibility of it being Amalia. Despite everything, I couldn't deny that fighting with her and touching her filled me with a thrill I hadn't experienced in a long while.

"There you are," Eva said, eyes on Derek. He leaned back and smiled at his wife. "You didn't tell me you were home."

"Peeked in and saw you putting Vali down for a nap, and I didn't want to wake her."

She slid onto his lap and gave him a quick kiss before turning to me.

"Heard you met the family this morning. How was that?"

"They surprised me," I said with a shrug. "I hadn't expected them to be so welcoming. But then again, they'd have no reason to be suspicious. She's making them believe we're in love."

Eva had intended to speak, but Derek gripped her by the back of the neck and kissed along her jaw.

"Do you need me to leave?" I asked my brother with a laugh.

"Don't be ridiculous; this is your room."

"Derek," Eva scolded, playfully swatting his hand.

"I haven't seen you all morning, angel." Standing, he swiftly tossed his wife over his shoulder. "Let's go catch up." He turned to me. "I'll swing by later."

I offered him a nod and leaned against the closed door once they exited.

"Fuck."

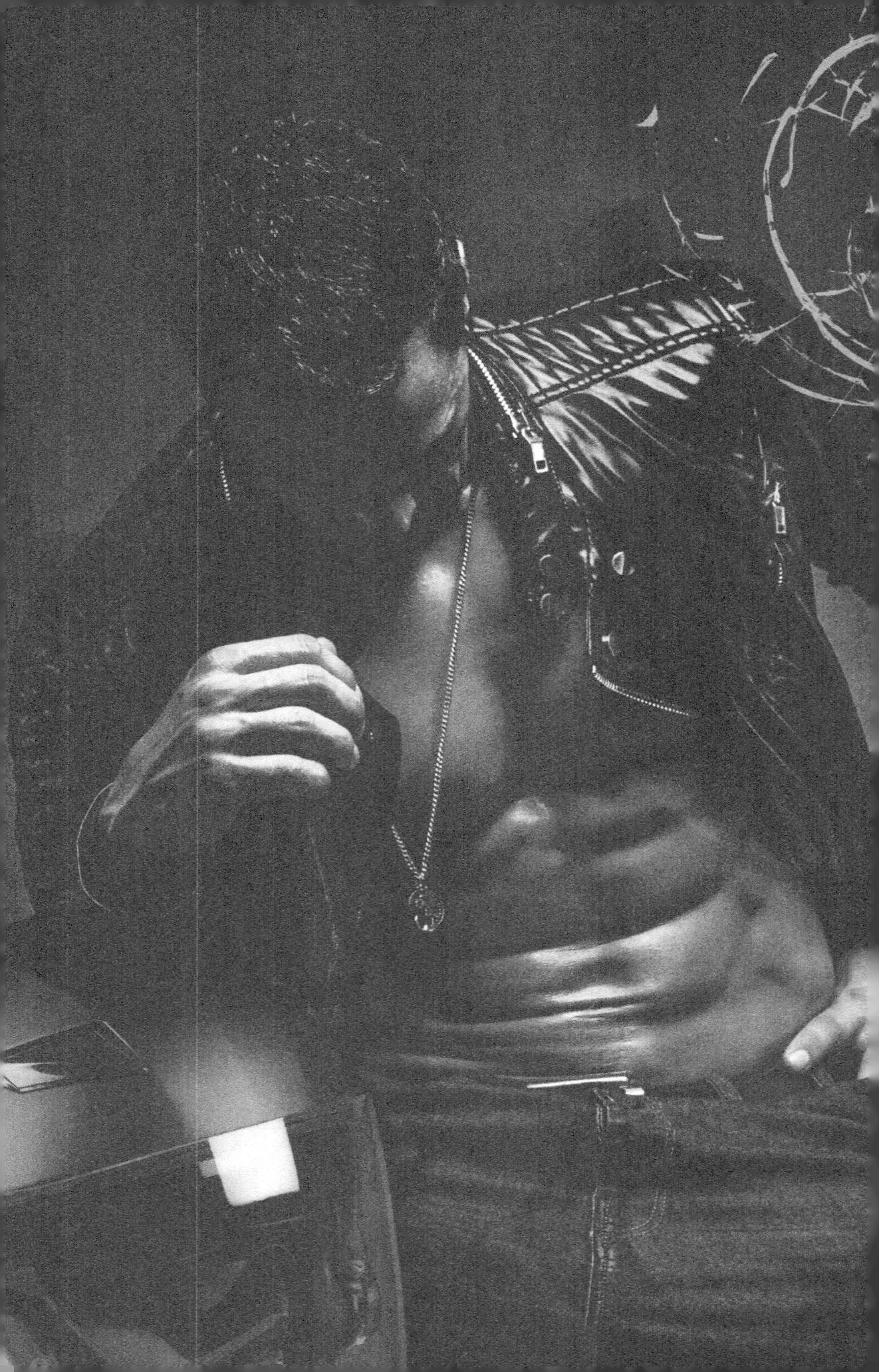

Chapter 8
Kai

"**YOU** clean up nice."

Gio stopped and glanced down at his navy dress shirt before cracking a smile. "Thanks."

I could see what Amalia meant. The kid seemed out of place in this family. He didn't have a malicious bone in his body, which made me wonder about his upbringing and what differences had made her into the woman she was versus this boy who beamed when paid a simple compliment. We all had a story, a rhyme or reason as to what led us to shed vital pieces of our conscience and morality.

Hers intrigued me.

"You know, she's not so bad," he said, breaking the silence.

"Who?" I tried to play it off as if I wasn't aware of who he was talking about. I didn't want him to know that I had those thoughts about Amalia. It was clear they were close.

"My sister. She's not as bad as people think she is."

The men she'd maimed and buried through the years would disagree.

"She's beautiful." It was the only honest answer I had to give.

In the week since I'd been here, we'd done nothing but fuck with each other. It was a strange sort of relationship off the bat, but maybe it was our way of avoiding the implications that our union would ultimately bring us.

Gio didn't say another word for the duration of our walk to the dining hall. This gave me time to analyze his comments and the possible intentions behind them. Speaking highly of her meant that, in some ways, he approved of our relationship.

But if he believed the engagement was genuine, he wouldn't need to sell her to me.

He knew.

I caught Gio's arm and tugged him to a stop. Voices poured in from around the corner, so I made sure to lower mine to a whisper. "What do you know?"

"I know my sister. And that's enough to know this whole marriage thing is for my parents and the lawyers." He focused beyond me. "I won't tell. I know why she's doing it. And I'm glad it's you and not Rocco."

"Rocco?" I remembered he'd brought up his name a few days ago.

"You'll meet him at dinner. He wants to marry Amalia."

"Does he?"

Gio nodded again and peered nervously around the corner. "But she doesn't love him."

"She doesn't love me either, kid."

"No, but she can learn. Show her."

Show her.

Of all the impossible…

We stepped into the formal dining room, and I never knew what it felt like to experience a rush of air leaving my lungs unless it was due to a fist to the abdomen, yet there I was, eyes on her, attempting to catch my breath.

Amalia's once-long black hair was cropped, sitting just on her shoulders. The ponytail I'd wrapped in my hand days ago was gone. But I wasn't mad. She looked goddamn edible. My perusal was short-lived when a man's hand snaked around her waist. I had never seen him before, though I imagined it was Rocco.

I cracked my knuckles and clenched my fists. Real or not, touching what was mine was outright disrespectful, and I didn't appreciate being made a fool.

Maybe Amalia noticed the hole I was searing into the side of Rocco's face.

"Kai," she said, moving toward me immediately. As if rehearsed, I pulled her to my chest at the same time as she levered up to press her lips to mine. But I crushed her to me, hand in her hair, deepening the kiss.

Our first kiss.

My cock stirred at the sound and sensation of her soft moan inside my mouth. Amalia tasted fucking divine, and I couldn't help the urge to know what the rest of her would feel like on my tongue.

Conscious of her family's presence, I reluctantly pulled away, kissing her one last time before combing my fingers through her freshly trimmed hair.

"Maybe that was a little too convincing," she whispered.

"You cut it," I said, ignoring her.

"You're observant."

"Why?" The question tumbled out, and when the edges of her mouth twitched, I quickly regretted possibly making her feel as if I didn't like it. As if she didn't look fucking exquisite.

Since when did I care about hurting her feelings?

Amalia fisted my shirt and dug her nails into the side of my ribs. "Have you already forgotten your little stunt from the other day?"

I leaned into her ear. "It's perfect, vicious. Just means I get to hold a little tighter while you scream for me."

"You're a cocky son of bitch." She laughed, lips brushing my ear. "You'll *never* hear me scream for you, Cain."

My arm curled around her waist. "Challenge accepted."

A throat cleared behind us, and Amalia clapped my chest, twisting around to introduce me.

"Rocco, this is my fiancé, Kai Cain."

His smile was tight, eyes on me for just a fraction of a second before they were back on Amalia. I decided then that I didn't like him, didn't like the way his grin shifted and his eyes darkened. And it wasn't my M.O. to play nice with people I preferred to see choking on their own blood.

"Kai!" Isabel looped an arm through mine and escorted me toward the table. Amalia resisted, but I dragged her with me.

"Fuck him," I whispered near her ear.

"Have I fucked him, you ask?"

My hold on her wrist tightened. It was meant as a joke, a dig at me, because she loved this game of seduction and provocation as much as I did. And while I knew she had a past, the thought of her sleeping with this bastard made my blood hot. He wanted her. That much was clear.

"Don't provoke me. Not here."

Her deep red lips dipped between her teeth as she mulled over my words, nodding subtly as understanding dawned. Killing Rocco wouldn't exactly bode well with her family.

Dinner was, for the most part, uneventful. The food was delicious and kept everyone occupied enough that the conversation was slow. Aside from the fleeting glances between Rocco and me, the atmosphere remained light. It was a strange feeling, but in some ways, comforting. I couldn't pinpoint a time in my life when I sat at a table as a 'family' besides Derek and Eva's.

This was different. In a good way.

"Kai." Isabel's voice broke my thoughts. "I assume my daughter has shown you her studio."

"Mamá," Amalia interrupted with an annoyed groan, forgetting for a split second that I was supposed to be the love of her life. "I mean, of course, I have. But—"

"Oh, stop! I know you hate the attention," Isabel said with an eye roll. "But let me brag. I'm your mother. It's what I'm supposed to do."

Amalia brought her fork to her lips and forced a smile. "Please, continue."

"Thank you." Turning back to me, she said, "Amalia donated a beautiful portrait to next week's local art auction."

My future wife was an artist, a talent she had yet to share with me other than as part of a cover story and strict guidelines on a contract. I'd been curious to see her talent and wondered which of the paintings displayed around the Villa had been created by her hand.

"All the proceeds will go to an organization back home called *Carrusel*, a home for orphaned children. Her idea!"

I covered Amalia's hand with mine and squeezed as an unfamiliar emotion filled my chest. She met my eyes.

"That's very generous but not surprising." But that was a lie. I was stunned to hear of this side of her, and her choice of charity did not go unnoticed.

A woman's heart had never mattered much to me, but maybe she was changing my mind.

"So, how did you two meet?" It was the first time Rocco had addressed me since we'd sat at the table. He had a glass of scotch in hand.

I reached for Amalia's hand. The story she'd spun and had made me memorize was hanging off the tip of my tongue, but I thought I'd give it my own spin just to fuck with him.

"I'm glad you asked," I said, knocking back my drink. "Even though we've been together for the last six months, we actually met four years ago."

Amalia choked on her water and gave my hand the grip of death. "Breathe, baby," I crooned into her ear, and she tensed before releasing a breath. "Good girl."

Her eyes slid toward me, and I met her gaze and winked.

"Oh, you never told me this part of the story!" Isabel set her elbows on the table and leaned forward enthusiastically.

"That makes two of us," Amalia muttered quietly from between her teeth.

"My brother and me, were out having the time of our lives, just tearing up the town. You know how that goes." It was mostly true. "Derek was meeting his wife, but there was a communication issue, and they lost contact. So, while we were trying to locate her, that's when we ran into my girl here." I scooted her chair closer, and she pinched my thigh under the table. But I played it off and looped my arm around her shoulders. "You two have been together for a while, so you know that feeling when you see someone for the first time, and they take your breath away."

Amalia was staring at me, intrigue written all over her face.

"She is stunning, isn't she?" Rocco said from behind his glass.

Leaning over, I kissed the corner of her lips and watched her slowly close her eyes at the contact. "The most beautiful woman I've ever seen."

Gio snorted from his seat, suppressing a laugh into his glass of water.

"So, how did you find your sister-in-law?"

Amalia cocked her head and narrowed her eyes. "Yeah, Kai, tell her what happened."

"Amalia. She saved the day."

"The hero, huh?" Rocco chuckled darkly.

"Sure was," I said, kissing her temple. "It took me a while to come back into her life, but I'm glad I did."

"Oh, ¡*que belleza*!" Isabel proposed a toast, and we all joined in, clinking our glasses together, with the exception of fucking Rocco.

"Amalia, I found this gorgeous little boutique—"

"Sorry, I need to get some air." Amalia hurried out of her chair and left the dining room. My smug grin was gone. The point had been to mess with Rocco, not to upset her.

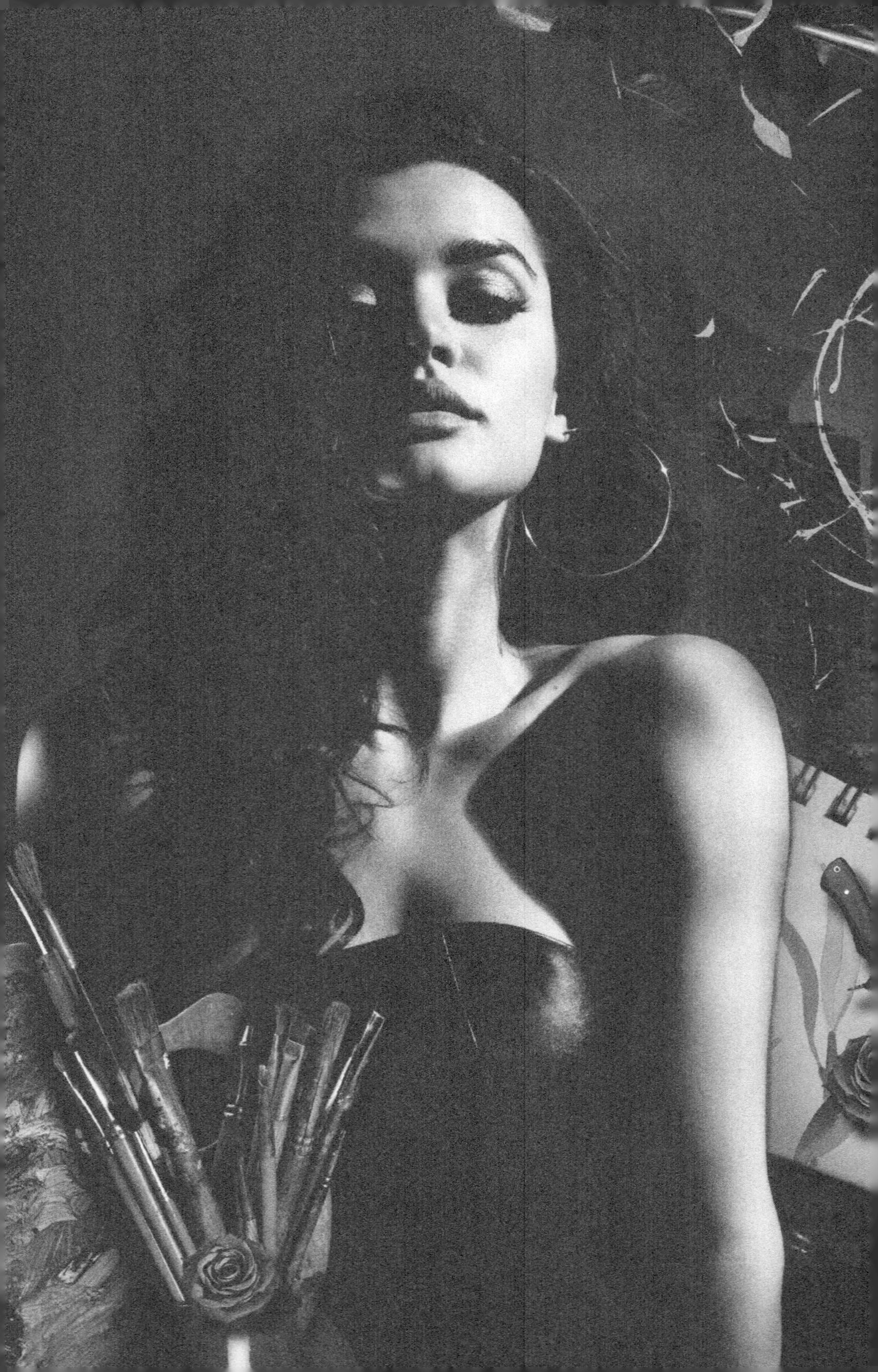

Chapter 9
Amalia

I SLAMMED my glass on the metal workbench and braced myself against the edge, letting the whiskey slide down my throat, hoping to ease my nerves. I wasn't a big drinker, but if there was ever a time that called for a buzz and temporary amnesia, this was it. Kai was messing with my head, my parents and their expectations, the death of Cassie, Alba, and Felipe, hell, even Derek and Eva.

It was almost too much.

Sighing a heavy breath, I refilled my cup and brought it to my lips.

"Celebrating alone?" Kai's voice rattled me, and it made me want to chuck my drink at him, especially when I glanced up to find him leaning against the doorframe of the garage, looking too good to be so damn infuriating.

"Keyword, alone."

He snickered, his full attention now on my car as he stepped inside.

"Hellcat Widebody. Sexy," he said, as he ran a hand along the sleek black hood.

"You into cars?"

"Who doesn't love a Charger, but I'm into another type of ride."

I rolled my eyes. "Of course you are."

Kai's laughter shook his chest. "I didn't mean that. Not that that's not a favorite of mine, but—"

"I don't care," I said, throwing back another sip.

"Tell me, vicious, what's got you bailing on dinner and out here alone drinking your feelings?"

"Leave."

"No," he said, then pulled up a chair next to me, taking a seat.

"Fine, stay." I'd started to walk away when he grabbed my wrist and pulled me back. The sudden switch in direction caused me to stumble and trip on his boot, my ass landing in his lap. "Kai, consider yourself extremely lucky that I need you. Otherwise, you'd be buried under my stables." I tried to push out of his hold, but it was a vise. "You don't need all your limbs for the wedding. Don't test me."

"Come on, Amalia. Dinner was going smoothly. What's got you so bent out of shape?"

"How about your little love story back there? Are you crazy?"

"We have a love story?"

I shrieked out of frustration. "Kai! You can't go off script, especially in front of Gio and Rocco."

His smile vanished the instant I mentioned Rocco's name.

"I don't like him."

"It doesn't matter who you like. That's irrelevant. Is he the reason you put on that act? Like some pissing contest to see whose dick is bigger?"

Kai huffed. "You slept with him?"

"Who I've fucked before you got here is none of your goddamn business."

He tipped my chin, meeting my eyes. "That's where you're wrong. He clearly wants you, and if you're my wife, I won't tolerate another man lusting after you and flaunting it to my face. I've buried bodies, too."

I briefly wondered if he could feel how wet I was through the fabric of my skirt. He just admitted to being willing to kill a man in my honor. Frustration ate away at my insides, the feeling suffocating and nearly insufferable. I took what I wanted when it came to men and never held back. I wouldn't deny that I wanted Kai Cain. That I wanted to straddle him in this fucking chair or get on my knees.

I had visions of him taking me over my workbench, on the hood of my car, hell, even right here on the floor. But giving in to him meant I'd lose.

I found his eyes again, the ire gone from them, replaced by a different flame, one that seemed to ignite my own. He said nothing as his thumb rubbed my cheek.

Giving in would be so easy. I just knew he would make me feel things I'd never experienced and reach places that had never been touched.

"Why haven't you given me the grand tour of your studio?"

I knew this was coming. Talking about my art was too intimate. It wasn't something I wanted to get into with Kai.

My mother and her big mouth.

"Because no one is allowed in but me."

He slid a strand of hair behind my ear and flashed an infuriatingly sexy smile.

"All that talent and you want to keep it hidden. The portraits hung in your home without signatures, they're yours, aren't they?"

"It's late." I attempted to get up, but he held me tighter.

"Why are you so afraid to be alone with me?"

"Afraid," I snickered. "Don't flatter yourself. You're not as scary as you think you are."

He drew soft circles underneath my shirt with his thumb, and satisfaction lit up his face when goosebumps scattered across my skin.

"I'm not trying to be scary to you, vicious."

I couldn't handle the velvet tone of his voice and that hungry look in his eyes. Had he been anyone else, I would have been naked, waiting for him, long before he crossed the threshold.

But my pride was a bitch.

"I just have two questions."

"That's two too many."

Kai tipped his head and laughed.

"Humor me. Please."

I was disgusted at how easily he chipped away at every wall I put up, just by the way his stupid blue eyes penetrated my soul.

Huffing an exaggerated sigh, I relented. "What's got your curiosity so piqued you're willing to risk a throat punch by not letting me up?"

Another hearty laugh sent a jolt straight to my pussy.

"Can I watch you paint?"

"No."

"Why?"

"Because I'm always naked."

Kai stiffened beneath me, fingers digging into my flesh. "Are you fucking with me?"

"No. Last question."

He remained quiet. Pensive. And licked his lips, immediately drawing my attention to his fleshy mouth.

"Why did you choose that specific charity for your auction?"

There was something different about the way he posed his question. The smoky tones in his voice were gone, replaced by vulnerability.

It was my turn to watch him with curious eyes. I knew why he'd asked. But if I confessed the truth, that I'd thought of him and his upbringing, he'd look too much into it. Because it was just an idea, from the experiences of what I knew of his childhood.

An inspiration.

Fuck.

"You know why."

He nodded. "I like that."

"Kai Cain has a heart." He laughed, taking my hand and pressing it to his chest.

"You feel that?"

I felt it all. The fast pace of his heart, the electricity buzzing between us, his hard cock against my thigh. I was fighting a losing battle and I knew it.

Rules be damned.

"You want a drink?" I asked, grabbing the bottle of Macallan and readjusting so that I straddled his lap. My body took the reins of this internal battle, if only for another taste of him.

"I thought you wanted to drink alone," he said, his hand on my hip.

I popped open the bottle and grinned. "So, is that a no?"

Kai's free hand smoothed up my back, settling at my bra line and making me shiver. "That's a fuck yes."

I brought the whiskey to my lips and took a long swig. Our eyes connected, and neither of us said a word as I leaned forward and spit the liquid into his mouth.

"Shit," he groaned, grabbing me by the nape and crushing his lips to mine. Anything holding me back flitted away within a blink.

My first theory proved to be true. Kai devoured me in a way that made me question if I had ever been truly kissed before. I couldn't hold back the moans he pulled from my throat, born from the need to be completely taken by this man. And my body reacted on instinct as I ground my pussy over his cock until we were both panting and ready to shed our clothes and our sanity.

No.

Placing my palms on his chest, I pushed him back, and his kisses and counterthrusts slowed.

"Stop. Stop, please."

"Baby, I stopped. But what's wrong?"

"We can't do this." I got to my feet. "I have to get to bed anyway. I have a long day. Meeting with someone potentially connected to the ambush on the highway."

I stood, attempting to catch my breath, when he grabbed my elbow and hauled me back.

"Repeat that again."

"Pretty sure I was clear the first time."

It was easier to be annoyed with him than resist fucking him, so I'd channel that.

"I heard you loud and clear, but I'm not quite understanding your logic."

"Would you like me to grab some crayons and draw you a picture?"

His mouth twitched, and he swallowed his irritation. "A man who tried to murder you wants you to meet him tomorrow?"

"I'm glad you're finally keeping up."

"Amalia, stop. Enough with the bullshit. You're not going."

My laughter made him roll his eyes and sigh. "I think you might have had a little too much to drink because you're absolutely delirious and out of line." I poked his chest with my finger. "You don't tell me what I can or can't do. I don't answer to you or anyone. The quicker you get that through that pretty head of yours, the better."

Again, I attempted to leave, but he tugged me back a second time, my back flush to his chest while his arms locked around me.

"I don't doubt you're good at what you do, but you're not bulletproof. You're five-foot-nothing; when a man wants to take, he will."

"Fuck you. Let me go." I tried to break free, but he squeezed tighter to the point I could barely take a breath.

"All he needs to do is get you in the perfect hold." His lips grazed my ear. "And you're done." I was one second from breaking his nose with the back of my skull, but the following words out of his mouth lit a fire in my belly. "No one touches what's mine."

I froze. "I'm not yours. And I can handle myself."

"I know you can, and it's sexy as fuck. But that doesn't mean—"

A loud grunt left his lips when my elbow connected with his abdomen.

"It means everything."

Kai doubled over, hands on his knees as he attempted to compose himself. "Okay…you got a cheap shot in." His breaths were ragged. "But that's not how it always goes down in the real world."

"Let me apologize for the cheap shots to all the men who have died by my hand in the last decade."

"You wanna do this?" he questioned, with a wild look in his eyes. As he ripped off his shirt, a grin pulled at the corner of his mouth.

"You like pain?" I asked, tugging my shirt over my head.

His eyes fell to my lacy red bra, and he licked his lips. "Sometimes it's worth it."

"It's always worth it," I added, then caught him with a right hook to his abdomen.

Kai was ready this time, abs tight, and only a slight grunt escaped. But fuck me if it wasn't sexy.

"Hit me again," he said, dodging another punch.

"Fuck you. This isn't a lesson."

"I know it's not." Tackling me to the floor, his hard body covered mine. "It's fucking foreplay."

"You're crazy."

"So you're telling me, your pussy isn't dripping wet for me right now?"

I couldn't even bring myself to deny it. My panties were absolutely wrecked. Kai slid his hand under my skirt, hiking up the fabric, and

I shuddered with anticipation.

"This is beautiful," he said, fingers brushing the tattoo running up the length of my thigh. "It's very fitting."

I wasn't sure if his comment was backhanded, considering the ink was that of a pit viper—the Mexican cantil—entwined in vines and roses.

"Yeah, well, that's saying something, isn't it?" I challenged.

His eyes journeyed up my body until they met mine. "I've lived at the edge of death my whole life. I'm drawn to it." He squeezed my thigh. "Drawn to you."

"What are you doing?" My voice was a whisper. His gaze stayed locked on mine as he climbed off and hooked my underwear, sliding them down my legs with no resistance from me. The red fabric was visibly soaked, and he bit down on his bottom lip and sucked in a breath.

"Oh, fuck," he groaned as he brought the thin fabric to his nose. The sight had my thighs clenching for friction. "Go, vicious. Now."

I stood up on my elbows. "Now you want me to go."

"I'm about to fucking devour you, and if that's not what you want, then you need to leave."

With my panties clutched in his fist, he got to his feet. I followed, adjusting my skirt back down over my thighs. "Maybe you should keep those," I said as I crossed the threshold.

"Oh, and Kai, be ready at eight sharp tomorrow."

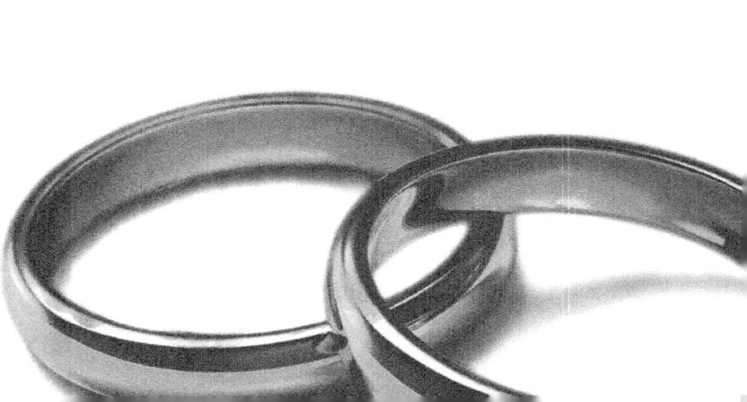

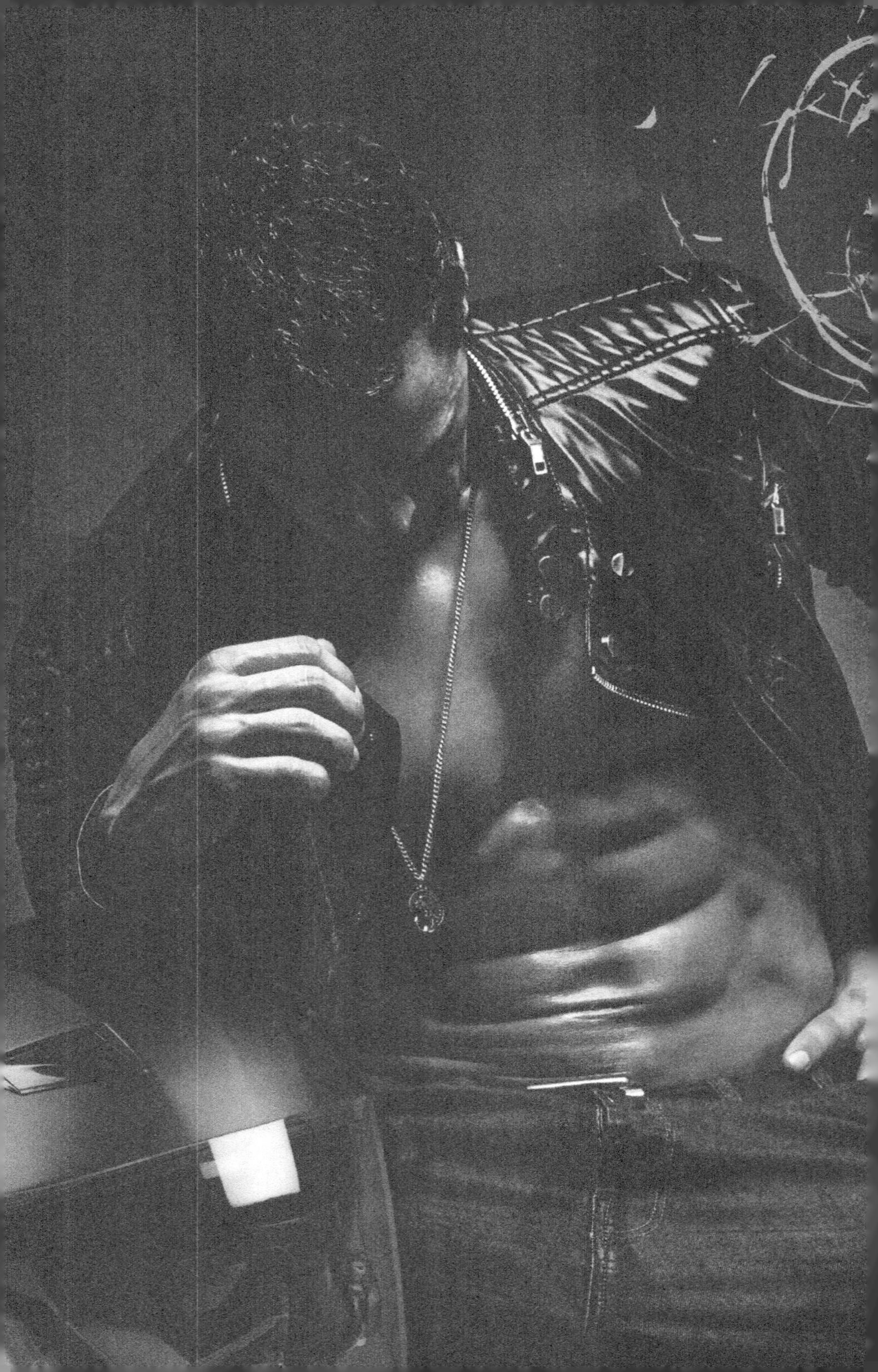

Chapter 10
Kai

> You left without me.
>
> I had some last-minute prep for this meeting.
>
> And you don't dictate my schedule, Cain.

ROLLING my eyes, I stuffed the phone into my back pocket and leaned against a metal railing as the elevator ascended. Amalia had asked me to accompany her, but she was already gone by the time I woke up. Being with her was a constant game of whiplash—hot and cold. One moment, she was in my lap, spitting whiskey into my mouth, and the next, I was doubled over by an impressive right hook to the stomach. But I had to admit, I enjoyed every second.

When the doors slid with a ding, a tall blonde woman stepped inside. Her smile brightened, and she stood beside me instead of moving to a far corner. I shifted away, feeling slightly suspicious and uncomfortable by her sudden proximity.

"Eighth floor, too," she said with an excited chirp. "You must be Kai." Her gaze was on my signet ring. "Amalia said you were on the way."

She had my full attention. "Oh, yeah. And who are you?"

"A friend," she replied with a wink, patting the black briefcase under her arm. "She said you were handsome, and she wasn't lying, but that bitch was definitely holding out on me."

While it was clear she was speaking with affection, her choice of words regarding Amalia affected me in all the wrong ways.

Before I could ask any more questions, the doors shifted open, and she hurriedly moved forward, her eyes on her watch. "We're a little behind schedule. Come on, Mr. Cain."

Mr. Cain.

As curious as I was, I'd get my answers from the source, so I followed her down a short corridor until we reached slate metal doors. The woman threw them open without knocking, and a dozen pairs of eyes fell on us. I was immediately drawn to the front of the office space, where Amalia stood, one hand on her hip, the other braced against the table. My future wife wore a pantsuit with a plunging neckline, pulling my eyes down the soft, bare skin of her chest beneath a navy-colored blazer. Irrational as it was, I scanned the room, Glock at my hip hot, as I searched for wandering eyes. That's when I spotted none other than that sack of shit, Rocco.

"Nice of you to join us, Kai." Amalia's lips were moving, but I heard nothing after she'd said my name. All I could do was stare as she glided across the room, stealing the attention of every swinging dick. I stepped closer before I was conscious of my actions, and she startled for a heartbeat when I crushed her to my chest.

"I might just have to gouge out the eyes of every man in this room."

"Distractions are a necessity sometimes."

"Not a fan of this one," I said, trailing the back of my fingers over the exposed skin of her abdomen. "I don't like men lusting over what belongs to me."

She rose to her toes, one hand on my shoulder—her touch sizzling. "Like I said, you don't own me, Cain," she whispered, ghosting a kiss over my ear and sending a jolt of heat straight to my cock. "You'd do well to remember this is business. Nothing more."

"That would be more believable if I hadn't stuffed your dripping wet panties in my pocket last night," I countered, rolling my thumb over the black engagement ring on her finger. "You're wrong, vicious. You're already mine."

"Senorita Amalia, not to interrupt you and your—"

"Husband," I finished, daring him to say the contrary.

"I wasn't aware the ceremony date had been pushed up. Please accept my congrats."

The tone of his voice and the daggers in his eyes let me know there wasn't a shred of sincerity in his words. Alarms went off and continued to blare when his eyes shifted to Amalia.

I clenched my teeth.

"Kai." The sound of my name on her lips a second time and the warm press of her hand against my chest cooled my rage. "Sit down," she said with a tenderness to her tone I'd yet to hear directed at me.

Covering her hand with mine, I nodded and sat in an empty chair on the far side of the office, across from the woman from the elevator. I realized I hadn't caught her name, but Amalia had greeted her with a smile when we'd entered, easing my nerves.

Everything and everyone in that room ceased to exist the moment she began speaking again. Maybe I should have been paying attention, but it was impossible to focus on anything but her painted lips and the smooth dip between her breasts.

She had to feel the heat of my gaze because her words faltered before she lifted her attention to me. We made eye contact from across the room, and I spotted the hint of a smile before it faded and her expression hardened. It was then I noticed the asshole from earlier had raised his voice and straightened in his seat. A little too bold for my liking. I wasn't sure when I'd developed this sense of protectiveness, despite knowing damn well this woman was capable of handling herself. But with every harsh word he spoke, how his mouth twisted into a cocky smirk, and the way his arms came up as if he challenged her to disagree, the murderous heat in my chest swelled. I motioned to get to my feet, but before I could react, Amalia rounded her desk, and in one swift motion, she pulled a gun and sent three rounds into the now-dead bastard.

Gunfire broke out in the small space, causing echoes of broken glass and ricochet to boom around us and ring in my ears as chaos erupted.

The men at the table hit the floor, their own weapons drawn as blood spilled around them. I couldn't see Amalia anymore, and my heart suddenly felt weighted with worry.

"Amalia!" I shouted, disregarding my own safety as I let off round after round toward men behind chairs and under the long table.

A hand on my forearm made me jerk, and I hesitated just in time to realize it was the blonde woman.

"Let's take care of these bastards first. Our girl can handle herself." I took cover when a bullet exploded against the wall behind us. Crouching beside me, she dropped her mag and reloaded.

"What the fuck is going on? Where is she?"

"Hmm, that was fast," she said, before taking off without answering a single goddamn question.

I sprung to my feet and scanned the room, eyeing a wounded man huddled in a corner. I didn't know who the fuck he was or why my Glock was shoved inside his mouth, but at that moment, my priority was my future wife.

By the time I'd pulled the trigger, the gunfire had stopped. Twisting around, I was met with the barrel of Rocco's weapon. I lifted mine, and we were suddenly in a tense standoff. I had no problem pulling the trigger, even if it meant I'd also take one to the chest, but he was a friend of the Montesinos, so I hesitated.

"Careful, Rocco. Put it down."

Amalia stepped between us, her back to me as she confronted the man who'd been her childhood friend. I lowered my gun the second she walked into my line of fire, as did he. A sense of relief washed over me when I finally had her within my sight.

"Are you okay?" I asked, giving her a once-over.

"Of course." Her focus was still on Rocco, but she squeezed my hand reassuringly. "Rocco, is there a particular reason you were threatening my fiancée's life?"

He sucked his teeth and holstered his gun. "Just a lapse of judgment, *muñeca*. Everything happened so fast. Didn't know who he was for a second. That's all."

"Is that so?"

"Of course."

He was full of shit. But I'd let it slide…for now.

I shot him a wink and slipped my hand beneath Amalia's chin, tilting her head back and kissing her. She insisted we act the part, and I fully intended to take advantage of the opportunity, if only to see the look on that son of a bitch's face.

"Holly," she called for her friend. "I see you've met Kai."

"I have."

Holly said nothing else and began punching messages into her phone as she walked into the hallway. Rocco had slipped out before we realized he was gone.

"Why did we just kill a dozen men?" Amalia smiled and patted my cheek.

"I like that you shoot first and ask questions later, Cain."

When she tried to push out of my arms, I tugged her back.

"I'm just Cain again?"

"You'll always be just Cain."

I read between the lines, her words meant to sting. But I knew better. "You're a terrible liar. You stood between me and his bullet. Maybe you do care."

Her laugh and the way her body shook against mine had my cock thickening.

"Now, Cain, who would take your place on such short notice if you're dead?"

My teeth caught the soft skin of her ear, and she squirmed.

"Why is your heart racing?" I caressed between her breasts, and Amalia released a small breath of air.

"I just murdered three men."

I pulled her closer, my hand now journeying down the length of her torso and hesitating when I reached the waistband of her pants. Feeling no resistance from her, I continued, dipping inside her panties and parting her with two fingers.

"Tell me, does murder also make your pussy wet?"

She let her head fall against my chest, eyes closed, and her face split into a grin.

"About as much as it makes your cock hard," she replied breathily.

We were having a moment, both of us high on the adrenaline of what had unfolded minutes before, but when I caught sight of a pair of lifeless eyes, it was a bucket of cold water.

"What happened here?"

Amalia opened her eyes but made no effort to shift out of my arms.

"Our families have been doing business with Fernando and his men for over five years. But they can't be trusted." She placed her hand on my forearm and pulled away. "I received word he had plans to double-cross my father and sell him out, and one of the plates recovered from the highway was traced back to one of his men, which made him the prime suspect in the ambush. But now, I'm not so sure."

"So why kill him before getting answers?"

"He threatened to fuck me into submission, and I don't tolerate disrespect. You missed all that?"

I'd been too distracted. Guilt made my stomach heavy.

"How about a little heads-up next time?"

Her eyes were on my hand and the way my wet fingers glistened. "I wasn't sure which way things were going to go. I trusted your instincts would kick in, and I was right."

"You trust me?"

Amalia looked up at me from her thick lashes, red lips curved into a smile. "I trust you'll follow through with our contract."

"What makes you so certain?"

She tightened her grip around my wrist and nudged my fingers against the seam of my mouth. Our eyes locked as I slipped them inside and sucked them clean.

"I just have a good feeling about you."

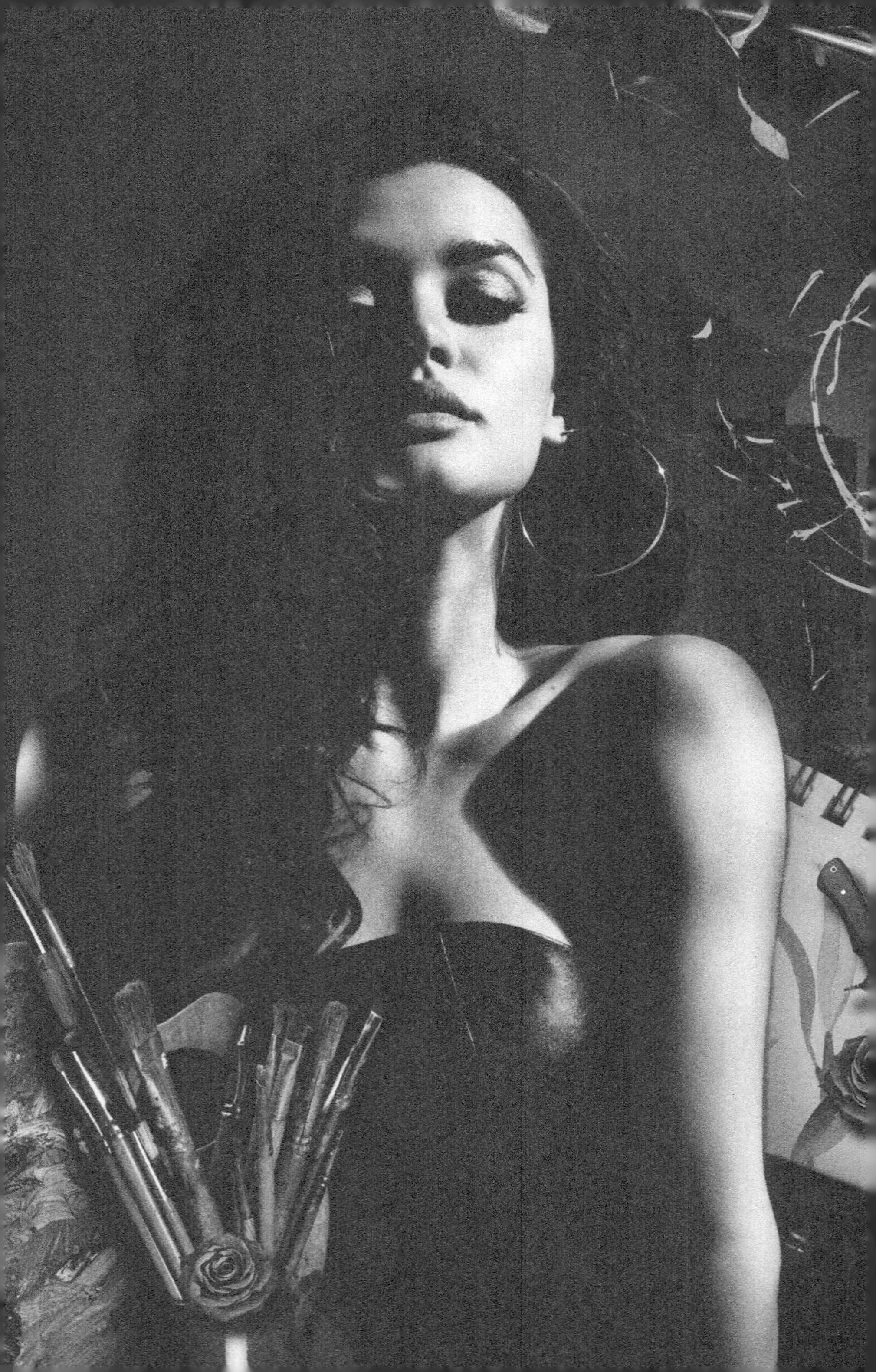

Chapter 11
Amalia

"**AMALIA,** wait!"

My brother's hurried footsteps echoed behind me as I tore through the dark corridor. I'd tried to make it to my room without anyone noticing, especially Gio. I said nothing and moved faster.

"Mali," he sing-songed, calling me by my childhood nickname.

Clearly not getting the hint, I came to an abrupt stop and wiped at the dried blood I knew was still smeared on my clothes before twisting around. The hours had turned grueling between wrangling the clean-up crew and combing and deleting surveillance. I needed a shower as soon as possible.

"Gio, what are you doing up at this time?"

"Waiting for you," he replied, matter-of-fact. "I was worried."

I stepped closer, careful to stay in the shadows. "The last thing you should be is worried about me. I had some last-minute wedding errands and stopped by Holly's. Nothing out of the ordinary."

"So why are you bleeding?"

"I'm not."

He sighed an exasperated breath. "Okay, then, why do you have someone else's blood on you?"

I loved my brother. He was a beautiful soul, and although it pained me to be away from him as much as I had been throughout his life, distance was for his own good. Gio didn't deserve to be tainted by this life. We'd tried to keep him sheltered as long as possible. Boarding schools and time abroad with relatives and close family friends. But he was older, more observant. Curious. And I often wondered if the taste for blood and chaos ran deep in our veins. If his hands were always meant to be drenched with the souls of dead men.

Like mine.

"You ask a lot of questions," I said, mushing his face.

"They're valid ones."

"Maybe. But sometimes certain things are best left unknown, Gio." I tapped his cheek, flashing a forced smile that I hoped he couldn't see right through. "I'm okay."

"Until you're not."

"But isn't that true for everyone?"

He shrugged. "I don't care about everyone else. I worry about you like I did for Tony. And he's dead."

Tony and I weren't the closest, but we loved each other despite our fights and disagreements. He was hot-headed and impulsive, and I knew it would get him killed someday. And I'd been right.

"I'll be fine. Besides, I have Kai now," I added to appease him and ease his nerves. I could tell he liked him. "Get to bed." Gio was nearly a foot taller than me, but I'd always see him as my baby.

"You know, you could be a little nicer to him."

He suddenly made me second-guess my last thought.

After my shower, I paced my room—anxious, adrenaline reigniting. There was no way I'd get to sleep. I was too fucking wired. And before I could think too hard about my next decision, I was standing in front of Kai's door. As I leaned my forehead against the hard oak, I sighed nervously, annoyed with myself. Because since when had a man ever gotten under my skin the way he had? No matter how hard I tried, I couldn't stop thinking about his hands on me, inside me, his lips against my neck.

My panties never stood a chance.

I turned the knob to his door, determined to take back my power. Get him out of my system somehow, even if it meant throat-punching him. As I stepped into the dark bedroom, it was silent. At nearly three in the morning, what else had I been expecting apart from a sleeping Kai? He had one arm behind his head, a bare fucking torso, and no blanket. My eyes immediately centered on his dick.

I'd thought about how good of a fuck he'd be more times than I would ever admit to myself.

Three years. Could I really go three years alongside this man without touching him? I knew the answer. We were already dangerously close. And it had only been a week. What would things be like by the end of our contract?

I cursed into the dark with a hushed voice and turned to leave, my hand on the knob.

"If you walk out that door, make sure you're faster than me."

"Is that a threat?"

He brought his other arm behind his head, looking every bit like the smug asshole he was. "Take that whichever way you want. But you came here for a reason, didn't you?"

"Maybe." I pulled a knife from my waistband. Kai eyed the sharp steel as it glinted under the glow of a nearby window.

"Is that what you're into? Because I've been there, done that. It doesn't faze me."

One name suddenly came to mind, and I found myself gripping

the hilt of my knife a little tighter.

Helena.

I knew they'd been together for a time. She'd said as much herself. And while she and I weren't exactly friends, she had my respect. And I hers.

However, at the moment, the thought of Helena and Kai together made my teeth clench.

"I was thinking a bit more drastic."

"Were you? Why don't you come here and show me what you have in mind."

Decisions, decisions.

I twisted the knob, intent on getting the fuck out of there…

"I couldn't sleep either." I froze. "And I was probably minutes from coming to you, too."

Releasing the brass knob, I turned and leaned my back against the door. "And why is that? Too shaken up about what happened today?"

"I was trying to figure out why I was so upset when I didn't know where you were or if you were okay."

His admission electrified the air between us, rendering us both silent until my knife hit the floor with a clang, and I stalked forward. Kai sat up when I crawled on his bed and straddled him. In a matter of seconds, his hands were on my waist, gripping my cami and tearing it up over my arms. The shirt hadn't even hit the floor before his warm mouth was on me.

"We're not…having sex." My voice grew ragged as he held my nipple gently between his teeth.

"I need you to sit on my goddamn face."

With my nails scraping across his scalp and through his long hair, I tugged his head back and grinned. "Straight to it, huh?"

Kai grabbed the back of my neck and slammed his lips against my mouth. But I was never one to be dominated in the bedroom, so I fought for control. And he met my challenge, fingers snaking into my hair, his grip biting and so fucking delicious. I moaned, and my voice vibrated down his throat.

"I haven't been able to think of anything else besides your sweet cunt. You got me fiending for you, vicious. Like a goddamn addict, and I've only had a taste."

I squeezed my eyes closed and arched into his eager mouth as he licked between the valley of my breasts.

"You want me to feed you my pussy, Cain?" As he tipped me back on the bed, I struggled to keep the taunting smile on my face and in my voice, but when he gripped the edges of my shorts and panties and nearly tore them from my body, my resolve crumbled.

"Like I'm a fucking starving man," he growled into the wet skin of my inner thigh, the tip of his nose ascending to where I craved him the most.

This wasn't part of the plan. I'd set boundaries, and he'd scorched the line of every single one.

"Shit," I gasped as he suctioned my clit into his mouth.

Just this once. That's it. Just one time, I repeated to myself as I bit down on the corner of my lip, almost drawing blood.

Just one…

"Kai…*más. Así.* Don't stop." (More. Just like that.)

Curving two fingers inside me, he ran the flat of his tongue vertically until he was over my belly and up my torso, then he circled one nipple and slid past my collarbone, until he hovered over my mouth.

"I told you not to stop."

His tongue swept across my teeth. "Since when do I ever listen to anything you say?"

I nipped at his mouth until he hissed and sunk his fingers deeper inside me, forcing my body to arch off the mattress.

"Lie back."

"Make me."

He released a dark chuckle against my parted lips and sat back on his legs, retrieving his hand and eyeing me as he licked his fingers. "Okay," was all he said before he gripped my hips and pushed me over the edge.

There was no time to protest or brace myself for the assault of his tongue on my clit because my head and upper torso hung off the side of the bed as he held me in place, hands digging into my skin.

"Kai...wait." I clawed at the sheets, trying to leverage myself, but he spread me wide and ate until my whole body was shaking, and I felt light-headed from the blood rushing to my head.

"God, when you say my name..." Lifting my hips off the mattress, he surged deeper until I came apart in his mouth. But no matter how loud I screamed and squirmed in his grasp, he wouldn't stop.

"Kai, are you trying to kill me," I said between whimpers.

"You can take it. I want more. You taste so fucking sweet when you come." The palm of his hand suddenly came down hard on my clit, causing me to jerk and yelp at the sting. "Again."

Tears gathered in my eyes when his hand came down again. "No...fuck!" Fisting the sheet, I stuffed it inside my mouth and bit down as another sinful wave of pleasure roared through me.

"Harder," he growled and spanked my pussy one last time, making me writhe until my entire body felt like Jell-O.

I wasn't aware of how much time had passed since I'd gotten my breathing under control while staring aimlessly at the spinning ceiling fan above our heads.

"Are you going to say something, or did I finally fuck you into silence?"

Shaking my head, I breathed deeply, feeling confident enough in my muscles to lift onto my elbows, my eyes falling on Kai, who had laid back against the headboard. His big cock was still erect as he stroked himself.

But it was then, when I realized how badly I wanted more of him, that everything came rushing forward at once.

"What's wrong?" He sat up and moved toward me, his expression showing his concern. Somehow, I summoned the strength to get up, trembling legs landing on the floor.

"I'll see you tomorrow, Cain." And I was out the door before he could stop me.

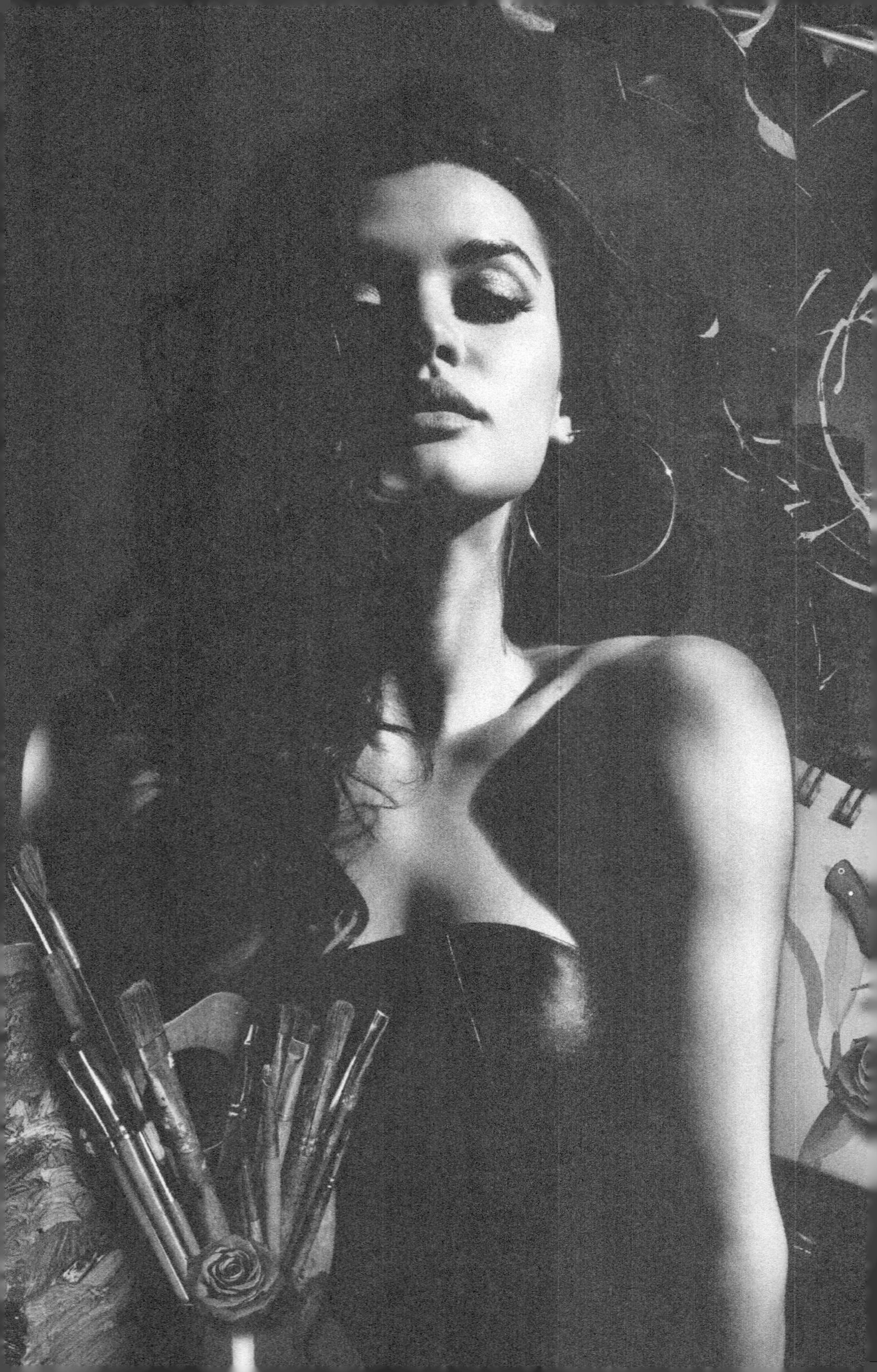

Chapter 12
Amalia

RUBBING out the soreness in my neck, I stepped out of my room and pushed all thoughts of Kai and his skilled tongue from my mind. It wasn't like I hadn't had those experiences with other men. He wasn't special.

I found myself repeating those words in my thoughts, and it annoyed me when I realized it was as if I was trying to convince myself rather than be reassuring.

Movement, followed by a soft thud, had me whipping around, my nerves oddly on edge.

Valentina's bright eyes stared back at me, and a broad smile adorned her pretty cherub face. I glanced down both directions of the hall and saw no one.

"Valentina, ¿que haces aquí solita?" (What are you doing here all alone?)

Surely, Derek and Eva would keep better tabs on their little girl, especially in a stranger's home. Intrusive worries suddenly sent my heart spiraling, and I bent down to pick up the one-year-old, stopping to listen for anything out of the norm. The unusual silence did nothing to ease my nerves.

Had Fernando's men retaliated?

I checked the baby for blood spatter or any signs of injuries. But she seemed too happy to have witnessed any distress. However, that meant nothing, as she was still so young.

The booming sound of a motor revving startled us both. I squeezed her to my chest, popped open a false compartment in a hallway table, pulled out a shotgun, and darted for the door. Once outside, I was met with varying expressions.

Gio was smiling, hands over his ears. Eva's wary eyes moved between my gun and her daughter as she gripped Derek's forearm as if holding him back. I knew that look in his eyes and where his thoughts had drifted. He was calculating, assessing all the ways he could kill me before I harmed his baby. Did he think me that much of a monster? I might have been a heartless bitch when it came to my enemies. But this sweet angel. Never.

As if she could read my thoughts, Valentina placed her hand on my cheek and giggled before smearing my lipstick, and I couldn't help but smile back.

"Did she escape her crib?"

I snapped up at the sound of Kai's voice. He was on an all-black motorcycle, legs sprawled on each side, keeping him balanced and looking entirely too good after having been left with blue balls just hours prior. But what captivated me the most was his easy smile and amused expression.

He hadn't reacted like his brother or Eva. There was trust in his eyes, and I appreciated that he knew I'd never be capable of harming this baby.

Warmth kindled from somewhere inside me as I returned his gaze and nodded.

"I found her wandering the hallway."

Eva's body visibly relaxed, and a quick breath of relief blew past her lips. It was all I could do not to roll my eyes.

Fuck it. I did anyway.

Derek was still on edge. Any more tension in his jaw, and he'd crack every single tooth.

I had a new favorite pastime. Fucking with Derek.

"Maybe you should keep better watch of your child, Mr. Cain," I taunted, walking down the steps and handing the girl off to her uptight father as he trailed me with a murderous gaze.

Kai stepped off his bike and moved in front of me as I set the gun down and pretended to become enraptured with the damn thing, one eye still on my future husband and expert pussy eater while he subtly shook his head at his brother.

Moments later, I heard the front door open and close behind me, and I could only assume Derek and Eva had gone back inside to have a chat about their little escape artist.

"You like it?" Kai asked close to my ear. The feel of his warm breath sent goosebumps all over my body.

"Since when do you ride?"

"I don't remember a time when I didn't. Had my girl Gloria delivered today."

Turning to him, I arched a curious brow. "Gloria, is it? Is there a story there I should know about?"

He inched closer, his devious grin letting me know he'd thoroughly enjoy whatever he was about to say. "Why, vicious? You want to know if her cunt was as sweet as yours?"

"Fuck you," I whispered from between my teeth, conscious of Gio standing just feet away.

He kissed my cheek tenderly, and I instinctively leaned into the gesture. "I let you slide last night, but next time—"

Snatching him by the collar of his shirt, I murmured, "What

makes you think there will be a next time?"

He stole a kiss, mouth stretching into that sexy fucking smile of his. "You know there will be a next time." Tugging me by the waistband, his thumb lifted my shirt, caressing my skin. "I'll never forget the way you screamed for me." His lips were on my neck. "And what you tasted like when you came on my tongue."

"I think it's cute you think you're the first man to tongue-fuck me."

I shoved him back, intent on walking toward Gio, when Kai curled an arm around my waist.

"But I sure as hell will be the last."

On the inside, I was burning hot, my stomach flipping at his words and the way his feral eyes darkened into threatening slits.

"For three years, maybe."

Kai gritted his teeth and released me, our little game suddenly over, leaving a slightly hollow feeling in my chest. He looked away, and I heard him exhale. There was a heaviness to his sigh.

"You done over there?" Gio asked as he crouched by the bike's exhaust. I bent down next to him, trying to determine what had caught his attention.

"What are you doing?"

"You think I want to see my sister kissing and groping a man?"

"I was *not* groping Kai."

"Sure," he said with a laugh. "I'm not blind." My brother suddenly crept closer, his expression serious. "Newsflash, Mali, your whispers aren't as quiet as you think they are," he added with a shudder.

"*Gio!*" Heat crept up my face.

"What? Don't act like *you're* the one offended. I might need therapy now."

"Oh, God." I pushed him over so that he tumbled onto his ass, and he broke into peals of laughter.

Tires on the paved driveway and the purr of an engine caught my attention. I straightened in time to see Rocco climb out of the back of his SUV and smile brightly the moment he saw me.

It wasn't a secret he had a crush. He'd asked me to marry him during my *Quince* and again at graduation. He'd also offered to help with my grandfather's will and that stupid marriage clause. But as easy as it would have been to choose Rocco, I'd never be able to see him beyond anything more than a brother, making that option an impossibility. I knew he'd want more and somehow use his position as my husband, fake or not, to his advantage. Because while he cared for me in his own ways, I wasn't naïve enough to think he was a righteous man. Without hesitation, Rocco would slit the throat of anyone he thought looked at him sideways.

But then again, were we any different?

I shifted my gaze toward Kai, who was polishing Gloria, the fucking bike, and chatting with Gio. My eyes lingered on them for another beat, and I felt a smile pulling at my lips. I'd never seen my brother take to anyone so fast. It both warmed my heart and aggravated the hell out of me.

"*Muñeca*, sorry to stop by unannounced, but I have some news." He dipped down to drop a kiss on my cheek. "Is Antonio home?"

"My father? Why can't you tell me? Sounds important."

Rocco looked down at me, and his brow creased. "You look… different today," he said as he lit a cigarette.

Maybe my face was still slightly flushed from hanging upside down while Kai's tongue was inside my body.

"I couldn't sleep that well—Roc, what news?"

"Antonio's warehouse in Nogales was set on fire late last night. Four of his men were murdered."

"How did he not know about this? His men always keep him well-informed."

Rocco lifted my chin with his forefinger. "Dead men don't speak."

I shook off his touch and crossed my arms over my chest. "So, who told you?"

"My connects were picking up a shipment, and imagine their shock when they found an inferno instead."

Rocco's father had passed away twelve years ago, and mine had taken him under his wing, mentored, and treated him as if he were his own. Rocco had been nothing but loyal and devoted to my father's business dealings. I shouldn't be questioning his honesty, but something in his eyes put me on alert.

"Did I say or do something wrong?"

I hadn't noticed I'd spaced out until he spoke, jarring me back to the moment in time to catch him motioning behind us where Kai and Gio stood side by side, watching with grave expressions.

"Your bodyguards are burning holes through my head as we speak."

"Go inside and talk with my father. He's probably in his office or having breakfast. I'll catch up in a few."

Rocco nodded and leaned into my cheek for another kiss, but I moved away, causing him to narrow his dark eyes at me. "Everything okay?"

"Of course. But we need to discuss boundaries now that Kai is in my life."

"Hm," he scoffed. "Never thought I'd see the day when Amalia *La Mercinaria* lets herself be dominated by a man."

"It's not like that."

"I would hope not, especially not someone like him." Rocco moved in closer, speaking through his teeth. "I'm not stupid. I know this is just a sham to fulfill your *abuelo's* will. You don't know this man's history. He's trash, Amalia. He doesn't deserve to have someone like you by his side."

Grabbing at his wrist, I met his glare. "Trash? You mean, he lost his parents and was taken in by another family? Now, where have I heard that story before?"

Rocco took a long pull of his cigarette before dropping it on the ground and snuffing the flame with his foot. "See you inside."

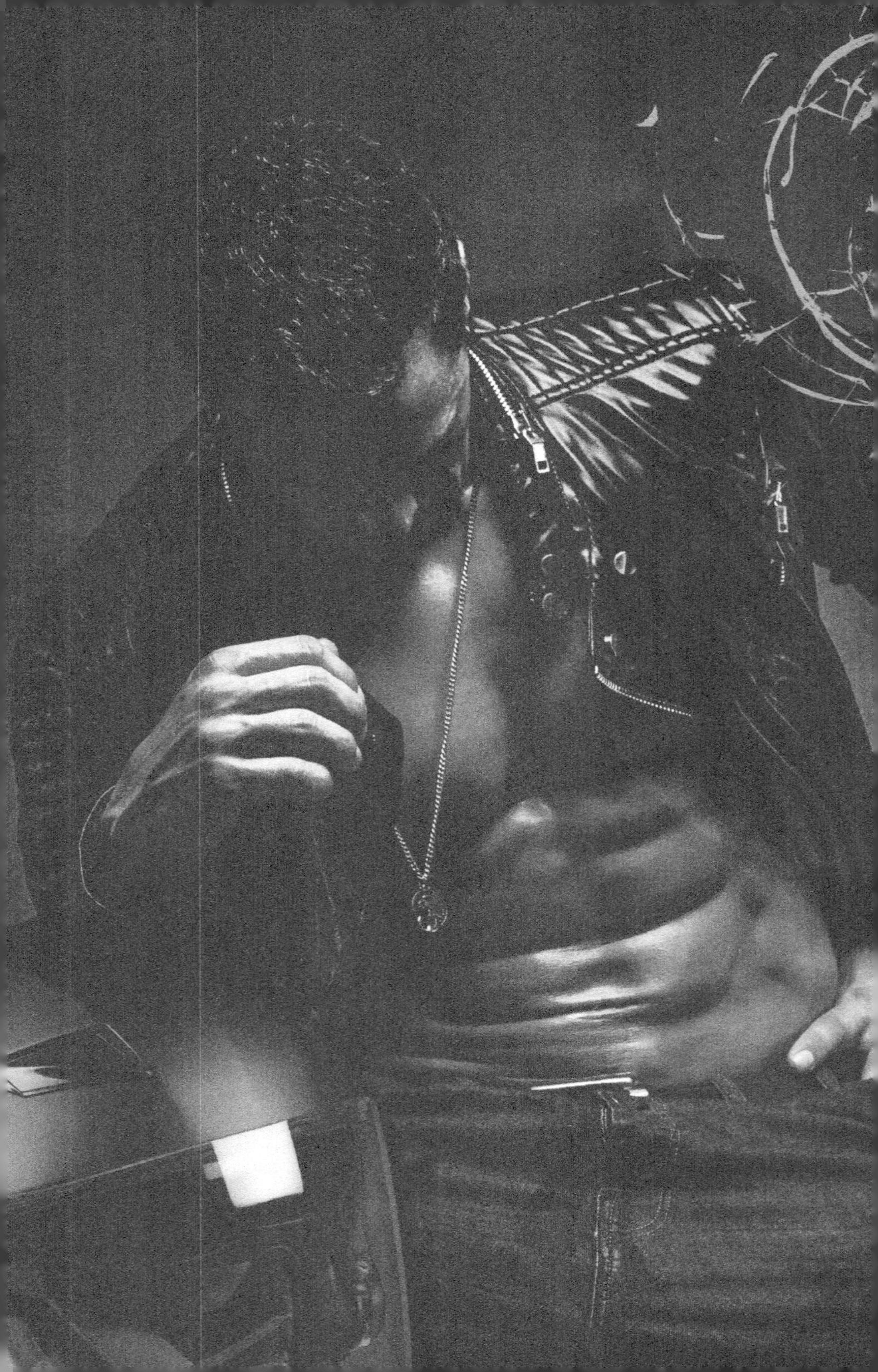

Chapter 13
Kai

    THAT bastard Rocco shot me a look and nod that was anything but cordial as he walked past and made his way inside. It took everything I had to stay rooted in place and not make him swallow that goddamn cigarette while he spoke to Amalia. But I didn't want to give her another reason to fight me. The story of Gloria, or rather, what she thought was the truth, had gotten under her skin. My poorly timed dig had backfired when she threw the reality that she and I were temporary in my face.

    But that's what I wanted, what I'd agreed to, even if thoughts I refused to acknowledge told me otherwise.

    "Kill him."

    I slowly turned toward Gio, shocked by his words and even more taken aback by his face, which was void of emotion, as if he'd just asked me the day of the week.

    "What did you say?"

    "*Kill* him. Do it. I know you can."

Raking my fingers through my hair, I shook my head in disbelief.

"Gio, do you hear yourself? Even if I entertained the thought, Rocco is like a son to your father. I don't think that would go over too well."

The boy's eyes found mine, and they held a mix of fear and anger. "He's going to hurt my sister. You can't let that happen."

A rush of blood whooshed past my ears, and I gripped his shoulder, twisting him toward me. "Why would you say that? Did you overhear something?"

His gaze was downcast as he huffed a breath. "No. It's…just a feeling."

"What's going on?" Amalia's hand was over mine, the one with the death grip on Gio's shoulder. "Cain?"

"I-I asked him if I could go for a ride."

She rolled her eyes. "Sure, you did. You refuse to sit on a horse, not even a carousel, and somehow, you expect me to believe you want to *ride* this crotch rocket?"

"Hey, Gloria is a masterpiece. Don't say that in front of her."

She flashed me a hard stare. "You're sick."

On second thought, maybe messing with her wasn't all bad. She looked fucking adorable when she was pissed off.

"Gio, get inside."

"You're my sister, not my mom."

"I can still kick your ass. Get inside. I need to speak with Kai."

Every time this woman said my name, my cock stirred.

"Gio, listen to your sister." My command spilled out harsher than I intended.

He looked between us briefly, that emotionless expression back in place before he shuffled up the steps and through the front door.

"Do you trust him?"

"Gio?"

"No, that fucker, Rocco."

"Well, it's obvious you don't."

"I'm being serious."

She shrugged. "Is he an honest man? No. But he's been loyal to my father his whole life. Take that answer as you please."

"I don't like it when he touches you."

"There you go again, trying to claim something that's not yours."

My hand trailed down her slender throat and tightened, thumb lifting her chin. "You can deny it all you want, but the way you broke for me, called out for me, and how you were so goddamn wet—that was all mine."

Amalia closed her eyes. "Kai, you and I…this, us…it's not real. Remember that."

"Maybe. I'm not trying to fall in love with you, vicious. But I do plan to fuck you. Own you. And ruin you for anyone else."

She chuckled and rose to her toes, running her lips over mine. "We'll see who ruins who." Pushing out of my arms, she started for the steps. "Come on, my father is going to need us. Rocco said one of his warehouses was hit last night. That is, unless you need more alone time with your girl over there."

"Amalia, Gio asked me to kill Rocco for you." She froze, her breath catching. "He said he was going to hurt you. Do you have any idea what that's all about?"

"How does he know that you—"

"He's not stupid. You think he can't see what goes on around him?"

She rolled her eyes and sighed. "Stop acting like you know him more than I do."

I stalked forward, passing her. "All I'm saying is, be careful with this guy. I know he's your father's right-hand, but if he does anything to hurt you…"

Amalia gripped my shirt and shoved me against the door. "I already told you I'm not your damsel. And trust that if Rocco attempts to hurt me or my family, I'll slit his throat myself."

She let me tug her into my arms and melted into me as I whispered into her ear, "That's my girl."

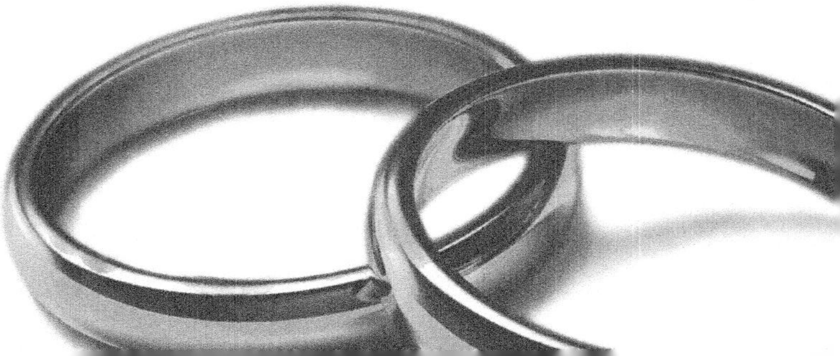

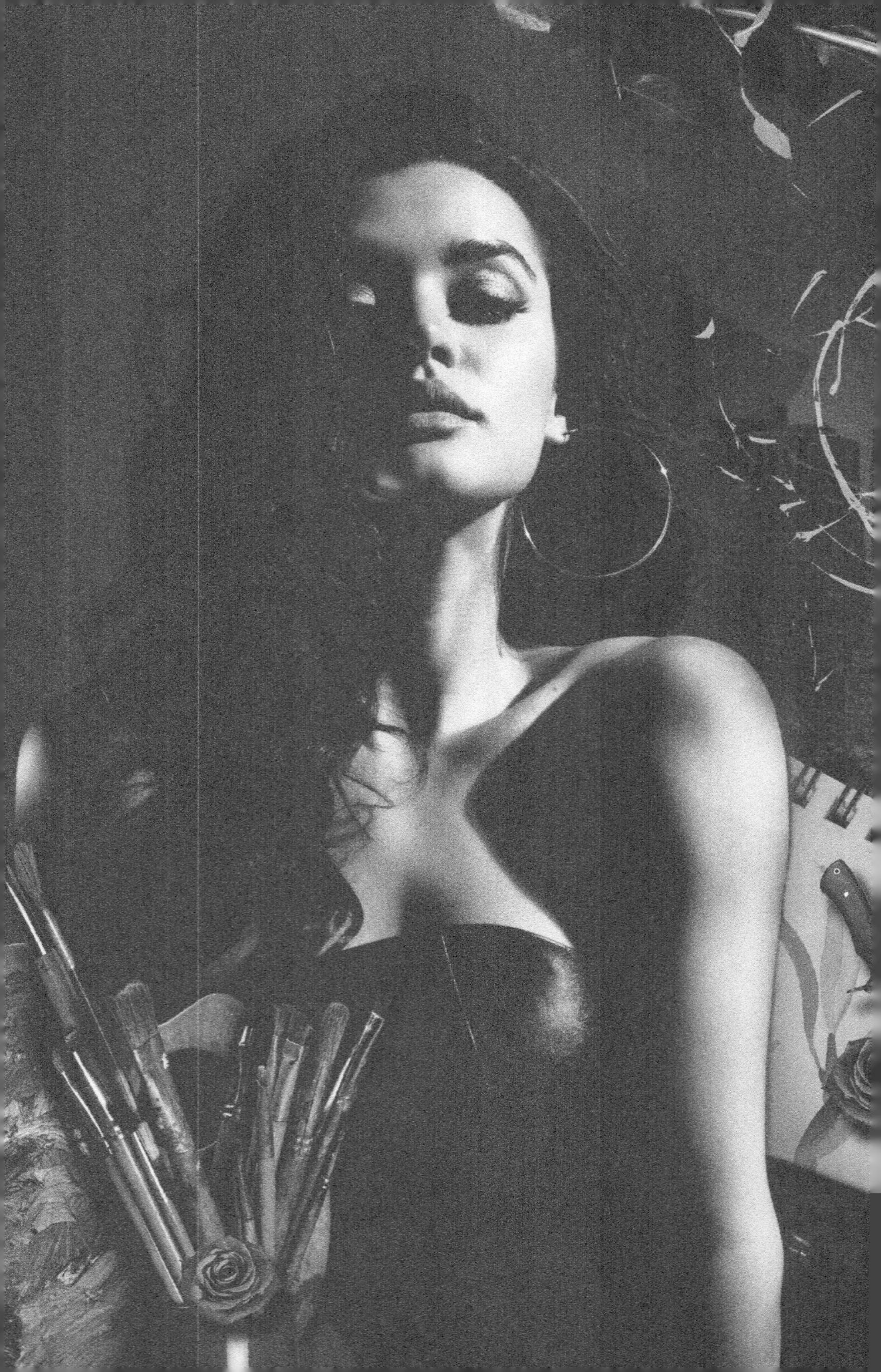

Chapter 14
Amalia

"AMALIA."

Eva called for me as I set off for my studio, but I kept moving, not in the mood to deal with her shit. I needed to unwind. It was barely noon, yet I already felt the world's weight on my shoulders. Soon, I'd be married to a man I didn't love; in two days, I had to gather my girls, some out of retirement, and knock on doors in retaliation for my father's losses.

And then there was Gio.

"Hey," she called again, catching up to me.

"I don't have time for you, princess."

Evangelina grabbed my arm. "I just wanted to apologize for earlier. And also, thank you for finding Vali. I had no idea she could climb out of the crib."

"It's fine," I said, waving her off and continuing through the courtyard.

"And Derek..."

I came to an abrupt stop and turned to face her. "You're not trying to apologize on his behalf, right?"

"Of course not." She let out an unamused laugh. "I love that man with everything I have, but I know he can be a dick."

"Do you, now?" I moved closer, our faces just inches apart. Eva wasn't intimidated, though I hadn't expected her to be. Sure, she'd been naïve and stupidly blind to all of Derek's bullshit and lies all those years ago, but I could admit the woman had a backbone. "How do you do it?"

"What do you mean?"

"*Hipócrita*. Derek agreed to accompany his brother, me, and my girls in two days for a little fun. His body count will be higher when he comes home to you than when he left."

Eva looked away.

"So I ask again. How do you do it? Work as a detective, fuck a monster, raise a child—what will you tell her when she's older? Or will you keep her in the dark like your father did to you?"

I was in a bad fucking mood and taking it out on someone who'd done nothing to me. Sure, I'd felt some way when she thought I was trying to harm her baby, but who could blame her? Either way, I didn't care. And I'd warned her to leave me alone.

Evangelina schooled her shoulders. "I don't really think that's any of your business. But maybe I should ask your parents which way worked best for them."

I knew I deserved that, so I couldn't even be upset.

"I like you, princess. So I'll let that slide," I said with a wicked grin.

"It's *Eva*. And you call me princess, but look around you. Who's the hypocrite?"

I had already turned around and started down the path toward my studio.

"That's because in here, I'm the *fucking* queen."

"You can't be serious."

Kai was sitting on his bike, backpack slung over his back, dressed in all black with a matching helmet.

"What?" He gestured the question with his hands out.

"Why don't you just strap on a fucking siren and lights? Just in case they don't hear you coming."

Kai chuckled and patted the seat behind him. "Actually, I was hoping you'd ride with me."

"Cain, I don't trust you enough to hop on the back of that thing while you speed down a highway. And we're trying to get in and out without being seen, heard, or *killed*."

He pulled off his helmet and shook out his hair, smoothing it back with rough fingers.

Fuck. This man, sitting on that bike, all but begging me to straddle him. He knew what he was doing.

"Are you sure you don't want to go for a ride, beautiful?" He sent me a wink.

I did. I absolutely fucking did. But before I could belittle him with a response, an SUV pulled up from around the driveway. Eva and Derek climbed out, meeting by the passenger side door. She had started to say something, when he tugged her forward, lifting her just enough to damn near inhale her entire face.

"Don't wait up for me, angel."

I heard him say before looking away. Kai and I locked eyes, and something electric sizzled the air between us.

"How do you stand to be around them?"

Laughing, he pulled his helmet back over his head.

Three more SUVs pulled into my property. I glanced at the lovebirds one last time just as Derek wiped tears from Eva's cheeks. Sometimes, I wondered what a love like that would feel like. She sacrifices her morals and her oath as an officer every day, and in turn, he attempts to change his life to be a better person and father—for her. Romanticism aside, their relationship seemed toxic and stressful. But I couldn't deny they seemed happy.

Kai and I…we were different. We wouldn't have to change or be other people for one another…

Stop it, I scolded myself. There was no us. He was just the means to an end.

I slid into the passenger seat of the first vehicle as Kai revved his engine and pulled out in front of us.

"What's wrong?" Holly peeled out, her attention shifting toward me. "You look like you're a thousand miles from here. And that's not a good place to be with where we're heading."

Leaning my head against the seat, I scoffed. "You doubt me?"

"Of course not, babe. But that man has you all kinds of twisted."

I let out a small bark of a laugh. "You're delusional."

"Oh, am I the delusional one? You think I missed the two of you after the incident with Fernando's men? The tension was thick, okay. And he gave you a pet name, Amalia." Her eyebrow quirked as she glanced my way. "Maybe not the sweetest of pet names. But it was the way he said it!" Squealing, her hands gripped the steering wheel tighter.

"He's unbearable, crude—"

"Hot, fuckable, and he rides a bike, for fuck's sake! What else do you need?"

"That's just it. I don't *need* anything. I hate that I'm bound to this man over some archaic, misogynist clause on a piece of paper, as if I've needed him all this time. It leaves a bad taste in my mouth. And if I accept it, then they'll win. I can't lose the last shred of dignity I have left."

Holly was quiet momentarily, chewing on her lip as she turned over my words.

"Listen, I hear what you're saying, I do. But choosing to be miserable for the next three years isn't exactly winning, either. One thousand ninety-five days is a *lot* of days, babe. A lot of lonely days tempted by that hot piece of man candy."

"Did you just do that math in your head just now, or is that some random fact you already knew?"

She snorted a laugh as we came up behind Kai at a red light. "Don't change the subject. Look." She motioned forward with her chin. "Look at his shoulders, those legs. That man will break you in the best way."

I couldn't help the smirk crawling across my mouth as the memory of Kai between my legs sent a shudder through my body and all the way down to my toes.

In my peripheral, I saw her double-take. "You fucked him. I see that look on your face."

"No, I didn't."

"Amalia Isabel Montesinos, there are no secrets between us. Spill! I could die tonight and, trust me, I'll come back and haunt your ass if you leave me in suspense."

My smile grew bigger, and I turned away, eyes on the side mirror, the other cars in view. "It was the other night. I felt confused and vulnerable…so I went to his room."

"Oh, so you took the pussy to him?'

We broke into laughter.

"I didn't plan it. It just happened."

"Stop being so fucking cryptic and tell me. What did he do, throw it in your ass, mouth, what?"

"Let's just say, the man can eat and clean his plate."

Holly chuckled and shook her head with amusement. "I knew it. I can tell these things, you know?"

"I bet you can."

We shared another laugh before the cabin grew quiet. My eyes and thoughts were on Kai. I knew Holly was right. What was the point in torturing myself? Why not just enjoy the time we'd spend trapped together? Let the pieces fall where they may—and part ways a bit more experienced and a hell of a lot more limber. Getting under Kai's skin was entertaining and all, but getting *under* Kai promised to be a whole other level of fun.

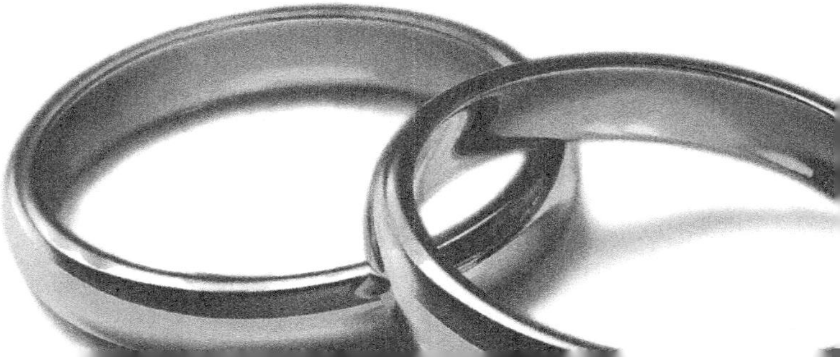

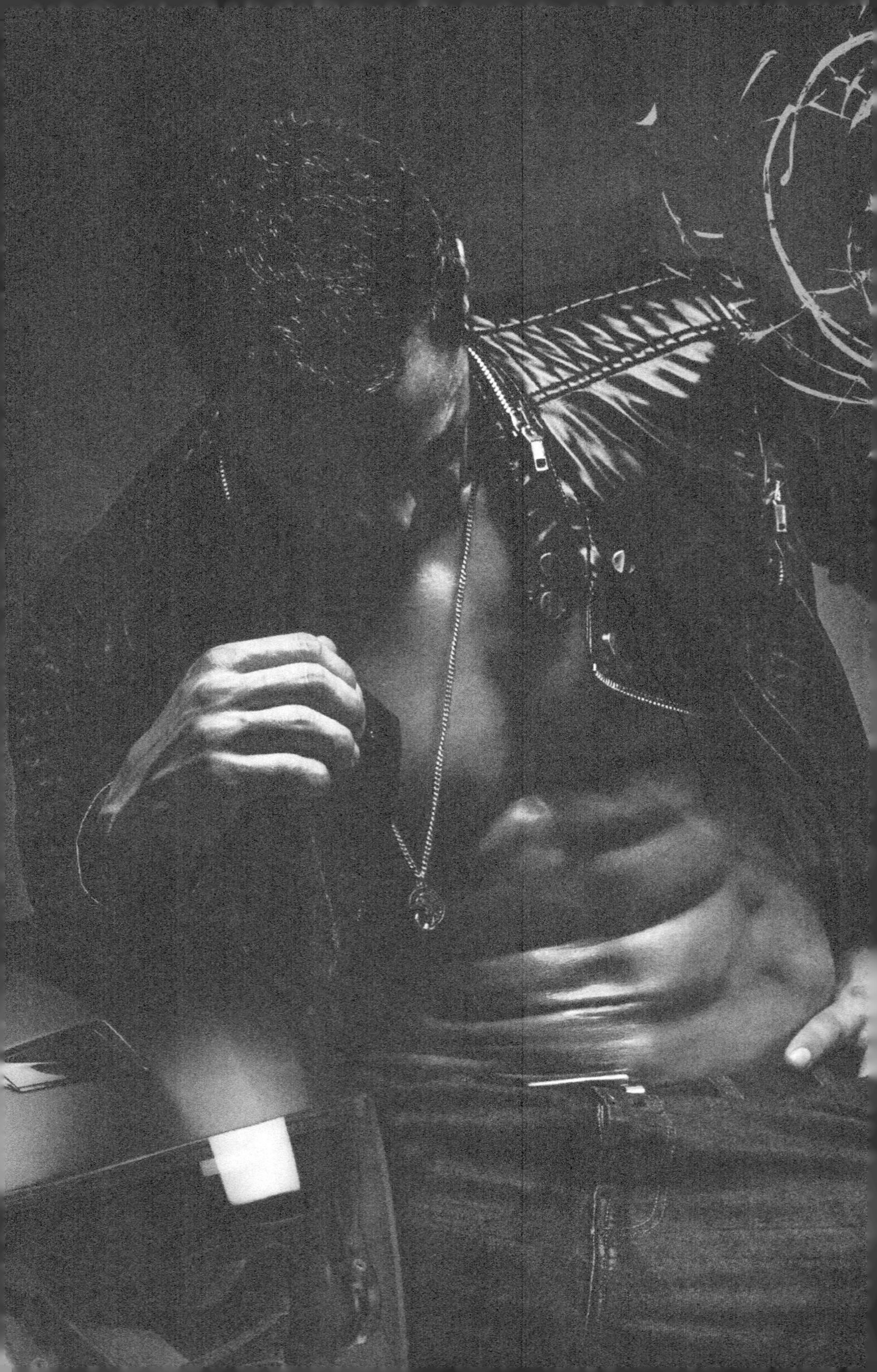

Chapter 15
Kai

THE compound's basement floor was flooded with about two inches of water. We sloshed forward in the dark and damp hallway, trusting the facility's security footage was on a loop, courtesy of one of Amalia's girls who had set up in a van just out of sight. Holly and a taller woman took the lead while Amalia and I brought up the rear.

"How are you holding up, Cain?" she asked, glancing back at me briefly. The glow of red emergency lights above our heads highlighted her profile, and I caught her smirk.

"This is a typical Tuesday for me, baby."

My wrist lit up with a text from Derek, who was with another team on the other side of the building. He was checking my status and letting me know they were about to make entry onto one of the main floors. I knew it had taken a lot for Derek to be here. He'd promised Eva years ago he was done with this life, but he wasn't willing to let me go alone. Fucking up on my own was one thing, but putting my life in the hands of others, especially ones I was barely acquainted with, was another level of trust neither of us had reached yet. And while we didn't like the idea of splitting up, I wasn't going to bitch about it and give Amalia the ammo to shit talk later.

"Does your little friend Rocco ever make it, or does he just send you to do his dirty work?"

She turned to me and fisted my shirt. "I'm no one's errand girl, and I'm here for my father, not Rocco."

"You look fucking adorable when you're ready to kill someone."

"I'm sure I'll look just as cute when I put my foot up your ass."

"I know you will."

"Cain. Vicious. Head in the game. We're about to breach the main level stairwell."

We both snapped our attention toward Holly.

"Don't do that," Amalia said, shaking her head and falling back into step with the others. We heard an amused chuckle from the entryway where Holly and her partner had disappeared.

"That's my thing," I whispered. "She can't just take it."

"Of all the names you could have—"

"It's perfect for you."

As hard as she was probably trying to hide her smile, the small lights on the pipes above us were on my side.

She was fucking beautiful.

"Hey." I caught her wrist, and while she didn't turn around, she stopped walking, waiting to hear what I had to say. "Don't chew my head off, but I just feel like it needs to be said. "Be careful."

"I didn't know you cared."

I leaned in, inhaling her soft, unforgettable scent. "You still owe me."

"Ugh." She mushed my face back and hurried after the group.

In the next several minutes, we were up three flights of stairs and busting through the door to what should have been a banquet hall occupied by our targets. But it was empty.

"Are we in the wrong place? Bad intel?"

Amalia didn't answer. She scanned the room, her expression both perplexed and flustered. "No, this was what he said. We confirmed with his guy, and he wouldn't betray my father."

"Vicious, everyone has a price. I keep my circle small for that very reason."

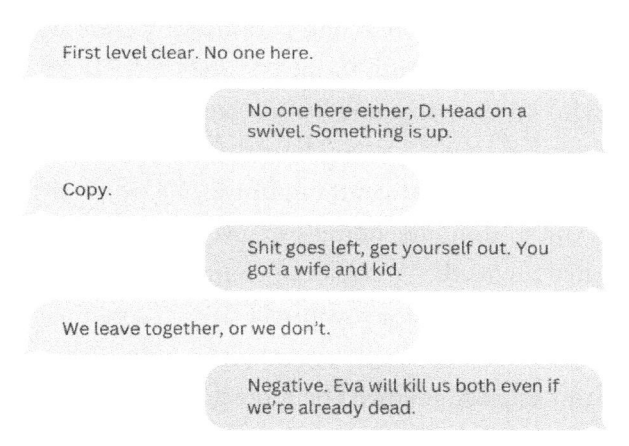

> First level clear. No one here.

> No one here either, D. Head on a swivel. Something is up.

> Copy.

> Shit goes left, get yourself out. You got a wife and kid.

> We leave together, or we don't.

> Negative. Eva will kill us both even if we're already dead.

I waited for another text from Derek, but nothing else came through.

"Amalia, I can't get ahold of Simone. I have no way of knowing if the signal is still blocked. And we've got no eyes on the outside. I say we bail before we get caught with our asses out."

Holly had barely finished speaking when gunfire erupted from the floors below us. We scattered in different directions, taking cover. I took off after Amalia into a narrow hallway seconds before bullets began to impact the walls around us.

She returned fire, but we were outgunned, and fighting back was useless. We'd be dead within seconds. I dragged her into a utility room as she clawed and kicked to escape my grasp, even as the echoes of automatic guns were coming at us from all sides.

"What are you doing?" she shrieked, shoving me hard against the chest and diving back toward the door. My arms came around her from behind, pinning her arms to her sides. "Let me go. We can't just hide in here. Holly, all of them. *Derek*—they need us!"

"Sshh, Amalia, shut the fuck up. Derek can handle himself. And we can't help them if we're dead. So stop fighting me and listen to reason."

I released her slowly as her thrashing ceased, but the moment she was free, Amalia turned around and pounded my chest with her fists. "You're such a fucking coward, Cain!"

"Enough," I growled, caging her in against the wall, wrists held in my hand above her head. "Do you hear that? That's what you want to run into? Stop being so goddamn impulsive. We won't survive."

"I told you to stop pretending you give a damn about me."

I clenched my teeth. "You're exasperating."

"You're not exactly a peach yourself."

Gruff voices filled the hallway, spewing commands in a mixture of Spanish and English, followed by more gunfire.

"We're fucked," she whispered, backing into a corner when I let her go. As Amalia slid to the floor, three bullets pierced the room's metal door, and I threw myself over her body, our eyes connecting through the madness. "Kai, if they find us, they'll kill you…but they'll take me. And I can't…I won't…" She lifted her gun to her temple.

"The fuck they will," I seethed, as my hand wrapped around the barrel of her Glock. "I won't let that happen. I already told you no one touches you."

She scoffed and flashed me a frail smile. "Don't be stupid, Cain. You're not bulletproof, and it's only a matter of time before they come through that door, and then we're both fucked." Amalia tugged at her gun, but I held firm. "Let go."

"No."

"Fuck you. I'd rather choose how I die. And I refuse to become one of their whores. You're not going to save me. So *let go*."

With her free hand, she reached for the rifle at her back, but I gripped her wrist, again holding it above her head. "I get it. I'm not just going to sit here waiting to die, either."

Her eyes were on my lips, a grin on her pretty face. "Going out in a blaze of glory, huh? Perfect. I'm right behind you."

"Maybe later." I kissed her jaw. "I figure I better collect what's owed to me while I still can."

She chuckled and loosened her grip on the gun, and as I slipped it from her hands, Amalia reached forward and grabbed my already hardened cock.

"I've never been one not to pay a debt," she murmured. Climbing into my lap, she positioned her warm little cunt exactly where I wanted her. "What will happen when they come through that door?" Her hips rocked forward. She felt so goddamn good.

"I won't let them hurt you."

"You care about me, Cain? You don't know me." A sharp hiss left her lips when my fingers dug into her skin, guiding her movements. "I'm not a good person."

"Good, because I'm not either."

Her soft moan sent a jolt to my dick. Fuck, I needed to be inside her.

"You're different…from your brother. I can see it. Feel it," she rasped.

She tipped her head back, eyes closed as I bucked into her, desperately seeking relief. "Same monster, different skin, vicious."

She smiled, undulating her hips with more momentum.

"Vicious, vicious," she hummed.

Faster, harder. The pressure in my balls intensified with every thrust. "You don't like it?" I asked, lips trailing across her collarbone to the hollow of her throat. "Then tell me to stop."

She shook her head from side to side. "No…don't stop. Don't you fucking stop."

More gunfire and shouting boomed from the hallway and what

I could only assume was the banquet hall, but we were so far gone, so lost in each other, and on the verge of coming apart, that the whole goddamn building could have crumbled around us and we would have been hard-pressed to care. If we were meant to die in this shithole, then like Amalia said, we'd die on our terms, even if it meant coming in my goddamn pants.

"Kai," she moaned, "don't let me die with a debt on my shoulders." Her eyes were locked on mine, swollen lips between her teeth. "Come for me."

Leaning forward, I tugged her lip free, kissing her hard enough to break skin. "You first." I gripped the waistband of her pants and pushed them down over her ass. "If we're going to die here, I need to die touching you."

Amalia smiled against my mouth, lifting her body just enough for me to slip my hand between her thighs. "Always so wet for me. I told you, this pretty pussy is mine." I dipped two fingers inside her and she bit down on my shoulder as I found that sweet spot that made her feral. "That's it." I wrapped a hand around her throat and her mouth gaped open slightly as I squeezed and slid another finger inside. "If there was ever a reason to fight my way out of here..." I kissed her roughly, savoring every second, knowing it was my last taste, "it's to know how it feels to have you wrapped around my cock."

Amalia's nails dug into my skin the faster my thrusts and the tighter my grip on her neck became. She came so hard, her body jerked, her nails finally breaking skin.

"Fuck..." she whined, collapsing into me. But we had no time to bask in the moment we'd just shared.

Bullets pierced the wall above our heads, causing pieces of sheet rock and dust to rain down over us. I brushed the white ash from her cheek, where a single tear had escaped, carving a trail along her skin.

"I'm sorry," I whispered.

She offered me a slow smile. "For what?"

"For not protecting my wife." Nipping at my neck, she chuckled between soft pants.

"I'm not your wife yet."

"Yet? So there's still a chance."

Her laugh was thick with emotion, and she shuddered in my arms. I brought my hands to her face, our foreheads together. More ash fell over our heads, her lashes white. "Don't be afraid, Amalia. Wherever we're going, we'll get there together."

She shook her head. "I'm not afraid of dying, Kai. I'm afraid of leaving my brother and parents behind. Gio will never forgive me…or himself." She gritted her teeth. "But I won't die on my knees."

"Blaze of glory?" I asked, wiping a tear.

"Fuck yes."

I helped her adjust her pants as we got to our feet, ready to face our fate. Amalia reloaded and racked her Glock. "I owe you twice now."

"Don't worry, I'm keeping tabs."

When I reached for the doorknob, Amalia's hand suddenly fisted my shirt from behind, tugging just in time to avoid the shrapnel of a shotgun to the chest.

"The vent!"

We'd been so caught up in dying that neither had noticed the partially hidden grates of an air duct. Wasting no time, we lunged toward our only way out, gripping the metal and tearing it open. I shoved her inside and quickly followed down the winding pipe, hoping the damn thing was strong enough to hold our weight.

"Faster!"

"I'm trying. If anyone follows, put a hole in their fucking face."

"A woman after my own heart."

Gunfire still boomed around us, but the vent acted like a vortex, making it impossible to guess where the threat was coming from. Our only option was to keep moving.

I shot a glance at my watch. Not a single message had come through since my last text to Derek.

Don't you fucking die on me, D.

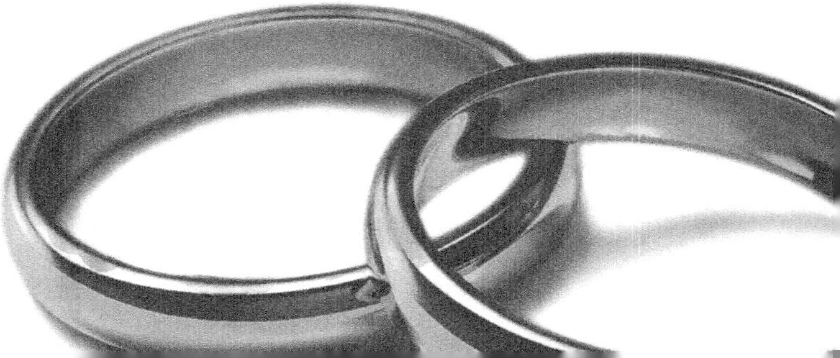

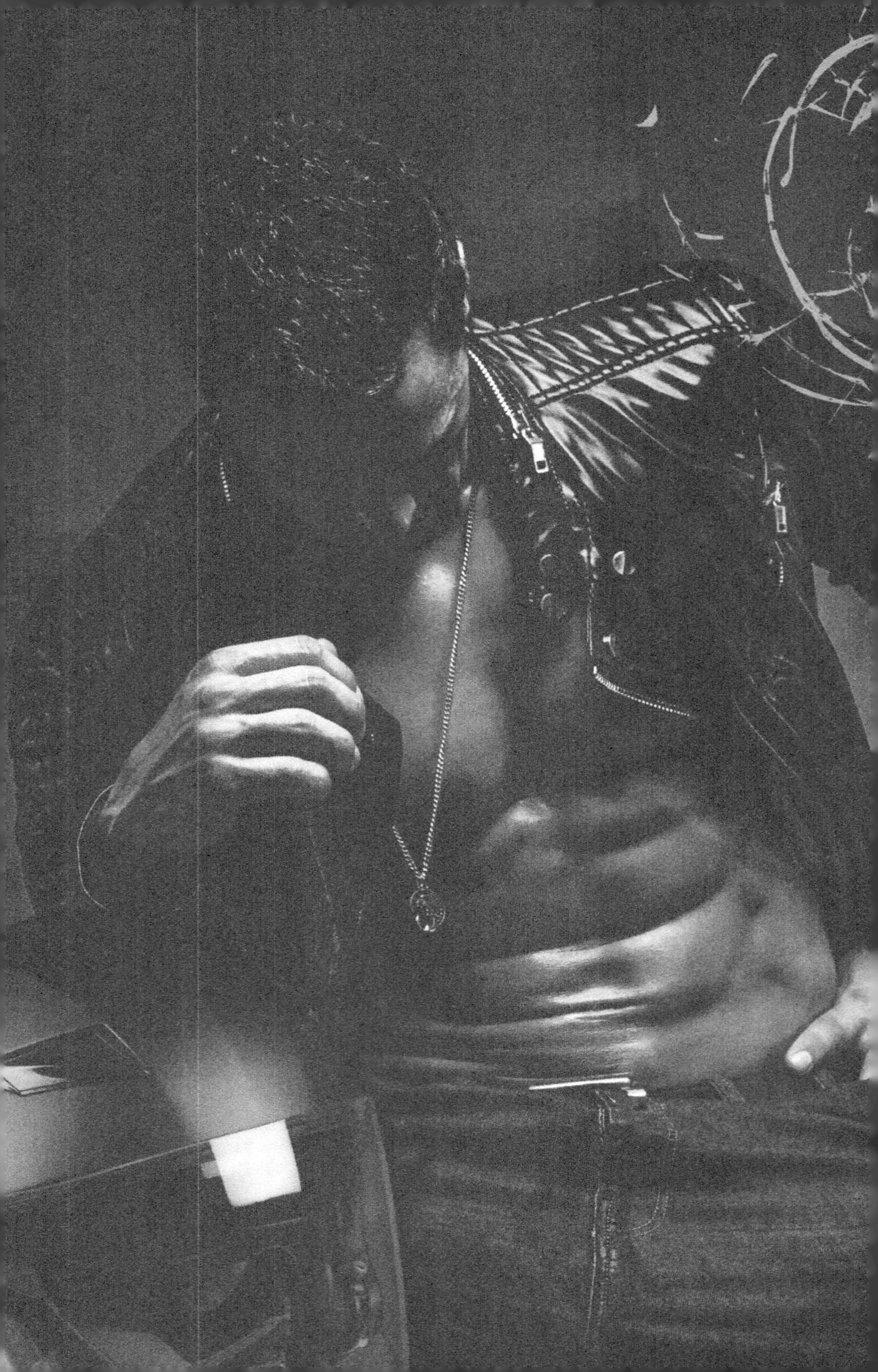

Chapter 16
Kai

I CURSED as I sent three more messages to Derek, but every single one went unanswered.

"Kai, we have to keep moving."

"I won't leave without my brother."

She stopped and crawled toward me, a hand on my neck. The filtered lights streaking in from the vents highlighted her beautiful brown eyes. "No one said anything about leaving."

"I want you to go."

Her laugh was cynical. "I think you've got me confused with someone else. Holly is up there, probably dead." She sucked in a breath before continuing, reeling in her emotions. "I know how you feel right now because she's like a sister to me. And I *won't* let what happened here slide. Whoever did this knew we were coming. So that means we either have a rat in our ranks, or our connect betrayed us. Either way, they die. The more creative, the better."

Her lipstick was smeared, her skin covered in dust and streaks of mascara, but I'd be damned if I'd ever seen anything more beautiful. I swept my thumb over her lip. "Has anyone ever told you how goddamn sexy you look when you talk murder and mayhem?"

While the world fell apart, being in her company somehow helped ease the grief I felt without news from Derek.

"You just have a way with words, don't you?" With one last half smile, she crawled forward toward the grates of what could potentially be an exit. Considering our situation, I knew indulging in how her ass swayed from side to side and the alluring vision of her crawling on all fours was wildly inappropriate. Still, we could be dead inside of fifteen minutes, so why the fuck not.

"How much ammo do you have left?" she whispered.

Through the thin slits, I could make out three men, all equipped with automatic rifles. One slip-up, the slightest noise, and all they'd have to do was spray in this direction, and we'd be done.

"We're outgunned. By the time we kick this open, they'll be on us."

"Not if I go out first."

"Fuck that. No."

"I'm flattered you care so much, Cain. But I'm not exactly asking, so you either help me or watch them take me. Those are the only two options."

I grabbed her by the shoulders. "You don't know who they are or what they want. You're goddamn gorgeous, vicious. But that means nothing right now. They weren't exactly being too selective earlier when they shot up the place."

Her expression hardened, and she tugged her shirt up over her head and tossed it, which left her in a black lacy bra barely covering her nipples.

"Again, I'm not asking."

I gripped her arm, eyes on the swell of her breasts. "Is this what you normally wear for these occasions?"

She flashed me a grin. *"Antes muerta que sencilla."* (I'd rather die than be basic.)

A flare of possessive heat rolled through me as I thought of how those men would lust for what was mine.

Yeah, she was fucking mine.

But I knew nothing would stop her from following through with her plan. I huffed a resigned breath and pulled her closer, my other fist in her hair. "If something happens to you…"

I smoothed my thumb over her nipple and felt it harden under my touch. "Be careful out there. You owe me, remember?"

"I'm glad you have your priorities straight."

"Always."

As I kissed her, she smiled against my lips.

"You better not miss." Amalia slid her rifle off and positioned her boots quietly against the metal. "Out of sight until it's time." Those were the last words she spoke before kicking open the vent and quickly exiting.

A commotion ensued between the men as they shouted instructions and raised their weapons.

"On your knees," one commanded.

"*Es la reina*," another said with dark amusement.

"Alvaro, check the vent. Make sure she's alone."

I knew what that meant. He wouldn't be coming by and sticking his head in to say hello. Things were about to get ugly, but before they did, Alvaro got a new hole to breathe from when my hollow point ripped through the side of his neck. Without wasting a second, I fired more shots through the narrow opening when I saw Amalia hit the floor. The bastard in front of her went down with two bullets to his chest.

Holes the size of quarters opened up around me as the third man began firing. I ducked just as the metal behind me broke open, and aimed my weapon, hoping Amalia was out of my line of fire. But when

I squeezed the trigger, I realized my gun had jammed. As if sensing what had happened, she jumped on the man's back and plunged a blade into his throat twice before he even knew he was as good as dead. By the time her assault registered, his eyes were wide, mouth agape when she slid the serrated edge against his Adam's apple and sliced deep into flesh.

He threw his weight back, attempting to buck her off, but the stained steel disappeared again, deeper, until his knees hit the floor.

"Kai! We gotta run. Incoming!"

We picked up the abandoned AKs and dashed toward a stairwell, where a hail of gunfire awaited us, reverberating like clashing thunder against the long, hollow space. As we descended, our gazes met, and she reached out to me, briefly squeezing my forearm. While no words were exchanged between us, it was all I needed.

"This was where the other team was supposed to be," I said, fear tinging my voice.

A puddle of blood pooled on the floor from the other side of the door, and Amalia placed a firm hand on my chest. "Kai, whatever we see in there…we have to keep our heads clear, okay?"

Her tone was vulnerable and empathetic, as if she knew that whatever awaited us on the other side could be equally devastating to us both.

Something was happening between us.

Changing.

But there was no time to dwell on those thoughts. I just hoped we'd get the chance to do so later.

"It's quiet," I said, as I pushed open the door. Emergency lights illuminated dark corners just enough to see a crouched figure on the far side of the room as soft squelching noises filled the air. Amalia raised her weapon.

"Wait." Her shoulder twitched, hand shaking, desperate to make the kill. But I just had a feeling… "D, is that you?"

The fleshy noises ceased for several seconds before continuing, and Amalia steadied her aim again. But I shook my head, a broad smile on my face. Anyone else would have startled or reacted to the threat, but my brother was too busy handling business.

"About time you made it. My hand's starting to cramp up," he joked dryly.

"You've been down here finger-painting all this time while Amalia and I have been doing all the heavy lifting."

Derek scoffed and straightened, twisting around to face us. He and I had been through a lot and done some wild shit. Unimaginable shit that would traumatize the average person, but the way Derek looked right now, was straight up a thing of nightmares. There wasn't an inch of him not drenched in blood. His face looked like he'd applied crimson war paint and used it to slick back his hair, with the exception of a few thick strands hanging over his forehead, dripping red down his skin and onto the floor.

"Goddamn, Derek. We're going to have to take you out back and hose you the fuck down."

He shrugged his shoulders. "There's a little back spray when they kick and scream."

"A little?" Amalia chimed in. "You sure you weren't playing in it? You look absolutely vile." Her sneer suddenly lifted. "Amazing."

"Is that what I need to do to impress you?"

She looked up and hip-checked me. "You can impress me in other ways, Cain. But first, we need to keep moving…" I put a hand on her arm as she stepped under the glow of a red light that highlighted her sheer bra. Setting my weapons down, I quickly shrugged off my shirt and forced it over her head.

"Really?"

"Yeah, come on."

Amalia shoved her arms through without another word, then cautiously approached Derek. "What happened down here? What did you see? Did anyone else— Is it just you?"

He swiped the blade across the front of his shirt in a futile attempt to wipe it clean.

"The same that probably happened up there—an ambush. We all scattered. I didn't see anything else apart from that."

I had barely settled a comforting hand on her shoulder when a blast shook the room and sent us tumbling forward, the heat of a fire at our backs.

There came a point where defeat was inevitable. I would rather live to fight tomorrow than die here a pointless death.

"Amalia, we have to go. I'm sorry."

She nodded, mouth tight as the reflection of flames danced in her irises. Derek and I helped her to her feet, and she swatted us both and started for the exit.

"*Reina.*" The voice was hoarse and unfamiliar. I couldn't turn around to see his face because the barrel of a gun was pressed against the base of my skull. Derek reached for his side piece.

"This is a 12 gauge, so unless you want to wear your friend's brain as a new accessory, I suggest you keep your hands nice and high above your head. You too, *reina.*"

My brother's nostrils flared, chest rising and falling with every harsh breath as he reluctantly complied.

"*Reinita*, I need you to look pretty for me on your knees."

"I'll kill you if you think about touching her."

He knocked the sawed-off edge of the shotgun against my head.

"All talk. But how will you do that without that pretty face of yours?"

Amalia and I exchanged worried gazes, and she shook her head slowly.

"You will come with me or die with them."

"Fuck you. Go ahead and kill me," she spat at his feet.

He released a mocking laugh and shoved the barrel harder against me.

"As you wish."

We made eye contact through the darkness, and her lip quivered.

"NO! I'll go…just don't do it. Please."

Barking another laugh, he motioned for her to get up and remove her shirt, and I clenched my fists at my side, feeling so goddamn helpless.

"*La reina, la mercinaria*, begging me? Ain't that a bitch."

The pop of a bullet against flesh had us all hitting the floor, that bastard on top of me. Blood trickled down my temple and over my face, and my first thought was that I'd been hit. Until I realized the man draped over my back was no longer moving or speaking. It was his blood. Fuck. That was close. Too damn close. I exhaled harshly against the floor.

"Gio!"

I couldn't understand the name flying from Amalia's lips until I saw her look of horror.

With a gun in one hand and eyes and face scrunched with fear, Gio stood above us. His breaths were coming so quick and shallow that I feared he'd start hyperventilating.

"What the fuck are you doing here?" She charged and disarmed him.

"No time for a reunion. I hear them coming, and I'm trying to make it back to my wife while I'm still breathing."

I shoved the dead weight from my back and sprang to my feet before moving toward a frozen Gio and grabbing him by the scruff of his shirt. We stumbled outside into a back lot, where two SUVs were waiting. Amalia sighed a breath of relief when she was met with Holly in the driver's seat.

"Where are the others?" she asked, throwing her arms around her friend.

"Everyone made it except Simone. They came at the van from all sides…I'm sorry."

Amalia was quiet for several moments. "Is everyone out?"

Holly nodded and once we reached a safe distance, she pulled out a burner phone and detonated the explosives we'd planted in the basement level of the compound. The aftershock of the blast shook our vehicle. And we sat in silence until Amalia turned around from the passenger seat to face Gio.

"Start talking."

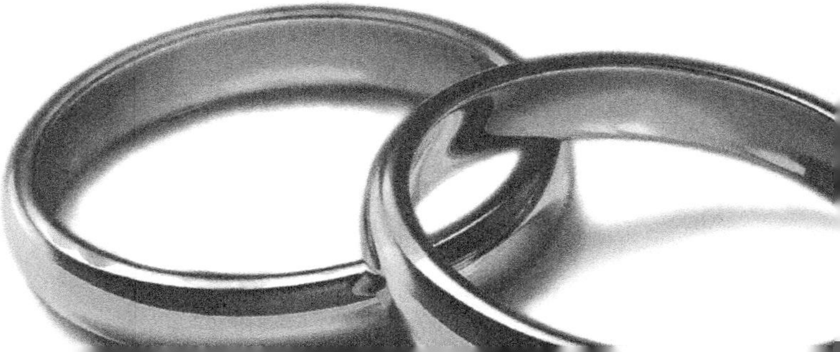

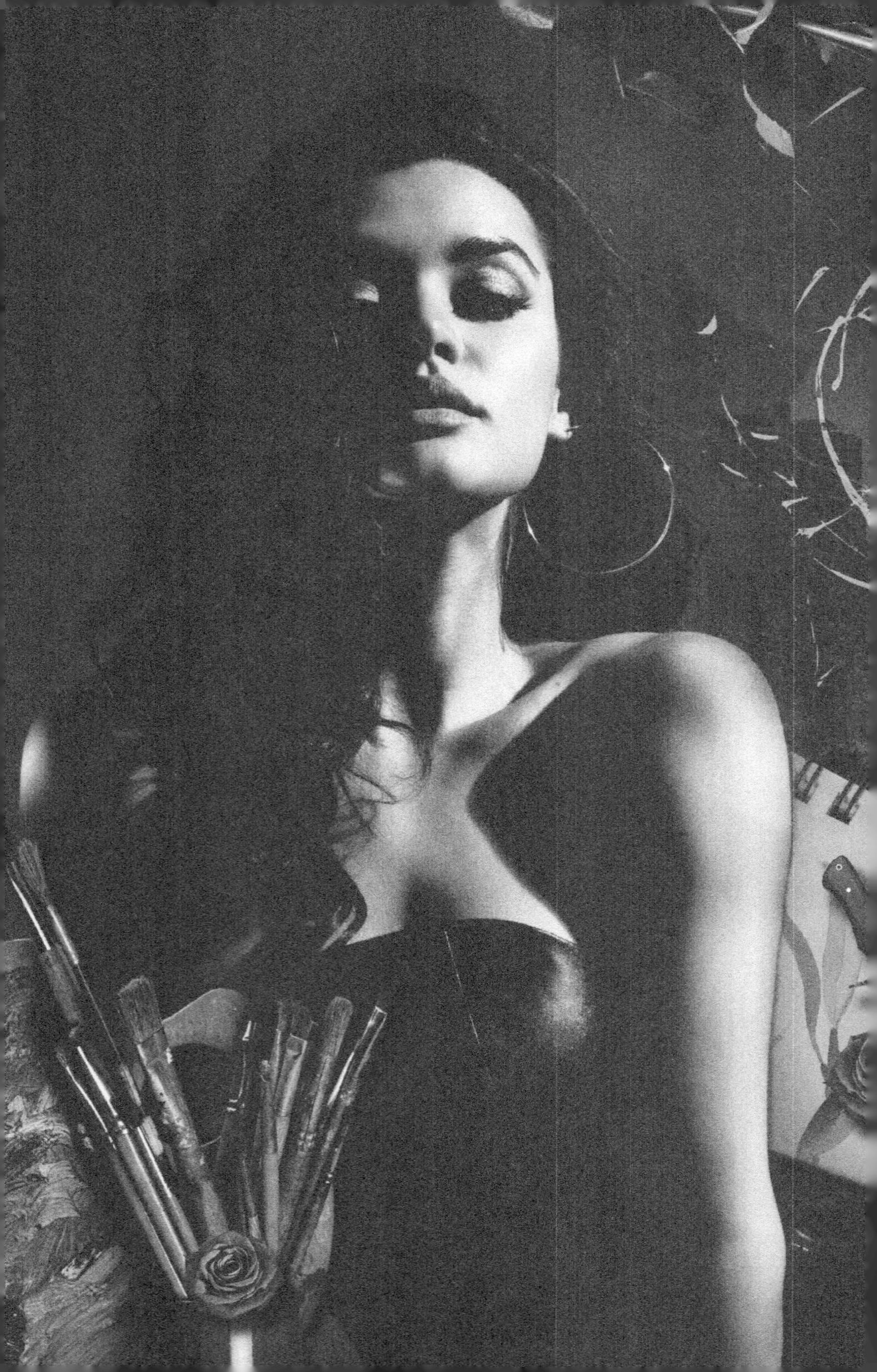

Chapter 17
Amalia

GIO slouched in his seat, pulling the front of his hoodie up to partially cover his face.

"I'm sorry," he muttered from beneath the thick fabric.

"Sorry? You're fucking sorry? What are you—How did you? Why, Gio? You could have been killed. We barely made out ourselves, and we…" I paused and looked at Kai, whose expression was a mix of concern and sympathy.

"You're what, Amalia?" He pulled down his hoodie. "A professional? Stop treating me like I'm stupid. That's all you've ever done. You, Mom, Dad… Tony. All of you." Tears glistened in his eyes as they connected with mine, filling my heart with anguish.

"We were just trying to protect you."

"Because you think I'm not capable? In case you didn't notice, I saved your asses back there."

I sucked in a deep breath and closed my eyes before continuing so that I wouldn't be compelled to strangle my baby brother. "Fine,

Giovanni. You want in on the family business? You want to kill people? Run drugs, make arms deals like Tony did. Is that really what you want?"

"Is it what you want?"

His question was a gut punch. If I said yes, would he see me as a monster? And If I said no, would it be a lie? I wasn't sure.

"It's been one hell of a night. Maybe we should just make it home," Kai interjected, his hand over mine, where I gripped the edge of the seat like a lifeline. "Call in and check with the infirmary."

His words were like a dagger to the heart, because despite this car carrying some of the most important people in my life, some of my girls had been critically wounded. I threw one last reproachful glance at Gio before turning back around and leaning against the headrest.

Holly reached over and squeezed my hand but said nothing. Her silence spoke volumes, as she was never one to be rendered speechless, and I feared the worst. But I was too overwhelmed to ask questions and have reality flip my world upside down.

When we reached our driveway, Eva was on the steps waiting, jumping to her feet as the car pulled to a stop. Derek must have told her we were on the way, and I could only assume my parents were asleep.

Somehow, we all fell into the same stride as we approached the house, and judging by Evangelina's horrified expression as she rushed Derek, we must have looked like quite a fucking sight. We were caked in dust, dirt, and blood as if we'd crawled out of a warzone.

Maybe we had.

"I don't have the emotional strength to deal with you right now," I said, fisting my brother's hoodie. "But I will deal with you tomorrow."

He shook off my hold. "You're welcome."

I said nothing more and stormed inside the house, sprinting up the stairs and into my room. The shower was on within the next several minutes, and I let the hot spray soothe my anguish. It wasn't long before tears spilled over, and my fists connected with the wall until drops of my blood ran down the drain. But tomorrow was another day. And Rocco owed me one hell of an explanation.

The door to Kai's room was a traitorous whore. It creaked loudly, announcing my arrival like a damn overhead speaker. Kai looked at me for a beat, and I suddenly felt strangely vulnerable.

"Deja vu," I joked halfheartedly.

He reached over and pulled the blanket down next to him in an unspoken invitation. I hesitated for a moment until I found his eyes across the darkness. Slipping under the covers, he immediately pulled me against his side, and my heart fluttered because he knew exactly why I'd come to him. Maybe it was what he needed, too.

"Are you all right?" he asked, breaking the ten-minute-long silence between us.

"I'm always all right…eventually."

"Tonight was…chaos. But we—you, me, Derek…Gio, we made it back."

"I can't believe he snuck into Simone's van. He barely made it out when she was attacked. What was he thinking?" I shook my head, still in disbelief. "Is this who he really is?" I wasn't sure why the thought of Gio being like me and like my parents was an unsettling one. Maybe because I'd always seen him as this beacon of light among the dark. But I'd been naive. This was our world, and even though he'd stood on the sidelines for so long, I realized now he was always watching.

Kai rubbed reassuring circles on my back, and I closed my eyes, letting the calm of his touch relieve my worries. Being in his arms felt so right. It was a terrifying thought in some ways because I'd never needed anyone like I needed him at that moment.

"He saved your life," I whispered, snaking my arm up over his bare abdomen. The soft thuds of his heart gradually accelerated…or maybe it was my own.

"He saved yours."

I propped my arms on his chest. "I wasn't the one with a shotgun to the back of my head."

"Maybe not." A slight smile tugged at his lips as his hand came up around the side of my neck. "But neither one of us would be here had he not snuck away. And I would have had the worst time in hell." Kai's hand tightened around my nape. "Knowing that son of a bitch had taken you."

"Is that right, Cain?"

"I'm back to being Cain?"

I laughed and lifted my finger to his lips, tracing the soft contours. "Always."

He pressed a kiss against my skin. "Will you?"

Montesinos was my family's name. If Kai and I would only be married temporarily, I didn't see a point in changing it.

"This isn't real, Kai. You know that."

"Feels pretty fucking real to me." Turning on his side, he hauled me closer so that our bodies were flush, his cock hard against my abdomen. But somehow, we both knew sex wasn't the plan here. Not tonight.

"Don't do that," I whispered, closing my eyes and lowering my face. "You know what this is and, most importantly, what it's not."

"Yeah," he said, barely audible.

Several minutes ticked by, and while Kai hadn't said anything more, his hold on me hadn't loosened in the slightest.

And I was glad.

"Do you think your—that man who adopted you—is behind this?" I'd heard what had happened with Silas and Helena. As far as I knew, it had been nearly two years since anyone had heard from him. But all the people he had a vendetta against would be in one place together. And after all, my girls and I had a hand in his downfall when we took out that Russian prick.

"I don't think so, but I can't say for sure. Maybe you should ask your friend, Rocco, how they knew we'd hit that particular compound since he planned it."

His words held accusatory undertones. I knew where his mind had gone, and maybe I'd had those thoughts, too. But this was Rocco. We'd known each other since the two of us were in diapers. He'd never put me in a position where my life was at risk—that much I was sure of.

"I plan to."

"I'll go with you."

I scoffed. "I don't need you to protect me, much less from Rocco."

"Are you always this obnoxiously stubborn?"

"Always."

His laugh vibrated against my body, and it replied accordingly. Heat settled in my belly.

"*Reina*," he whispered to himself. "It means queen." I nodded. "*Mi reina*," he said again, as though testing the way the words rolled off his tongue. I squeezed my thighs together, my pussy throbbing. The phrase did things to me coming from his lips.

"Cain?"

"Hmm?" he said, his voice now thick with exhaustion.

"Go to sleep."

Kai dropped a kiss to my hairline and drifted off without another word, and I burrowed against him and closed my eyes.

What the fuck was I doing?

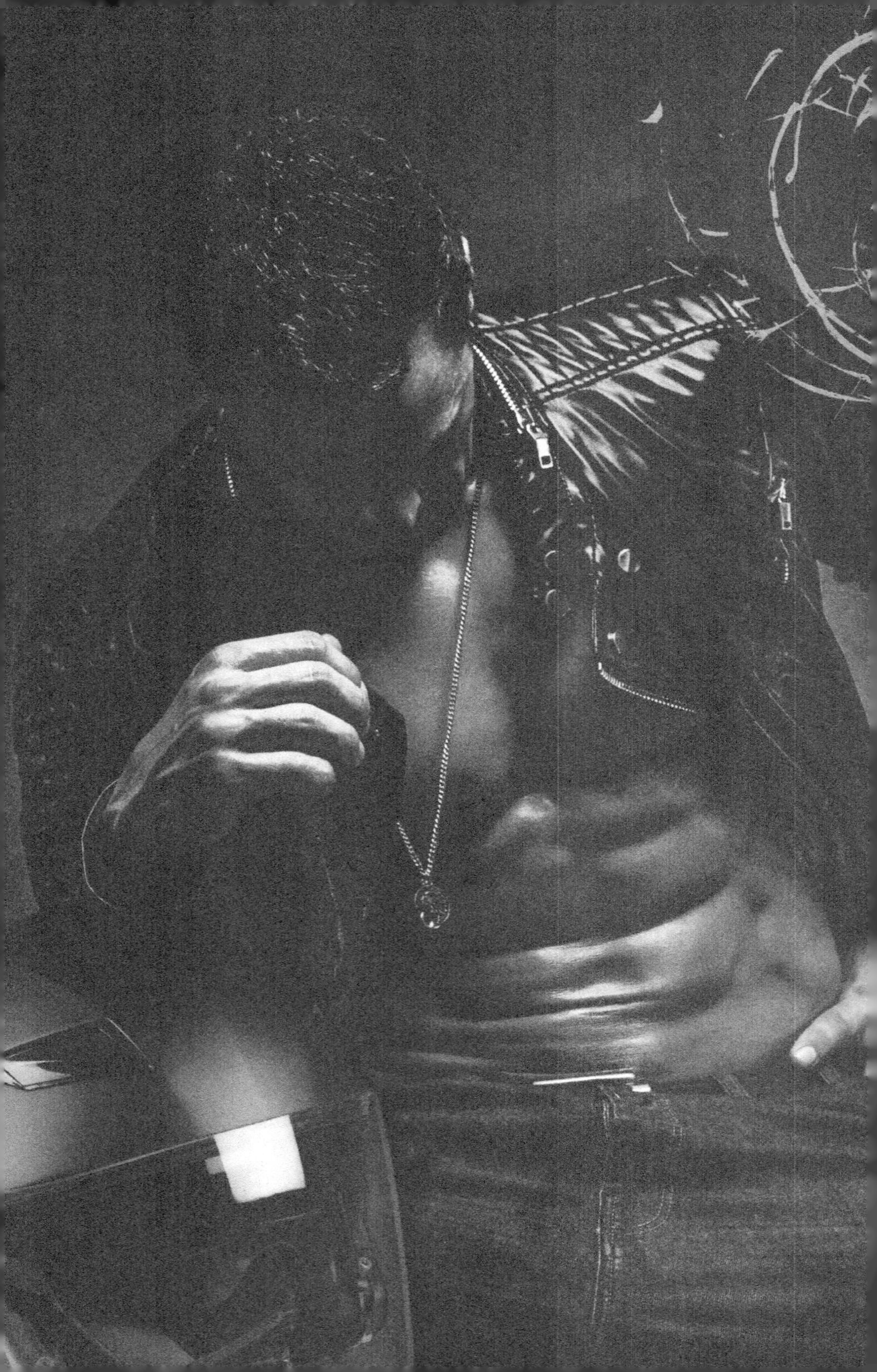

Chapter 18
Kai

"KAI!"

I slipped on my helmet when I heard Gio calling my name. I liked the kid, but I needed to go for a ride and clear my head. Luckily, one of Amalia's people had jumped on my bike and rode it back that night. Two days since the compound ambush, and everyone has been on edge since. Amalia's father hired extra security on all his properties, and at least a handful of men suspected of double-crossing him and Amalia had been tortured and executed. While she'd had no part in those punishments, she'd weighed in on their possible involvement and made the final call that sealed their fate. Yet there were still no answers. Rocco, of course, denied any knowledge and pretended to be just as shocked. His days were numbered.

"What's up?" I tucked my helmet under my arm and waited for him to speak. His eyes were on the ground first, then on Gloria as he fidgeted with his shirt sleeve. I waited until impatience and the need to relieve some stress got the best of me. Shifting my weight, I put a hand on his shoulder and squeezed. "Something wrong?"

He shrugged, and his whole body seemed to deflate. "It's Amalia. She won't talk to me. She's avoiding me." His glassy eyes finally met mine. "I think she's disappointed."

"She's still shaken up about what happened. She'll come around."

Gio's eyes glistened with unshed tears. "I just wanted her to be proud of me."

"I know for a fact she is. You should see how her face lights up whenever she talks about you. But what you did was reckless. Hell, we barely made it out alive." I gave his shoulder another squeeze. "Hey, I don't think I ever said thank you for what you did back there for your sister, for me. That was very brave." Gio wiped at his tears with the back of his sleeve.

"You think so?" he asked with a watery smile.

"Yeah, kid, but also very stupid. Don't you ever fucking do that again."

He nodded with his head down. "You think she'll tell my parents?"

"Nah. She won't. Nothing came of it. No harm, no foul, right?"

"You going for a ride?" He gripped the handle of my bike.

"Yeah, need to get some air. Sometimes, it's the only thing that helps me relax. Feeling the wind, the speed…it's freeing, you know."

"Was Gloria someone special to you?"

I flashed him a grin. "You heard that?"

He chuckled, swiping at the last of the moisture from his eyes. "Yeah, and I think my sister is jealous."

"She'd have to feel something for me to be jealous."

Ever since the night of the ambush, when she slept in my bed, Amalia seemed distant, like she was avoiding me too, now that I thought about it. And I found myself missing our banter and arguments. Replaying our conversation over again in my head, what we went through that night, and how close we'd come to dying, I wondered if I'd said or done something wrong.

Did I snore?

"Now, who's the stupid one?"

With my attention back then, I regarded him with knitted eyebrows. "What do you mean?"

"My sister definitely likes you, Kai. I'm not saying she wants to have your babies or anything, but I know how she is around people she *doesn't* like. And that's not you."

She kicked my ass hard enough. I'd hate to be someone she didn't like.

"You think so?" I asked to humor him.

"I know so. And she trusts you, because if you know Amalia, trust is crucial to her. I was never sure what she did or what she was capable of, but now that I'm certain, so much of it makes sense."

His amused expression found mine again. "You two are a lot alike. Maybe even perfect for each other."

"Because of who we are and what we do?" Gio nodded with a somber expression. "Does that bother you?"

"I killed a man, and I know I'm supposed to feel some remorse, but I don't. Is that bad?"

I whistled out a long exhale.

"I lost my ability to judge anyone's morals and what keeps them up at night a long time ago. That's for you to decide. This is my job. It's who I am and all I know. But when I kill, there's a purpose, Gio, whether it's an assignment or in self-defense. It's not a sport."

"I'm not trying to be a serial killer, if that's what she's worried about. I'm just tired of being the outcast or being treated like a kid. I want to prove to her and my parents that I'm just as capable."

I climbed on my bike as the climate of our conversation drifted into territory I wasn't too comfortable with. We all had our demons, and maybe I hadn't been all that truthful.

"Sometimes it's more important to prove certain things to yourself."

He shrugged. "Yeah. Maybe."

"You should let me take you for a ride one day."

Gio's eyes widened like goddamn saucers, and he shook his head almost violently. "No, thank you. Have you read statistics on motorcycle deaths?"

"You think they're as bad as sneaking into an ambush, in a building with armed men trying to kill you, then pointing a gun at one of them?"

The corners of his eyes crinkled into a smile. "Touché."

I couldn't help laughing as I tugged the helmet over my head. "I'm heading out, kid. Remember what I said. Just give her some time."

I needed to take my own advice.

"Kai, I wanted to say thank you." I wondered if he could see my perplexed look from beneath my visor. "Thank you for being my friend and for not treating me like everyone else—as if I'm a child. I knew I liked you."

"Well, at least one of you does." We laughed, and I clapped him on the chest one last time.

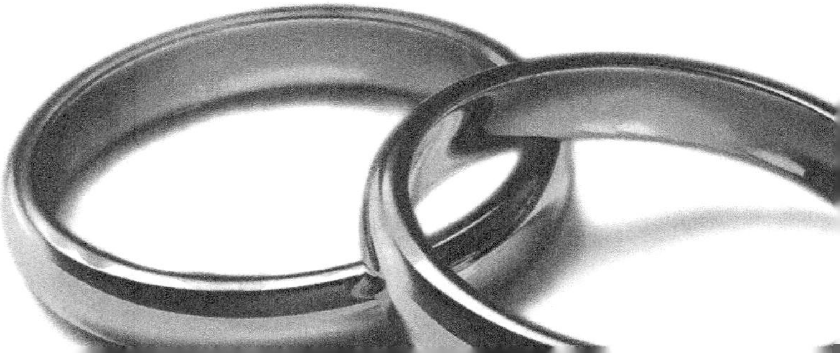

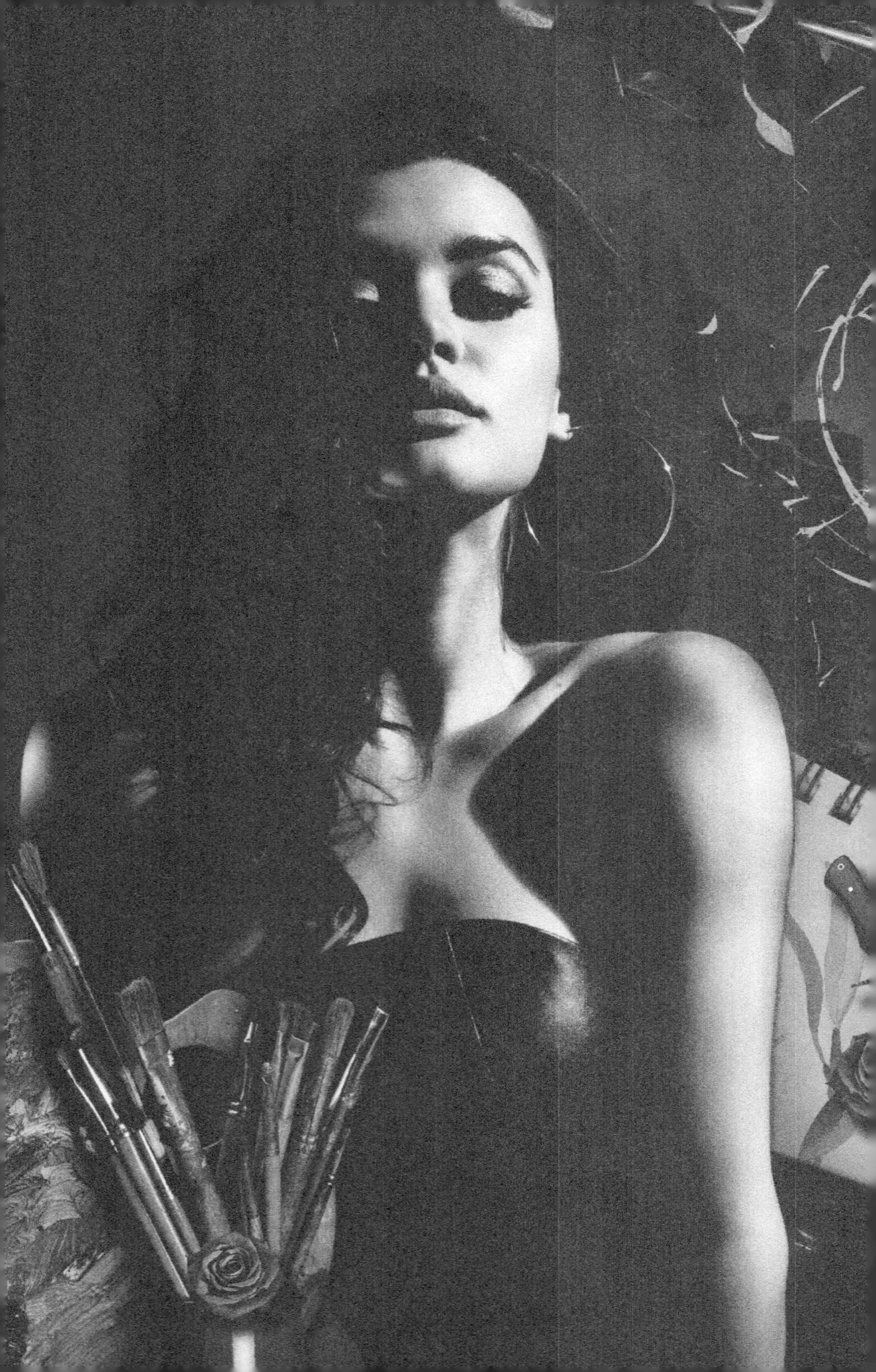

Chapter 19
Amalia

COOL leather pressed against my bare skin as I lay on the massage table and slipped my face into the headrest, waiting for Daniel to finish his prep. My muscles were practically buzzing for his gifted hands to work their magic and relieve the stress weighing on me over the last several days. With everything going on, I'd been overdue for my weekly massage, and fuck was I feeling it.

"Señorita Amalia, would you like me to start your usual playlist?"

"Yes, please." I wanted to tell him to hurry the hell up, that I didn't care what was playing so long as he worked out the knots in my shoulders and neck.

His warm hands were finally on me, and he tensed slightly before applying more pressure. "I see you needed me today."

I didn't answer and closed my eyes, letting his touch and the music take me far from the hacienda, from Texas, and all the worries and doubts plaguing my soul. The wedding was just days away. We amped up security for the occasion and changed locations to avoid unwanted guests at my home, but that did nothing to ease my concerns. Someone on our family's payroll had been bought off. That was the only explanation that made sense behind the attack on my father's shipment and the ambush at the compound.

Daniel's hands were suddenly gone a little sooner than I expected, though he probably needed more oil. Seconds ticked by longer than it would have taken, and I grew impatient.

"Is there a problem?"

Instead of words, I was met with a firm stroke at the base of my neck. His hands were no longer soft and smooth but rough and firm, hitting all the right spots in the best way.

Kai.

That unique scent of his was unmistakable. Calloused fingers smoothed up the back of my nape and into my hair. I clamped down on my jaw as I moaned and attempted to escape as his other hand moved down my back and over my bare hip. He pushed the towel aside just enough to give him better access, though he was obviously trying to avoid suspicion.

A smile crept along my lips when an idea came to mind.

"Daniel, your hands are magic, you know that? No one has *ever* touched me the way you have."

Kai's movements ceased for a moment, and I thought I heard him say something low under his breath, but the soft music in the background drowned it out.

"I'm sorry I rescheduled our last appointment. Things have been crazy. I missed you."

The fingers in my hair squeezed an ounce tighter, setting my skin ablaze. "Yes," I moaned. "Harder. You know exactly how I like it." Again, there was a moment of hesitation, and he released my hair, both hands now on either side of my hip, working their way onto my ass cheeks. "Just like that," I breathed. "Touch me."

I closed my eyes and bit my lip as he flipped the towel onto my back and spread my thighs open. I was already so damn wet for this man. "See what you do to me?" Kai gripped my ass with so much pressure that I was sure he'd leave fingerprints while the other hand slid down the seam of my pussy. He used two fingers and trailed them back and forth, spreading the wetness before massaging my clit in slow, deliberate circles.

"Fuck, Daniel…I missed your touch."

The music and his hands were suddenly gone, until I felt them snake around my throat and squeeze.

"You say that man's name one more time, and no one will ever find his body."

He loosened his grip and tore the towel away.

I chuckled. "How did you convince him to leave?"

His lips swept across my shoulder. "Easy. I gave him a choice, and he opted to keep his hands."

"Mm, I knew it was you," I murmured, gripping the edges of the table as he ran his tongue up the back of my thigh.

"I know," he said, lips hovering over my pussy.

"How?" I managed to ask in a strangled whisper as his tongue darted out and flicked my clit.

"Because this pretty cunt only gets wet for me." Kai hauled my hips back and smoothed his hand down my ass, spreading me open to get a better angle. "You know, vicious, even though I knew you were just fucking with me, every time you said his name, I wanted to choke the life from his body."

"Why?" My voice sounded more like a whine than a question when Kai suctioned me between his lips.

"I don't care about a goddamn contract, Amalia. My ring is on your finger, and your pussy is in my mouth. You're mine."

My nails nearly tore into the leather as those words vibrated against my clit. I wanted him to devour me, to die between my thighs, and to take me over the edge like only he knew how…but I'd been greedy.

I owed him. And I was suddenly ravenous.

I rocked against his face for three more sinful swipes of his tongue, but then I crawled on hands and knees toward the edge of the table. Glancing over my shoulder, I saw his look of confusion and tossed him a cunning grin.

"Where are you going?"

"No way are you going to make me owe you three times over." I hopped off as ladylike and leonine as I could muster, even on shaky legs.

I immediately grabbed his belt buckle and rose to kiss him. Kai's strong hands framed my face, deepening the kiss and nearly lifting me off the ground as he slid his tongue against mine and along my lips.

"And what will you do to clear your debt?"

"Easy." I dropped to my knees, never breaking eye contact, and tugged his pants down, pulling him free. Kai was a big boy with a pretty dick. "Swallow your cock."

He cussed between his teeth.

Fisting the base, I ran my tongue along the underside of his shaft, flicking the bead of precum dripping from his tip.

He grunted and tangled his fingers into my hair, tipping his head back as I took him entirely into my mouth, sliding up and down until it was soaking wet.

"Oh, fuck," he groaned as I worked him, hollowing out my cheeks when he hit the back of my throat. "I don't think I've seen anything more beautiful than you on your knees with my cock down your throat."

His hands were in my hair, squeezing, guiding me forward. Not that I needed it. While I wasn't out there giving random men blow jobs, I knew I was good. And by the look on Kai's face and the expletives falling from his mouth, I'd say he agreed.

"How much can you take, vicious?" He pushed until tears spilled from the corners of my eyes and black dots spotted my vision. "That's it. I'll feed you every inch of my cock until you cry some more and beg me to stop."

I was never one to back down from a challenge. I knew I'd never reach the base, but I sure as hell would enjoy how I made this man weak in the knees. The way he hissed and bit his lip as I sucked his cock so fucking good, he'd never remember there was anyone before me.

Reaching around his hips, I took his plump ass cheeks in each hand and squeezed, nails digging into his flesh, marking him as mine. For the next three years, that was who he would be. Who he'd belong to.

The moment I gagged and reached an impossible point, he reared back before driving into my mouth again and again. Tears streaked down my face, my legs shaking, pussy throbbing.

My hand lowered between my thighs, craving a release. But in the next moment, Kai wrenched his dick from my mouth and yanked me to my feet by my hair, fingers diving between my legs and stroking my aching clit.

And fuck, I was so turned on, I might have even let him slap me.

"I need to come inside this sweet pussy, vicious. I need to feel you. Can I do that? Can I fuck you, wife?"

"I'm not your wife yet, Cain." I swept my tongue across one of his nipples and looked up at him from beneath my lashes. "But I'll be your whore."

He spun me around so fast and bent me over the edge of the table that it almost made me dizzy. Maybe it was just the haze of lust, but I was drunk and wholly gone for this man, like nothing was more important than his cock buried inside me.

"Look at you. Fuck, you're beautiful," he whispered against my back, dropping soft kisses as he nudged my entrance.

"Kai, please…" I shamelessly begged. But now his teeth were

open against my ass, pulling a whine from my lips as he bit down. "I can't get pregnant... Just fuck me already before I cut you."

He laughed and straightened, pushing me farther into the table until I no longer touched the ground and spread me open. Glancing back, my breath caught in my throat when I saw how his eyes devoured me. How his lips parted and his breathing accelerated as he admired every exposed inch.

"Goddamn," he muttered, pressing inside me. The deliciously painful stretch of his cock had me gripping the edge of the table. He eased in slowly, feeling the slight resistance. "Easy, baby. Relax." A man telling a woman to relax is the equivalent of fighting words, but the tenderness in his voice, the way he cared about my pain and pleasure, caused something warm to flutter in my belly.

"More, Kai. More, please."

It was all the reassurance he needed to drive inside me as far as he could. A gasp left my lips at how utterly full of him I felt.

"You're so tight. So fucking perfect." Every time he eased back and plunged inside, a loud moan vibrated in my chest. "You feel that, vicious? Your pussy was made for me."

I clenched around him with every thrust and cried out his name into the cushioned surface of the table.

Kai's hand smoothed up my back until his fingers were in my hair, and he tugged my head back as he bent over my body and groaned into my ear, "I told you I need you to scream for me."

I bit my lip and grinned. "You said you'd make me...so make me."

In one swift move, he pulled out and flipped me over onto my back, and without so much as a moment to breathe, he threw one of my legs over his shoulder and fucked me so deep, I arched off the table, mouth open in a silent scream.

"I can't hear you," he said, circling his thumb over my clit. I shook my head and pounded the table with my fist as the whole damn thing scraped slightly across the floor.

"Kai," I cried, lifting my head just in time to catch him spitting on my pussy, nearly sending me over the edge into oblivion. I didn't need extra lubrication because the sounds rising from the slickness between us were filthy, sexy, and intoxicating. He was marking me.

I was his.

He rolled his thumb again, forcing another jolt and his name to echo against the walls of my studio. "Beautiful," he said, cupping one of my bouncing breasts and squeezing, ripping another gasp from my lungs.

"Fuck, fuck," I panted as his strokes intensified until my core tightened, and I felt myself reach the peak before shattering completely. My eyes rolled to the back of my head as I fell, but Kai hadn't slowed. Both of my legs were on his shoulders, and he bucked into me, gripping my thighs until my skin paled.

His grunts were loud, his cussing even louder, until he finally came inside me.

Letting my legs slide off, he laid his head over my trembling stomach as he caught his breath.

My eyelids fluttered closed when his hands came up around my waist and he kissed my belly tenderly at first, then with more passion. "You're incredible," he murmured over my dampened skin.

Kai straightened, grabbing my hand and taking me with him. "Mission accomplished."

We laughed, and I looped my arms around his back, meeting his eyes. "What are we doing?"

"Whatever we want."

"I don't know if this is smart."

He held my face. "Why?"

"You know why."

"How about we take this one day at a time."

I nodded my agreement. "Go get cleaned up."

I pulled a black lace robe over my body and tied it off at the waist. The hem barely made it past my ass, but it would do for now. Kai was near a window, looking at one of my paintings, his jeans loose around his hips, belt still undone, and bare chest beckoning to be licked despite my muscles still singing from just minutes ago.

"Amalia, these are—amazing. I had no idea you were this talented." He glanced back with a knowing grin. "As an artist."

"Nice save."

He winked and turned back toward my painting, brushing his fingers along the edges of the canvas. "Who is she?"

The aged face of a woman with deepset eyes and a crooked smile took me back to several weeks ago when I thought I was alone in the stable, crying like a damn baby because I'd been coerced into marrying a stranger. Milly's good friend, Daisy, snuck up on me. She didn't ask questions or show pity. She smiled that crooked grin and held me until I could hold myself. Not one word was exchanged between us, but they weren't necessary. I was sure Milly had told her everything.

"She's someone special who showed me kindness when she could have just pretended I didn't exist."

I hadn't noticed when he'd returned to where I was standing. Not until his arms were around me, his lips to my forehead.

"Impossible. You're a presence everywhere you go. I remember being taken by you that day you showed up. Every time you spoke, no one else existed. You owned the room."

"Well, I don't remember hearing from you afterward either."

He laughed into my hair. "You didn't exactly seem to be interested."

"I noticed you, Cain. And that's all you need to know."

"Fair enough." His gaze was set beyond me, to a far corner of my studio. I didn't have to turn to know what had caught his attention.

"What's that, under the white sheet?"

"Something I'm working on."

Kai's hands slid down to the small of my back. "Sounds important."

"It is. But you can't see it…yet. And if I find out you were snooping, I'll gouge out those pretty eyes and keep them as souvenirs."

"I'm just flattered you want to keep them," he said with a chuckle, sliding his hands farther down until he pulled me onto his waist. "So, you're beautiful, good with a knife…" He kissed up my neck, forcing my head to tilt back and my eyes to close. "A good shot…" His teeth nipped gently at my lips. "You have the sweetest fucking pussy."

"Keep going," I said, as I tangled my fingers into his soft hair.

"You can take a cock." Laughter bubbled up my throat. "And you're a goddamn talented artist. I've wanted to come here since your mother mentioned it at dinner that night. But I wasn't sure if—"

"All you had to do was ask."

"Well, we haven't exactly been on the best of terms. Though I'm not sure why. I'm not that ugly, and I think I have a shining personality."

I found myself laughing again, and I honestly couldn't remember the last time anyone outside of my family had made me feel this way in…maybe forever.

"I won't disagree. But I have my reasons."

Kai brushed his nose along my jaw, making it hard to catch my breath.

"Have or had?"

"You think that because you fucked me, that all is good?"

"I fucked your throat too. That has to count for something."

Kai met my grin. "It's not that simple. Don't take it personally, Cain. I just loathe that my hand is being forced. I've always made the rules for myself. I don't abide by the laws of men who think that because I have a pussy, I can't make decisions and be successful without relying on cock."

I pushed at his chest, and he set me down. "I've done just fine on my own. And I hoped to keep it that way until it was on my terms, not on those of bastards who aren't even alive." Kai was serious now as he listened unwaveringly. "I never wanted this responsibility on my shoulders. This was my brother Tony's burden to bear. Not mine. So excuse me if I'm just a little pissed off."

Kai tipped my chin with his fingers. "Can I ask you something?" I nodded. "Why me?"

I sighed and offered him a faint smile. "As you know, it was supposed to be Derek. But his circumstances changed and, well, you were the obvious second choice."

"Ah, the default."

He tried to play it off as a joke, but I saw the twitch in his jaw and the slight flare of his nose. I knew he loved his brother, but I wondered if he somehow felt overshadowed by Derek. He didn't have a reason to be. Kai was a force in his own right. If it wasn't for the circumstances surrounding our engagement, he was everything I coveted in a partner. Someone who could stand beside me, who loved all the dark parts that held my soul together. A man who knew I was just as capable. Who listened and was patient with all my highs and lows. He was all those things.

Touching his cheek, I smiled and said, "No, the upgrade."

He stared at me for what felt like forever, and I held his gaze and waited with anticipation for him to say whatever I knew was on the tip of his tongue.

"Fuck," he whispered, shaking his head.

"What?"

"Marry me," he said with a laugh, resting his forehead on mine.

"Give me a few days, and maybe I'll be forced to say yes."

"Done." With that said, he scooped me up again and tossed me back onto the massage table. "Do me a favor, tell Daniel he's fired."

"Cain, absolutely not. Daniel has magic hands."

"You liked what I did with mine."

I reached between us and grabbed his cock. "Do it again." Kai's lips were on my neck, my legs circling his waist when I felt him slow until his mouth hovered over my earlobe. "You see a ghost or something, Cain? Because I can't imagine anything grabbing your attention more than my wet pussy against you."

"Just wondering when I'll get to see what's under that sheet?"

"Someday. When I'm ready."

He looked down at me and nodded in understanding. A part of me hated that he didn't press, that he respected my privacy, because it did strange things to my stomach and put terrifying thoughts in my head. But then there was that woman I didn't recognize—or maybe I'd just lost her years ago—who craved love and sweet gestures from a man. That woman who was swooning and falling…

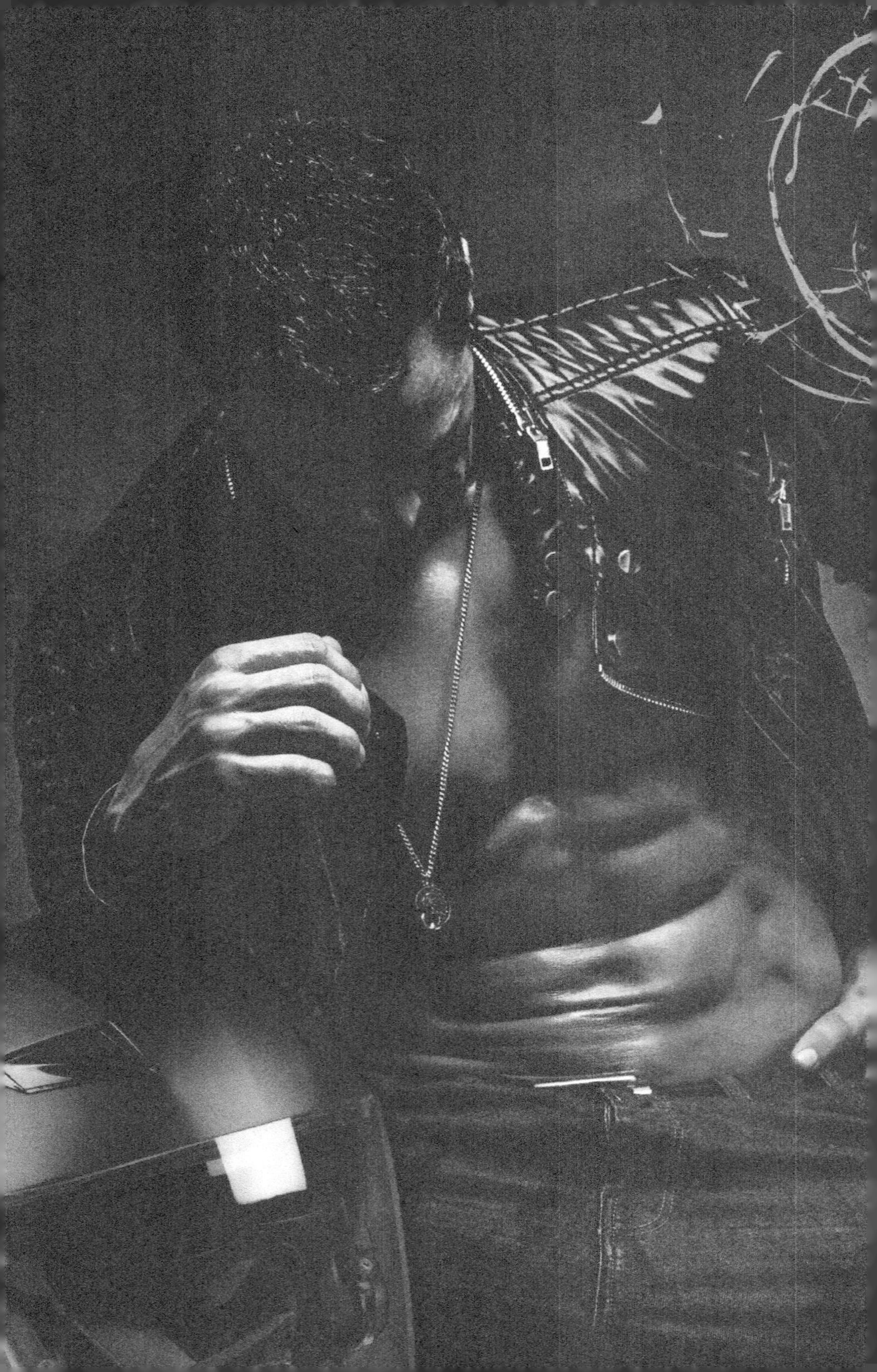

Chapter 20
Kai

"**TOMORROW** is the day."

I gripped the stone balcony, tightening my hands around the cool surface as I tipped my head toward a starless night sky.

Tomorrow was indeed the day Amalia and I would solidify our contract, and I wasn't sure how to feel about being bound to this woman who'd forced herself into my life. Nothing could have prepared me for the flurry of emotions: doubt, apprehension, anxiety—I was fucking terrified. Three years was a long time to coexist with someone by means of coercion.

But underneath it all, I knew those thoughts were just a survival mechanism—a way of protecting myself from what I knew was slowly unfolding between us—or worse, just me. We'd crossed a line, and there was no crawling back.

Derek's hand was on my shoulder, the other holding a cigar. He tilted his chin, huffing smoke into the darkness.

"I'm going to be with you every step of the way, Kai. I almost feel responsible for getting you into this mess, especially with a woman like Amalia."

"What does that mean?" The harshness in my tone had him whipping toward me, and his forehead creased in confusion.

"What does *that* mean?" he asked, taking another puff, though his eyes didn't stray away from mine. "I've noticed small things between the two of you, but I didn't know that you—"

"That I what?"

Derek nodded, gaze focused on the vast courtyard below. "I want you to be happy, brother. Whatever that looks like is up to you, and I'll respect it. If this woman—if she makes you feel things, don't deny yourself just because of how this started." He chuckled lightly, gazing at the cigar between his fingers, as if recalling a memory. "If anyone knows what that's like, it's me."

With a scoff, I leaned forward, forearms on the stone. "You trying to give me marital advice?"

We shared a laugh.

"I guess I am." Derek turned to me. "I'm sorry. Maybe things would have been different if Amalia and I hadn't met under those circumstances. It's possible you and her would have—"

"We wouldn't," I interrupted. "While we move in similar circles, she and I were always meant to live parallel lives."

"I would have said the same of Eva, but here we are. She made me a husband and a father, giving me things I never imagined I would have or want. Maybe I don't deserve them, but you know I'm a greedy bastard," he said with a grin. "And I'll never let them go."

"Those girls wouldn't let you even if you tried."

He glanced over his shoulder into his room, where an open sliding glass door revealed a crib and a small figure sleeping on her side against the wooden rails. "Over my cold, lifeless body."

As if on cue, Vali opened her eyes and outstretched her arms, and without a second of hesitation, Derek put out his cigar, picked up his daughter, and brought her out onto the terrace. Her sleepy eyes widened, and she smiled when she saw me, laying her head on her father's shoulder.

"Hey, you're supposed to be asleep," he said with a soft tone reserved for his baby girl. Kissing the top of her head, he gently rocked her from side to side. "Mami is going to come up here and get mad, thinking your Uncle Kai and I woke you up."

Valentina stopped suckling on her pacifier and giggled at his words.

Eva had taken a liking to Milly. I couldn't blame her. The woman was as sweet as they came, making it easy to forget she held all the family's secrets. They were busy prepping homemade appetizers despite the food being catered. She'd said she wanted to give Amalia that personal touch as she had all her life.

Derek kissed his daughter's forehead when her eyes fluttered closed and her grip on his shirt slackened.

"I know I say this a lot, but I'm happy you found happiness, brother. It looks good on you, and you do deserve it. We were dealt some shitty-ass cards. And life owes us big, especially you."

Derek grinned and returned to the room, carefully placing the baby into her crib. I turned my attention back to the courtyard and the seemingly endless horizon of the Montesinos property.

Someone suddenly emerged from a blind spot on the west side.

Amalia.

I didn't take long to notice the difference in her walk and how she carried herself. Where Amalia was always confident and deliberate in her steps, it almost seemed like walking was a chore, her movements heavy and uncoordinated.

Was she drunk?

Derek was returning when I hurriedly walked past him. "I gotta run," I said, and in typical Derek fashion, he didn't ask questions.

Just as I reached the bottom of the main stairway, Isabel came around the corner, eyes lighting up the moment she spotted me.

"Kai! I haven't seen you all day. I know you've been busy with last-minute fittings and errands, but I'm so glad I ran into you."

Suddenly antsy, I hugged her and intended to keep moving, but she hooked my elbow and tugged me backward, leading me to a downstairs office.

"I was just about to—"

"I know," she said, closing the door. "I know." Her bright smile faded the moment we were alone. And she motioned for me to sit. Isabel was about three inches shorter than her daughter, but both women possessed this way of being intimidating with just a look. While neither affected me, it was impossible not to give in to my future mother-in-law.

Fake or not.

I sat my ass down, even though I was itching to check on Amalia.

"Kai, I know about the contract and how this was an agreement between you and my daughter to appease my husband and the lawyers."

I said nothing. She could have been calling my bluff and trying to trick me into confirming her suspicions.

"It's okay, *mijo*. I know she probably threatened your life if you spoke," she said with a chuckle and poured herself a drink. "Amalia always did have this way with persuasion and getting what she wanted. She reminds me a lot of myself when I was younger." Tipping her head, she shot me a knowing look and knocked back the glass of scotch. "I just spoke to her, and she told me everything. In fact, she got to this bottle before I did."

I sprung to my feet once she confirmed what I'd suspected.

"Kai, Amalia isn't going anywhere. Please sit."

"I can't leave her out there like that."

Isabel's beaming smile was back. "I knew it. You care about her, don't you? At least, you're starting to."

"Call me a glutton for punishment."

She laughed outright and leaned against the desk. "That's my girl. Always taught her to be strong and never take shit from a man." Her frown made another appearance. "But maybe she learned that lesson too well."

"Is she all right?"

Isabel downed the last of her drink and sat, observing me with a pensive look. "She will be. Take care of my girl, Kai. She plays tough because she needs to, but deep down, Amalia is just as beautiful as she is on the outside. She just doesn't know it. Show her."

"I mean no disrespect, but if you know this is temporary, then you also know that we'll go our own ways three years from now. I'll be back in Philly. She's here. At best, we remain friends."

She scoffed, her lips parting as if she was about to speak, but decided against it and replied, "Of course."

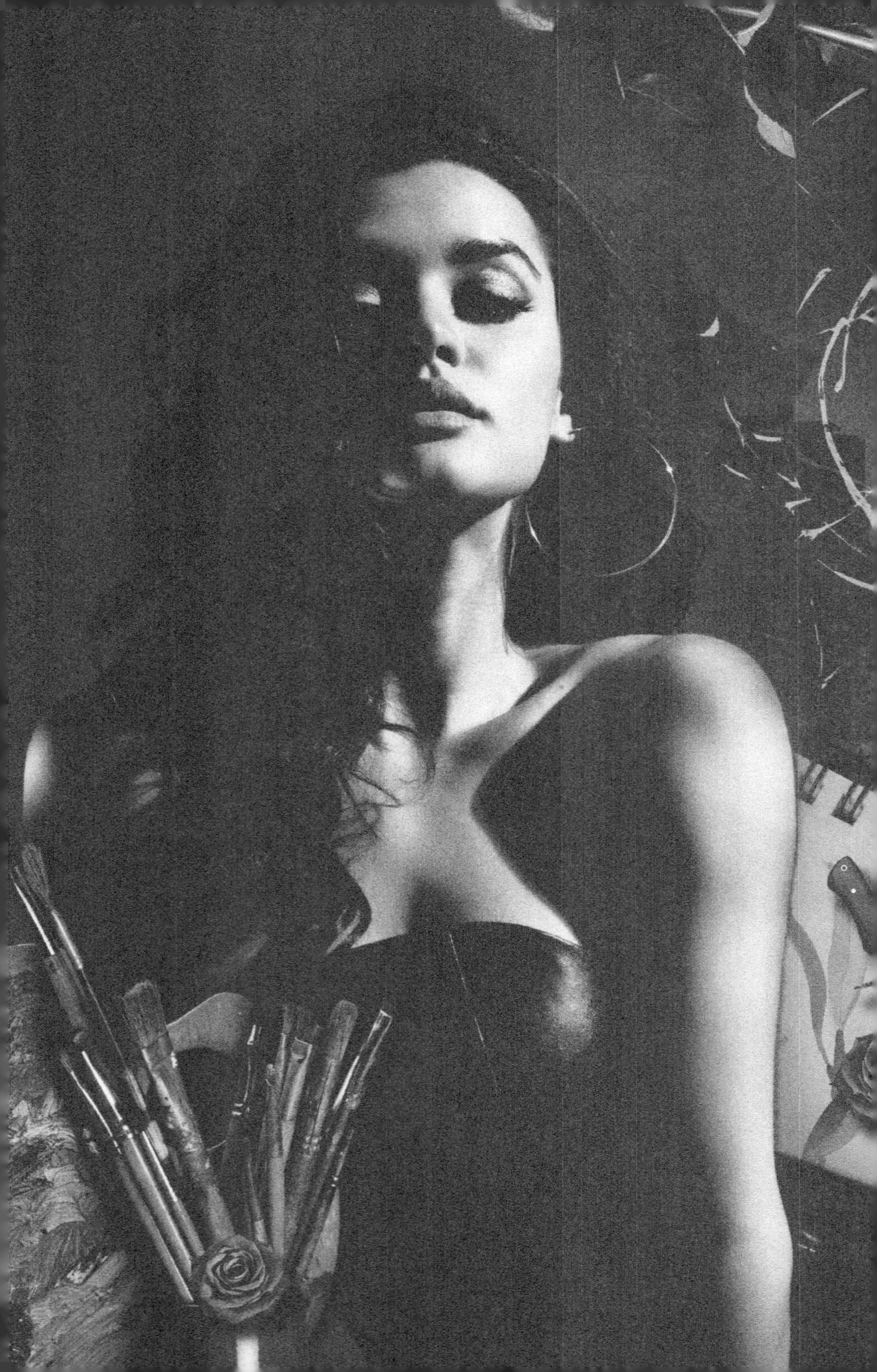

Chapter 21
Amalia

KAI'S slow footfalls drew close, but I didn't turn around. I didn't need to. As crazy as it was to admit, I felt his presence and the calm he brought with him every time he was near. The night of the ambush was when I realized he was safe. That I didn't need to be anyone else but myself with him. That he wouldn't judge or take advantage of me. Before I could swipe the tears from my eyes, his arms came around my waist, and he pulled me to his chest.

"Thought you could use a little company."

"I'm out here because I needed to get away."

His lips brushed my ear.

"Okay, let me rephrase that. I thought you could use *my* company."

I leaned into his embrace, and he held me in companionable silence, giving me time to speak when I was ready.

"I told my mother everything."

"What happened?"

"She walked in on me trying on my dress, and she…" I couldn't reveal that she'd gotten upset at my choice of dress. It was supposed to be a surprise—one to spite him that I'd purchased shortly after he arrived. Now, the enjoyment I would have gotten from the look on his face seemed so trivial and pointless.

"She what?" he pressed, concern lacing his tone.

I whipped around and swiped harshly at my eyes, aggravated that I couldn't hold back my tears.

"My mother has all these expectations, Kai. A honeymoon, and babies, a memorable first dance, and a *fucking* happily ever after. All of it. But we both know that I can't give her what she wants. That you and I…that none of it is real. And I'd never seen her so happy, especially after Tony's death. I just couldn't lie to her anymore."

"Amalia, you knew what this was from the beginning. What changed?"

I shoved out of his arms and trudged through the courtyard. My heels against the cobblestone and the shots I'd taken beforehand made the trek much more difficult than I remembered.

"Hey," he called softly, catching my wrist. "Now that she knows, none of that should matter. So what's really wrong?"

Closing my eyes, I let out a breath. "I don't know. I'm a mess. And it's not like me to feel…nervous. But I am. Can we pull this off? Can I actually go through with it?"

"I'll be at the end of that aisle, no matter what. I gave my word."

"Ugh, that's just it. I feel like I'm selling myself off to you and them—it goes against everything my girls and I stand for." I bowed my head, feeling foolish. What did I expect? For him to love me? Was that what I wanted?

"Vicious, there are things in life that are inevitable. We know that more than anyone. It is a means to an end, even though it takes a piece of us every time."

Kai's arms were around me, his lips against my forehead. "What happens when there's nothing left?" I whispered, clutching his shirt. He didn't answer and simply held me closer. But maybe that was precisely what I needed.

"Whether ours is a marriage of convenience, I know one thing for certain."

"What?"

"You're going to be the most beautiful goddamn bride."

I laughed and shook my head, regarding the black diamond around my finger.

He must have noticed because he took my hand and slipped off the ring before dropping to one knee. My heart fluttered at the sight of him.

"Kai, what are you doing?"

"Making this right." He cleared his throat and swallowed. "Amalia Isabel Montesinos, will you do me the honor of being my wife." This man. Fuck, this man. I swallowed the knot that formed in my throat, overcome with emotions that threatened to make me start blubbering like a fool. What was he doing to me?

"Are you trying to get laid or something, Cain?" He laughed as he slid the band over my finger again.

"No, that was already on my list of plans for tonight."

"How bold of you."

Kai straightened and crushed me to his chest. "So, is that a no?"

"Oh, no, you're going to put that pretty dick inside me, Cain."

He smiled while peppering kisses along my neck.

"I told you this, you and me, it's…effortless. So I know tomorrow will be fine."

"Why are you so good to me? I've been such a bitch. I was determined to make this as difficult as possible for you." I looped my arms behind his nape, meeting his gaze.

"Are you sorry?" he asked. Reaching down around my ass, he scooped me up, and I straddled his torso.

"No," I said, grazing his lips in a slow side-to-side motion. "Not one bit." His laugh vibrated against my mouth, and he squeezed my ass cheeks tighter, pressing me against his hard abs, and I wondered if he could feel how wet I already was.

"Wrong answer."

"Sounds like that warrants a punishment."

"Fuck, vicious. Anything you want."

I leaned forward and kissed behind his ear, reveling in the way he squirmed and grunted my name. "Remember when you said that I'd be on my knees, begging for your cock?" He nodded, his eyes hooded, drunk with need. "Do it, Kai. Put me on my knees, and make me beg."

"Can I take you somewhere?"

Kai was speed-walking through the courtyard. His muscles flexed as he carried me while also trying to keep balance on the uneven cobblestone.

"Don't drop me," I whispered into his ear as he rounded a corner, where the space opened up to the back pool area.

"I'd never drop you…on the ground."

There was only a millisecond to inhale a breath before I was airborne and squealing his name. One loud splash later, and I was submerged in the cool water. I didn't kick to the surface. Instead, I let my body slowly rise as I contemplated all the ways I'd murder and dissect my future husband.

Another splash exploded beside me, and Kai's arms were around my waist, pulling me to him as we broke the surface together.

"If you wanted to die to avoid marrying me, all you had to do was ask. I'm creative."

He barked a laugh and tugged me to the edge of the pool and toward a shallow ledge that allowed him to sit chest-deep in the water, me in his lap.

"Don't you feel better already?"

"You're still breathing, so I can't say I do."

Kai pushed wet hair from my face and leaned in for a kiss. I was tempted to turn away and tell him to fuck off, but who was I kidding. His white tee clung to every dip of hard muscle, and strands of his hair hung over his forehead, dripping down his face and the seam of his lips. I ran my tongue across that pretty mouth, licking the water droplets.

"That's better," he crooned, fisting the back of my hair, tipping my head back, and dragging the edges of his teeth along my jaw.

"Why are we wet and in a pool?"

"Wet was a given. The pool? Spontaneous idea. Believe it or not, I've never had sex in a pool."

My hand smoothed up his thigh until I reached his dick, and I stroked him until he groaned over my lips.

"So what you're saying is, I'm about to pop your pool cherry?"

Kai snickered and tightened his hold on my hair, "Are you, wife?"

"Just a few more hours until I'm your wife," I said, working his belt and zipper. He lifted slightly and pushed his pants down enough to free his cock, and I wasted no time before my hand was around his thick shaft. Kai allowed me to pump him twice, then gripped my wrist, forcing me to stop.

Our eyes locked, and he shook his head with a teasing smirk. "I'm going to need you to beg a little harder than that."

Releasing me, he slid his hands down my hips, hooking my shorts and panties with his thumbs as I helped slip them off, and tossed the sopping-wet denim on the stone deck.

I steadied my body, positioning myself over him, when he wrapped a hand around my throat and pulled me close. "You're going to ride my thigh with that sweet cunt, and when you're about to come, I won't let you…" He kissed me hard. "Then you'll beg."

Kai was unknowingly teaching me things about myself I didn't know I was into. I'd never let a man hold this much power over me, much less during sex. But fuck me, if I was ready and eager to please, to do every damn thing he asked. And I would beg for his dick until he was so deep inside me, I'd feel him days later.

With my hands on his shoulders for leverage, I slid my pussy over his thigh.

"Good girl. Just like that."

"I've never…been a good girl," I panted, rocking against him, my nails carving into his skin.

"That's why you and I are perfect for each other, *mi reina*."

His words spurred me on, igniting a fire so hot I felt like I would combust if I didn't come soon. I moved harder and faster against his thigh as soft moans flowed from my lips.

"Kai…please," I pleaded, needing to be full of him, but he held me in place, his grip around my neck tightening.

"Do you trust me, Amalia?"

My circle had always been small—my family, my girls—and that's where my trust in others died. But there was something about Kai. He was safe, he cared, and I knew without a shred of doubt that his loyalty was solid.

Losing myself in his eyes, I nodded, and he lowered me underwater. Words were unnecessary. I knew what he wanted, and I shuddered with anticipation until my mouth was around him, and I took him inch by inch until he bottomed out. I was in a state of absolute euphoria between his grip around my neck, being submerged, and his dick down my throat. It was filthy, depraved, risky—and I fucking loved it. My eyes stung with unshed tears as I worked him while struggling to stay conscious, but I was seconds from passing out. Maybe I tapped his thigh, or he noticed the tension in my body, but he lifted me out of the water, and I sucked in a big gasp of air.

"Fuck…" he rasped and kissed me fast and desperate.

My pussy ached. I needed him. God, I needed him. "Please…Kai."

"Please, what?" he asked between kisses.

"If you don't fuck me, I'll slit your throat." I felt the vibration of his laugh inside my mouth, and he lifted me over his lap. Kai released my neck and grasped my hips, guiding me down.

"Fuck, vicious. You look like a goddamn goddess bouncing on my cock."

He tore my shirt above my head, almost violently yanking down the straps of my bra until it was bunched somewhere around my abdomen.

We knew there was a possibility we could get caught, but neither of us acted like we gave a damn. No one else existed but us. And if this was what the next three years would be like, I felt foolish for ever being upset.

"Tomorrow…you'll be mine." Kai hissed when my nails dug deeper, marking him. "Three years."

"No," he said, my nipple between his teeth. "I'm yours right now." As he bit my shoulder, I threw my head back. "Yesterday." He slammed me down, over and over. "From the day I walked off that plane." He met my thrusts, and water splashed over our faces. "You were mine."

"Yours," I whined, shattering in his arms. His name danced off my tongue as he followed me over the edge.

Tomorrow was the day. And maybe my heart was no longer afraid.

Maybe it was hopeful.

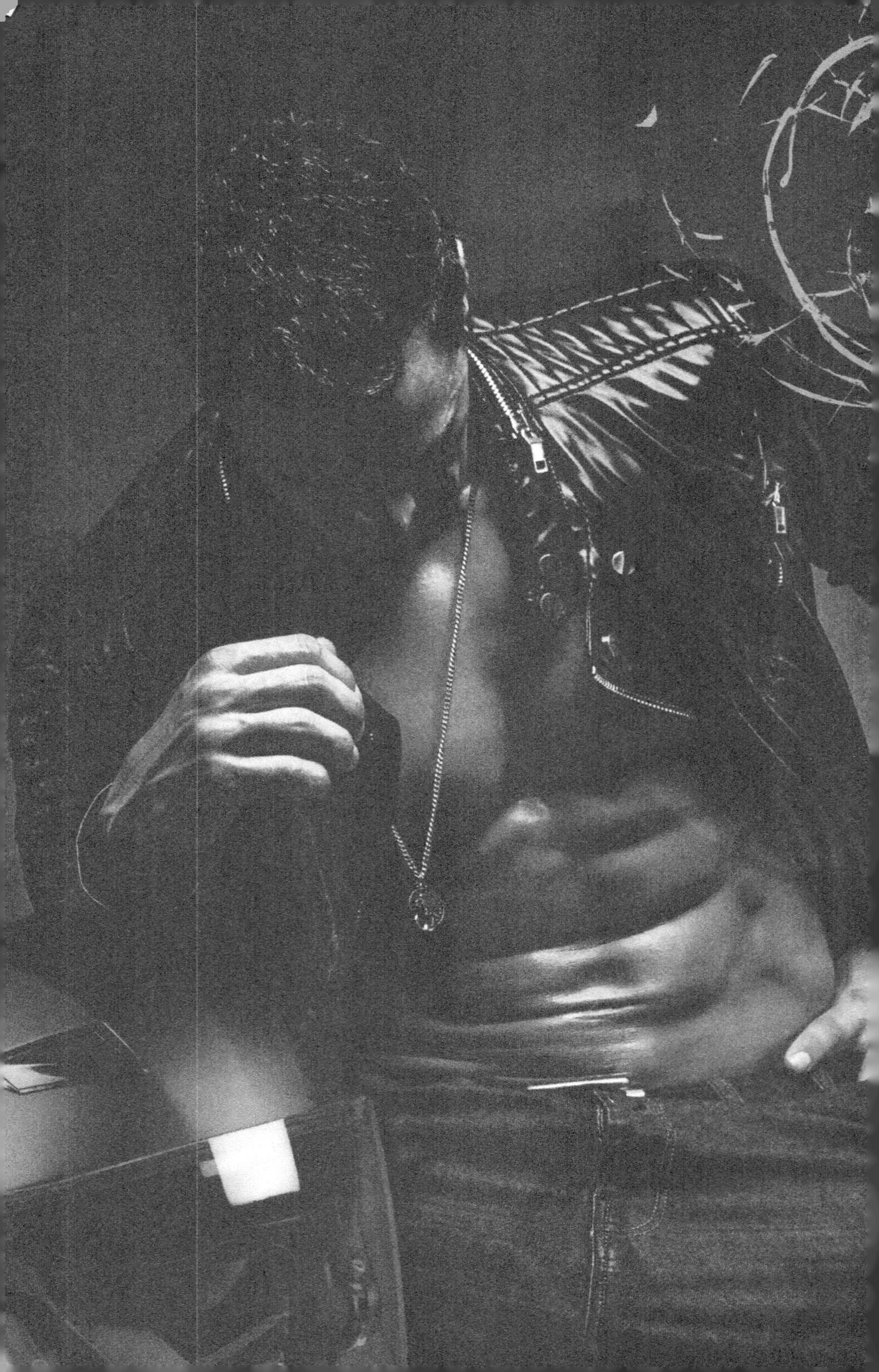

Chapter 22
Kai

"**LENI,** girl! Come here."

One of my favorite faces beamed at me the moment our eyes connected. She threw her arms around my neck as I hugged her tightly. Leni and Silas had been on a month-long trip to Greece and the Philippines before I left Philly. I was happy that she'd found love and fulfillment, and Silas couldn't have been more perfect for her brand of beautiful chaos.

We'd once thought our attraction to each other could have been more—we were part of the same world, the sex was goddamn good, and our chemistry and friendship had felt so natural. What more could we have needed? It wasn't until we fizzled out that we realized that we could go longer stretches without sleeping together or hanging out the way we once used to. In hindsight, it was easy to see how and why we came together and then quickly fell apart.

Leni would always have a piece my heart and my loyalty in the same ways as Derek. She and Silas were family.

"You look beautiful as always."

"Kai, look at you." She patted my lapels and whistled her approval. "Now, I have to admit, I'm surprised Amalia hasn't murdered you yet," she teased, stepping to the side and letting Silas through.

"You owe me $50, love."

I peered around him, a look of mock indignation on my face. "You bet him money that I wasn't going to make it?"

"Hey, I've known Amalia longer than you. She must like you, at least a little bit, since you're still standing without so much as a scratch on that pretty face."

When Silas clapped my back, it was a reminder that Leni's comment was half true. Sharp nails had carved my back last night, but no matter how much they stung, I was ready for her again tonight.

"Kai bear, are you ready for today?" Despite the nickname, Leni's expression was etched with concern.

Parts of me would never be ready for today's events, of getting married and having such an extravagant wedding to someone I didn't love…

I paused for a beat. Feeling those words out in my thoughts.

Marriage was never on my radar. That was Derek's thing, oddly enough. But what I had once thought would be the worst three years of my life had turned into something…something else.

"I'll be fine. And I thought I told you never to call me that again."

"You know that's not going to happen." She laughed and twisted around, eyes roaming the courtyard. "Where is my baby?"

"Eva was getting her up and ready from a nap. She'll be happy to see you."

Leni suddenly took Silas's hand, and with a nod, motioned to a young boy sitting by the fountain. He was looking aimlessly at the water, light brown hair hanging over his face.

As if he knew she was pointing him out, the boy raised his head, and while it had been a few years, I would never forget that face. Silas waved him over, and after a moment's hesitation, he was at their side, leaning into Leni.

"Hey, kid. Been a while."

"Maksim, you remember Kai?"

"I do," he said, eyes on mine. He looked to be about twelve or thirteen now.

"Maksim Belov." I'd often thought of that boy Derek and I orphaned years ago, though maybe we'd done him a favor. His mom was a piece of shit. Tried to use him as a shield and a fucking bargaining chip for her pathetic life.

But what the hell was he doing with Leni and Silas?

"Maksim is staying with us," she said, reading my thoughts. "Pulled some strings, and he was able to accompany us on our trip."

I realized years ago when I was younger than Maksim, how small and deceiving the world truly was. So it didn't surprise me that our paths had crossed again, and in a seemingly more permanent situation—similar to mine and Amalia's. There was a reason he was spared that night and was standing in front of me, looking more confident than a kid his age had any right to be.

"Valentina!"

Leni darted past me and scooped up Vali, Eva and Derek just steps behind them.

Derek zoned in on Maksim immediately, but the boy's attention was on Leni and the baby.

"Fucking small world, brother."

Familiar faces lined the front row while strangers occupied the rest of the seats, all there to witness the marriage of Amalia Montesinos. I was never one to feel nervous, but as I skimmed the crowd, I quickly realized all eyes were on me. Many must have been asking themselves who the fuck I was, where had I come from, and how had

I managed to win over *la reina*.

Derek tapped me on the arm with his elbow, maybe sensing my nerves, as he gestured a reassuring nod. A little over four years ago, he'd been in my shoes, and I was his best man. Though the event was much smaller and more intimate, it was one I'd never forget. His fond expression, the emotion in his eyes, it was all I ever wanted for my brother. And now here we were, roles reversed, but in a much different circumstance.

As the music started to play, my heart thudded and blood whooshed in my ears, causing me to nearly sway.

This was it. I knew she was close, and the distance between us felt electric. When Amalia finally came into view, I felt an overwhelming need to grip my chest.

She was fucking breathtaking.

A black wedding dress adorned her beautiful body while a long veil of the same color carved a trail behind her. When her signature red lips curved into a smile the moment her eyes connected with mine, time was suddenly suspended. Not a single soul existed in that venue. The emotion burned my throat, and it was then I realized I hadn't taken a breath.

"Easy," Derek whispered, his hand on my forearm as I swept in a lungful of air.

Shaking off his touch, I focused back on my bride as she walked past Gio and sent him a wink.

I reached for her the moment she was close, my arm around the curve of her back, nose against her cheek, as I took in every gorgeous inch.

"You wore this for me, and I'm going to spend all night thanking you for it."

"Is that a promise?" she asked with a smile in her voice and a touch of emotion in her eyes.

The sound of a man clearing his throat behind us snapped me

back to the moment. That was when I lifted my gaze to the sea of guests, though none of them were distinguishable because no one else mattered.

Even as the officiant began to speak, my attention was solely on Amalia.

"With this ring, I vow…"

As I slipped the black band onto her finger, and lost myself in the depths of her eyes, I had never been more sure of anything else in my life:

I was completely fucked.

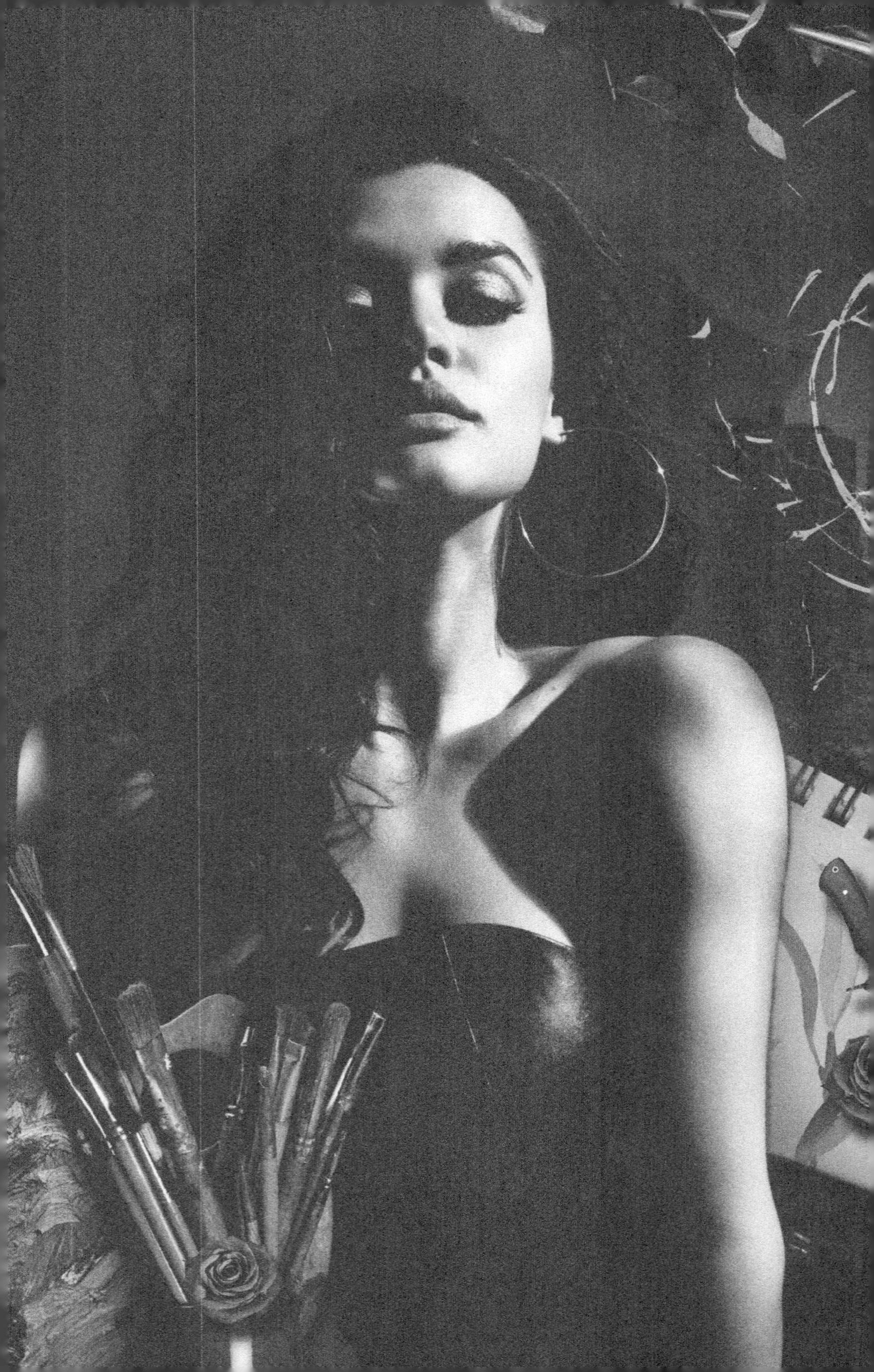

Chapter 23
Amalia

"**EVERYONE** is watching us."

"I promise you there isn't a single person in this room looking at me." His lips were at my temple, and his hands were on my back as we swayed to the smooth musical notes. "Amalia, you look stunning."

My face flushed, and I leaned into him, taking a moment to breathe in the crisp scent of his cologne. "You clean up pretty good yourself, Cain."

"I believe that title also belongs to you now. *Wife*."

I laid my head on his shoulder and sighed. "We did it," I whispered. "We pulled it off. Everyone seemed convinced."

"Effortless, vicious. You and I don't have to try. You know that. Anyone can see, even now, that the last place I want to be is on this dance floor."

I lifted my gaze, confused by his words and maybe slightly insulted, until I saw the fire in his blue eyes and how they darkened. "And where exactly would you like to be right now?"

"My favorite place. Inside you."

Closing my eyes, I swallowed the moan fighting its way up my throat. "Come to my room tonight, Kai."

With his thumb and forefinger, he tilted my chin. "*Our* room?"

Ours?

Against my better judgment, I nodded, because no other response would do.

Maybe this arrangement wouldn't be the hell I'd envisioned and dreaded for so long. Life beside this man excited me in ways I hadn't felt in a long while. My belly dropped to my feet at the thought. It was unnerving for so many reasons, but the biggest was, what if I couldn't say goodbye at the end of it all?

"Mind if I cut in?"

Gio tapped Kai's shoulder, and his handsome face lit up when my new husband pressed a kiss to my lips and handed me off.

"You look beautiful."

"Thank you," I said, throwing my arms around him in a tight hug. "I'm sorry."

"What for?"

I sighed heavily. "After what happened at the compound, I've purposely avoided you."

"I noticed. I'm sorry, too," he whispered, emotion thickening his voice. "What I did was reckless, I know. But when I overheard your conversation, I was afraid for you. I don't want to lose you, Amalia. Not you, too."

His face blurred behind the tears that had gathered in my eyes. "Gio, you won't even ride Miss Oscar because you're afraid she'll throw you, but you snuck into one of my cars when you knew that we…that things would get dangerous."

He wiped my tears. "I did that for you."

I squeezed him until he grunted, but I didn't care, and I held him tighter. He did nothing to shove out of my embrace. "Don't you ever do that again. If something had happened to you, I would have never forgiven myself." Gripping his shoulders, I said, "Promise me."

"I promise. But you…"

"Gio, I've been doing this a long time. I can't promise that things will always go as planned, but for now—"

"But why? We don't need the money, Amalia. And I know Kai is loaded."

Despite the seriousness of our conversation, I couldn't help but find humor in his knowledge of Kai's financial background.

"It's not just about money. There are things you don't understand. Our family can't just walk away from… from…"

Gio's eyebrows knitted together as he watched me stutter my words while looking past him.

"From what? What is it?"

It had been days since I'd felt the urge to sink a blade into flesh or empty my mag into something that had once been moving. The feeling rolled over me in hot, pulsing waves as I advanced to the other side of the wooden dance floor.

"Helena, losing those pretty nails would be a damn shame."

She twisted to face me, her arm still around my husband's neck. "Amalia, I never took you for the jealous type."

"I'm not."

"Hey," Kai said, stepping between us. When he attempted to thread his fingers with mine, I swatted his hand away. I was being irrational, and I knew it because Helena had Silas. But I suddenly couldn't unsee the image of her and Kai fucking, and now she was here, with her arm around him.

What would people think?

"How are we supposed to be convincing when you're cozying up with your ex at your wedding? How do you think that makes me look? You will *not* disrespect me, Cain, especially not here."

"Amalia, you're being—"

"Watch how you finish that sentence. You say crazy, and I'll cut off your dick."

Helena had the audacity to cross her arms and grin as she watched us. "I knew I always liked you," I heard her say as I turned my back and walked off the dance floor. I kept pace until I reached the end of the paved walkway, and I tossed my heels, crossing onto the grass toward an iron bench.

Heavy steps followed, and I knew it was Kai.

"*Muñeca.*"

Or not.

"Rocco, I didn't exactly want company."

"I'm sorry. You've been the center of attention all day, and I haven't been able to congratulate the new bride."

"Don't be a hypocrite. We both know you're not a fan of Kai's."

He chuckled and placed a hand on my shoulder. "You know me well."

I shrugged him off. Things had changed with Rocco ever since the compound. No matter how much I tried to convince myself, I couldn't shake the feeling that he was somehow involved. It was a hard truth to reconcile, considering I'd known him my whole life, and my father trusted him with his. But without concrete evidence, it was just a wild accusation.

His brow quirked when I moved away, and we regarded each other suspiciously, as if waiting for the other to say something or make a move.

"Amalia?" he questioned, stepping closer. "What's wrong?"

I wasn't the type to hold my tongue for anyone, but I suddenly felt strangely vulnerable, and with only a blade strapped to my thigh, if anything went down, I wasn't confident that it was a fight I'd win.

"Nothing," I lied.

He moved in closer and dared to lift my chin.

As I swatted him away a second time, another voice joined in.

"You know, the men in my life don't ask questions about another man's hands on what's theirs."

Helena took a casual stance beside Rocco, but I knew that every instinct was on alert.

"Are you going to call your boyfriend, the guy with the ponytail?" he asked, scoffing.

I sat on the bench and crossed my legs, suddenly intrigued.

"Oh no, he knows better than to steal my fun."

Rocco regarded her, eyes falling on the Ares ring that adorned her forefinger.

"Amalia, I was also coming by to let you know I'm heading out early." His stony glare slid toward Helena. "It's a little crowded here anyway."

"Bye, Ricky," she said with a smirk.

"It's Rocco."

"I know."

Rocco motioned as if he were going to say his goodbyes with a peck on the cheek, as was his MO with me, but even he knew that something had fractured between us. With a nod, he turned and disappeared down the dark walkway as I kept watch, paranoia getting the best of me.

"Who's the asshole?" Leni sat beside me on the stone bench, making no effort to conceal the blade she'd tucked in her thigh strap when the slit of her dress fell open.

I rolled my eyes. Clearly, Kai has a type.

"What do you want?"

"Come on, Amalia. We go back years. Kai is a dear friend. And I know you're not jealous."

"Jealous, no. But you hanging off my new husband isn't exactly a good look. There are eyes and ears everywhere, Helena."

She laughed and leaned both elbows on the back of the bench. "No one will believe that man has eyes for anyone else. In case you missed it, he looks at you like you're the only person in the room. Hell, maybe even the whole goddamn city."

There it was, that feeling like the pit of my stomach had fallen to my toes. Of course, I'd noticed because I'd also felt it. For just a moment, I had envisioned that our circumstances were different. That he and I were getting married because it was what we wanted.

Because we were in love.

Living in that reality was easier than the one where my hands were tied, as were his. I wasn't the woman who followed orders. I gave them, and it killed me that this was the one rule I couldn't break—one where I had to give up my power and choice.

"Are you ready to get back to the party? Kai is probably fidgeting like a kid, waiting for you. I had to threaten his life to come talk to you."

As I motioned to get to my feet, Helena put a hand on my forearm. "Hey, Kai is special. Don't hurt him."

We locked eyes. There was an unspoken warning in her tone, but the threat was loud and clear. I sent a smirk her way. It was one of the many reasons she and I had always gotten along.

Stab first and ask questions later.

Helena twisted as she got to her feet, but in the next breath, she plopped down beside me again, as if she'd lost her balance, and released a small gasp.

"What's wrong?"

"I—I," she stuttered and brought a hand up to her left shoulder, her eyes widening when she looked at the blood streaking her fingers.

"Amalia," she whispered. "Duck."

The impact of a silenced bullet hit the stone beside her, sending pieces of rock flying in all directions.

Fuck.

She and I hit the ground and hid behind a stone ledge. Fear gripped me at the realization we were under attack.

"This can't be happening. We hired extra security. Someone is fucking us over."

"Well, they ruined my fucking dress and shot me in my goddamn good arm. They're dead."

"Agreed," I said in a hushed voice, conscious that whoever shot at us was still close by. "But we have to go about this with a clear head. The bullet came from over there. If we stay on this side of the wall, we can round the corner and come up behind them."

Helena held her arm as blood spilled in a steady stream between her tightly clasped fingers. I tore several layers of tulle from my dress and made a tourniquet around her wound.

"Leni, there's no exit wound. This should help, but I need you to tell me if you start feeling lightheaded."

"It takes me getting shot for you to care and call me Leni?" Her smile was sincere but tight, the pain getting the best of her.

"Well, my probability of walking out of here is greater with you than not, so don't get your hopes too high. It's purely selfish."

"Noted."

Panic suddenly set in as realization dawned. If they were here, another group could also attack the reception guests. Had they done so already? Fuck. My parents, Gio.

Kai.

We'd only managed to crawl a few feet when three pairs of heavy boots landed beside us, the barrels of their guns pointed at the top of our heads. Dread snared my heart. Leni was a fierce and skilled fighter, but down one arm.

"I suggest you stay down."

"Who are you working for?" I asked, not expecting an answer, but I had to try.

"This is one hell of a party. Probably cost a fortune."

I gazed up at the three men, surprised to see them dressed as our security team. Though I didn't recognize them, that didn't mean they hadn't been here all along, as many had been hired by my father. I was sick to my stomach at the thought that we'd put our trust in these men, only for them to betray us in the worst way.

And on my wedding day, no less.

Rage.

It was hot and tasted sweet on my tongue, or maybe I was anticipating the smell of their blood at the end of my blade. I extended my hand to Helena and squeezed hers, hoping she'd understand that we only had seconds to act and that whatever we did had to be lightning fucking fast. No matter how much training we'd had, they could overpower us if we were disarmed, and I knew that was their next objective.

When she squeezed my hand back, I knew it was go time.

With no parting words or sarcastic comments, I slid my blade from where I'd hidden it between my thighs in the grass and went for the most vulnerable spot that would bring him to his knees.

Gripping the leather handle, I plunged the knife into his ball sack. His partner hesitated for a second when he heard his howl, and it was just long enough for me to slash and puncture the second man's thigh and disarm him.

A gunshot went off, piercing the dirt next to my leg. He didn't have the opportunity to try again. Leni buried her blade into the third man's gut, sliding the steel in a vertical direction, until his insides poured out and landed on his boots. Dropping his gun with panicked eyes and shaking hands, he attempted to put himself back together, but he knew it was pointless.

The first man cupped his dick and spewed every derogatory word he could think of. Unfortunately for him, his voice irritated the hell out of me, and he needed to be quiet in case more were on their way.

I cut into his throat and severed his vocal cords, blood spattering on my face and chest and down the front of my dress. With a smile, Leni was about to do the same to perp number two, but I shouted,

"No! Leave him alive. I have questions."

"You won't get shit out of me," he spat, saliva dribbling from the corners of his mouth.

"Maybe. But that doesn't mean I won't have fun in the process." I noted Leni's eager expression as she hovered over him. "Make sure he can't escape."

"Perfect," was all she said before slicing through the back of his ankles. The Achilles tendon made an interesting sound when severed and snapped out of place. Though it was nearly impossible to hear over the man's wails.

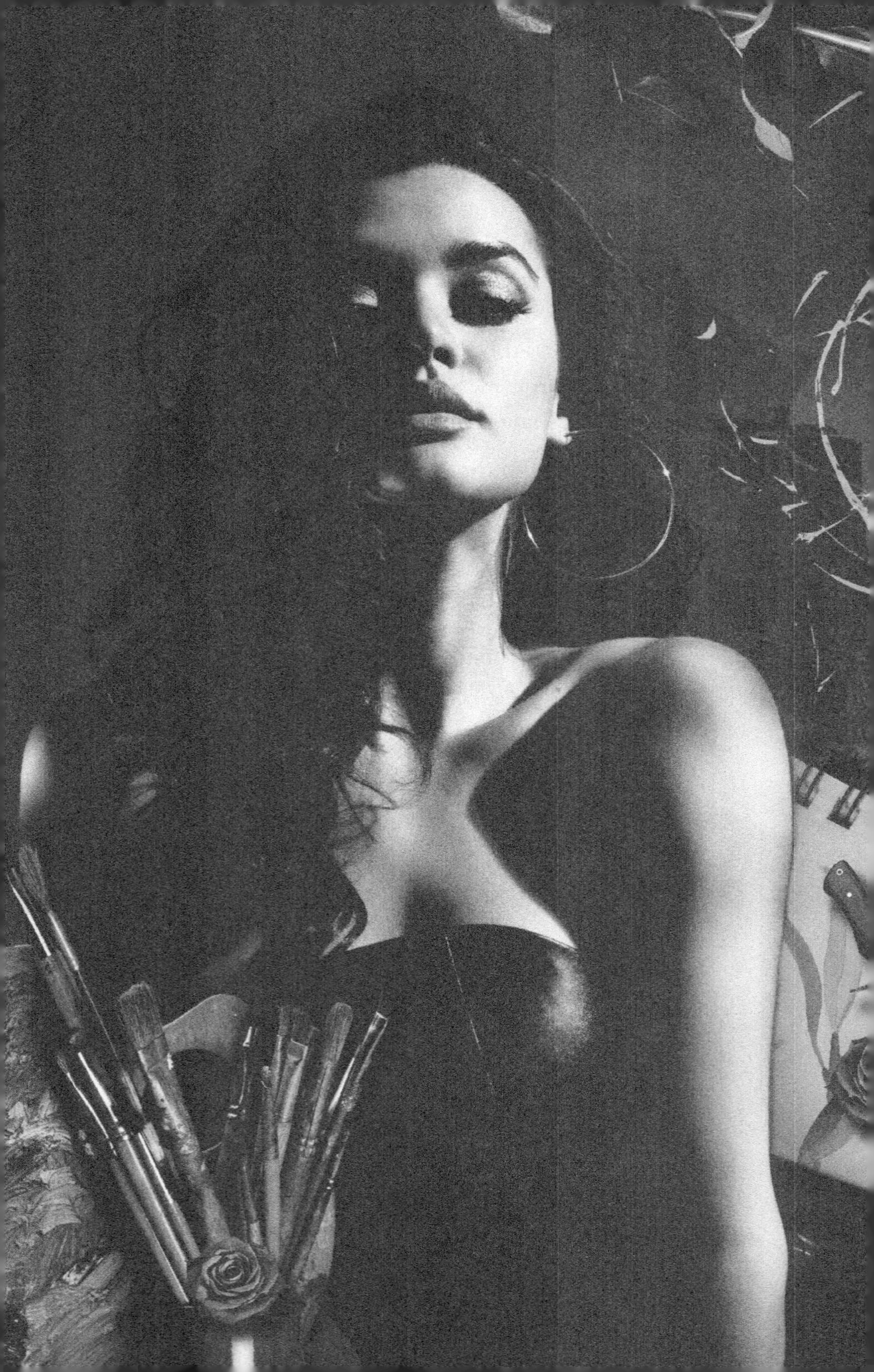

Chapter 24
Amalia

I WAS thankful I'd kicked off my shoes earlier as I ran through the grass and even as my feet collided with the path's hard cobblestone. Leni was beside me, keeping up despite bleeding profusely from her arm. I held her hand as we dashed toward the reception area, and my heart stuttered when we came upon a body. I didn't recognize the older woman, but I assumed she was a friend of my parents. She'd been shot through the forehead and maybe her neck. There was too much blood to be sure.

"Fuck, Leni."

"No…" she gasped, lifting her eyes to the other three bodies scattered on the pathway. "Silas." She tore her hand from my grasp and bolted, and when she reached the opening of the tent, she came to an abrupt stop.

My mind raced a mile a minute, chest tightening as every twisted scenario crossed my thoughts. "No…no…"

I squeezed the handle of the gun I'd taken as I cautiously stepped toward the entrance. Silas was first to come into view, covered with spatters of blood. Desperation was etched onto his face like he couldn't reach the woman he loved fast enough. It was then I saw Kai. He'd been running to Leni as well, but the moment our eyes connected, a host of emotions passed over him all at once. He mouthed something I couldn't quite make out, but I stopped trying the moment his body crashed into mine.

"Did they hurt you? Baby, please tell me you're okay." His hands were frantic, patting me down, searching for the origin of the blood painting my skin. At that moment, I was almost too stunned to speak. "Amalia, look at me. Look at me, baby." He cupped my cheeks. "Where is it? Tell me so I can help you."

My hands came up around his, a frail smile on my face. "It's not mine. The blood…it isn't mine."

Kai released a haggard breath and tugged me to his chest, arms wrapped around the back of my head as he squeezed and kissed my hair. "I thought they… And then, when I saw Leni and not you. Fuck—don't ever do that to me again."

"What happened? Is everyone else okay? My parents? Gio? The baby?"

"Fine. Security is doing a sweep. Two men attacked me and Silas."

"Kai, this is an inside job. The men who ambushed Leni and me were part of the security detail. We can't trust anyone."

"Shit. We have to get these people out of here. The kids and Milly are in a safe room in the main building—" He froze, eyes wide. "Can we trust her?"

"Of course. She's been with me since I was Valentina's age."

He sighed another relieved breath.

"Eva and Derek are on the north side of the property with some of your father's men. Should we be worried?" He was punching in messages to Derek before I could reply.

"I wish I knew. But we left one of them alive. He's down near the lake. Leni made sure he wouldn't escape."

Kai peered past me, his jaw set tight.

"I'm taking her to get this taken care of." Silas was carrying Leni. His eyes were red-rimmed, worry creasing into his brow. He jerked a nod in my direction and mouthed his thanks before making his way out of the tent.

Leni peered from around him. "Amalia, give them hell."

There was something uniquely thrilling about hearing the cries of a piece-of-shit man when faced with his mortality and all the creative ways one could find to test the threshold of just how far the human body can be pushed. Ten bloody nails and four teeth lay on the wooden table of a special cellar beneath the stables of my home. The bearded man's head bobbled back and forth, bloody drool staining his chin and the facial hair that had once been a salt and pepper color. He peered at me through swollen eyelids and mouthed another "fuck you."

"Kai." With a tilt of my chin, I gave him the go ahead. Clearly, this asshole needed more persuasion.

My husband fisted the top of the man's hair, yanking his head back and forcefully prying his mouth open. Muffled cries filled the dimly lit space as Kai removed another tooth.

"Please...." he begged, spittle spraying into the air as he wailed.

"Answer my questions, and I promise I'll make it quick." My patience was running thin.

"I don't," Derek growled from behind me as he paced idly in the background, practically foaming at the mouth for a turn.

I had no plans to take it easy on a man who'd set out to kill me and crashed my fucking wedding, threatening my family and guests. But if I only offered him a tortured death, then what incentive would he have to speak? I needed to know who was behind this and the attack at the compound, because there was no doubt in my mind they were related.

"I can't help you... Please, let me go. I have a family."

"*I have a family*," Kai taunted, his fingers still wound tightly in the man's hair. "Somehow, you think that will garner sympathy." I'd never seen this side of Kai. I knew he was in there. He was a Cain, after all. But fuck me if I wasn't already dripping wet. "You ruined her dress, and I liked that fucking dress." The sharp blade of a knife pierced the top of his hand, impaling it to the table. "You tried to kill my wife. I'm going to rip off your head."

Hell, Kai. I hadn't realized I was staring and biting my lip. It was wildly inappropriate, considering the circumstances. But as I'd always said, there was nothing sexier than a man defending his woman's honor in blood.

Feelings of jealousy toward Helena seemed so damn trivial now because Kai had never looked at Leni like he had me. And I would own that. He was mine. Temporary or not.

He was mine.

The man's mouth gaped open, and hoarse grunts replaced the shrieks from just moments ago when another knife effectively nailed both his hands to the table.

"Shit, shit...please stop."

"You know what you need to do. Now, give me names. Who gave the order?" I demanded through gritted teeth, leaning on the table's edge.

"I don't know. You know better than anyone how this works."

I pounded the table—just an insignificant lackey. Those men at the bottom who are anonymously given orders in return for a payday. It was insurance for scenarios like these because, no matter what, spineless men ultimately broke—every single time.

Twisting around to a stone-faced Derek, I nodded, giving him the green light. A devious grin crawled across his lips as he unfolded his arms and reached for his blade.

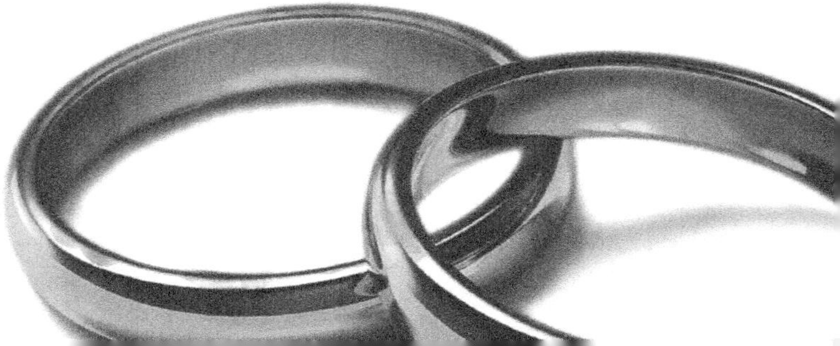

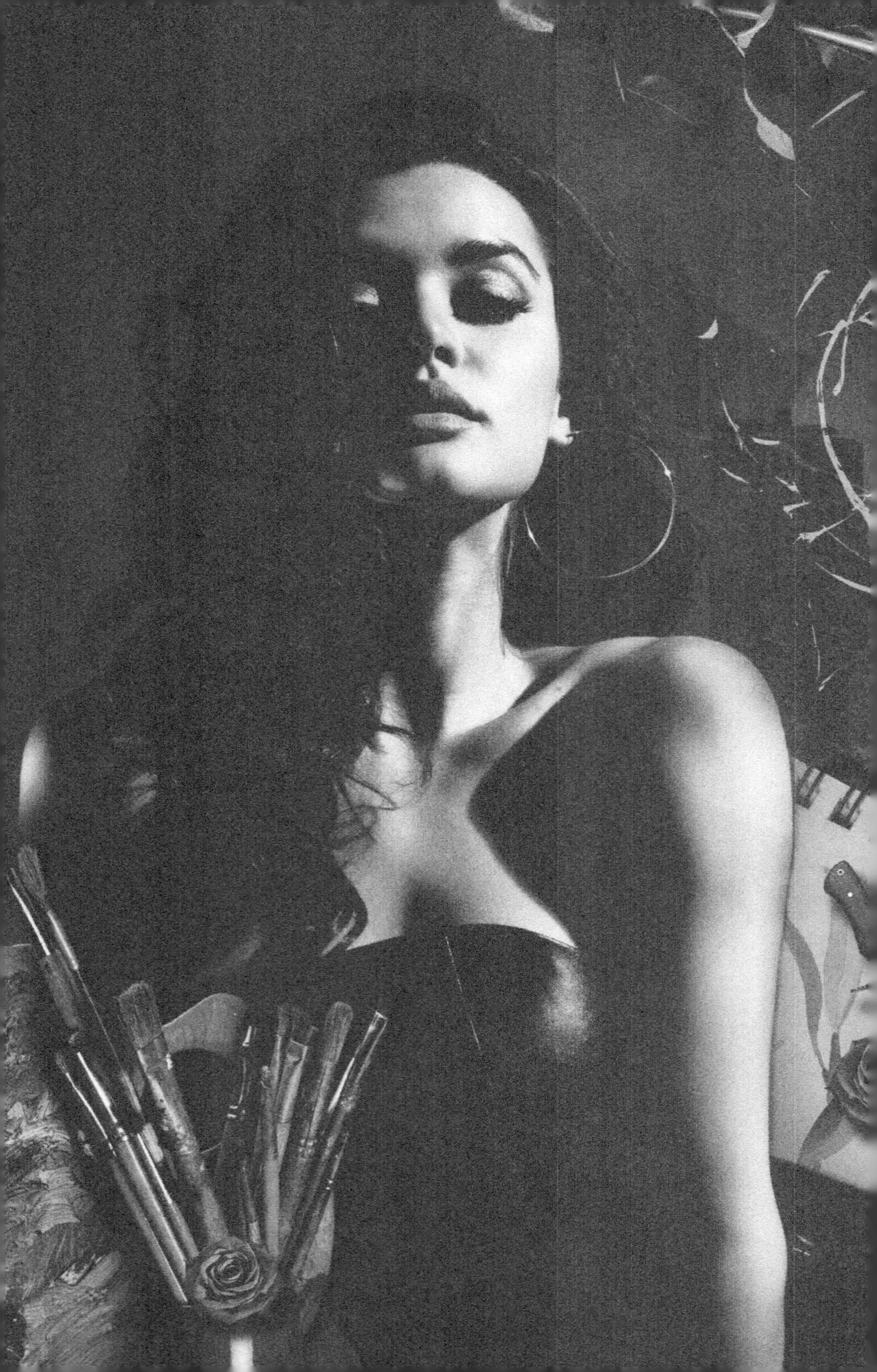

Chapter 25
Amalia

MERE hours felt more like days. Between combing the property, interviewing the staff, and quieting the witnesses not privy to our world, I had drained every ounce of strength left in my body. I was still in my bloody, raggedy wedding dress, dried blood still clinging to my skin. The sun would be rising shortly, but neither of us had the luxury of sleeping in, much less making a 6 a.m. flight for what would have been a honeymoon.

I leaned against a wall on the first floor, just outside Derek and Eva's room. He'd booked a private plane for his family, and I didn't blame him. He had a little girl to protect. Things here had gotten out of hand. Decades had passed since an enemy breached our walls, and I was determined to find who had betrayed my family.

"Amalia." Holly's soft voice and a hand on my shoulder pulled me away from Kai and Derek's goodbyes. "Are you all right?"

I nodded. It was better than lying out loud. "Are you?"

She forced a smile and pulled me in for a hug. "I'm so glad you're okay. What were you doing by yourself on your wedding day anyway?"

Looking back at Kai, I shrugged my shoulders. "Being foolish."

"Were you able to extract any information?"

"I don't think he had any to give. Either way, he's not a problem anymore."

My phone buzzed in my hand. I didn't need to look at the screen to know who was calling again. Rocco had been relentless, but I didn't have the mental or emotional strength to deal with his questions or, worse yet, his possible involvement. It was quite the coincidence that he'd left right before everything went down. And what's more, I wasn't even sure how he found out. Though things like these circulate quickly in our circles, I couldn't shake the suspicion.

I rubbed a rough hand down my face.

"You going to answer, babe?"

"It's just Rocco. I already told him through text that I was fine."

Her forehead creased. "How about I call him and tell him you're already asleep."

I pulled her in for another hug, kissed her hair, and whispered a thank you.

Holly had a crush on Rocco when we were teenagers, but he never reciprocated her feelings. There was a time I used to worry that she'd resent me for always having his attention, unwanted or not. But we were like sisters, and she understood I had no control over his emotions. Luckily, that puppy love dried up fast. Holly was a beautiful soul and deserved to be loved by someone who could appreciate that.

"Just because you two are canceling the honeymoon doesn't mean you can't have your fun," she joked, motioning toward an approaching Kai.

"Hols, I don't have the energy even if I wanted to, but also—mind your goddamn business," I said with a laugh as I playfully shoved her away.

"I'm going to go check on Gio, and then I'll be out."

"Thanks." I blew her a kiss.

"Where's mine?" Kai circled my waist and drew me into his arms. I wasn't sure when he and I had gotten this comfortable touching each other, but I wasn't complaining. If ever I needed comfort, it was at this very moment. "You look exhausted."

"Is that a polite way of telling me I look like hell?"

He chuckled and whirled me around. "Never. But I know you've been through a lot, and it's late."

"There's no time to sleep, Kai. Whatever this is, it'll be back. And what if next time, it's at our doorstep?"

"I really want to focus on what you're saying, but the words 'our doorstep' make that impossible."

I reached down, threaded my fingers through his, and raised our joined hands. "You're wearing my ring, and your cock has been in almost every hole of my body. I'm pretty sure you live here now." I grinned.

"Almost? Fuck, we should remedy that."

I laughed and let him pull me toward the bottom of the steps. "Have you ever felt so damn tired but also completely wired at the same time?"

He had already started to ascend the stairs when he froze before turning around. "Amalia, get cleaned up and meet me outside."

"Cain, it's nearly five in the morning. What do you mean?"

Kai brushed back a strand of hair, his eyes boring into mine. "You said you trusted me, right?"

The second those words left his mouth, my stomach fluttered in ways I hadn't experienced in a long time—quite possibly never. He had no idea how hard it was to trust anyone outside my family, but he had somehow scaled the wall I had put up for the world.

"I do." My voice was barely a whisper. He brushed his lips over mine, and I felt myself melting against him.

"Thank you." The way he spoke and his relaxed expression told me that he was aware of just how pivotal that admission was.

But did I?

Dawn had yet to break the horizon as I walked outside to wait for Kai. When the door opened behind me, I whipped around, fully expecting to find my new husband, but was met with Eva and Valentina instead.

"Derek told me you and Kai were about to head out, and I know we'll be gone by the time you come back, so I didn't want to leave without saying goodbye or clearing the air between us."

"I wasn't aware the air needed clearing," I said, calling her bluff and crossing my arms.

"Amalia, the last time we spoke, you basically called me a naïve, spoiled brat."

I couldn't help the smile that drew from my lips. "I don't believe those words came out of my mouth."

She scoffed. "Listen, I'm used to people thinking I'm—"

"Evangelina, I heard what you did for my mother. Kai told me you saved her life, and I could never thank you enough. So whatever you're about to say, I don't think that at all. And I didn't think it before, either. You just caught me at a bad moment. Besides, you're Derek Cain's wife, for fuck's sake." That earned me a laugh. "But let's spare ourselves a sappy goodbye. I'll see you when I see you."

She put a hand on my arm. "Take care of yourself. And take care of Kai for me." Eva nuzzled her daughter's cheek. "Someone also wanted to say goodbye and thank you for the hospitality. We're about to head out, too." When she leaned forward, Valentina raised her arms and reached for me. This kid was probably the happiest baby I'd ever seen.

"*Pórtate bien, chiquita.*" (Be good, little one.) I kissed her forehead, and we said our goodbyes. No sooner had Eva walked back inside, I heard an engine revving from around the corner.

"No," I said, shaking my head. "I'll take my car."

Kai pulled off his helmet. "As sweet a ride as that Hellcat is, I want you to ride with me, vicious."

"Are you sure you and *Gloria* don't need some alone time?"

He laughed and leaned over the front of his bike, looking so damn good I might have licked my lips. "The only woman I want alone time with is you."

"Oh, so you admit she's a woman?"

"She was."

"Was? Who? A lost love?"

"I killed her."

I'd seen more death than any one person should in a lifetime, many of those by my hand, but somehow, his admission sent a small shock wave through my body. He'd said it so casually, I almost doubted I'd heard it.

"You killed Gloria?"

"How about you hop on my bike? I'll tell you the whole story when we get to where we're going. And we should hurry. I want to get there before the sun."

I placed my hands on my hips. "You just admitted you murdered a woman who was significant enough for you to name your bike after, and you expect me to just ride with you into the sunset to some mystery location."

"Wrong. Sunrise, not sunset."

"Kai Cain, you better start talking."

"I thought you said you trusted me," he said with amusement.

"I did, up until three minutes ago." Kai tipped his head back and laughed. "I fail to see the humor here."

He extended a helmet to me. "Come on. We're already married. No backing out now."

Eyeing the black helmet, I huffed as I snatched it. "Kai, don't crash this goddamn bike, and don't kill me and hide my body in the woods."

"Never."

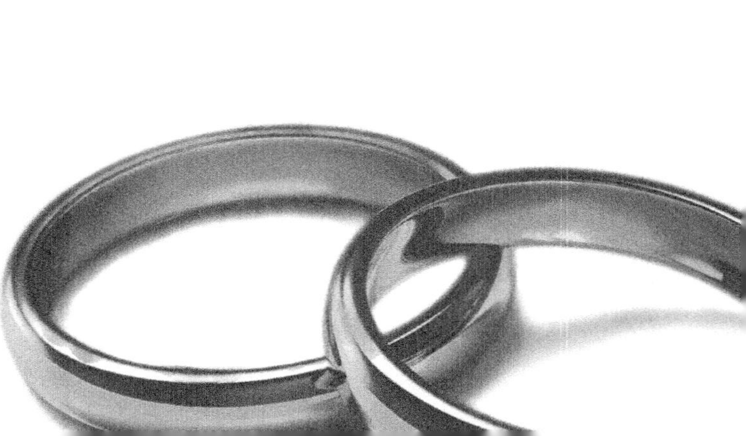

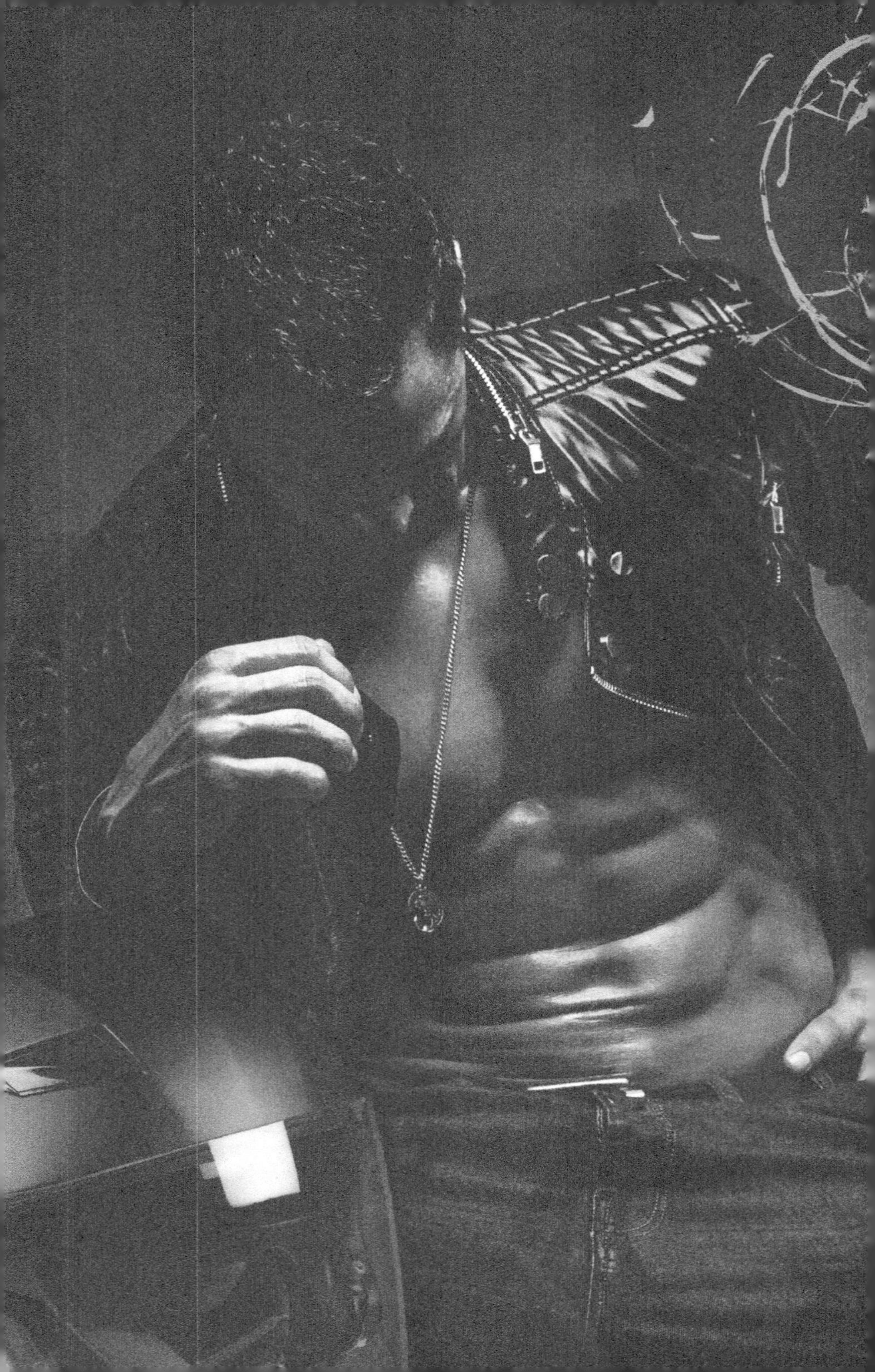

Chapter 26
Kai

AMALIA'S arms were wound tight around my waist, and I reveled in the feeling of her body flush with mine. She was warm, and her head rested on my back. I couldn't remember the last time I'd shared a ride with anyone. It had possibly been years ago when Leni and I had our thing.

But this—*her*—I could get used to this. The thought was terrifying because I felt it. The way I was becoming attached. How I craved to be near her all the fucking time. The fear I felt when I thought she'd been captured, or worse—killed.

I shook those thoughts from my head.

"Cain, where the hell are we going?"

Amalia's voice filtered into my helmet through the speaker.

"A couple more miles. How are you doing back there?"

"I'm fine. Regretting not bringing my lucky blade."

I barked a laugh. "You won't need it. Trust me."

"You keep saying that—"

Before she could finish, I accelerated down the stretch of dark highway, and she squeezed me to the point of nearly choking off my air.

"Kai, you bastard! You did that on purpose."

"I didn't take you for someone afraid of riding."

"I'm not. It's just, I have a hard time giving up so much control. You're literally holding my life in your hands."

I placed my arm over hers and interlaced our fingers. "Hey, I vowed to always keep you safe. I meant it."

She remained silent for several moments. "You vowed a lot of things that weren't true, Kai. So did I."

Her tone was somber, reality always knocking us down. She loosened her grip, but I promptly accelerated once more, ignoring the creeping uncertainties the future held. Cool air whipped past us, and I felt euphoric as always. Riding was my escape. It was the only thing that brought me comfort when the demons refused to quiet. Somehow, I knew that would no longer be the case.

Giving her hand another squeeze, I slowed as we came around a bend to a small clearing just off the road. I rolled the bike toward a thin hedge of trees and cut the engine. Amalia dismounted first, removed her helmet, and shook out her hair.

Fuck. She was beautiful. She couldn't see my eyes through the dark visor, so I took advantage and roamed every perfect little feminine curve of her body. My cock pulsed in my pants, painfully pushing against the seam.

"Okay, explain yourself. What is this place?"

I finally took off my helmet and hung it on a handlebar. "The other day, after the compound, I needed to clear my head. I took off and found myself here."

Dismounting the bike, I walked toward her and took her hand. There was a sliver of hesitation, but she relented and let me lead her through the trees. When I found this place, it was early morning, with the sun high in the sky. The darkness now masked most of the familiarity, but I knew this was the right spot.

The forest broke, and we came upon twinkling lights in the distance toward the edge of a mountainside.

The city below was starting to wake, and a smile tugged at my mouth because I'd known the view would be so much more at night.

Amalia's pretty features softened, and she released my hand and moved forward, close to the rock's edge. "Kai, I've lived here most of my life and never thought to venture this way. It's gorgeous."

"Breathtaking."

She caught me staring at her and smiled. "So, are you going to tell me about Gloria finally?"

"Why are you so invested in who she was?" I asked, tugging her to my side.

"Why did you kill a woman and name your precious bike after her? I'm not going to lie, that's a bit creepy."

"Are you scared or something, vicious?"

"I'm not afraid of killing people. Sometimes I think I like it more than I should." She turned to look at me. "That's a warning," she added with a wink.

"Duly noted." Moments ticked by in silence. But it was a calm reprieve from the chaos of the last few weeks. Oddly enough, I wouldn't change a thing…well, mostly.

I felt her shiver, and I slid off my jacket and placed it over her shoulders.

"Tell me," she whispered, as she leaned into my chest.

I sighed a long breath. My eyes fixated on the faint tendrils of color stretching from the horizon. "I've been part of Ares for a long time. I almost don't remember my life before joining. But more in the sense that time seemed to be suspended before them. Derek and I… we survived as best we could. He took me under his wing the day I arrived at that home. Younger, smaller at the time, he protected me."

Another shiver rolled through her body, and I held her tighter.

"I owe him a lot. Punishments meant for me...*other* things meant for me—he took the brunt of them. And for that, he'll always have my loyalty. And he'll always be my brother, because while I wasn't spared completely, he never was."

She turned in my arms. "Kai, what brought you to that place? Where's your family?"

The wind kicked up, and strands of hair whipped across her beautiful face. I cuffed them behind her ears and kissed her forehead. "I never knew my father...I don't know if my mom knew either. Could be anyone, if you know what I mean. But whoever he is or was, I probably look like him since the only thing I inherited from Clara Roth were her eyes."

"They're certainly pretty," she said, offering a faint smile.

"So I've been told."

She rolled her eyes with a bigger smile, though her happy expression was short-lived. "What happened to her?"

"Clara was murdered."

I waited a few beats, wondering if she'd give her condolences, but Amalia watched me with intrigue. And I was grateful, because though I may have loved my mother at some point, she hadn't been anywhere near fit to be responsible for herself, let alone a child. I'd woken up alone in a cold train station bathroom more times than I'd like to remember. So, in some ways, her death relieved me of the guilt I felt as my resentment toward her grew.

"And with no other known family, I was tossed in the system when I was eight. And the rest is history, as they say."

"And then Ares found you."

I nodded. "That's where Gloria comes in."

"Did she train you?"

"She was my first mark—the wife of a wealthy real estate mogul. A mistress was involved, and there was an inheritance, insurance money, and the works. That day, my rifle jammed, and she was on me before I could use my secondary, so I had to drown her in her fountain."

Amalia listened with rapt attention, brokering no emotion. "Then her kid came around the corner. And that's when I understood why she'd fought so hard. For her child." I looked away from her as I thought of Maksim. "I'm kind of two for two on that front."

"So you named your bike after her out of guilt?"

"Not just that. I became consumed with every aspect of her life and discovered that she was an outstanding mother. And that I'd stripped that little girl of happiness, only to leave her in the custody of her bastard father and his revolving door of whores."

"Kai," she murmured, reaching up to touch my cheek. "You couldn't have known. Most of those who die at our hands have families. It comes with the job."

"I know. I've worked through my guilt over the years. Besides, I pulled some strings, used some connections, and ensured her daughter would inherit everything and leave the father penniless."

Amalia swatted my chest. "If you could do that, then why are we here? Where were you six months ago?" she joked.

My hands slid down her waist and over her hips as I pulled her closer. "Waiting for you."

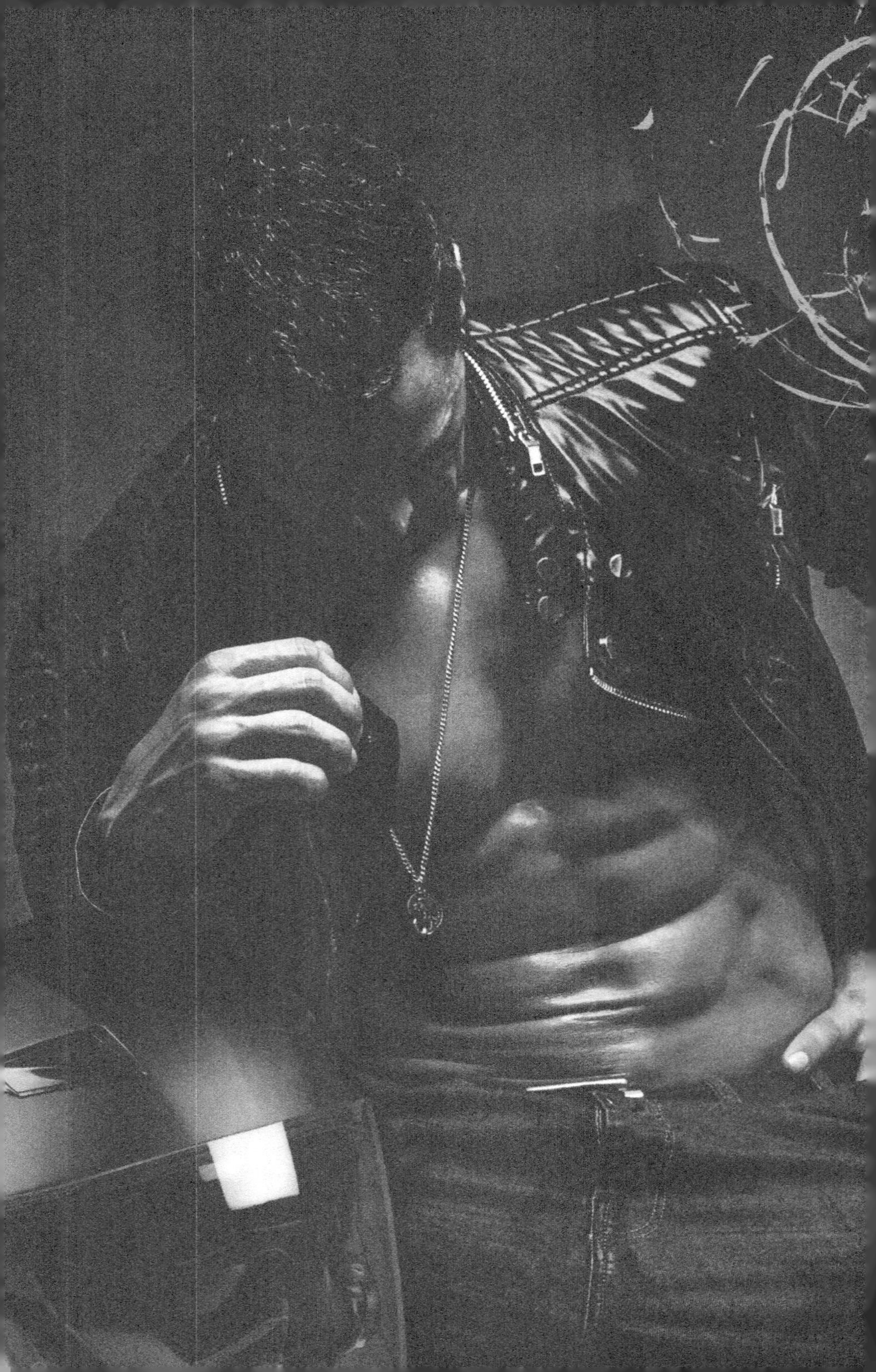

Chapter 27
Kai

THE sun finally peaked from the city's edge, and I shifted us around, wanting her to see the view but refusing to let her out of my arms.

"I can't remember the last time I watched the sunrise, at least not like this. Thank you for bringing me here. I needed it, especially after everything."

"It wasn't all bad, wife," I said, kissing her neck. She leaned her head back and looked up at me.

"No, it wasn't."

Tilting her chin, I dipped down to kiss her. "What happened?" I asked. Her eyes were still closed, the whisper of a smile curling her lips. "You and me, what changed?"

"Don't be a mood killer, Cain, and just fucking kiss me."

I laughed against her mouth, smoothing my hands farther down her body until I had a handful of each ass cheek. Giving her a little squeeze, I hoisted her onto my waist.

"I'm going to fuck you on my bike, vicious." Amalia shuddered in my arms and kissed me harder, grinding that sweet little pussy over my abdomen.

I carried her back to where I'd left the bike and lowered her to the ground. "Take off my belt."

"You give a lot of orders," she said, hiking up the front of my shirt, running her lips along my stomach, and setting every inch of me on fire. "Maybe you should ask nicely."

"Okay." I fisted the top of her hair and yanked her head back. "Take off my belt, wife."

With a grin, she slowly reached up, unhooking the black leather and grabbing my cock. I closed my eyes and tipped my head back as she stroked, then fell to her knees.

Amalia pumped my length and ran her tongue in circles around the tip before taking me fully into her mouth.

The sound of an engine approaching caused her to pause, and our eyes met as we waited to see if anyone would be coming around the bend. But the car sputtered and then took off for one reason or another.

"Would have been caught with your pants down, Cain. At least you have a pretty cock."

Tipping my head, I gripped her hair tighter and warred against the urge to come inside her mouth and watch as I dripped from the corners of her lips. So I let her suck me off until my balls tightened and tugged her back, needing to lose myself inside her.

"Hands on the bike." Amalia did as she was told and looked over her shoulder as I shoved the fabric of her black skirt up over her ass. The pink thong she wore was nothing but a sinful piece of cloth buried between her plump cheeks. "This is cute," I said, slipping a finger beneath the T and giving it a slight tug. Before she could say anything, I used my other hand to grip both sides of the lace and pull until the fabric gave.

"You ripped it."

"Looks like I did."

"How am I supposed to ride back home?"

"If you leave a mess on my seat, vicious, you'll just have to clean it."

"I could," she moaned as I slid two fingers over her clit. "But I'd much rather see you do it."

Amalia squealed when I suddenly lifted her by the waist and laid her on her back, over the seat. She reached above her head and gripped the handlebars, looking like a vision from heaven.

Shoving her cami up over her tits, I leaned in to swipe my tongue across a tight nipple.

"How strong is that kickstand?" she asked, closing her eyes as I licked my way to her other breast, and reached under her skirt.

"I guess we're about to find out."

Her fingers clenched the front of my shirt as she hauled me down and kissed me. "Good answer."

I grinned and circled her clit with my thumb. "A test?"

"Maybe," she hissed, back arched as I slipped inside her.

"Baby, there's only ever been you."

My lips moved over her abdomen with hard, open-mouthed kisses. I needed her to understand, she was the only woman occupying space in my thoughts. The only one I craved and wanted by my side. And the one quickly consuming my heart.

"So what you're really saying is I get to pop another one of your cherries?"

I chuckled into the crook of her neck and squeezed her breast as I dragged my mouth to her nipple.

"I almost feel like this is a new challenge," I said, hooking my fingers inside her and thrusting until her lips parted and her knuckles whitened against the handlebars. "How many new places can I fuck my wife?"

"Sounds like a fun game," she managed to mutter as I put pressure on her clit.

Caught off guard, my eyes widened when Amalia grabbed my cock and pumped me as I slid a third finger inside her.

Cars could be heard in the distance, and some were close enough to catch a glimpse of us from the road. But when we were together, nothing else mattered. My only goal was to claim her, taste her, and ensure she was properly fucked and satisfied.

"Let go, baby," I groaned as her pussy clenched around me.

The sight of her coming on my bike nearly had me busting in her hand.

It was fucking beautiful. As much as I enjoyed watching her come down from her high, the need to be inside her was damn near painful.

I lifted her like my little fuck doll and flipped her onto her stomach, climbing on the bike behind her.

"What are you doing?" she asked between heavy breaths.

"I said I would fuck you on my bike." I shoved her forward and readjusted my pants, pulling out my cock. "And I plan on following through. Now, scoot your ass back toward me."

"What if we fall over?"

"You think I'd let you fall?"

She regarded me, looking over her shoulder, with an easy smile. "No…because you don't want me to cut off that dick of yours."

"Neither do you."

"Touche."

Her playful expression shifted when my hand wound around her neck. I pulled her upright and ran the edges of my teeth on her shoulder.

"Amalia?"

"Mm?" Her eyes were hooded, head falling back.

"You're mine," I growled into her ear as I helped her ease onto my cock.

"Yeah? Show me, Kai. Fuck me like I'm yours. Only yours."

With a hand on her hip, I thrust inside her. It wasn't the most comfortable position, and I hoped not to catch my dick on this goddamn zipper, but being buried so deep, fucking her on my bike, was well worth the effort. Every pump sent her body forward as she braced herself on the dash. Taking it all like a fucking champ. Her moans rose every time her clit rubbed against the ridges of my seat, serving to drive into her harder.

Releasing her neck for a brief moment, I reached under Amalia's cami and cupped her breast, squeezing as I increased my pace.

"Is that…the best…you got?" she taunted between thrusts, peering back with a grin and her bottom lip tucked tightly between her teeth.

I chuckled and put more pressure on my feet for better leverage, pushing her forward, a position that gave me a clear view of her tight little asshole. We hadn't gone there yet, but it was certainly on the list.

"Don't tempt me. This slick cunt of yours tells a different story." I leaned over her back and whispered in her ear. "My seat is a goddamn mess, vicious. And I can't wait to watch you lick it clean."

Both of my hands were around her throat as I bucked harder, feeling the pressure coil in my balls. I had run out of patience for her counterthrusts, so I slammed her down on my cock, and her moans and gasps fell in tune with each stroke.

Nothing would ever compare to the feeling of being inside this woman. Every cell in my body was electrified, hard-wired to all the little noises that fled her quivering lips.

"K-Kai," she choked out, unable to form a coherent sentence the tighter I squeezed and the harder I fucked.

Amalia's movements had slowed, her muscles loosening, and I knew she was on the verge of passing out, so I reached around and found her swollen clit. It wasn't long before she cried out, her pussy clenching around me like a vise as loud groans echoed against the tree line. I broke with one more thrust, pumping until my legs gave out and my fingers imprinted on her skin.

Moments later, I reluctantly climbed off and tugged my shirt over my head, using the damn thing as a cum rag. I glanced up and caught Amalia watching me, still sprawled over the dash, cheeks bright pink and looking every bit like a woman who'd been properly fucked.

Walking over to her, I offered my hand as she sat up. "Lean back," I instructed, my eyes never straying from her beautiful pussy where I saw myself already leaking out. "Fuck."

With a devious little grin, she hiked her legs higher, letting them fall open.

"My wife—fucked, swollen, and dripping with my cum."

I touched her face and kissed her red lips while using my shirt to clean her up, remembering to wipe in a downward motion.

"You still expect me to take care of this?" she asked, stepping off the bike and motioning to the wrecked seat.

"Nah," I said, swiping at the black leather before tossing my shirt toward the embankment.

"Littering on this beautiful piece of land, Mr. Cain?"

"It'll be fine. Come on. Let's go home."

Home.

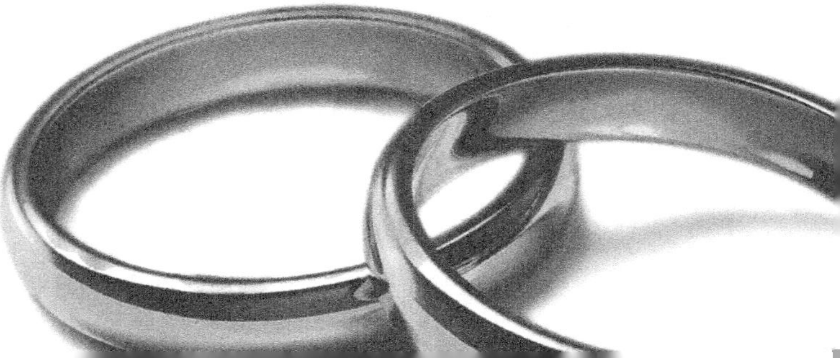

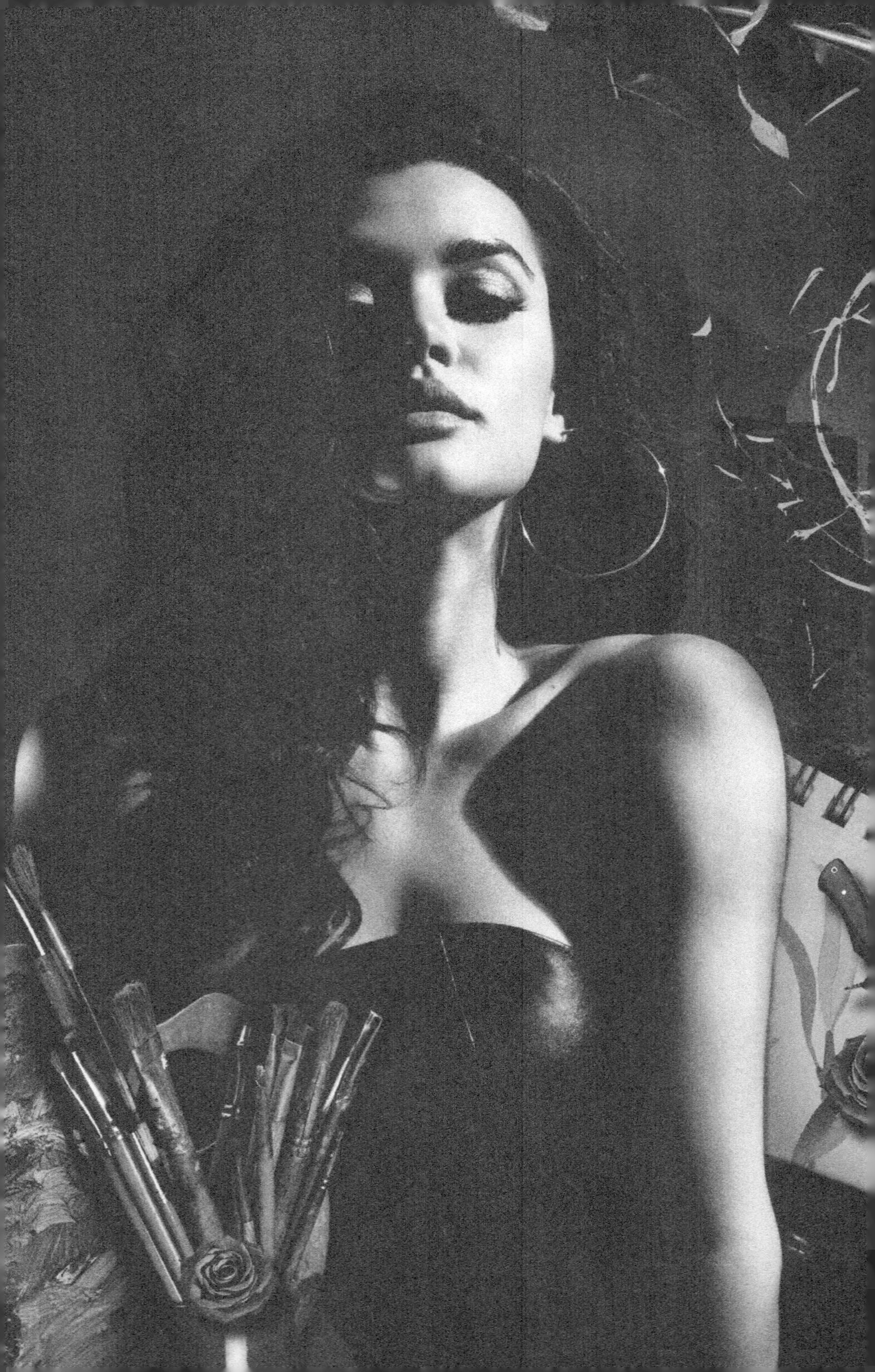

Chapter 28
Amalia

I CLOSED my eyes and let the vibration of the bike's engine soothe me as Kai and I tore down the highway. Exhaustion from lack of sleep and from quite literally being fucked into oblivion was finally catching up. But it was impossible to nod off despite my body begging for sleep. I was still too sensitive, and every change in acceleration jolted me. It was almost unbearable, but I couldn't decide if that was a good or bad thing.

As if feeling how I tensed, Kai used one hand to stroke my thigh gently and gave it a quick, reassuring squeeze. This man made me feel so many things I never thought I would, especially not with him. Our agreement was supposed to be a business transaction and nothing more. We were never supposed to get close. Yet somehow, there I was, jumping deep into potential heartbreak and wanting to hold on to things—to him—even though I shouldn't.

"I'm sure Milly is serving breakfast by now," I said as Kai cut the engine. "But I can't keep my eyes open any longer." I shook my hair out and handed him back the helmet. "And I need my energy for the heads that are about to roll. But you can go ahead and—"

Kai climbed off and swept me off my feet, bridal style. "Let's go to bed."

"We need to shower first."

"Even better."

My nose led me down the stairs into the corridor toward the kitchen, where Milly was busy at the sink, rinsing dishes despite having a fully working dishwasher at her disposal.

"*Mi niña*, you're finally up. Where is Kai? Did you want me to set your dinner in the dining room?"

I leaned against the counter and smiled, plucking a warm tortilla from its pan and savoring it. "He'll be down in a bit," I said, stuffing my mouth with another bite.

I was up before Kai and took the opportunity to take another shower while he was still asleep. Our attempts at cleaning up after getting home were useless, and showering together was counterproductive. The phantom pleasure still vibrated between my thighs at just the thought.

"You look well-rested," she said with a wink.

My neck warmed as a blush crept up to my face. Even at twenty-six, Milly had this aura, this way of making me feel like I was still that innocent little girl whose favorite pastime was helping her prepare meals while listening to stories. And I was okay with that. Being in this kitchen was comforting and safe, and as of late, I only felt that peace in one place.

Kai's arms.

"I am." Pulling a wooden stool, I sat across the island, holding another tortilla. "Do you miss your little helper?" I had to admit that Milly's kitchen was already quieter and missing the spark of Valentina's giggles and squeals.

I raised my gaze, expecting to see her smiling, but instead, I caught Milly wiping her eyes.

"It's been a long time since I've had a little one around."

The inflection in her voice gave me the sense that her words had a double meaning, and when our eyes met again, hers crinkled with amusement. I knew I hadn't been wrong.

"Milly, I just got married yesterday. And you know that things between Kai and me—"

"Are what? Complicated? ¡Por Dios!" she said, throwing up her hands. "I have eyes, you know."

"Eyes that look too deeply into things that aren't there." Except it was all there. I knew it, and she knew it.

"Ah, denial."

Exactly.

"Realistic. Because no matter what, he and I won't work like that. He has his life in Philadelphia, and I have mine here."

Milly shrugged her shoulders. "Okay," she replied in that sarcastic tone that drove me crazy. "I'll get the table ready."

"That's not necessary. We'll eat here. We have to run in a few anyway."

Her expression soured, a frown replacing her smile. Milly was privy to everything our family was involved in, and she was there from day one of my training. I knew she hated all that encompassed the dealings and lifestyle the Montesinos were a part of, but she was loyal and had helped raise me since the day I was born. She'd bury a dead body for me even if she'd hate every second.

"Already, *mija*? The blood is still wet."

"You know we can't let things like what happened yesterday slide. There's a breach somewhere, Milly. And if I don't find it, we're all in potential danger. And I can't wait to act until the threat is at our door."

She walked around the island and cupped my face with her hands.

"*Que Dios te cuide siempre.*" (May God protect you always.) Without another word, Milly kissed my forehead and was gone.

"Can I come with you?"

I twisted in my stool at the sound of Gio's voice. "*No.*"

"Why."

"You know why." I swiveled back around to my appetizer. "So please drop it, because my answer won't change. And I will be thoroughly checking to make sure you don't pull the same crazy shit from last time. Please don't make me kill you."

He chuckled and sat beside me, shoving my shoulder. "Fine, this time."

"Always."

Despite what I did and who I was, the fact that Gio murdered a man, and it hadn't fazed him in the least, worried me. Unless he was trying to create a facade to prove he was capable.

"Smells amazing in here."

My body's reaction to Kai's voice seemed wholly inappropriate while my annoying brother was just inches away. I turned to what was quickly becoming one of my favorite faces.

"Hey, kid," he said, acknowledging Gio with a nod.

"Kai, can you teach me how to ride?"

"Absolutely not," I answered before he could.

"You know, you used to be fun. I'm disappointed."

"Yeah, well, I'm sure others would disagree."

He looked from me to Kai and scrunched his face in disgust. "That's low. Excuse me while I go puke."

Gio slid off his chair and sprinted out of the kitchen.

Kai's warm breath was over my ear, arms around my shoulders. "*Mi reina*, you left me." His words oozed over me like warm honey, causing my skin to break out in goosebumps. Something about the way the phrase rolled off his tongue and the things it did to my underwear—I never wanted him to stop.

"I didn't want to wake you. And your blanket had slipped off, so trust me when I tell you it took a lot of willpower not to slap your tight ass."

When he laughed, it vibrated down the column of my neck, and I bit my lip to keep a moan from spilling out.

"I can't think of a better way to wake up," he said, pulling out the chair Gio had vacated. I ripped a piece of my tortilla and brought it to his mouth.

"I can think of a few. Hungry?"

Kai nodded and grabbed my wrist, bringing the food to his lips while his eyes locked with mine. "Are you dropping hints? Let's go back upstairs."

"As enticing as that sounds, we've already effectively fucked the day away, and we can't ignore the bigger issues. I'm going to pay one of my father's men a visit today."

"I'm going with you."

Last week, my first instinct would have been to say no and possibly become defensive at his thinking he needed to protect me or keep watch as if I was helpless.

But today...things were different.

"But first food."

"Good, because I'm starving," he said, stealing the rest of my tortilla and popping it into his mouth.

"Hey!" I laughed and swatted his arm.

"This is really good." His words were muffled, full of the warm snack, a staple in our home.

"Milly and I used to spend days in this kitchen when I was a little girl."

My thoughts briefly drifted to those warm afternoons, after church, rolling dough and stealing licks of dessert. They were some of the happiest times of my life.

Kai eyed me with amusement. "I thought Gio said you couldn't cook."

"I'm slightly insulted you believe him over me."

He put his hands up defensively. "Hey, I haven't seen otherwise, so I can only go by the information given."

I tossed a piece of dough at his forehead. "Good to know I have your trust."

"Come on," he snickered, leaning in for a kiss. "I'm just messing with you. Tell me, what's your favorite dish."

He snorted a laugh when I pretended to think it over while tapping my chin.

"Milly never misses, but if I had to choose a favorite, my top three would be *pollo con mole, tamales*, and the best dessert to eat on a rainy day—*Arroz con leche.*"

"Have I had those?"

I chuckled and fed him another piece of tortilla. "You've been here a while, Cain, and you have no idea what you've shoveled into your mouth."

A sly smirk lit up his face, and he grabbed my chin and hauled me forward. "Is that a trick question? Because I know exactly what I've been putting in my mouth."

"Yeah, and are they among your top three?" I asked with a coy smile.

Kai ran his hand up my thigh. "I would never be able to narrow it down to just three." I knew we were no longer talking about food, and I was suddenly wet again.

"What about these." He tore a small piece of the tortilla in my hand. "You make these too?"

I nodded with excitement. "I was seven when Milly taught me. Burned the hell out of my arm but sucked it up and made a batch for my mother's birthday dinner." I stretched out my forearm and showed him the faint scar near my elbow, and he brushed his finger over the disturbed skin.

"Teach me?" he muttered, lips against my scar.

My face ached from smiling so much. This man knew exactly what to say, how to gaze at me with those eyes that told a thousand stories. My insides melted into puddles at his request.

"You start with flour."

"This one over here?" he asked, reaching into a white bowl.

"Of course."

I'd barely opened my mouth when Kai pinched flour between his fingers and flicked it at my face."

"Kai! You bastard," I gasped.

"Baby, I had to."

My husband was too busy laughing his stupid head off to notice when I grabbed a fistful of the flour and let him have it.

His mouth hung open, face white as he stared at me in shock. But his expression quickly changed from surprise to mischief.

"Kai, don't you dare," I warned, sliding off my stool.

Grin widening, he reached across the counter. "I'm not sure I know what you're talking about."

"I'll kill you."

"If I let you suffocate me with your pussy, does that count?"

I backed away another step. "No pussy for you, Cain."

"Really?" he growled, our eyes locked.

Enough.

I straightened and placed my hands on my hips. "Kai, if Milly finds out—" A breath later, I was spitting and blinking away flour. "*You son of a bitch!*"

His hearty laugh was all the distraction I needed to make my move. In a blink, chaos ensued between us. Flour, salsa, beans, and even Milly's freshly shredded cheese went airborne, covering our bodies and every surface in that kitchen.

It was madness—complete and utter madness—but neither of us cared. We fell to the floor in fits of laughter, and he pulled me onto his lap.

A tingly feeling circled my belly, and I suddenly felt the world's weight wash away, even for just that moment. The sensation traveled through me and made me feel light and carefree, like that little girl so many years ago.

"I'm sorry," he chuckled, picking black beans from my hair.

"No, you're not," I laughed, as I smeared the mess across his face.

"How badly is she going to kill us?"

"Us? Milly is like a second mother to me. She barely knows you. It's been fun, Cain."

"That's some traitorous shit, wife," he joked, his mouth on my neck.

"Did you just…eat off me?"

Kai's chest shook with laughter. "Best I ever had," he said with another lick.

"You're disgusting."

He tightened his hold on my body and pushed to his feet, taking me with him. "Baby, I'll be fucking filthy for you any day. Come on."

"Was this your plan all along to get me naked again?" I asked, circling my arm around his neck. "There are easier ways to get laid without making a mess."

"This way is double the fun."

I was smiling like a fool. "Agreed."

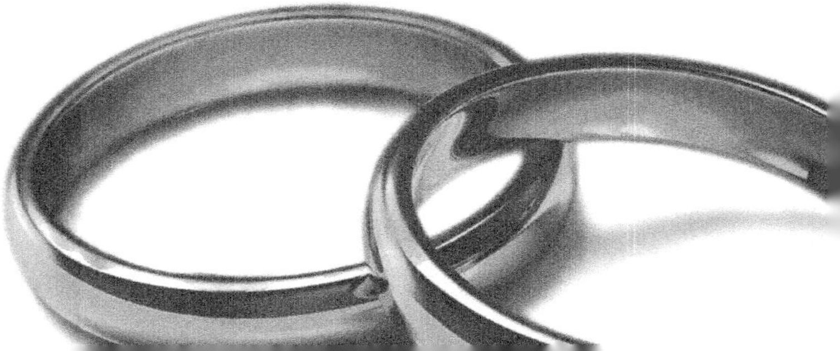

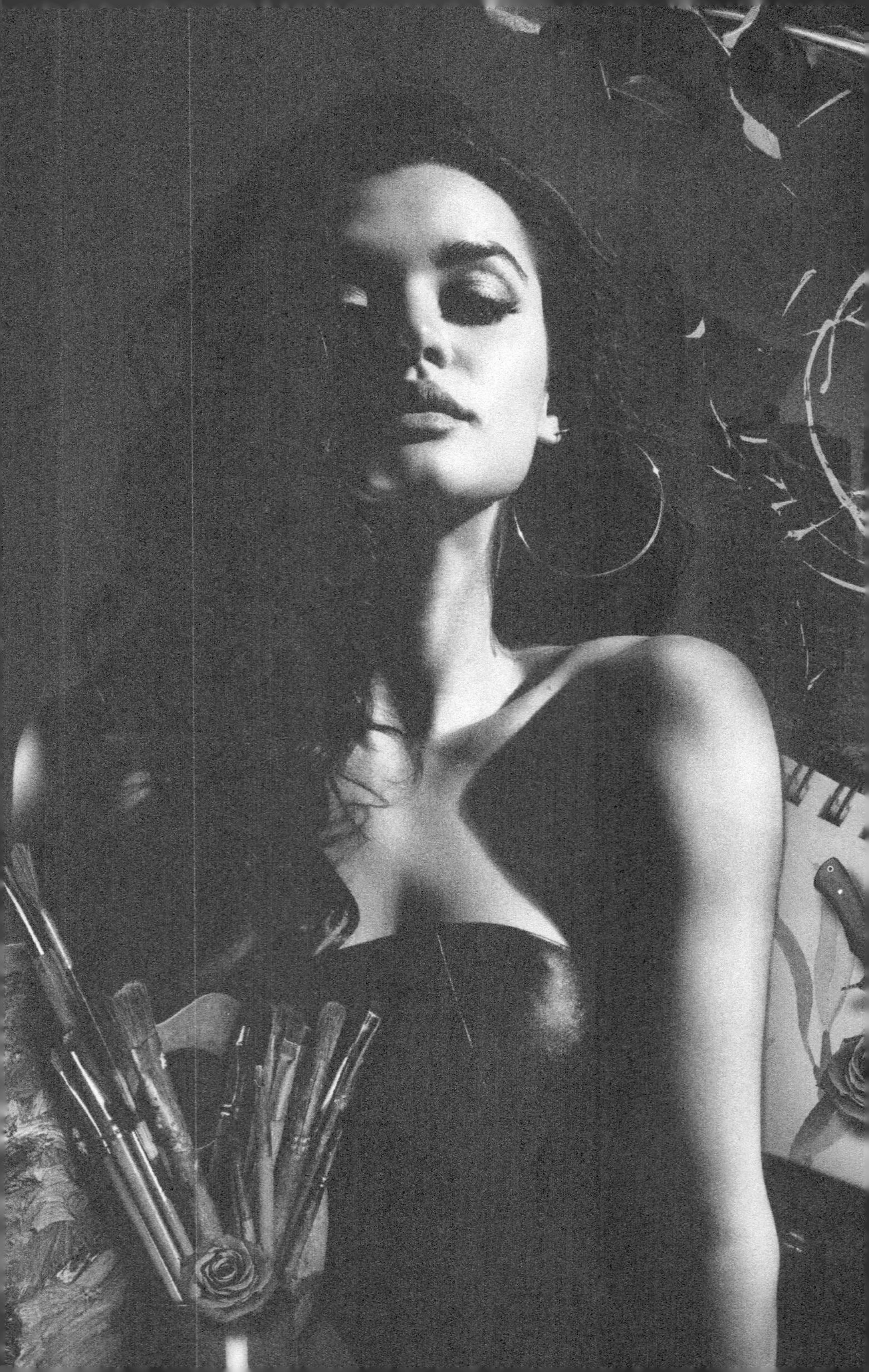

Chapter 29
Amalia

"**I COULD** get used to this."

I smoothed out my hair and handed Kai the helmet. "Maybe I should buy my own."

"Maybe. But I'm getting used to you riding with me," he said, placing the palm of my hand over his heart. "Always enjoyed the solo aspect of the ride, but with you, it is just something else."

"You're just Mr. Romantic, aren't you? You're going to get laid tonight, Cain. Stop trying so hard." I clapped his chest and moved toward the iron gate surrounding the home of my father's business partner, who also happened to be the CEO of the security detail hired at our wedding.

"Why on foot?"

"In case we have to make a quick exit. Wouldn't want to get trapped inside."

Holly's SUV pulled up behind us. "You brought the calvary."

"Of course. He thinks we're here to talk—which we are—but if things go south, and I don't like what he has to say, he'll be dealt with."

Holly squeezed me from behind and fist-bumped Kai. It took several more moments until the gate slid open and another five minutes before we were in front of a 10-foot glass door. An older gentleman with platinum hair greeted us and escorted us to a main-level office without asking questions, where a heavy-set man, who I knew as Rojas, leaned in his chair with a cigar between his fingers and a devilish grin on his face.

"Amalia, my dear, please sit. And congratulations. I'm sorry I couldn't make the event."

"I'm sure."

His lackey eyed me from the corner, where he stood like a sentinel, shoulders tensed, ready for the slightest signal from his boss. I wasn't naive enough to think he had no knowledge of the men he hired turning on me and my family. But we needed to play it cool.

"Let's address the issue. Cut the bullshit. You've been doing business with me for five years, longer with my father. What happened yesterday was unforgivable. And I need answers."

"I was just as shocked as you were."

"How are you going to sit there and tell me you had no idea your men were paid off."

Rojas chuckled and blew a puff of smoke. "Probably the same way you weren't aware."

I hated to be made a fool. It made me ragey and homicidal. What was more frustrating was that I knew he had a point, and that alone made me want to stab someone. Preferably the bastard checking out my ass from the corner.

Kai hadn't said a word, but I clocked him. His eyes were focused but everywhere at the same time. I was thankful he let me take care of things while staying vigilant.

"Three people were murdered in front of witnesses. The strings we had to pull and the money we had to pay to keep this story out of the press is on you. You won't get the remainder of your pay, and you'll owe me. And I don't tolerate unpaid debts."

"Bullshit!" he roared, jumping to his feet. "Those men came from one of the many agencies I own but don't directly oversee. It was out of my hands."

"And now it's not. You have forty-eight hours to pay up, and I want a roster with the names of every man and woman who works for you."

He rounded his desk and reached for me. "That's not how this works—"

"Careful. You put a hand on my wife, and she'll remove it. And I'll take the other for fun."

Kai's tone was menacingly calm, the threat palpable in the air. Rojas's hand recoiled as if he'd been burned, and he lifted his wary eyes toward my husband.

My husband.

"Forty-eight hours," Kai repeated. "Was she clear enough for you?"

"Crystal." He clamped down on his mouth, his eyes moving between us, lingering longer than I was comfortable with on Holly, then nodded his acknowledgment. But in my peripheral, I saw the signal he gave with the fingers at his side.

He'd sealed his fate.

"Kai."

A blade descended into my palm from inside my sleeve, and I plunged it twice into the side of his neck before he even knew what had happened. In that exact second, Kai sent five rounds into the tall man in the corner, who'd managed to pop off two of his own before he went down.

"I'm assuming this was the quick exit you were talking about?"

"Nice of you to keep up, Cain," I teased, snatching a laptop from the desk and bolting out of the office.

Thunderous footfalls beat against the hardwood above us and from unseen corridors on the main floor.

"Amalia, they'll be on us soon. Toss me the laptop if you're riding with Kai." Holly was just a step behind us as we tore out the door and onto the front lawn. I eyed Kai's backpack but knew the precious seconds I'd spend stuffing it inside could be the difference between life and death. Looking back, I hurled the device toward Holly, who caught it effortlessly.

We'd originally planned to scale the walls, but to our luck, the main gate was still slightly open, though it felt like it was miles away once bullets started whizzing by.

"Get in front of me." Kai reached for my arm and slipped behind me to shield me from the gunshots. It was unnecessary but a sweet gesture, nonetheless.

I'd thank him on my knees later.

"Fuck." A loud thud against the dirt had me glancing back in time to catch Holly taking a tumble, possibly having tripped over her own feet. At least that's what I hoped, not that she'd been hit. My first instinct was to run to her aid, but I heard Kai release a sharp hiss, and I knew he'd been hit.

"Kai!"

"I'm fine," he yelled back. "Flesh wound."

Despite his reassurance, I felt my heart pounding out of my chest. I knew I wouldn't be okay until I saw his wound with my own eyes. Holly had already caught up as we crossed the gate and split toward our respective rides.

"I dropped it," she yelled as she climbed into her car. "I dropped the laptop... I couldn't go back."

"It's okay," I yelled. Jumping on the back of Kai's bike, I pulled the helmet over my head as he did the same.

The engine roared to life, and we raced down the street just as one of Rojas's crew pulled out of the gate in a black SUV. Holly had taken off in the opposite direction.

"Baby, hold on tight."

My fingers interlocked around his torso. "Kai, where are you hit?"

"I'm good. Caught some lead in the arm, but it's nothing."

"Don't lie to me. Please." I hadn't meant to sound so vulnerable and afraid, but the thought of him hurt made my heart heavy.

"So you do care?"

"Kai, don't make me kill you."

Our moment only lasted seconds as more bullets were sent our way.

"*Malditos.*" I reached into Kai's holster and pulled out his Glock, returning fire while holding on to him with one hand.

The SUV's windshield shattered, causing the vehicle to swerve uncontrollably before righting itself and continuing its pursuit. When the gunfire stopped, I was sure I'd hit the passenger. "I'm out!" I shouted, dropping the empty mag and reaching for a new one.

"The bag, baby."

I noted the strain in his voice, and my stomach plummeted. "Kai? Talk to me."

"The bag. Get the bag. I'm fine."

"Fuck." Reaching into the black backpack, I pulled an MP7 and set it on full auto.

"Steady, vicious. Keep it steady. You can do this."

A bullet ricocheted off the body of the bike, causing Kai to swerve slightly, and I bumped my head on his back. "Easy," I said, giving him a reassuring squeeze. The moment he grunted in pain, a haze of rage rolled through me. Twisting around, I let it rip, spraying into the vehicle's cabin until my arm couldn't take the pressure, and it dropped onto the highway. But not before doing its job.

The SUV hit the stone median, clipping the edge and flipping twice.

"Did we lose them?" he asked.

"Yeah, we did."

Kai glanced back briefly and saw the fiery wreckage.

"That's my girl."

"I'm your wife."

"My fucking wife."

I circled his waist with both arms, and that's when I finally felt the wetness, and he flinched.

"Take the next exit."

"We still have another five miles."

"Kai, take the goddamn exit."

He said nothing and maneuvered through cars until we were off the highway. I gave him directions, and after the longest fifteen minutes of my life, we finally reached my condo and parked in a private garage.

Hopping off the bike, I tossed the helmet, opened his jacket, and frantically searched for the wound. Just below his right ribcage was a growing stain of blood. "Kai…no, no, no."

He lifted my chin, mouth tilted into a half smile. "Hey, I told you it was a flesh wound. I won't lie to you. Hurts like a bitch, but it's just—"

I suddenly threw myself in his arms, a wave of relief lifting off my shoulders, and kissed him hard. Kai returned the hug and tightened his hold on me.

"I think you like me a little bit," he whispered, grazing my lips.

"I do," I said, unable to suppress my smile.

"Good, because I fucking like you a lot."

"And here I thought it was the amazing sex."

He laughed into my neck. "That's a bonus."

"Come on," I said, tugging him toward the elevator. He seemed to look around for the first time, and his eyes narrowed.

"The garage is empty."

"I know. That's because only one other person lives here: Dr. Aaron Ward, on the third floor. He's on my payroll and has his expenses paid in exchange for his services."

Kai's face lit up with understanding. Ares had its doctors, lawyers, and judges—pretty much every profession that would allow its organization to continue in secrecy and remain above the law.

"I'm fine. I can patch myself up if you got a first aid kit."

"I'll be the judge of that."

He pulled me to his chest and kissed my forehead. "That was close. Too close, too soon."

"We kicked ass. That's all that matters. Don't get soft on me."

I was pretty sure a flock of birds had taken up residence in my stomach. This feeling was foreign, and I had to admit that I liked it.

The elevator doors slid open to a short corridor where the second lift awaited us. I placed my hand on a black panel, and Kai watched with intrigue as it scanned and alerted green a beat later. When the second set of doors opened, we ascended three more floors.

"This is impressive," he said when the last set of doors slid open directly into my condo's main living space, which also doubled as a second studio.

"Another one?"

"Of course. But before any questions, let's take care of you first."

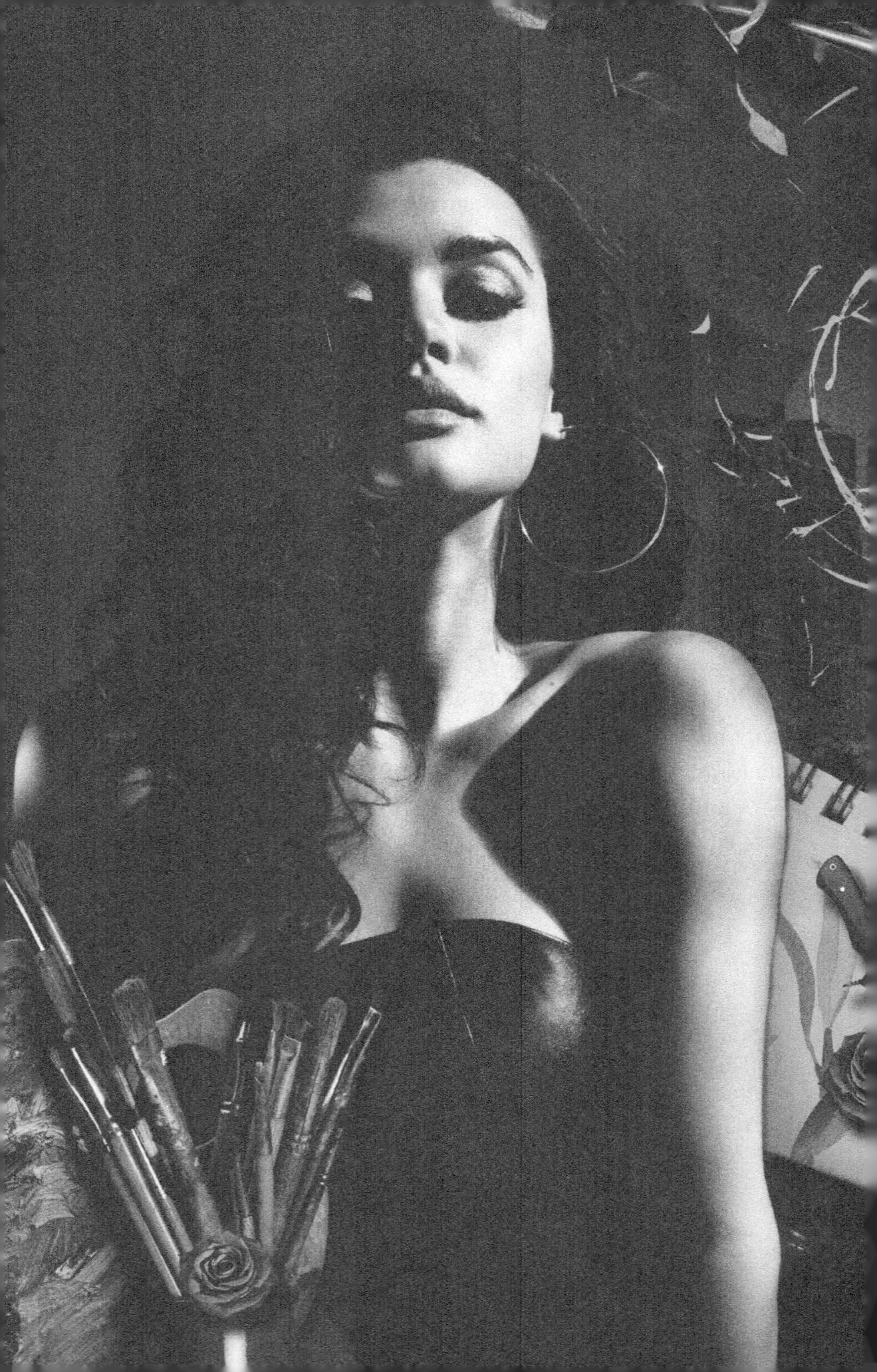

Chapter 30
Amalia

"**HOLD** still."

"I'm not going anywhere."

It was hard to focus when this beautiful man stood in front of me, his solid, bare chest on display. I'd never tire of looking at his hard body and the art that covered it.

"You were right. It looks like it just grazed you, but it's still pretty deep. Are you sure you don't want stitches?"

Kai clenched his mouth tightly when I pressed the wet cloth against the broken skin. "You have that glue stuff?"

"And I'm the stubborn one?" My phone suddenly vibrated in my pocket before he could hit me with a sarcastic comeback. It was the text I'd been waiting for, and I breathed a sigh of relief when I saw Holly's name.

> Hey, babe. Got your text. Glad you're safe.

> Lay low, Hols. I've got the girls running extra security at my place. Get there if you need to relax a bit.

> Okay. Thanks.

> Amalia, I'm sorry about the laptop. I feel like I fucked this up.

> It's okay. It was a shitstorm. We're lucky we made it out. There's going to be press regarding the shootout on the highway. Get our people ahead of the damage.

> Got it, boss.

I rolled my eyes and grinned.

> Love you, pendeja. And I'm happy you're safe. Text you later.

Text bubbles appeared and disappeared twice, and I waited to see if she would respond, but nothing came through after several minutes.

Placing the phone on the bathroom counter, I turned toward Kai, who was just about done gluing himself back together. A twinge of heartache pricked at my chest when I thought of how close he'd come to being seriously injured. The angst swirling inside me at the possibility of losing him, especially in that manner, was crushing.

"What's the matter?" he asked, concern pulling his eyebrows together. I hadn't realized I was wearing my emotions on my sleeve lately.

"I'm sorry. I was reckless today. We should have gone with more backup." Kai wrapped me in his arms. "I would have never been able to forgive myself if something had happened to you…or Holly."

"I'm good. Just another scar to add to the tally."

I met his eyes, those beautiful ocean eyes, and smiled. "The only scars I want to see on your body are the ones I give you," I said, digging my nails into his back.

Kai's hands came up to the side of my neck. "I'm yours to mark, *mi reina*."

We shed our clothes and stumbled into the shower, my legs wound around his waist, teeth clashing together as we each fought for dominance. Growling into my mouth, he pushed my body against the tile. The impact bordered on pain, but I needed more. More of him. I wanted to feel him claim me, stretch me open, and fill me until I was on the fringes of death, if that's what it took.

"Fuck me, Kai…please."

"My wife is so fucking needy, isn't she?"

"Yes…say it again. Who am I?"

He popped my nipple out of his mouth. "Mine."

Water droplets gathered in his full lashes and rolled down his face.

He was so fucking beautiful.

With my thumb, I pushed his bottom lip, and he kissed it. "Mine," I whispered.

Nothing about how I felt being in his arms, being his wife, his partner—none of it felt temporary, and it scared me. But I didn't give a damn anymore. If Kai and I were meant to be more than that godforsaken contract, I would let the pieces fall where they were meant to. In the meantime, I would enjoy every single second in the company of this man.

Kai set me down on the bench and threw my legs over his shoulders, lips brushing up my inner thigh.

"I missed this."

"It's only been a few hours."

"Too long." His laugh vibrated against my clit, and I closed my eyes as he chased it with his tongue. "My wife tastes so fucking good."

A grin broke across my face as I tipped my head back and tangled my fingers into his hair. The sting of a sore wrist from today's chaos had me suppressing a hiss, but the pain was quickly drowned out by pleasure as Kai devoured me as if I were his last meal.

"*Dios*," I moaned as he gripped my hips tighter, drawing me closer and burying his tongue inside me.

"Kai," he growled, fingers replacing his tongue, sliding against the slickness before he pushed it against the rim of my ass. "Call my name when your pussy is on my face."

Rocking against him, I murmured his name, urging him on and biting my lip when he pushed inside me.

"You look so goddamn beautiful when you break for me," he said, pumping inside me with each thrust of his fingers and a swipe of his tongue. "I'll never get enough of this sweet little cunt."

"It's yours…baby, only yours."

"I need you to mean it, Amalia." He suctioned me hard into his mouth, and mine gaped open. He locked eyes with me.

"I…I do," I whined, my legs shuddering around his head, voice broken.

My orgasm rippled through every inch of my body, from my toes to the very top of my head. I cried out his name between ragged pants and whimpers. But he continued feasting, stealing my breath.

"My wife," he groaned, then flipping me over without warning, he pushed my head against the bench.

I attempted to spread my thighs to give him better access, but he spanked my ass cheek so hard it made my whole body jolt forward. He pressed his lips where my skin was on fire. "Leaving my mark."

"Again," I whispered. With my nails digging into the bench's surface, I braced myself for the impact. The sting spread deliciously. "Fuck," I moaned, my teeth open over my arm, closing against my skin as I rode out the waves of pain and unimaginable pleasure.

Kai spread me open and lined himself at my entrance, thrusting inside with a groan from deep in his chest. He was the epitome of *hurts so good*. Birth control was well worth the goddamn headaches at this moment because all I wanted was to be savagely fucked and taken by this man, to feel him lose himself inside me so that I'd erase the memory of every woman that ever came before me.

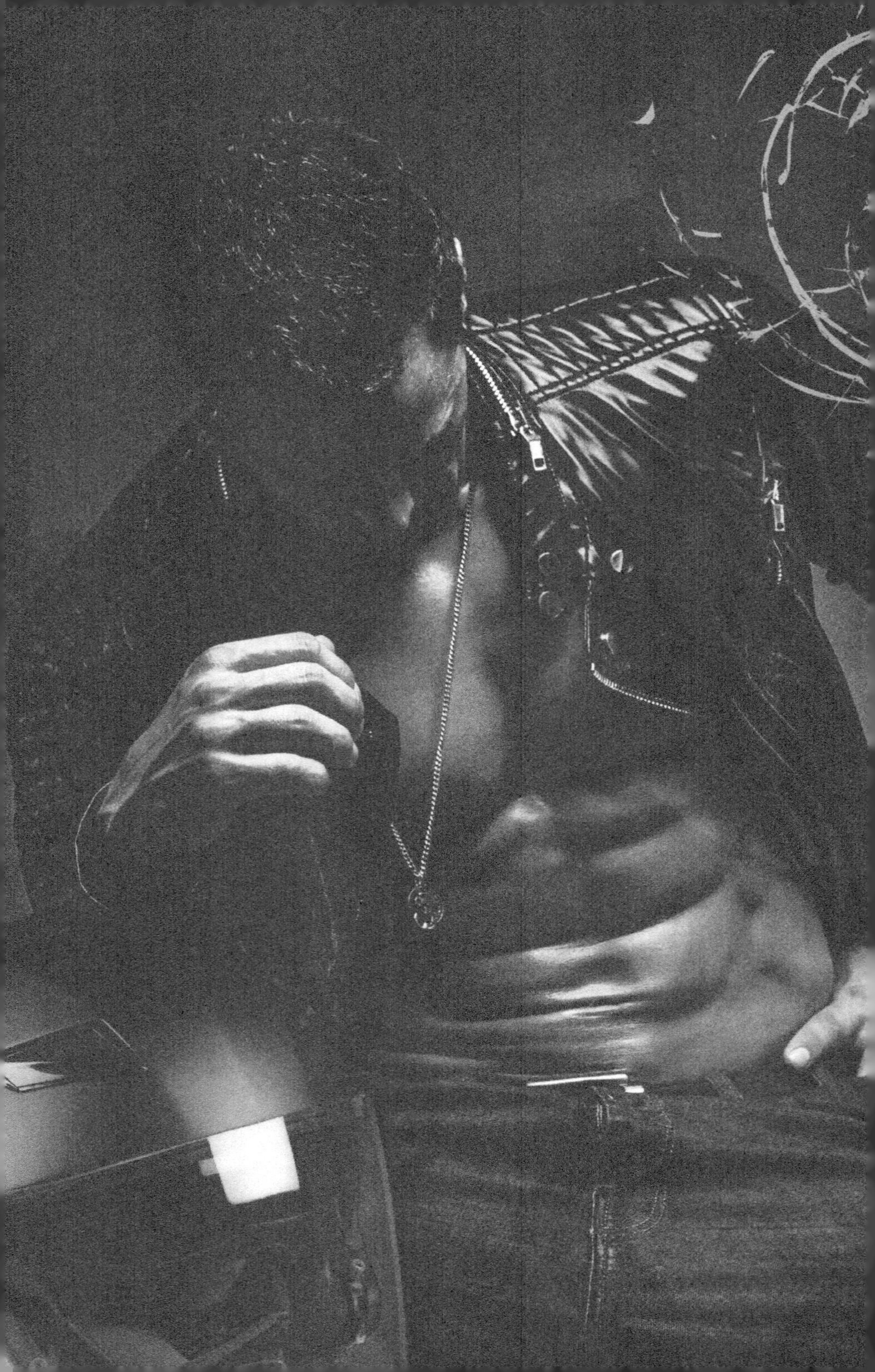

Chapter 31
Kai

THE soft vibrations of my cell phone against the nightstand pulled me from a light sleep. Derek's name lit up on the screen, and I immediately went on high alert. It was just past three in the morning, and he wouldn't be calling unless there was an emergency. I crept out of bed, careful not to wake Amalia, and answered the phone from the hallway.

"What happened?"

"Nothing. Got up to check on Vali—she was crying. And something told me to give you a call. Everything good?"

I let out a breath of relief. "Yeah, all good. Had a little run-in with some men who have very bad aim and even worse driving skills."

Derek listened without a word as I relayed the day's events. Even when I'd finished speaking, he remained quiet for countless seconds.

"You were shot?" he finally asked.

"Grazed. Nothing serious."

"Kai, maybe you should consider returning home—bring her

with you."

Always on the same page. I didn't have to tell him that Amalia had become important to me, just like I understood when Eva became his whole world. Leaning on the doorframe, I watched her sleeping figure. Derek's suggestion was tempting, because I'd do anything to take her away from the threat. But if there was one thing I knew about Amalia, she wouldn't leave her family behind, nor would she walk away and forgive a betrayal.

"Once we figure things out here, I'll bring it up."

"Watch your six, Kai— No, don't look at me like that."

"What?"

"Not you, Valentina. When I say your name, she wants to pretend she's not sleepy anymore."

"Tell my nugget I'll see her soon."

"I need you and Silas to find another nickname for my daughter."

We laughed and said our goodbyes, and I slipped back into bed and pulled Amalia toward my chest. I wasn't trying to wake her, but I needed to hold her. She stirred when I kissed the back of her head.

"Can't sleep?" she asked, her voice groggy.

"Derek called." Amalia stiffened in my arms. "Everyone is okay. He was up with the baby and decided to check in." Her body relaxed into mine, and she interlaced our fingers and kissed my hand.

"What about you?"

"What about me?"

"Are you okay? Sure you don't want Dr. Ward to look you over in the morning?"

I dipped my face and nipped at the shell of her ear. "*Mi reina*, I quite literally fucked you to the point where I had to carry you out of the shower. What else do I need to do for you to believe that I'm fine."

She turned in my arms and buried her face in the crook of my neck. "I believe you…it's just…you make me feel some type of way, Kai."

"How?" I asked, stroking her back.

"At peace," she whispered, kissing my jaw. "Soft." Another kiss. "Vulnerable in the best way." Her lips grazed along my skin, making my cock hard and raising goosebumps on my arms and the back of my neck. "Safe. Like I don't have to be on all the time because I have you."

Her admission stirred something inside me, warming every inch of my body. I'd never experienced feeling wanted and needed so wholly, not even with Derek.

She sat up and straddled my pelvis. "No one has ever made me feel safe the way you do. Not my girls. My father. No one. Until you. Is that crazy?"

"I love crazy."

She smiled and kissed me. "Good, because I heard once you called me certifiable."

My eyes opened wide, and I couldn't help the laugh that roared out of my mouth. "Did Derek tell you that?"

"So it's true?" she asked, pretending to feel offended.

My hand trailed up her naked waist to her breasts. "I didn't know you. But the moment I saw you—I know you caught me looking," I accused, flicking her nipple.

"A man checking out my tits isn't anything new and surely not someone who would be on my radar. But I noticed you, Kai. The 'tall guy with the pretty eyes.'"

"Could have been Derek."

"Of course it was. It was both. But if you need an ego stroke, Cain, I was definitely looking at you."

"Come here," I said, reaching for her and kissing her lips, soft and slow. "And you were so down bad you forced me into marriage, huh?"

It was her turn to snort a laugh. "You're delusional."

"Maybe, but I'm not a liar."

"Go to sleep," she said, a faint blush on her cheeks as she slipped beside me again and turned around.

"You pushing that ass against my cock, baby, is going to get you nothing but fucked again."

"It's almost like that's the point."

We were both sore as hell. But fuck me, how could I pass up a chance to drown in her.

I stepped out of Amalia's ensuite, towel-drying my hair from a shower and fully expecting her to be already dressed since she'd gone in before me. But there were no signs of my girl. Tossing the towel on the bed and foregoing a shirt, I crossed into the living area and searched around the condo for her. Nothing. A surge of panic rose in my chest, but before I let my imagination get the best of me, I checked one last room at the end of a long corridor. The black wooden door was slightly ajar, and I pushed it open.

My heart thundered for entirely different reasons. I had probably seen and tasted every gorgeous inch of this woman. Still, something about her sitting behind her easel, paintbrush in hand, a sheer shirt covering nothing but her elbows as it had fallen to the crook of her forearms, made the moment nearly magical.

"Your breakfast is on the table."

"I'm looking at my breakfast."

"Kai, I love you, but…" Her eyes widened in panic, but my chest warmed. "It's just a saying…I didn't—"

"Didn't mean it?" I asked with a smile, moving toward her as those three words echoed in my mind.

"Of course. You know that you and I—"

I reached down a hand on either side of her torso and lifted her before slipping into the seat and setting her down over my lap. "Are just temporary?"

"No," she said, so matter-of-fact that I snapped my eyes to hers, waiting, my heart pounding harder. "That you and I are so good together. And maybe someday we could get there."

Nothing else needed to be said, and I watched as she continued painting. It was a portrait of a young child with a toothless grin and dimples on each side.

"Valentina," I said. It was a statement, not a question. Her eyes were unmistakable, even in this older version of my niece. Amalia nodded. "It's beautiful. Your talent is amazing."

"I'm a woman of many trades."

"Indeed."

She snickered.

"Eva would love to see it."

"There's something about that little girl. A beautiful soul despite her..." She hesitated.

"Since when do you bite your tongue for anyone?" I said with a laugh. "Say it. Despite a father like Derek?"

"Nail on the head, Cain."

"Well, she has Eva. And Derek's not so bad," I joked.

She was quiet and focused on her art. "My mom is convinced she'll never have grandbabies. Not any time soon anyway."

The thought of Amalia carrying my child made my stomach fucking fluttery.

Fuck. I was the one down bad.

"Someday?" I asked, and her hand froze mid-stroke.

"Someday."

I kissed her shoulder and inhaled the fresh scent of something sweet on her skin.

"What happens today?

"We have to get back home. Face my father. And fix this mess I caused by killing Rojas."

"He deserved it."

"Of course he did. But dead men don't speak, Kai. And we're not any closer to figuring out who the rat is or what this person or persons want from me besides having me killed." I knew of her suspicions where Rocco was concerned, and I could only assume her hesitation in taking his head was because he was a family friend and didn't have the evidence to prove his involvement. But he was no one to me, and if Rocco Solis ended up hanging from a bridge, innocent or guilty, the world would be better for it.

I wound my arms tighter around her waist. "No one touches you."

Amalia placed a hand over mine. "We can't always control or prevent what happens." She leaned her head against my shoulder. "If anything, I'm terrified of what can happen to you in the name of revenge against me."

"I'm impossible to kill. You've seen that firsthand," I joked, trying to lighten the mood.

"The last man who said that to me ended up with my pistol in his mouth and his brain as new wall decor."

My dick pulsed at her back. "Is that supposed to scare me, vicious? Because I'm strangely turned on."

Amalia shook her head. "You're gross."

I slipped my hand between her thighs, two fingers over her clit. "Maybe. Filthy? Always."

"My pussy is so fucking sore, Kai. I don't think I can…" Her voice was ragged, a moan slipping past her lips as I stroked her.

"Look at you, baby. You're already a mess, and it's all for me." I brought my fingers to my mouth and licked them clean as she watched. "Goddamn, *mi reina*, so sweet." Instead of mine, this time, I brought two fingers to her mouth, and she eagerly opened for me. "Just like that. See how good you taste." I pushed my fingers deeper until I heard her gag, and it was fucking music to my ears. "You know what my new goal in life is?" I asked while pinching her clit with my other hand.

She moaned, shaking her head and rocking her hips as the paintbrush and palette dropped to the floor by my feet.

"My one goal in life is to make sure you break for me *every* day." She gagged again, and I could feel the tears sliding down her cheeks. "Every fucking day, I need to feel you this goddamn wet. And hear you sing for me, just like that."

She arched her back and lay her head on my shoulder, hips moving at a steady rhythm. Another gag as I pushed deeper down her throat. "Use me, vicious. Show me how you want me to fuck you."

Her hands were in my hair, tangled tightly the faster she climbed to orgasm.

"You always paint in the nude?" I asked, eyes on the tempting sight of her tits bouncing up and down, making my mouth water.

It wasn't long before she was shuddering in my arms, her cries muffled by the fingers in her mouth. Amalia slid off my lap, and just when I thought she needed a break…and a breather, I was wrong.

She looked up at me through wet lashes, knelt between my thighs, and grinned as she undid my belt and zipper. "I haven't had breakfast today either and, wouldn't you know, your pretty cock was exactly what I was craving."

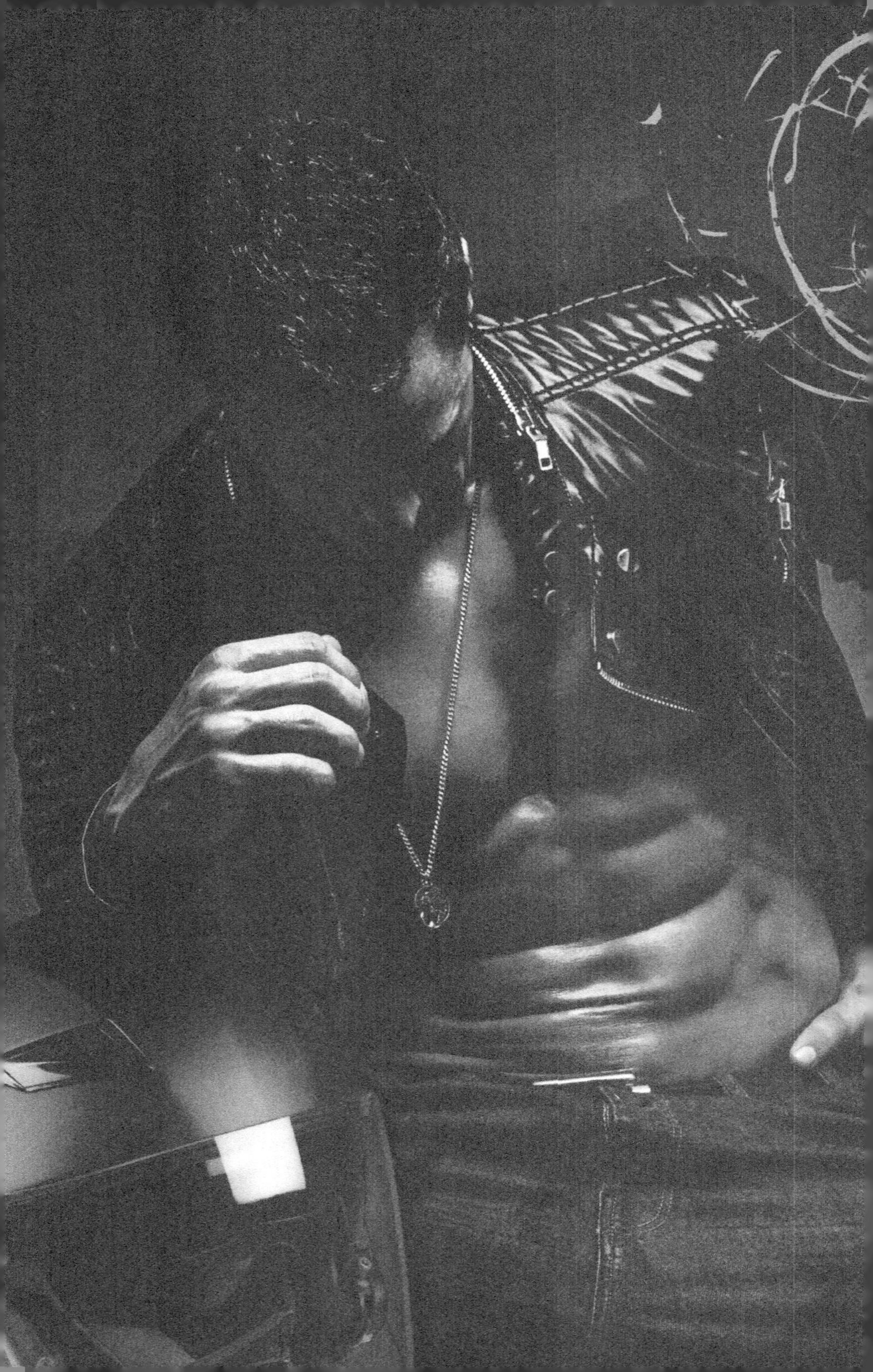

Chapter 32
Kai

"FUCK."

Gloria had taken a hit to the fuel tank. We'd had her towed from Amalia's condo two days ago, and I hadn't had the stomach to look at the damage until now. But I'd take a totaled bike in exchange for Amalia's safety any day.

Wiping the sweat from my brow with the shirt I'd torn off ten minutes ago, I reached for my bottle of water, but instead of drinking, I poured the damn thing over my head. The Texan sun would take some time to get used to. It was a world away from Philly's four seasons, but I'd go anywhere she was. Hot, cold—it didn't matter, because when I thought of my wife, only one word came to mind.

Home.

"Milly tells me you've been out here for quite some time." Amalia's father's footsteps stopped just behind me. "You know, we have people who do this. All you have to do is say the word," he offered, regarding a freshly hand-washed Hellcat sitting in the drive.

"And miss the opportunity to admire that work of art?" I said, straightening and drying off my face. It wasn't just the car. Doing these small things for her filled me with a sense of pride and purpose—anything to make her smile.

"You seem the type to have had your hands on a number of specialty vehicles…and yet you choose this"—he motioned toward my bike—"as your main means of transportation."

"It's fast and perfect for a quick getaway, if need be, and it's a hell of a lot of fun."

"I heard," he said, eyes dropping to the bandage at my side. "Dr. Ward said he took care of that for you."

Amalia had ultimately convinced me to get treated by her doctor friend—it wasn't my choice, but when a goddess is on her knees, my cum sliding down her throat, she could have very well asked me to jump out the goddamn window, and I would have obliged with a smile.

"Yeah, it's nothing serious."

"Thank you," he said, a hand on my arm. "I always worry about her. And there are many days, if not most, I regret ever getting her involved in this life."

"So why did you?"

He hesitated, eyes slightly narrowed as he studied me. "I'll be the first to admit it was for selfish reasons. Greed. Ambition. Amalia has always been beautiful…" Antonio Montesinos sucked in a deep breath, as though deciding whether to continue his story. "I wanted to capitalize on that," he finally said.

Anger raged inside me at the thought that Amalia's own father had all but sold her soul for money. Used his daughter's beauty as a tool to gain more power. To this day, he was willing to risk her life for his own greed. The same way Ronan had used Derek and me.

It was my turn to exhale forcefully and relax before I did or said something I'd regret, if only because I knew she and him were close, and I'd never do anything to hurt her.

I said nothing and used the rag on my shoulder to polish a random spot on Gloria's dash.

"Kai, I know that makes me sound like a piece-of-shit father. I used my daughter's pretty face for my own gain, but it was also the best way to keep her from the same fate that most women in our world are subject to. An arranged marriage."

I stopped my frantic wiping.

"I know about you and Amalia."

"Then you know this is exactly that."

"No, what exists between you and her is completely different than what would have happened to her if I'd been forced to marry her to some drug lord's son. I would have lost my only daughter."

I hated that he made sense. And I hated even more that we seemed more alike now than five minutes ago because, selfishly, I'd prefer to have her in my life the way she was than married off to some spineless bastard who would have treated her like nothing more than an object to showcase, fuck, and discard when he pleased.

"Isabel and I are headed back to Sinaloa tonight. Gio asked to stay until the end of his vacation. But I know you two are newlyweds and probably want—"

"You're leaving? In the middle of all this?" I tossed the rag to the floor and eyed him, face twisted in disgust at his disregard for his daughter's safety.

"I don't have a choice. Business doesn't wait for personal matters to resolve. And despite what you might think, Amalia has protection and can handle herself. Gio, on the other hand…"

If I had to guess how much of what's happened in the last weeks was due to Antonio's shady dealings, I knew my assumptions would be right. I knew he loved his daughter but loved money and power even more. After all, he hadn't done a damn thing, but allowed her to risk her life, time and time again.

"Gio can stay, but with everything going on, I'm not sure if—"

"That's not fair, Kai. I thought we were friends." Gio was standing by the door, leaning against the frame with a reproachful look. "And besides, this is nothing new. Growing up a Montesinos, there's a new threat every week. Just because you all thought I was in the dark doesn't mean it was any less *dangerous*," he added with air quotes.

Maybe the kid had a point, but it would have been easier not to have to babysit or worry about him getting caught up.

"Kai is right, Gio."

"*Papá*, I'm not a kid anymore. Please stop treating me like I'm not part of this family." His voice was tinged with hurt and resentment, and I suddenly felt like I was intruding. "I'll stay out of trouble, I promise. But don't make me leave because you think I'm too weak. It's what you've thought about me my whole life."

Antonio looked away and said nothing, not even to deny his son's claim. I never knew what a good father was growing up. Never had one. The father figures in my life were scum. I'd convinced myself that because of that, I'd never be worth a damn at being someone's dad. But Derek had proved me wrong. Maybe it was the circumstances, the fact he'd had his daughter with the woman he loved. But I found myself contemplating the idea that maybe someday...

Maybe.

As if I'd manifested her in my thoughts, my wife was pulling up in the passenger side of Holly's vehicle. I didn't realize how big I was smiling until the sides of my cheeks started to burn. Amalia hopped out, looking too goddamn good for me to express how much I missed her, while her father and brother stood just steps away. Her smile widened the moment we made eye contact.

She'd been at a meeting this morning with her girls, then called to tell me she'd be running errands with Holly. I felt like a pathetic bastard because I missed the hell out of her after just a few hours. Maybe that's why I washed and waxed her goddamn car and sat in the driver's seat because the interior and seatbelt strap smelled like her perfume.

Fuck me, I was gone. Completely fucking done for.

"Hey, handsome," she said before wrapping her arms around my neck and climbing onto my waist, her legs around me, and I held an ass cheek in each hand. "I missed you." Her mouth was on mine in the next second, and for that moment, I didn't care that we weren't alone. That I was sweaty, filthy, and missing a shirt, while she was dressed in sleek beige pants and a silky white tank top, looking every bit like a powerful woman.

"Come on, Gio. Let's give the lovebirds a moment to get reacquainted after a grueling morning apart." Amalia peered around me at the sound of Holly's laughter as she dragged Gio inside the home. I hadn't noticed when Antonio left or seen where he'd gone off to, but nothing else mattered but the woman in my arms.

"You're bad for business, Cain." She nipped at my bottom lip.

"How so?"

"You have any idea how hard it was to focus on anything going on around me? To have to get up and speak, schedule, and arrange shipments when all I wanted to do was come home to you and get fucked."

Every ounce of blood in my body migrated to my pants.

"Fuck, vicious. I missed you too."

"What's wrong with us? I've never been this pathetic."

I laughed over her lips and kissed her again. "It's because I like you, wife."

"A lot?" she asked, wiping her lipstick from my mouth with her thumb.

"A *lot*."

"Is that why Milly called to tell me you were sitting in my car for an hour?"

Barking a laugh, I walked us over to the Hellcat and sat her on the hood, wedging myself between her legs.

"Milly is a *chi...chi...*help me out here."

"*Chismosa*," she choked out in laughter.

"That's it. Exactly. I was detailing your car, not missing you or smelling you or thinking about you on your knees and how fucking beautiful you look choking on my cock."

Her laughter quieted, and she placed a hand on my cheek. "How romantic of you."

"I thought so." My hands journeyed up her blouse. "Any updates?" I asked, flicking her hardened nipples.

Amalia rested her forehead on mine, closed her eyes, and reveled in the pleasure of my caresses.

"No, but I've got Holly looking into possible leads and tracing phone calls. As you know, a lot of these transactions happen anonymously from burner phones and accounts— Fuck, Kai," she whispered, tipping her head back as I kissed behind her ear. "Just like that."

"So what's next?" My hands dropped to her hips, and I hauled her forward. The heat of her pussy on my abdomen made me want to take her right here on the hood of this car.

"Unfortunately, wait until they strike again. Or we can set up a drop and see if they take the bait." She bucked against me as I kissed down the valley of her breasts. "It seems like I'm the target, so if I'm alone, it might entice—"

"The hell with that."

Her eyes snapped open.

"Excuse me?"

"You alone? No, absolutely not. Fuck that."

Amalia rolled her eyes and shoved me back. "Again, I wasn't asking, Cain."

"No, maybe you weren't, but I *am* telling you, that plan is shit."

Her laugh was cynical and maybe downright diabolical, but it didn't faze me.

"Oh?"

"Putting yourself at risk is out of the question."

"You mean, my every day? I think you forget that I cut the dicks off cocky, pieces-of-shit men for a living—in heels and a skirt, no less."

"And you look goddamn sexy doing it, woman, but deliberately putting yourself in danger is different. I know you're capable, so get over yourself. This isn't me trying to be an overprotective husband or underestimating you or whatever bullshit it is you're thinking."

She arched an eyebrow. "And what is it then?"

One of my hands wrapped around her throat, and I tugged her close. "This is me letting you know that as long as I'm breathing, no one touches my fucking wife." Amalia's eyes closed, her nails digging into my arms. "That's my ring on your finger, *mi reina*. Whatever needs to get done, you and I do it together. I'll burn this whole goddamn city to the ground for you. Just say the word."

"Kai." Her voice was barely a whisper as her lips grazed the shell of my ear, followed by the tip of her tongue. "You owe me an orgasm today. Every day. Your words."

"I made sure you started the day properly satisfied. Don't tell me you already forgot."

"Hmm, I might need you to jog my memory a bit."

"Join me in the shower? I've been out here all day, messing with this bike and your car. I'm filthy."

"I noticed," she said with a slow smile. "I wasn't going to say anything."

"Is that right?" Maybe she recognized the mischief in my voice because her eyes went wide, and she attempted to wriggle away, but I was faster. Snatching her from the hood, I tossed her over my shoulder and ran inside as she laughed in my arms.

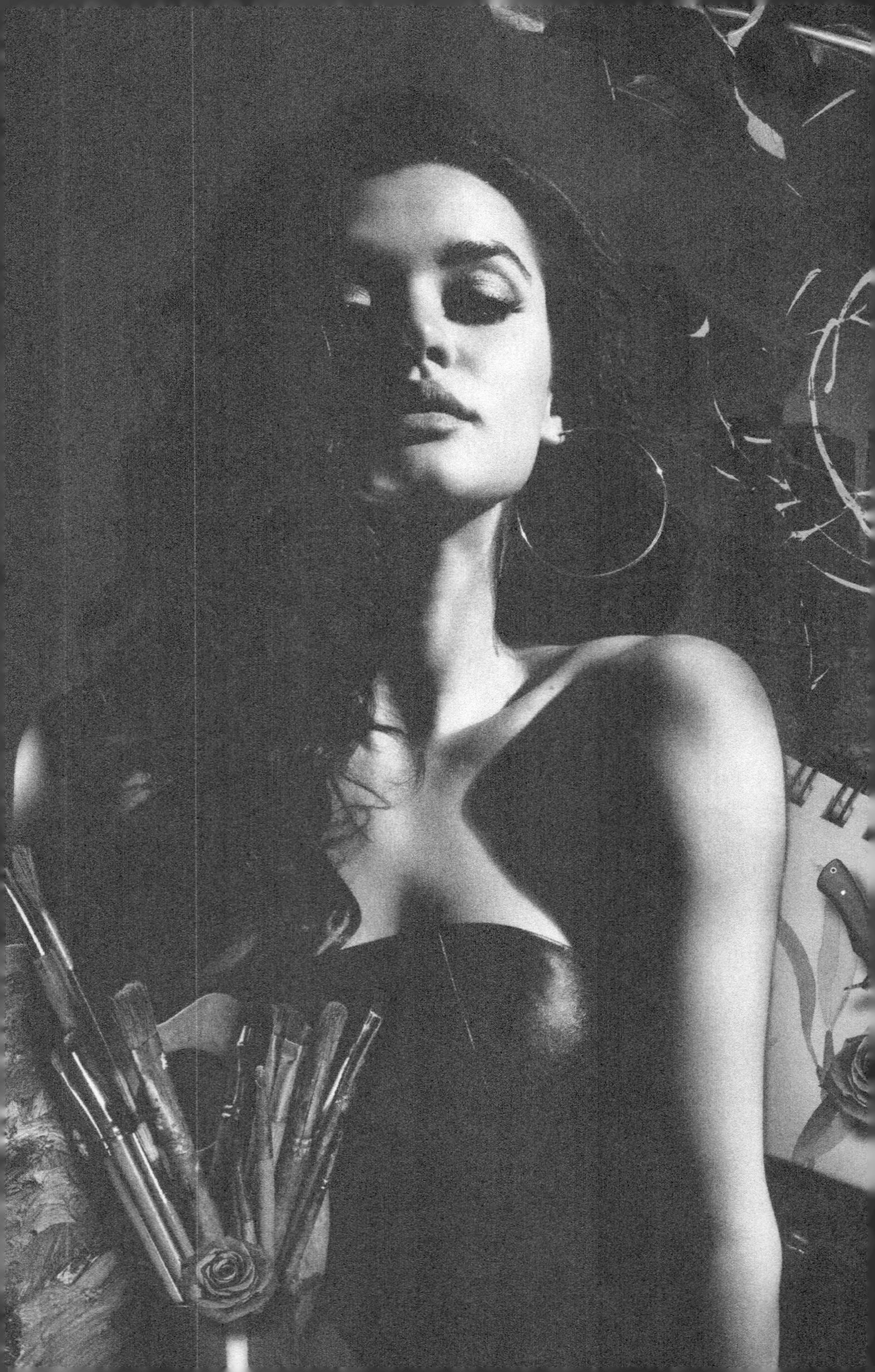

Chapter 33
Amalia

I ALREADY knew who was on the other side of my door without having seen the surveillance footage. Having arrived from his trip late last night, Rocco had been texting and calling me nonstop, but I wasn't in the headspace to deal with him or whatever he had going on. I should have known better. Known he was bound to come around sooner than I was ready. I couldn't shake the feeling that he could somehow be involved in the recent attempts on my life and against our family. Threats on our lives and livelihoods weren't anything new, but something about this seemed personal. I didn't want to believe that my childhood friend, the man who had grown up like one of my brothers, whether he saw me that way or not, had orchestrated the chaos of the last few weeks.

"So you are alive?"

"Surprised or disappointed," I asked, casually leaning on the doorframe but ready to react if the need arose.

One of his eyes narrowed, jaw twitching as he regarded me. "Is that really what you think? That I'm behind everything that's happened?"

"I didn't say that. But it's a little telling when you know exactly what I'm talking about."

Rocco chuckled and attempted to let himself inside, but I extended my arm, blocking him. He froze and stared at me like I'd sprouted an extra head.

"*Muñeca*, you can't possibly be serious. Me? You think I did this to you?"

For a second, my heart plummeted. Rocco wasn't the type of man who showed emotions or made attachments, but something in his eyes told me my accusation had stung.

"Roc, you have to understand where I'm coming from." I put a finger to his chest. "You were the first to know about the ambush at my father's warehouse. The one who put together and coordinated the retaliation at the compound."

"Bullshit. I chose a random day and time when I knew they'd be there."

"Only they weren't, at least not how we expected. Instead, they were waiting for us. They knew exactly the moment we'd breach the facility. That can't be a coincidence. And how convenient for you to leave the wedding reception just before all hell breaks loose."

He balled his fists and punched the wall. I'd be lying to myself if I denied the sliver of fear that crept up the back of my neck at his sudden rage.

"Dammit, Amalia. You think I'd send you into a death trap? And hire men to kill you on your wedding day?"

I removed my arm from the frame and positioned myself in the doorway. "A month ago, I would have said no. But today, things are different."

"Of course they are, aren't they? There's a new man in your life, and you can't have old friends putting a damper on that. So, it's easier to blindly throw accusations. Did he put these thoughts in your head?"

"Since when do I base my thoughts and actions on someone else's judgment?"

"I don't know you anymore. The you from one month ago would have never ignored my calls or accused me of trying to harm you."

There it was again—the pain in his eyes. But I couldn't let emotions blind me. I had to think logically, and all of it added up—as much as it hurt.

Rocco extended his arms at his sides defensively. "So, what now? What is *La reina* going to do? Kill me?"

Again, he raised a good point. He would have already been bleeding out on the ground at my feet had he been anyone else, even with the doubts clouding my brain. But this was Rocco, and even with the evidence stacked against him, a little voice at the back of my thoughts told me to wait.

It was stupid, and maybe I was holding on to that little girl and the boy who had once been her best friend, but—

Rocco's hands were suddenly cutting off my air supply, his eyes crazed and unrecognizable. He shoved me against the metal door, the impact painful as my head spun.

"I had our whole future planned out, *muñeca*. You and I would have been so perfect. We could have burned the whole fucking world to the ground and made it better. Just you and me. *El rey y la reina*."

I clawed at his hands, the need to breathe taking over rational thought, but Rocco was unfazed and dragged me through the doorway, closing it behind us and away from security and other staff.

"I tried to make you see. Show you that I was who you were supposed to be with," he snarled through gritted teeth. "But you chose some bastard you didn't even know." The pressure at the back of my eyes was unbearable as was the sinking feeling in my stomach. "Do you have any idea how that made me feel?" Rocco's face twisted into a sadistic smile. "Sshh, don't say anything, beautiful. It's okay. He won't be a problem for much longer. I've got plans for Kai Cain."

There it was, the words to slap me back into reality and shake me from the shock of Rocco attempting to end my life.

As black splotches clouded my vision, I reached into my side and pulled out a blade. Too disoriented for precision, I drove the knife wherever I could. It took two stabs for him to realize what had happened. His grip loosened, and I sucked in one gasp of air before stabbing him a third time.

With wide eyes, Rocco put a hand to his side where blood was now dripping in a steady stream onto the floor. He regarded his bloodied fingers and flashed me the same insidious grin as before.

"So it really is over between you and me, huh?"

"Fuck you," I choked out, still attempting to catch my breath.

He chuckled. "Now *that* is my biggest regret. Not having fucked you." Rocco took two unsteady steps toward me. "Mostly because I was trying to be the good guy. And what did that get me?"

"Fucked anyway," I said, throwing the knife into his abdomen.

He fell to his knees and looked down at the black handle protruding from his body. "Bitch, I liked this shirt."

I fisted the top of his hair, tilting his head back while I pushed the knife deeper, forcing grunts and growls from him as he jolted. Tears burned my eyes as I mourned for who I thought was a friend and how this tragic moment was our end. Despite everything, I felt his loss, his betrayal deep in my soul, a scar I knew I'd never heal from.

"Amalia," he whispered, reaching for me.

"Shut up," I cried. "You don't get to speak to me." Tearing the knife from his abdomen, I pressed it to his throat. "See you in hell, friend."

"How about…we get there together?" Rocco gripped my hair with one hand and my wrist with the other, yanking me forward and laying me out on my back. The knife flew and slid across the floor too far for me to make a run for it in time.

"Come here!"

He attempted to pin me, but I sucker-punched him in the jaw and twice in the wound on his side. I cursed having left my gun in the bedroom.

"Stop fighting me," he seethed. And before I could react, he slapped me across the face. Ringing exploded in my ear on impact, leaving me vulnerable and disoriented again. Blinking rapidly and holding the sides of my head, I attempted to get to my feet, but he tackled and slammed me against the floor, causing a rush of painful air to leave my body.

"F—fuck…Rocco…stop." I wasn't sure if he hit me a second time. My thoughts were jumbled, my vision blurred, and there was no oxygen.

Fuck. He was strangling me again, only this time, I had nothing left to fight him off.

I clawed at his face, but it was impossible to get a grip. He was sweating, bloody, and fucking rabid.

They say your life flashes behind your eyes when you're at death's door, but maybe they're wrong.

Kai's face appeared first, followed by my parents, Gio, and even Milly. It was like hell's way of taunting me, of showing me everything I'd be missing in my life.

"Let her go!"

No, Gio. No.

My brother's voice gave me an extra dose of adrenaline, oxygen I didn't know I had, to keep fighting. His blurry figure was doubled, but I could see he was holding a gun.

I couldn't let him do it. Not again. Desperation set in, stealing the last of my oxygen reserves.

"Do it, kid. Prove you're not a weak little fuck."

From the corner of my eye, I saw a black object to my left, and I reached blindly, hoping beyond hope that it was my knife.

Rocco didn't have time to react before I plunged it into the side of his throat. His grip loosened just enough for me to scrape in some air and the strength to tear it out and, this time, drive into his skull from beneath his chin.

A burst of blood poured out from his body and all over me. I tried to keep my mouth closed, but it was impossible as I was still panting. Gio dove forward and pushed Rocco's convulsing body off me, gripping me by the shoulders and into a sitting position.

"Are you okay? Talk to me!" He was frantic and maybe hadn't realized he was shaking me too fucking much.

"Gio…stop," I managed to rasp out, still trying to relearn how to breathe.

"He was going to kill you." Gio turned toward Rocco's still body. "What happened?"

"It was him. This whole time, it was him."

The front door swung open. Kai walked through, with long-stemmed red roses and a smile, until awareness dawned, and he took in the carnage.

His helmet and the roses hit the floor, and he was on me in the next second.

"Amalia, where are you hurt? Where is it coming from?" His hands were all over, searching for wounds that didn't exist. "Baby, look at me."

"I'm fine." Despite the terror I'd just gone through, his arms filled me with a sense of calm and security. I buried my face in his chest and let myself be vulnerable for the first time in my life.

Low, labored moans had us both whipping our heads toward the noise. Without a word, Kai stood and emptied his mag into Rocco's body. He dropped the empty magazine and reloaded, taking off through the open door. Gio and I followed as he fired several rounds into Rocco's driver, who had gotten out of his car, most likely when he'd heard the gunfire. His knees hit the ground, and he took another bullet to the head before falling face-first onto the concrete. Another man from inside the SUV fired at Kai but missed, though he didn't share that luck, as Kai shot him twice in the chest, causing him to fall out of the vehicle.

I'd never seen that look on Kai's face—rage in its rawest form. His pupils were blown, his jaw tight. As he passed the driver's body, he sent another round into the back of his head. Kai moved as though on autopilot. Without a word, he dragged Rocco and the other men's bodies and shoved them back into the vehicle, then dashed inside the house and into an office.

"Kai," I called, but for once, my husband didn't acknowledge me. It was like his vision was tunneled, and he had one objective. He walked out with a bottle of Vodka and a piece of his torn shirt sticking out of the top.

Molotov cocktail.

Flames engulfed the car in seconds, but Kai remained emotionless until he was in front of me again.

"Amalia, baby, are you sure you're okay?" he asked, lightly touching a tender area on my lip from when Rocco had slapped me. "Gio, tell Milly to call clean-up."

Kai said nothing else as he scooped me up and headed for the stairs.

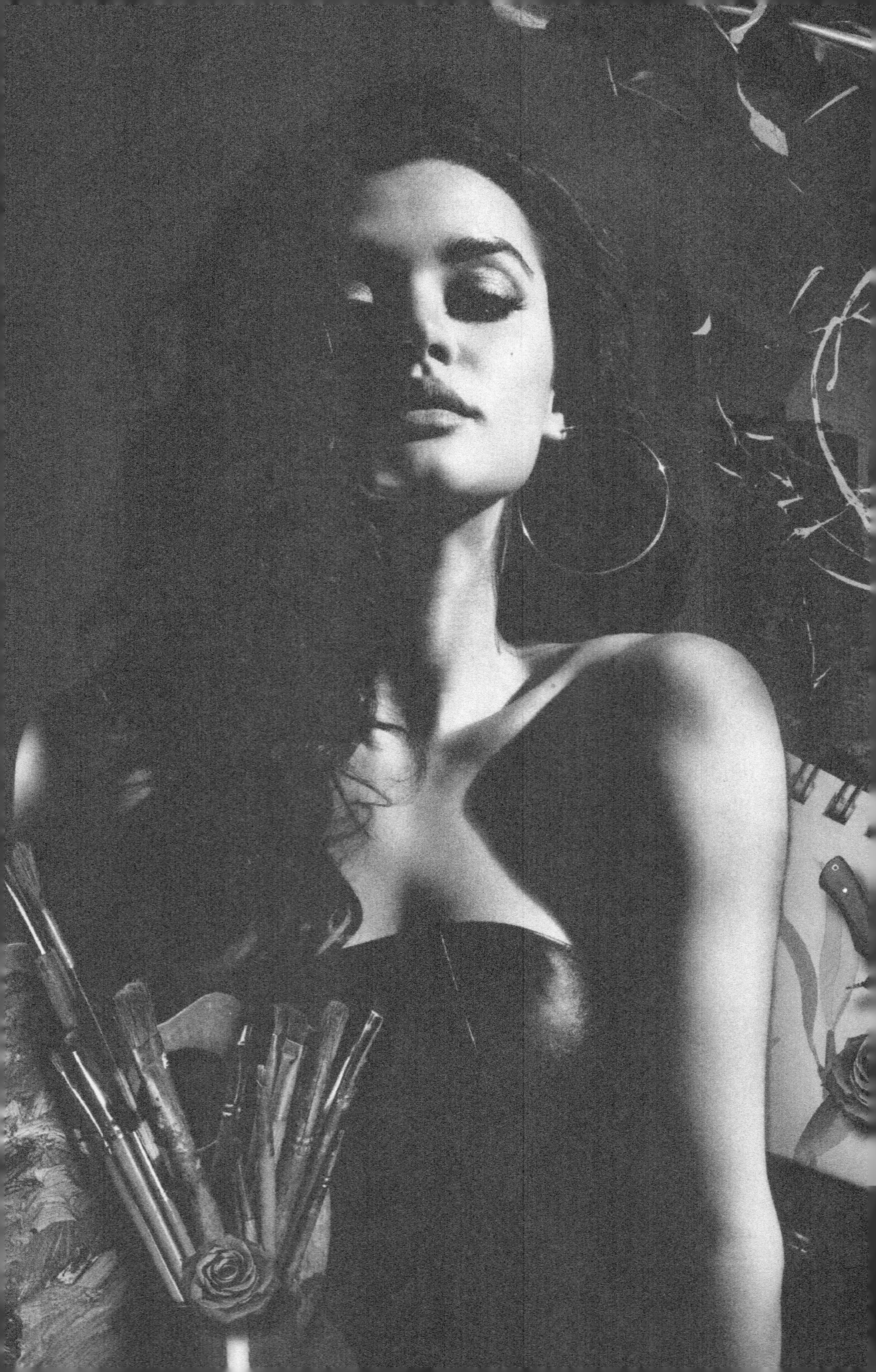

Chapter 34
Amalia

KAI hadn't spoken for ten minutes since I'd been in this tub. He was behind me, hyper-focused on lathering my hair and gently scrubbing the blood off my skin.

"Kai, talk to me."

His fingers stopped working through my scalp, and I felt his lips on my shoulder. Closing my eyes out of instinct, I leaned back and waited for him to break his silence. But he didn't. He rinsed out the shampoo and towel-dried my hair. He was so sweet and attentive that I didn't have the heart to tell him I needed to apply conditioner. I let him lift me out of the water, and he continued to dry me off. His touch was soft and cautious as he worked his way down. I noticed his gaze would stray to the sorest spots on my body, where bruising had already begun. But even then, he refused to meet my eyes.

"Hey," I tried again, to no avail.

The same tension he wore while he finished off Rocco's men was still creasing his beautiful features. As he dabbed water droplets from my shoulders, he reached up to feather his thumb against a sensitive area on my neck. Kai's breathing suddenly accelerated, and his hand rolled into a fist. But I couldn't take any more of his silent rage. Ripping the towel from his hand, I tossed it.

"That's enough. Look at me. I'm *fine*," I assured him assertively, my hands framing his face.

His stormy eyes finally found mine, and he shook his head. "Fine? You have bruises everywhere. And have you seen your face?" I actually hadn't, but now I was curious. "Your neck— Amalia, he almost killed you. Do you know what that would have done to me? If I'd walked in and found you..."

"Kai, I've almost been killed more times than I could count. But I'm fine. Don't make me have to keep repeating myself, because I'm already getting aggravated."

Kai held my wrists and tenderly lowered them from his face. Taking a step back, he tugged off his shirt, then slid out of his pants, leaving just his black boxer briefs. He held my hand, led me to the bed, and motioned for me to climb onto the mattress. I obliged, and he slipped in after me and pulled me close until his chin rested on my head.

"I would have never forgiven myself had something happened while I was gone. I should have been home. I would have been home, but I stopped to buy you those damn roses."

"They're beautiful."

He sighed loudly. "Amalia, stop. Stop waving this off like it wasn't a big deal. Could you just accept that someone else gives a damn about you? That I give a damn. I don't know how else to tell you. I'm not here just because of a contract. I'm here because I want to be here. And you matter to me so fucking much."

My stomach flipped upside down, and I closed my eyes and inhaled deeply.

"Kai...are you happy here? With me?"

His hold on me tightened, but his touch was still gentle, conscious of the bruises. "I've always tried to put on the facade of the guy people could count on—of being happy and using humor to get by. But the truth is, I've always felt out of step, like something was missing. Even surrounded by the people who meant everything in the world to me, there was a hole inside me that maybe I wasn't aware of."

I touched his face, anticipating words I didn't know I needed to hear. "And now?"

He kissed my palm, his eyes burning through mine. "For the first time in my life, I'm home."

My breath hitched, and a smile stretched across my face as I leaned in and brushed my lips against his.

"I like you, Kai Cain. And I was planning on keeping you anyway."

He laughed and rolled us over, his large frame over mine. I'd never felt so safe and so…loved.

"I'm not going anywhere," he whispered, his thumb smoothing back and forth along the bridge of my nose.

I held him at the nape with both hands and pulled him in for a kiss, my legs spreading to allow him room to settle between them.

"No, baby. You're hurt."

"Hurt me more," I begged, arching against him. "Make me forget, Kai. Make me yours."

He shook his head slowly. "That's a done deal. You're already fucking mine."

I'd never been run over by a bus, but I was pretty sure the way I was feeling and how every muscle in my body was aching was damn near the equivalent. I pushed into a sitting position and propped myself against the pillows. The breakfast of scrambled eggs and toast Kai had made and insisted on having me stay and eat in bed still lay untouched beside me. My appetite was non-existent. I had too much on my mind, but at the same time, nothing at all. Mostly because I pushed away thoughts of Rocco. There was far too much pain associated with the memory of everything that had transpired last night and over these last few weeks.

I tried to convince myself that I'd seen his betrayal coming, building for years due to his obsession because Rocco was ruthless and cold-hearted, yet I was still blindsided. Maybe because while I knew he'd cut off the heads of his men for smaller transgressions, he was different with me…or at least that was what I'd been dumb enough to think.

"Can I come in?"

Gio poked his head through the partially opened door, a frail smile on his sweet face. "Of course," I said, placing the food tray on my nightstand and patting the mattress beside me. I did my best to hide the pain by measuring my breath and focusing on returning his smile.

"Kai said to come up and keep you company while he talks to those men downstairs."

The clean-up crew.

Initially, he'd instructed Milly to call our local agency, but he quickly changed his mind and called Ares to have his own trusted team take care of yesterday's problem. We all hated that we'd had to sleep with the corpses of dead men outside our door, but on such short notice, the fastest they could arrive wasn't until this morning.

"You're the best company," I said, tousling his hair like I used to when he was a kid. Only this time, he didn't laugh or try to get me to stop. Instead, Gio remained silent and hung his head. "Hey, I'm so sorry you had to see that."

A tear slid down his nose as his shoulders trembled subtly. "I'm sorry, too." He reached for my hand and squeezed it. "I thought he was going to kill you."

"He was," I whispered, my voice on the verge of cracking. "But you saved my life. Again."

Gio turned to me, his beautiful brown eyes blurred behind tears. "I don't want you to die, Amalia. Let's leave from here. Please," he begged.

I cupped his face and kissed his forehead. "You know I can't do that, even if I wanted to."

Gio broke from my arms and stormed off the bed. "That's bullshit! You're the self-proclaimed queen, aren't you? You make the rules, don't you? So why not leave someone else in charge?"

"It's not that simple," I tried to explain, pushing to stand a little too fast. I wobbled, and I caught myself, but not before unwillingly showing how much pain I was in. Wearing just a cami and shorts, the extent of my bruising was on full display.

Gio shook his head in horror.

"What is it going to take, Amalia? You're not immortal. You dole out punishment and death, and one day, the bill will be due."

His words hit my core with the weight of a premonition. "Stop." I reached for him, but he recoiled from my touch. "Maybe you should go."

"Kai said—"

"No, I mean back home."

He folded his arms with an indignant scowl. "You don't want me here?"

"I love you, and I want you safe."

He scoffed. "Oh, there's a crazy concept."

"Giovanni, I can't guarantee your safety here."

"Rocco's dead."

"That means nothing. Another Rocco will take his place soon enough. Wash, rinse, repeat." Maybe I needed to hurt him to protect him. I hated the idea the moment it was born, but I knew it was the only way. "There's a reason I had to marry Kai and take Tony's place and not you."

His eyes narrowed, body stiff as if anticipating the following words out of my mouth. I fought back tears and the emotions burning a hole in my throat and instead gave him the Amalia Montesinos that ate men for breakfast. "There's a reason why you were lied to and kept in the dark all this time." He inched back as I advanced on him. "Yesterday, you got lucky because we know you're not cut out for this life, Giovanni. You'll never be Tony...or Kai. And you'll *never* be like me."

Pain.

His shoulders deflated, and he crumpled in on himself as tears streamed down his face.

"G-good," he stuttered, voice shaky. "Because I don't want to be anything like you. I'm not a monster."

He rushed for the door, bumping into Kai on his way out. Kai could have overheard everything I'd said to my baby brother, but I knew he wouldn't judge me for it. He'd understand my reasons without having to ask. This man just had a way of reading my soul and knowing exactly what I needed. He scooped me up, sat at the edge of the bed, and held me in his lap as I cried.

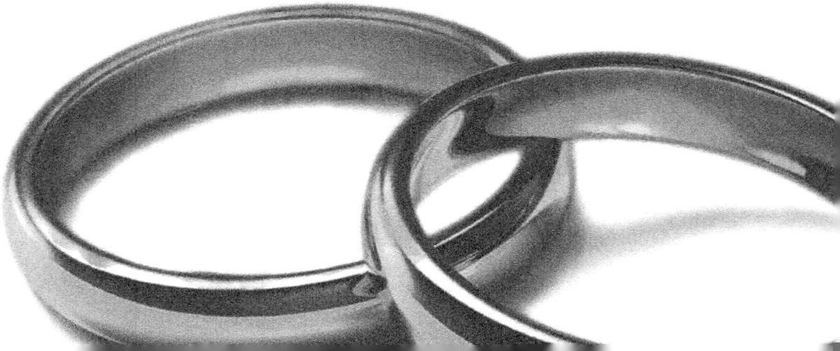

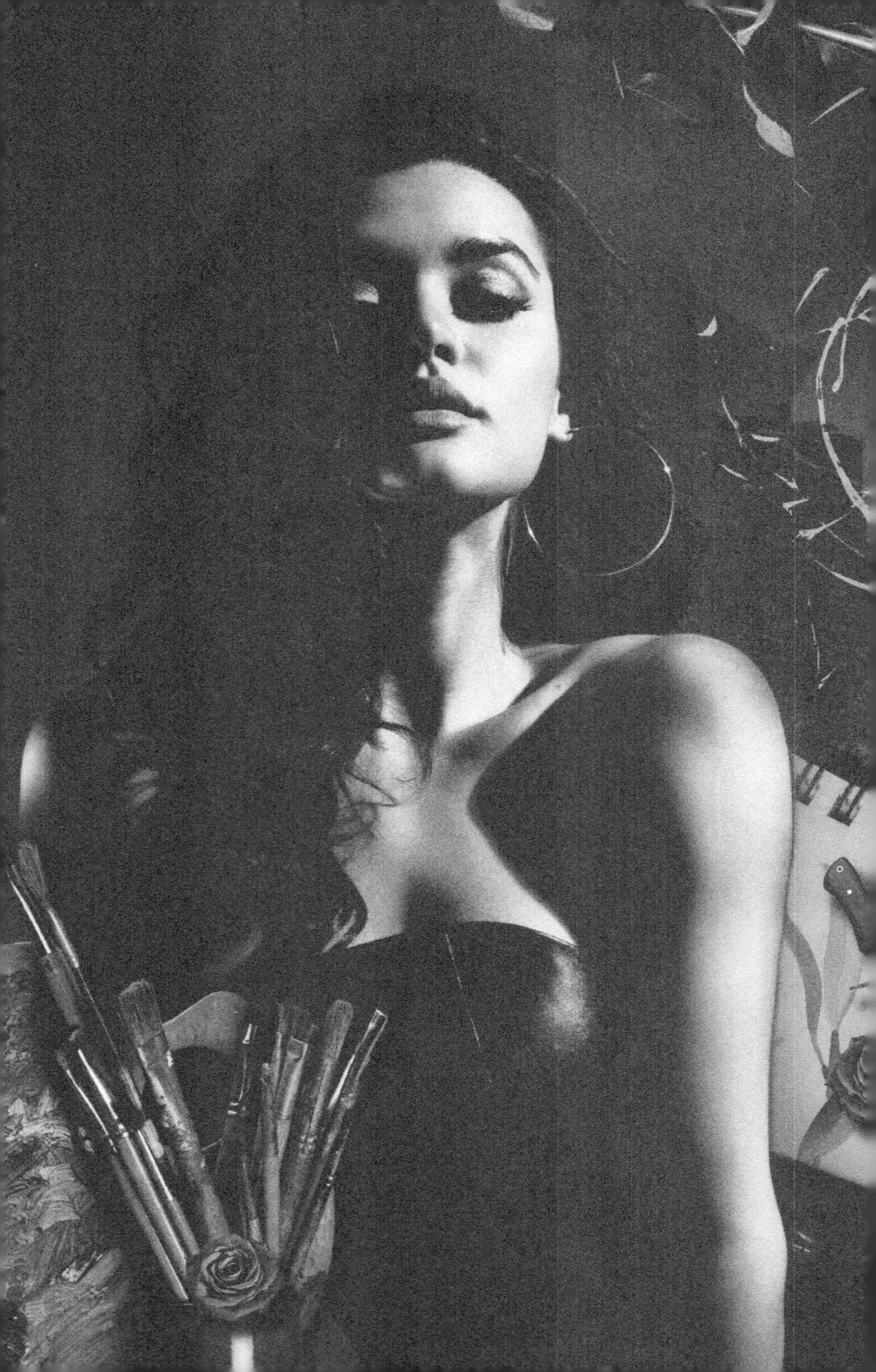

Chapter 35
Amalia

"**WHAT** do you mean, one more week?"

I slammed my paint palette and brush on the wooden table and began to pace as my mother threw excuse after excuse about why she and my father couldn't leave their impromptu trip to Brazil sooner than another six days. It had been nearly two weeks since Gio and I had fallen out. He wasn't speaking to me, and I was giving him space and time to sort out his feelings and forgive me. I knew all I had to do was apologize and tell him that I didn't mean what I'd said. That I'd intentionally hurt him and played on his insecurities because I wanted him to go back home where he'd be safer. But it was better this way. He'd move on and forgive me one day.

He always did.

"You're being hysterical for nothing, *mija*," she said, dismissing my concerns. "It's been two weeks, and things have calmed down, no? Rocco is gone. Anything else, you can handle."

"That's not the point," I gritted out.

"If anything, have him stay with Holly— Listen, I have to go. We'll be in touch. I love you." My mother hung up in a hurry before I could respond.

Placing my hand on my hips, I stared at my phone's black screen, contemplating her words. Maybe she was right, and I was just overthinking. What's another week? Holly had her own thing going on.

Since Rocco's death, she'd been quiet and somewhat secluded herself. In the days that followed, I was reminded of her feelings for him. She tried to remain strong in front of me, unwilling to diminish the pain and trauma I'd gone through at his hands.

A light knock at the door saw me lift my head, and a smile instantly formed on my face at the sight of a shirtless Kai stepping through the threshold with a lunch tray in hand.

I wasn't a stranger to the leering eyes and words of men, but from Kai, the way he took me in, gaze sweeping over me from head to toe, eyes darkened—with no panties as a barrier, I felt the slickness of my arousal between my thighs.

He crept closer, and set down the food and pounced, sliding his arms down my ass and lifting me onto his waist.

"You spoil me, Cain. Lunch on the go. Are you planning a picnic?"

Pressing slow kisses to my jaw, he worked his way down my throat. "You wait for me, looking like that, and somehow you think there's anything else on my mind besides me touching you…" I tipped my head back as his tongue swept back up and over my chin. "Tasting you." His fingers tangled into my hair close to the scalp, just enough to sting so damn good. "Fuck you and make you mine."

There existed a special sense of peace when I painted, wearing nothing but skin and creativity. My staff and family already knew never to enter my studio while I was at work. Kai was obviously the exception, and the reason I kept the doors unlocked these days.

"Did you come to eat or watch me work?"

He chuckled darkly over my lips. "I came to fucking eat."

"Don't let me stop you," I whispered, squeezing my legs tighter around his waist.

He kissed me and set me on the table, but his expression suddenly shifted, and I was perplexed.

"But first, tell me what's going on with your parents and Gio that's got you throwing things around," he said, eyeing the palette and brush on the floor by his feet.

I groaned and laid back on the table, giving him an eyeful of my wet pussy in the hopes he'd shut up and fuck me.

My eyes were closed when I heard him sigh and felt his hand squeeze my thigh, and I knew I wasn't making things easy.

Good.

"So what's another few days? He's fine. We're fine."

"Kai, remember what I told you once? You don't get wealthy from blood money without making enemies…or friends who become enemies because they covet what you have. You and I are one thing, but I won't chance my brother and what's left of who he was before this trip."

"Amalia," he said sternly, tone serious, as he pulled me back into a sitting position. "He's already killed a man. That first time changes something in all of us. You can't just send him away, not without clearing the air." He scooted me forward by the back of my knees. "Think about it. In the meantime…"

Goosebumps rippled across my skin when his lips grazed below my navel and journeyed between my thighs. He pressed a kiss to my pussy. "You've been in here for hours. I miss you, *mi reina*." When Kai's tongue split me open, I leaned on my elbows and let my head fall back as waves of sweet pleasure swept through my body. It was exactly what I needed.

"Yes," I moaned softly, closing my eyes and slowly lying flat while he continued feasting. My fingers were in his hair, tugging and smoothing as I called out his name. Kai knew exactly what to do, how long and where I needed him as if he'd memorized every whimper, how fast and slow I rode his face, and how hard or soft I gripped his hair depending on where I craved him most.

No sex clause.

I almost laughed out loud at the errant thought, how ridiculous I'd acted, and what I would have missed out on had I passed up on this man and his skilled tongue.

My thighs clamped closed around his head as I reached my climax. But he pushed them open, burying his face deeper, fingers digging into my skin as I fought to wriggle free.

Kai glanced up, his lips and chin glistening with my cum, and he grinned with malice. "My wife forgets that I own this sweet pussy, and that I decide when I'm done."

"Fuck…Kai," I groaned, punching the table as he suctioned my sensitive clit and had me stuttering. "Just wait." I panted through every stroke and thrust of his tongue.

We played this game of delicious torture every chance we got, and while I felt I would disintegrate or combust from another brush of pleasure, I loved every goddamn second.

"No…no…I can't," I whined. Scooting up the table, he followed mercilessly until I cried out his name and arched off the wood, coming so fucking hard I thought I would pass out.

My head hung off the edge on the opposite side, but I didn't have the strength to move. I wasn't even sure the rest of my body was still attached. I was floating.

Kai gently dragged me down and rested his head over my trembling belly. He was quiet for longer than usual. And I was eager to return the favor, but he seemed pensive, lost inside his head.

"Kai, what's the matter? Cat got your tongue?"

He looked up at me then and laughed. "How original."

"I thought so."

He quieted a second time, and used his forefinger to trace tender circles on my skin. Again, his blue eyes were fixed on whatever it was he was seeing inside his thoughts.

"You know," he finally said, "I never understood the way my brother looks at his wife. Like he sees the whole world in this one person." Kai stood up and held my face. His eyes were so intense that I felt him in my soul. "Until you."

I thought I felt my heart stop then thunder back to life. "And what do you see when you look at me?"

He leaned in and kissed me gently before reaching over and dipping his finger in the blue paint from my palette. With a blissful smile and a million words left unspoken, he drew a heart just below my belly button. "What do I see when I look at you? Everything."

"Everything…" I whispered back, my hand now over the blue heart.

"All of it."

I arched up and kissed him. "Can I ask you something?"

"Of course."

Reaching for the paint, I asked, "Is this mine?" As I drew a heart on his chest.

"Fuck, it's yours. All yours." It was as if we couldn't kiss each other deep enough to convey everything we were feeling.

It was desperate, turbulent—*beautiful.*

I clawed at his belt, craving to be full and utterly drunk with this man. His pants hit the floor, and he stepped out of them and tugged me off the table until my legs circled his waist. We stumbled into the easel, then back again against the table, knocking over the palette before accidentally stepping on it and slipping. Crumpling to the floor in fits of laughter, I trailed my hand through every color. Kai's eyes widened when he saw my intentions.

"You wouldn't."

He'd barely finished his sentence when I smeared more paint on his chest and shoulders. "Oh, yes, I would," I whispered in his ear, grinding my pussy against his thigh.

"Can I ask *you* something?" Kai dipped his hand in the paint and brought it to my chest, but before he could say another word, I adjusted myself, his cock at my entrance, and let my body fall, closing my eyes as he stretched me so damn good.

"You have it, Kai. It's yours," I murmured, my hand over his where it was pressed to my chest. "I'm yours."

He slammed his mouth so fiercely into mine it was nearly painful, but the unrivaled pleasure buzzing through my body only amplified every sensation in the best way.

"I'm keeping you," he whispered, taking one of my bouncing nipples between his teeth. I hissed at the pain and arched forward when he took those long pulls that made my toes curl.

"I know," I replied in short, breathy pants as I held his shoulders and rode him.

The paint made our bodies slick and messier the harder we fucked and rolled around the floor. I couldn't remember if it was the non-toxic stuff, but I licked him regardless, and he did the same.

"You're so goddamn beautiful," he said when he flipped me over and drove into me from behind as his painted hands smoothed over my ass. I clawed at the floor while on my hands and knees, trying to keep upright but failing miserably with each one of his frenzied thrusts. My hands were too slippery, and my upper body collapsed. "I wish you could see how gorgeous you look while I fuck you." He squeezed my hip and slammed into me with more force, jutting me forward. "And how perfectly your tight little pussy swallows my cock."

As if realizing there was a mirror across the way from us, he fisted my hair and tugged me back on all fours. "Look at yourself, baby. You were made to be mine."

Our eyes found each other in the reflection, and he flashed me a wicked grin, slowing his movements. He was lucky I really fucking liked him, or else I might have been inclined to stab him with the business end of a paintbrush.

"Kai, if you don't fuck me, I'm going to—"

Releasing my hair, he reached around to stroke my clit until my thighs felt weak.

"Beg…"

"Kai, please. Don't make me kill you."

He chuckled and drove back inside me until neither of us could speak. I clenched around his cock and broke with a soft cry. Kai followed soon after, his grip on my flesh painful as he spent every drop.

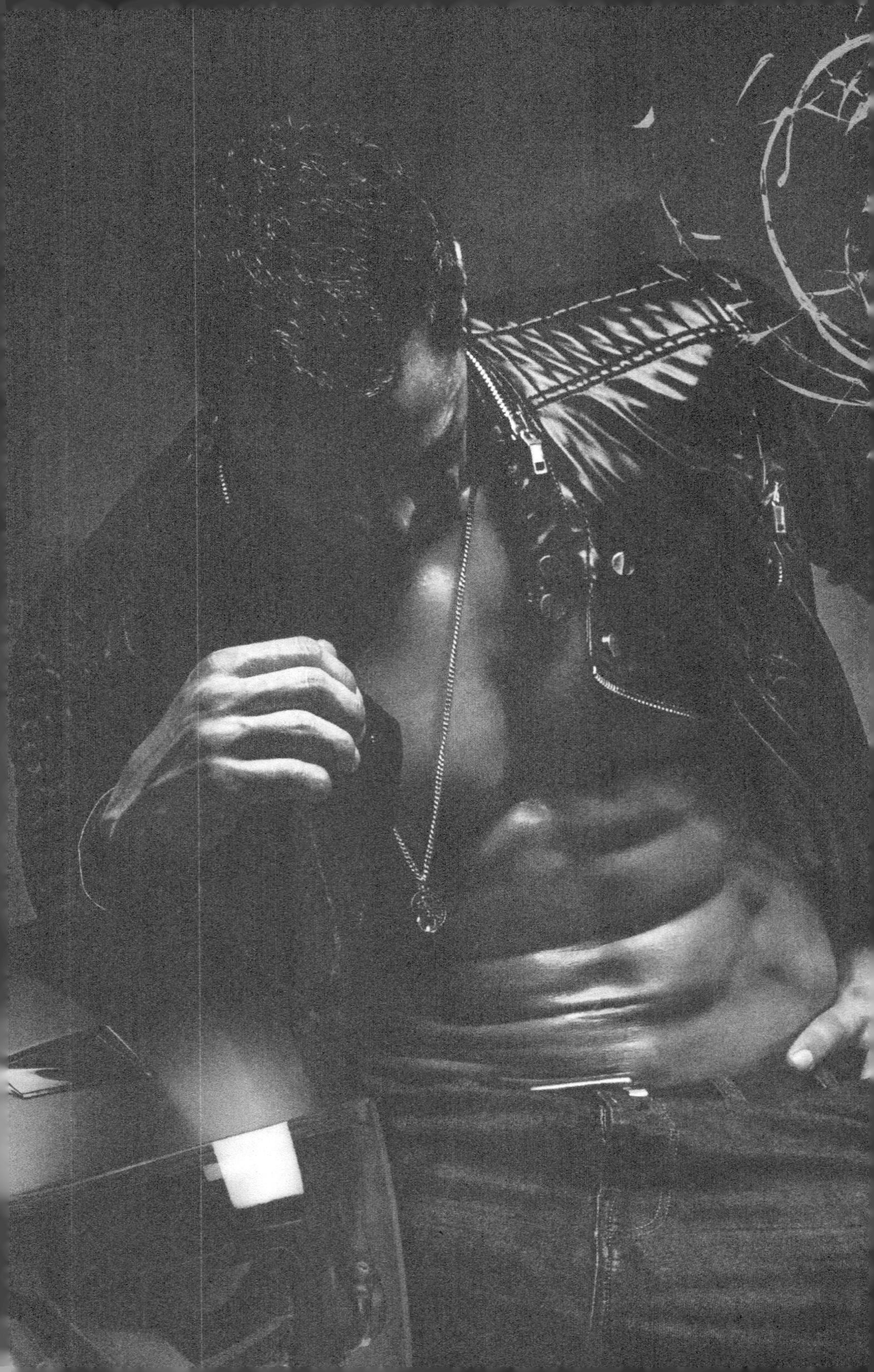

Chapter 36
Kai

"**I'm** glad you got your bike back."

I peered over my seat from where I was crouched and polishing a rim, catching the sight of Gio sitting on the steps, his elbows resting over his knees. I waited for him to return eye contact, but his gaze was downcast.

"That's the most you've spoken to me for nearly two weeks."

"Yeah, well, you're in love with my sister, so I know you'd take her side no matter what."

I chose to address the first part of his statement at a later time. "So I don't get a say? I thought we were friends, kid."

"Stop calling me kid," he said, finally meeting my eyes. His bravado instantly wavered. "Please," he added in a softer tone.

"Okay, Gio. I get that you fought with Amalia, and you're upset, but that doesn't mean your issue is with me."

He shrugged. "I just want to go home."

I set the rag on my seat and joined him on the steps. "Your sister is working on that. But either way, I know neither of you wants to say goodbye on bad terms."

"Tell her that. She's the one who needs to apologize." This conversation wasn't exactly going the way I'd hoped. "Kai, do you think she's right? What she said. I know you heard us, and even if you didn't, I know she told you."

I sighed and leaned back on my hands. "I think she cares about you and wants a different life for you than all this. That's really all there is to it."

He remained quiet, lost in thought.

There wasn't a doubt in my mind that he and Amalia would work through whatever this was, so I decided not to press. Pushing to my feet, I walked back toward Gloria, happy to be able to ride again, and climbed on the seat, eager to hear her purr for me.

"Do you, Kai? Do you love my sister?" he asked as I turned the ignition.

His direct question caught me off guard. Amalia and I had moments of deep connection, of admissions and revelations about our feelings for each other, but those three words had yet to be spoken out loud. I felt her in my heart, buried so deeply that I knew it was her home. I didn't need months or years to understand what she meant to me and represented in my life or that she was the only woman I saw when I closed my eyes and envisioned a future.

"Even if you don't want to answer, I know. I saw what you did for her that day."

"I'm sorry you had to see that."

"I'm not." Gio approached me. "Kai, would you do anything for her?"

I whistled a breath. "You're just full of questions today, aren't you?"

"Well?"

Gio wasn't ready to hear the lengths I would go to for Amalia.

Putting a hand on his shoulder, I nodded. "I would."

He grabbed my arms and attempted to shake me. "Then save her, Kai. Save her from herself. Take her away from here."

"Gio, you know who I am. What I do."

He squared his shoulders. "So stop. Sever your ties like your brother."

"How the hell do you know about Derek?"

"That's not important."

"Kid," I huffed.

"Gio."

"*Gio*, it's not that simple."

He clenched his jaw and swallowed hard. "You're all hypocrites."

Without another word, he stormed up the steps. On his way inside, he shoved past Amalia and Holly and quickly disappeared.

"He's still upset with you?" Holly asked.

"Seems that way." Amalia climbed on my bike, straddling the seat and looping her arms around my neck. "He'll get over it eventually," she said with a tinge of sadness. I brought her closer so that her thighs rested on mine.

"Would you mind if I took him out for a bit? Maybe a movie, dinner. It'll help us both clear our heads."

Amalia seemed to contemplate the idea for a beat, then smiled at her friend and nodded. "Maybe that's exactly what he needs. He's been cooped up here for two weeks. Surrounded by everything that's upsetting him, including me."

"I know that feeling…of feeling suffocated and trapped while holding a grudge. That shit will wear on someone."

I could only assume she was talking about Rocco. I knew of her feelings for that bastard, and it never occurred to me that a part of her could resent his death. But she also loved Amalia, so I could see how her feelings were conflicted.

"I'll call you as soon as we get there."

"Thank you, Hols."

"Of course, babes. See you two lovebirds later."

"How is she holding up?" I asked when she was gone.

"Better. She made it through our meeting and was mostly herself."

I scooped Amalia closer until her ass was in my lap. "You're back early today," I said, preferring to switch the subject.

"It went a lot smoother than I thought. Some things are still up in the air as far as filling in the void Rocco and his men left. No one knows what really happened. They just care that he's dead."

I leaned forward and kissed her as I reached for the handles. "How about we forget all of that and go for a ride."

"Mmm, that sounds like a good idea. Where's my helmet?"

"Your helmet?"

"Yes, mine."

"Fuck, yes," I said, my arm wrapped around her lower back as I revved the engine. "But you're going to stay right here."

"You want me to ride like this?"

"You can ride me any way you want to, vicious. But right now, I want you just like this."

I retrieved her helmet and quickly jogged back, unable to hide the smile on my face, when I realized Amalia hadn't moved. She'd waited for me exactly as I told her, and the fact that she trusted me to care for her caused heat to build in my chest.

"We're just going to take a little spin around the property. I wouldn't risk your safety out on the road like this," I said, adjusting her helmet and pulling her close by the mouthpiece. I pressed a kiss to the top of the helmet and gently tapped it. "Ready?"

"Always."

I took her slow at first, noting Amalia's death grip on my arms.

"If I fall, I kill you."

I laughed and gripped her hip. "Relax, baby. You trust me, right?"

"You know I do."

"Then you know I'd never let you fall."

Villa Dorada was an extensive property with acres of land and dirt roads. I knew she rarely visited these parts, but I wanted to teach her how to ride out here. I'd never been interested in having someone to share this hobby with until her. It was almost scary how much I wanted her to be a part of every facet of my life.

"Hold on. I'm going to open up a little here."

She crossed her arms behind my neck. "Is this okay?"

"Do you want me to teach you how to ride?"

"I'm two steps ahead of you, Cain. I'm having two delivered on Monday."

"Two?" I asked with a laugh.

"I couldn't decide. But I already have names picked out—Christian and Carlo. Twins."

I knew Amalia had a past. She wasn't a virgin when I met her, but as irrational as it was, I wanted to slit the throats of fucking Christian and Carlo.

"I know you're enjoying all the questions I haven't even asked yet."

She tipped her head back and laughed. "And I know what you're thinking, and not that I haven't been there because I'm not ashamed"—I knew she could feel how my body tensed with her admission—"but…I totally just made up those names to mess with you."

"Vicious."

She squealed and squeezed her legs around my torso when I gunned it.

It was just after sunset when we arrived back home. We'd spent the evening by a lake, talked, fucked, and talked some more until the rumbling in both our stomachs was too loud to keep ignoring. Opting to store the bike away later, I parked it near the front entrance.

The moment we stepped through the door, the smell of Milly's latest masterpiece hit our noses, and neither of us said a word as we made a mad dash to the dining room.

Amalia's cell phone buzzed in her pocket, and I saw the conflict on her face.

"Call them back later."

The buzzing was relentless until she gave in and reached for it, immediately answering when she saw Holly's name on the screen.

"Holly?"

She sounded fearful as if she knew that whatever news she received on the other end of that call would drastically change things.

"Amalia...they're all dead."

She gripped the phone with both hands, her mouth parted slightly, expression stoic. "Who? Who's dead?"

"The shipment. All of it. Another ambush. They killed the men and stole the guns. They knew the route, Amalia. It doesn't sound like some random hit."

She shook her head slowly, the shock of the news settling in.

"Rocco's men?" I asked.

"I...don't know. I changed the route yesterday. No one had any idea. It doesn't add up. Fuck!"

Amalia broke into a sprint and ran down the hallway.

"Hey, where are you going?"

"To end this."

"Amalia, wait."

She kept moving faster until I realized she was far from me and heading toward the garage. "Amalia!"

By the time I'd crossed through the doors, the Hellcat roared to life, and the garage door had just finished rolling all the way open.

"Amalia, open the door," I demanded, pulling at the handle. She didn't even look my way. "Amalia, open this goddamn door!" The tires screeched when she peeled off and down the driveway. "Shit!" Running as fast as I could through the open garage on foot, I reached my bike and took off after her.

I called her three times and was sent to voicemail. But I wouldn't stop until she listened to reason.

"You have two seconds," she hedged, finally picking up.

"Amalia, stop this. It's a goddamn suicide mission, and you know it."

"Time's up."

"Don't you dare hang up this call." Silence. "Listen to me. We can do this. We can do whatever you want, but we do it together. As a team. You, me, your girls. They don't stand a chance. But not like this. Not alone."

"No." The call dropped.

She was weaving in and out of traffic, driving erratically and nearly wrecking.

Fuck.

I called another three times. The fourth was the charm because she picked up but said nothing. "Listen to me, *mi reina*, please. You can't be this impulsive. It will get you killed, and so will your driving."

Her laugh was cynical and cold. "You're criticizing the way I drive right now."

"Amalia, I'm right behind you. You're going to get us both killed, either here on the goddamn highway or by Rocco's men."

"Go home, Kai."

"Do you hear yourself? You think I'm going to turn around and let you go out guns blazing? Is that what you want to do?"

She accelerated, passing a truck and nearly crashing head-on with a pickup but dodged death at the very last second.

"Amalia, when I fucking catch up to you, that ass is mine." The line went dead, and she sped up, zooming past a red light. I tried to follow, but a caravan of five or six cars blocked my way. I had to slow down and go around them, dodging two more cars. Horns blared, and obscenities flew. I'd lost her, and I suddenly had to make a split-second decision as there was an exit less than five hundred feet in front of me.

Shit.

I veered right and gunned it as soon as I came off the curve, and my stomach felt like it collapsed to my feet when I saw her car halfway in a ditch. "No, no, no."

Hopping off the bike, I darted toward the upturned vehicle, frantically calling her name as I ripped off my helmet and used it to shatter the driver's side window. There was no movement, no sounds, and I didn't see her anywhere. Blood thundered past my ears so loudly I could barely hear my thoughts.

"Amalia!" Fear seized my heart when I realized she wasn't in her car. Had she been thrown? I whipped my head around, and that's when I caught sight of her stumbling down the side of the road.

I called her as I ran, but she didn't turn or acknowledge me until I gripped her arm and whirled her around. Her first instinct was to fight me off, and I feared she'd hit her head and was disoriented.

"Baby, stop. Look at me. It's me. Are you okay?"

"I'm fine. Let me go!" she shouted, not looking at me.

"I'm not going to do that." I patted her down, searching every area of exposed skin for blood or apparent injuries, and a heavy breath left my body when it was obvious she'd walked away unscathed. "Amalia, I feel like I'm having a heart attack right now. Please, stop."

"I told you I'm fine." She shoved out of my arms and stormed down an embankment.

"You're not walking out here like this. Let's go."

"I'm fine," she said again, grating on my last nerve.

"Amalia, get on the bike."

"I need to walk. I need to think."

"Amalia, get on the goddamn bike before I make you." The authority in my voice made her hesitate for just a moment.

"Fuck off. I said I need to walk."

Left with no other option, I scooped her up and threw her body over my shoulder.

"You son of a bitch. Let me down!" she yelled, pounding on my back.

No sooner had I sat her on my bike than I felt the sting of a slap connect with the side of my face. I gripped her throat and slammed my mouth into hers, snuffing out my anger. Amalia attempted to pull away for the first few seconds, but then seemed to melt into my chest. I held her face and pulled back just enough to gaze into her eyes.

"I'm not the enemy," I whispered, kissing her again, softer this time. "Please, stop for a second and think. You know this is reckless—all of it. Just like you know, I'd never let you go on this crazy-ass mission alone. So you and I will die together tonight or plan this out properly. Either way, it's me and you. Always."

She fisted my shirt and rested her forehead on my chin, her soft cries cutting deep. Every word I'd said was heartfelt. I would die for this woman, just as I would kill for her.

"Tell me what you want, and we'll do it. If we have to take out every last one of them, I'm there."

She finally looked up at me, blinking away tears. "Sometimes, I don't deserve you, Kai."

Dipping my head, I smiled and dropped another kiss on her lips. "You're right. You deserve so much better, baby. But it's too late because you're mine. Till death, and I'm a man of my word."

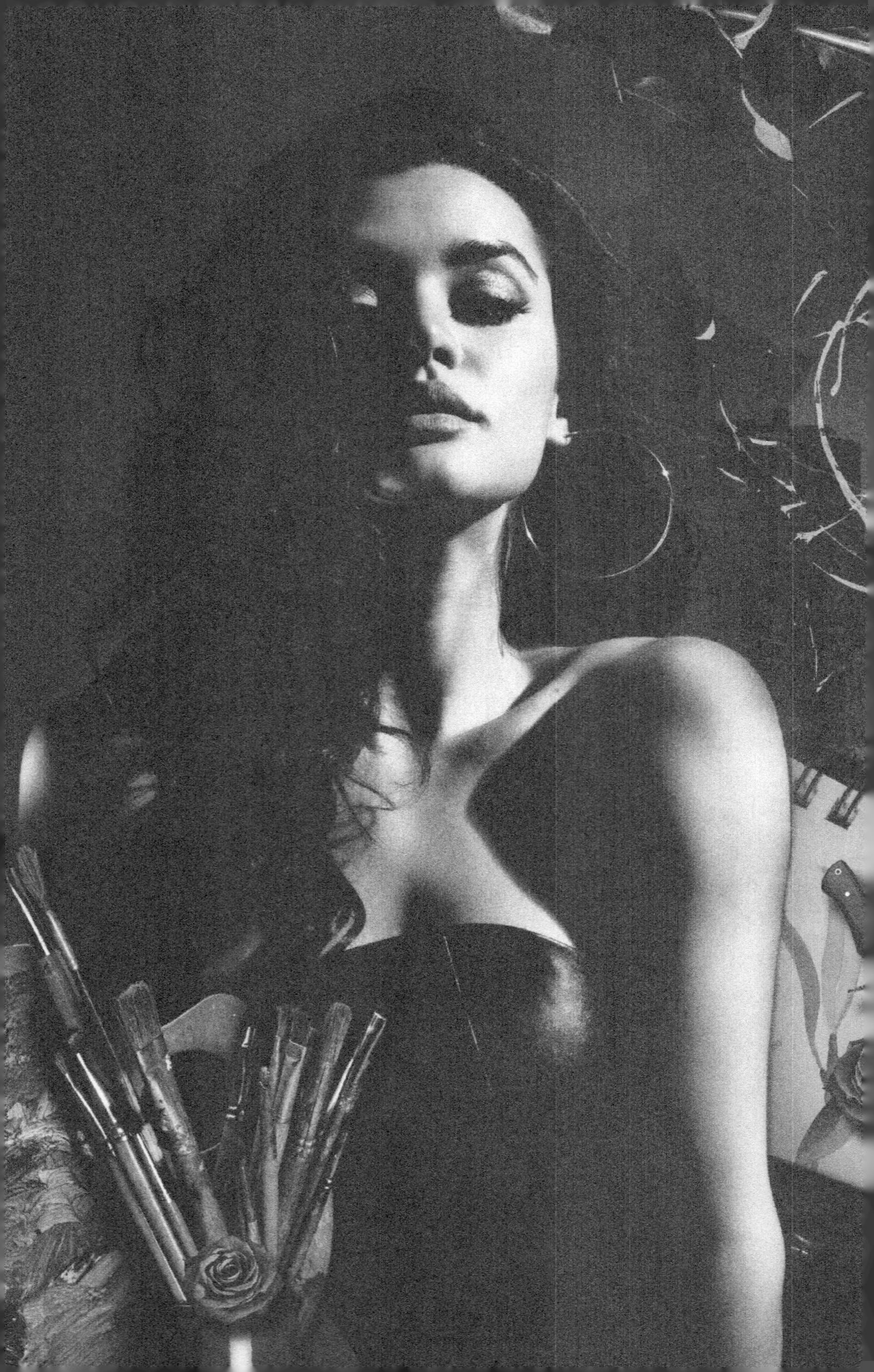

Chapter 37
Amalia

WHEN Kai cut the bike's engine, I didn't let go. Now that the world was quiet and it was just me and him, he let me hold him and listen to the sound of his heart. Guilt ate away at me as I thought of how rash and reckless I'd been, putting not only my life in danger but his as well.

"I'm sorry."

His hand came up over mine. "Yeah, well, I told you that if I caught up to you, that ass would be mine. And it's time to pay up, Mrs. Cain."

My laughter shook us both. "I guess it's only fair. Do I get a say?"

Kai climbed off the bike, and with one quick tug, I was over his shoulder again. "Nah, tonight you're going to be my little cum bucket. All holes are game," he said, slapping my ass as my core clenched. "Tomorrow, we'll talk and call in a tow truck—that is, if your car survives the night."

"It has a tracker, and house calls are my favorite."

Kai's grip on my legs suddenly tightened, and I waited for him to say something, but he just stood there. "Kai?" His hold slackened, and he set me down and quickly pulled his gun, racking it back. Without question, I did the same and aimed down his line of fire. But when my eyes caught up with my actions, I felt my soul leave my body.

"Holly?" Lowering my weapon, I stepped forward, but Kai's arm shot out and held me back.

"Hold on," he gritted out, eyes scanning down the drive.

Holly walked toward us, a slight limp in her step, face and arms bloodied. My breaths suddenly felt labored, my stomach hollowing out when I realized it was just Holly—injured, beaten, and covered in blood...and alone without my baby brother.

"Gio," I whispered. I took off down the driveway, Kai on my heels. Holly was hyperventilating, speaking too fast for me to understand what the fuck she was saying. "Where is he?" I asked, shaking her violently.

"I—I don't know. We stopped for ice cream, and a group of men rolled up on us, Amalia. There were too many. I tried...but they took him. They knew who he was."

She was speaking, and I understood every word that came out of her mouth, but it felt like an out-of-body experience because it couldn't be true—not my brother.

"Holly, who took him?" My voice was strained as hot, wild rage burned through me.

"I didn't recognize them. I'm sorry."

"Fuck!" I paced back and forth, cursing and trying to devise a plan of action.

"I'll make some calls." Kai touched my arm, momentarily anchoring my sanity. He pulled out his cell and started to dial when his phone chimed, indicating a text message. No name was attached to the bright text box, just a number. His brow furrowed, and just as he intended to open the message, my phone vibrated in my pocket, quickly followed by Holly's musical ringtone. All three of us had been contacted by the same number. My throat felt constricted as I tried to breathe and compose myself.

> 5436 W. Campbell Dr
> $5 mil
> Midnight

Ransom. Someone had taken my brother for ransom. Kidnappings were common in this business, but somehow, it was hard to believe that this was my reality. After everything…something wasn't right.

"I don't believe this."

"We're on the same page," Kai said, staring at his phone as if trying to piece it together. The timing and everything leading up to this were all too much of a coincidence.

"We have three hours. Someone dies in three hours, and it won't be Gio. Holly, get the team together. You stay here with Milly—"

"No fucking way. I'm going. They fucked me up, took Gio. Fuck that. I need my pound of flesh."

"You're hurt, which means you're also a liability."

Kai and I moved like a synchronized team toward the armory below the garage.

"That's bullshit, Amalia. I'm not sitting this out like some scared little bitch. Gio is like my brother, too."

I stopped abruptly, and Holly would have plowed into me if Kai hadn't steadied her.

"Holly, look at you."

"They're just flesh wounds. Nothing I haven't experienced before." She was stone-faced, determined. "I'm not letting you do this alone. I'll phone the team, you get the goods. They'll be expecting us. But hopefully, they're truly just after the money." Holly was punching messages into her phone. "Can you move $5 mil in the next hour?"

"I can have it in the next fifteen fucking minutes, but they don't want money. We both know that."

I slung a black duffel bag over my shoulder. Two hours and twenty-five minutes. Every second that ticked by was like another closer to my brother's possible death. I exhaled shakily, feeling as though I was coming undone at the seams. Steadying myself, I gripped the table's edge and hung my head as I attempted not to break down. Gio needed me more than ever. If someone were dying today, it would be me, not him.

"Till death, *mi reina*." Kai's arms wound around me, and he kissed the back of my head and whispered, "I love you."

My breath hitched, and I whirled around to face him. "Kai, I—" He put a finger to my lips. "Whatever happens tonight, I want you to know that meeting you, being with you, wasn't just by chance, Amalia. The road that led me here, every broken piece of my life, brought me to you, and I wouldn't change a damn thing. You're mine. You were always meant to be mine. I love you, and no matter how this night ends, somewhere, somehow, you and I will find each other again. I promise."

"Kai," I murmured, my voice breaking along with my heart. "Why does it feel like you're saying goodbye?"

He tilted my chin and kissed the tear sliding down my cheek.

"I need you to promise me something," he said, hoisting me up so that we were at eye level.

"No, absolutely not. I can already sense what you'll say, and my answer is no. I'm not leaving you behind."

"If you can make it out with Gio, you need to do it."

"Kai, stop it. That's not how this goes down."

He gritted his teeth. "We have to be prepared for every scenario. You know that better than anyone. And you're the only person who matters to me. You and Gio…" Squeezing me tighter, he kissed me hard. "I need you to be okay."

His voice shook. I'd never seen him cry, and it tore me open. This beautiful man was everything I never knew I needed in life. Holding the sides of his face, I gazed into his gorgeous eyes and offered him a watery smile. "We're going to be okay. We're going to wake up tomorrow, and you're going to put that big, beautiful cock inside your wife until I can't walk straight."

Kai laughed as I wiped his tears. "Are you ready?"

"Always."

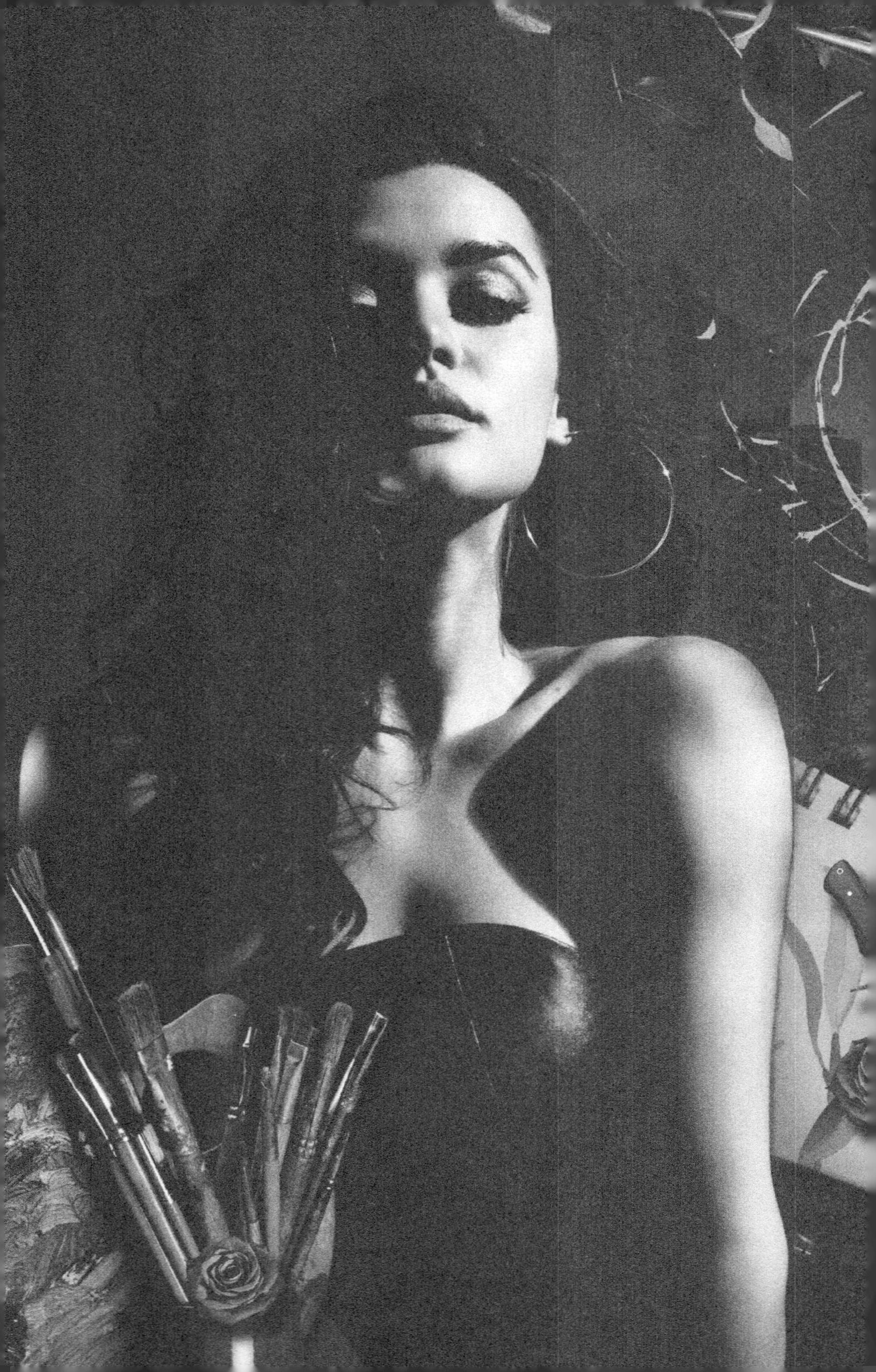

Chapter 38
Amalia

"**WHY** aren't they here yet?"

I glanced at my phone, expecting to see a confirmation of arrival text from one of my girls, but the silence was glaring. "Holly, did Gabi confirm with you?"

"She did, but I told them to hang back. Out of sight."

I nodded and peered across the dark lot and into the abandoned warehouse where they were supposedly holding Gio.

"So what would stop them from picking us off from this position and taking the money?" Kai questioned, his eyes fixed on the blown-out windows and rooftop of the building.

"Took care of that. I offered them half now and the rest through a wire transfer once we have Gio. They extorted another $5 mil from me, but I'd gladly pay whatever it takes to get my brother back."

Holly stretched out a hand and squeezed mine. "I'm so sorry. I feel like all of this is my fault. I should have done more." Her mouth quivered with emotion, and I pulled her into a hug.

"There's nothing more you could have done. You were outgunned and outnumbered. I'm just glad you're safe."

She blew out a heavy breath. "Okay, let's do this."

Kai took the duffel from me and hooked it on his shoulder, holding my hand as we made our way to an entrance on the side of the building, per our instructions. I jerked a glance across the parking lot one last time, hoping to catch a glimpse or signal from Gabi or one of my other girls. They were our muscle, as we weren't allowed firearms. But I trusted Holly's word. She was my right-hand for a reason, and if she said they were here, I knew they were doing exactly as they should—staying out of sight.

Kai didn't release his hold on me as we moved through a dark hallway, illuminated only by flickering emergency lights. The air was damp and smelled of mold and something that had possibly been alive at one point. The thought filled me with dread, although I knew it couldn't possibly be Gio, as it had only been a few hours since he'd been taken.

A slight sense of relief washed over me. He was alive; at least, that's what I prayed for. I'd never forgive myself, especially after everything I said to him, the days since I'd hugged him and seen his smile. I'd been so stupid and wasted so much time letting him stew in his anger and resentment because I thought it was what was best for him. But if anyone knew how fragile life was, it should have been me. I had stared into the faces of dying men more times than anyone should in one lifetime. Maybe this was my karma.

The bill was due.

We took a stairway up to the third-floor landing and through double doors with shattered glass windows.

"Remember what I said," Kai whispered, squeezing my hand. I said nothing because there was no point in lying. While I'd do everything possible to get Gio out, I'd never leave my husband behind. Part of me regretted not telling him that I loved him because the way my heart aches for him can only be love. I hoped I'd get another chance to make things right.

The closer we got to our destination, the more pungent the smell. It was unmistakable: blood in various stages of decomposition. It was clear this was a spot they frequented and used for ransom, torture and, subsequently, murder.

Kai pushed open the door and placed himself in front of me and between the two men on the far side of the room. They were very similar in appearance, almost as if they were related—all about the same height and build, with dark facial hair. I swept the room, and panic set in when I didn't see my brother.

"Where is he?"

The man on the right chuckled, making me want to put holes in his face.

"Easy. Let's see the cash first. And maybe I'll bring that little bitch up here."

"Maybe? Fuck that, we had a deal."

The other man joined in on the laughter. "You got quite the mouth on you, don't you?" he added with a leering smirk. "I'd like to teach you how—"

"Careful. You disrespect my wife, I take your tongue."

More laughter filled the dimly lit space, echoing off the walls. "You know what, since I'm in a good mood because we're getting paid today, I'm gonna let that slide. But one more threat out of you, and we'll see who starts losing body parts."

"Where is he?" I questioned again.

One man signaled to the other, ushering him forward. He stepped off the stage and beckoned Holly toward him.

"No," I protested, gripping her arm.

"We need to make sure you're not armed. So you either come here or strip. Your choice—or I can make it mine."

Holly widened her eyes, pleading with me to comply. My glare shifted back to the men, and I took a deep breath and clenched my teeth as I lifted my shirt and tossed it to the floor before shedding my shoes and pants. I'd never wanted to kill anyone more. My hands buzzed for it.

Kai's breaths were hard and fast, fists clenched at his sides. He hated that I had to strip bare in front of these sons of bitches, but I knew he'd prefer that over the groping they would have done.

"What are you waiting for, pretty boy? Take it off."

I looked up at my husband as he slowly shed his clothing. His eyes were trained on the boldest of the two men, and he stared back with a cunning smile and a wink.

Holly lowered her head and walked forward, allowing the vile man to pat her down and whisper something into her ear. She shuddered, and her eyes found mine as his hands lingered a little too long, moving roughly over parts of her body. She closed her eyes, and I caught the tremble in her lip.

"That's enough." My voice was sharp, causing him to snap his head up and smirk as he forcefully shoved Holly back toward us.

The room grew quiet, making me hyperaware of a glaring detail: We were alone. I felt a hollowing in the pit of my stomach.

No one was coming.

Before I could dwell on that nightmarish reality, soft whines suddenly filled the room, and a third man stepped onto the stage, dragging my brother with him. Out of instinct, I lunged forward, but Kai caught my wrist.

"Easy, baby."

I tried to control my breathing.

Gio was limp. He had swollen eyes and duct tape across his mouth. The bearded man slapped him twice, forcing him to come to and, again, Kai had to hold me back.

"They're dead," I gritted out.

"Agreed."

Gio startled awake, thrashing his body but unable to move as he was bound at the wrists and ankles.

"Gio!"

He froze at my voice and shook his head frantically the moment he saw us. Muffled cries filled the room as he thrashed harder, attempting to reach us in vain.

"Let him go. I have your money. Please."

But Gio wouldn't let up. He was desperate, like he was trying to tell me something.

"What was that?" the man teased, straightening him with a harsh tug. "I can't quite hear you."

He ripped off the tape…

"Amalia! No! She…she did it!"

The words he shouted didn't make sense… And then I felt it, hard steel pressed to my temple.

"Surprise, babe." Holly chuckled and stepped back, putting enough distance between us where she felt comfortable that I wouldn't disarm her.

I never knew what an ice bucket felt like, but I was pretty sure the chill racing through my body in painful waves was reality knocking me hard on my ass and blindsiding me in a way that I would have never seen coming.

Holly. My best friend. My sister. Had a gun pointed at my head.

"You goddamn bitch." Kai took a step toward us, but she steadied her aim.

"If you think you can reach me before I put a bullet in that beautiful face of hers, I invite you to try."

"I'm going to kill you," he threatened, cracking his neck as he stared her down.

Holly scoffed. "I'm sure you are."

"Holly…*why?*" My voice cracked, and I swallowed hard as feelings of nausea churned in my stomach.

"Oh, fuck. Here we go with the twenty-one questions. *Why are you doing this? I thought we were sisters. Please, let us go.* Blah, blah, blah." Her tone was taunting as she paced back and forth, enjoying every second of this reveal—of her betrayal.

That was the moment that hit me hardest. It had been her this whole time—the highway, the meeting, the ambush…my wedding.

Not Rocco.

Gabi and my girls weren't coming.

"I can see the light bulbs in your head going off like fucking Christmas lights. It's hilarious."

"What's wrong with you? Why would you do this? After everything."

"You're so far up your ass that you can't see anything beyond what you want to see. *La reina*," she seethed, rolling her eyes. "I've hated you my whole fucking life. But I had to pretend because my mother shoved you down my throat. And, of course, the man I loved only had eyes for you, as that story always goes. Most importantly, in case you haven't noticed, I'm just a damn psychopath who tortures men for a living. Did you expect any less? It's that simple. I hate you. I have no emotions beyond that."

"You sorry bitch. You're too much of a pussy to confront me, so you orchestrate all of this."

She shrugged and exaggerated a sigh. "I could have killed you so many times, but that would have been too easy, so I killed Tony instead."

Blood rushed to my feet, and I reared back as if she'd sucker-punched me.

"No," I whispered.

"Yes."

Kai wrapped his arms around me, preventing me from lunging toward her. "I'm going to kill you."

"Sure, babe. Like you killed Rocco?" She raised the gun toward

Kai. "You know that saying, an eye for an eye?"

"No! Don't you fucking do it."

Holly's eyes narrowed, her grin malicious as she winked. "Okay."

The gun swung around and pressed to the side of my brother's head, and for a split second, our eyes locked, and so many words and emotions passed between us, but it was gone in the next thunderous beat of my heart.

Pop.

Blood sprayed, and he collapsed.

There are moments in life that flash before our eyes and others that slow and play out like the reel of a movie. This was one of those moments. The movie went silent until there were just echoes. Every movement was agonizing. My voice seemed to remain locked inside my throat, the scream clawing its way out but just out of my reach.

My ears were still ringing long after the world crumbled. Gio's lifeless eyes were fixed beyond me as he lay in a pool of his own blood. There was no bringing him back. I knew that. He was gone. Everything he was. Gone forever.

Rage.

I lifted my teary gaze toward Holly, mouth gaping open. No matter how hard I tried, I couldn't fill my lungs with air.

"Oops," she teased.

I made a split-second decision before Kai could stop me, and Holly could see it coming. I pushed off my feet and lunged for her, determined to tear her apart. Her eyes widened, and she popped a round toward me, and I felt the sting of a bullet somewhere on my body, but I was too fucking high on adrenaline and bloodlust to care.

A hail of gunfire and chaos filled the room, but if I was going to die tonight, I was dragging her to hell with me.

My hand was on her gun, and another bullet shot off behind me as I twisted the barrel and broke her trigger finger, and I didn't stop until it was severed.

It was her turn to utter a soundless scream, but I'd show her no mercy. Two pistol whips to the face left her mouth bloody, fucked up, and missing teeth.

"Does it hurt?" I whispered into her ear as the hot barrel of her own gun singed the inside of her mouth. "I want you to feel the pain I'm feeling. I want you to suffer, to beg me to kill you— And I won't, because you deserve so much more."

Blood and saliva bubbled out of the sides of her mouth as she moaned in agony. I took a quick glance around and saw Kai crouched over one of the men, driving a blade into him repeatedly. Another lay dead on the floor, while the third grabbed the duffel bag and ran out of the room.

"I need you to wait right here for me, okay?" I said, getting to my feet and sending a round in each of her legs. "Kai, are you good?"

He nodded and started for me, but I put a hand up. "She stays alive. She's mine." With that, I was out of the room, catching a glimpse of that bastard as he turned the corner. I ran for the opposite hallway, knowing both paths linked up at the stairwell.

"Pretty sure that belongs to me," I said the moment his hand was on the knob. He thought he'd be faster than me, but he was wrong, and he hit the floor with a bullet to the side of the neck and one in his leg. I crouched next to his still-twitching body and slid open the bag's zipper, pulling out a blade and a pistol. As I stood, he made eye contact with me, hand pressed to the wound in his throat and tears slipping out of the corners of his eyes.

Pathetic.

"Let me help you die with some dignity." By the time the second bullet hit his forehead, he was no longer moving, but I thought I'd send him off with one more for good luck.

Leaving the duffel behind, I set off back to the room to deal with Holly, but in that instant, the memories of Gio barreled into me, and my knees gave out.

"No…no…" My throat spasmed, and I couldn't catch my breath with the vision of his death playing over and over in my thoughts. I hadn't realized when I'd fallen to the floor until Kai's arms surrounded me. He tugged me to his chest and let me have a moment to compose myself before he spoke.

"We can go, or we can do whatever you need. I'm here for you, and I've got Gio. Just say the word."

"She killed him. He's dead, right?" Kai closed his eyes. "Then she dies."

"Agreed." He glanced down at my thigh. "Baby, you've been hit."

I hadn't felt pain until then, but it was nothing compared to the loss tearing my soul apart.

"I don't care."

"Looks superficial."

He helped me to my feet, and I released another long breath, suspending the pain of my brother's death for just that moment and replacing it with hatred.

Holly was dragging herself toward a back door, but I grabbed her ankle and violently slid her back to the middle of the room. She wailed and clawed at the floor.

"Wait…Amalia, please. I'm sorry."

Pathetic.

"You will be."

I looked back at Kai, who had Gio's limp body in his arms, and decided then that I wouldn't drag this out more than it needed to be.

But she wouldn't get off easy either.

A bottle of vodka sat at the edge of the decrepit stage. I snatched it, and by the time I reached Holly and her pathetic attempt at crawling away a second time, Kai had already reached for his lighter and tossed it to me.

Having nothing else to say to her, I poured the liquid over her body, smashed the glass against her face, and flicked the lighter. Her body went up in flames, and she screamed for me, arms stretched out as her skin melted away.

A part of me mourned for her, for the loss of the sister I thought I had. But I snuffed that emotion and walked out of that godforsaken room, Kai behind me. I couldn't turn around. Couldn't look at my brother lifeless in his arms because my legs would give out and I might contemplate running back into the flames for an ounce of mercy.

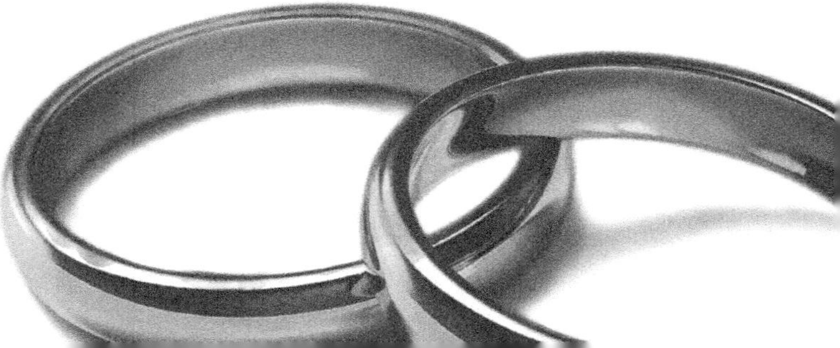

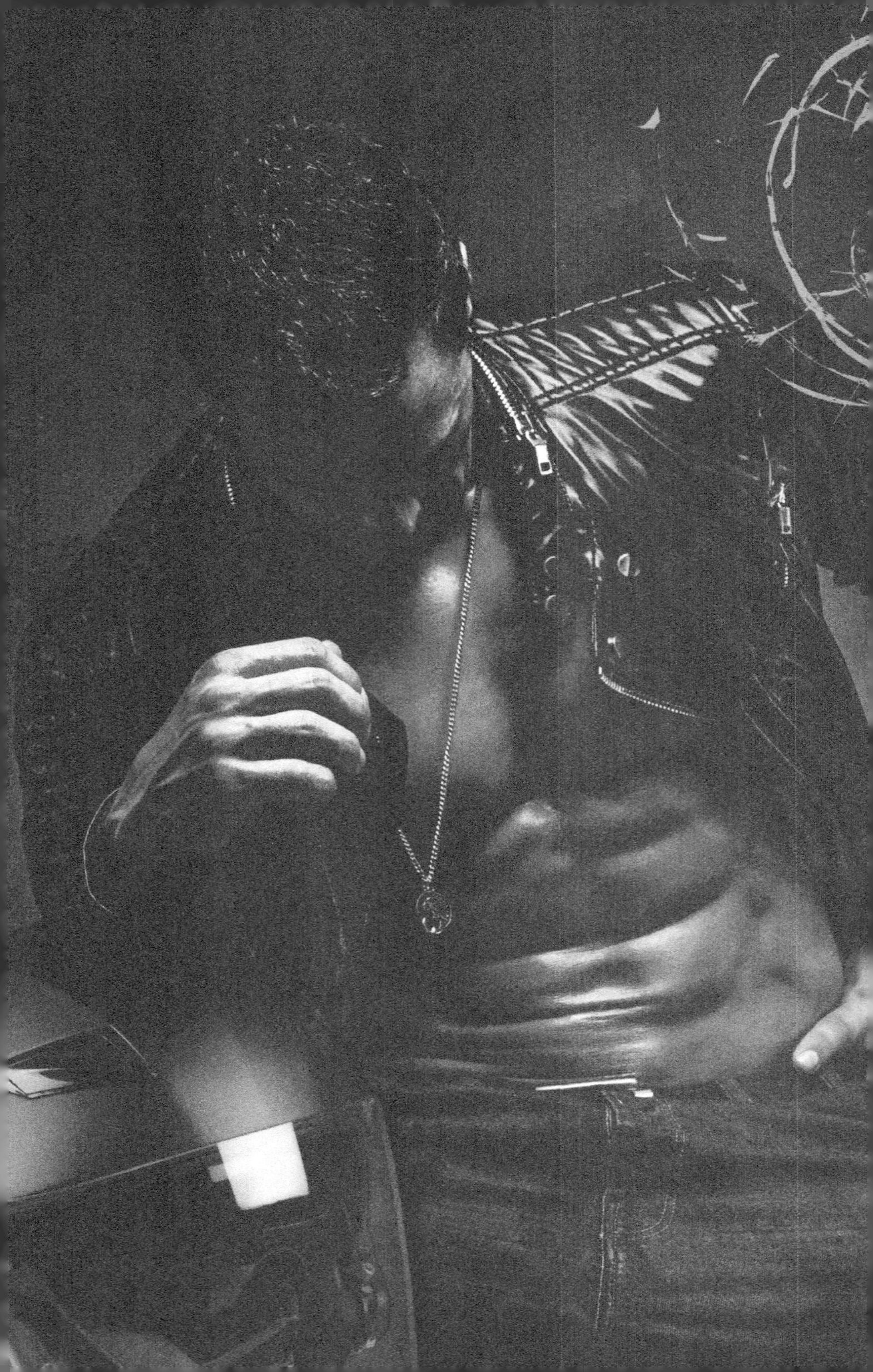

Chapter 39
Kai

One Month Later

WHEN I reached for Amalia this morning, the bed was empty, and her phone was still docked on the nightstand. My first instinct was to panic because the sun was barely halfway into the sky, too early for her to be awake on a Sunday. But I talked myself off the ledge, thinking she might have gone to the bathroom or to get a snack. Anxiety hit me a second time when it was apparent she wasn't home. I'd intended to look for her, but that's when I realized my bike was gone. I didn't know whether to be relieved that I was able to track her or scared shitless because she'd only practiced riding less than a handful of times.

I clocked my bike's location and went after her.

The dewy smell of wet grass filled my senses while the chill of a light rain bit at my exposed skin. I was too desperate to see my wife and make sure she was all right to throw on more than a T-shirt.

Amalia's shoulders stiffened as I approached, though quickly relaxing when I sat behind her and pulled her into my arms. We sat in silence for what seemed like hours, but I was willing to give her all the time she needed.

Nearly a month later, there were still days when she'd wake up screaming from a nightmare, or I'd find her crying in his room. She wasn't just grieving; his death had changed her in subtle ways. Amalia was quieter these days. Life moved slower. There were times she lashed out, trying to drive me away, but she should have known that I wasn't going anywhere.

"How'd you get here?" she asked, her eyes still focused on the endless horizon of headstones.

"Your car. I figure if we're trading, I might as well."

Her chest shook with a faint laugh. "Great. Now I'll have to re-adjust my seat."

"Well, if it makes you feel better, I nearly took out my knees, trying to climb inside in a hurry."

She twisted in my arms. "And why were you in a hurry?"

I clasped my hands behind her, our faces inches apart. "I didn't know where you were. I woke up, you were gone, and you left your phone—you can't do that to me. Not after everything."

Amalia averted her eyes. "I had a nightmare. I saw him, and he told me it was my fault…that he'd never forgive me." Her voice broke, eyes flooding with tears.

I held her quivering face. "Maybe you're the one who has to forgive herself. Gio loved you." She shook her head and sobbed, gripping my shirt like a lifeline. "And he knew how much you loved him. None of it was your fault."

"No!" she shouted. "I said awful things to him, Kai. Those were the last memories he had of me…and I don't know how to live with that. It hurts too much."

My heart sank, tears brimming in my eyes, distorting the face of the woman I loved more than anything.

"Amalia, let me help you. Please."

"I went to our spot on the hill," she whispered, lifting her broken gaze. "You know why? Because I wanted to be with him and Tony."

The air was knocked from my lungs, and I gripped her as if she were still on that hilltop, ready to end her life, and with her, the brightest source of light in mine. "No, baby…no."

She sobbed against me, her pain seeping through the walls of my chest. I would have given anything to switch places and take away her suffering.

"But I'll never see him. Gio is somewhere good, somewhere I don't deserve. And that kills me."

"Amalia, look at me."

"No, no…I want to be alone."

"And I need you to listen." I cupped her cheeks, the rain falling harder, slipping past my lips as I spoke. "Remember when I said that death takes a piece of us every time? What you're feeling right now is a gaping hole, and I know it feels like you have nothing left."

"I don't," she cried, squeezing her eyes closed.

"That's where you're wrong." My voice broke as I lifted her chin. "You have me. Let me fill all the hollow pieces of your soul, baby. I'd give you my very last breath if I could. But I need you to stay…or take me with you." Amalia cried harder and buried her face into my chest. "I love you."

As she shuddered in my arms, terror filled my heart at the thought that my love wouldn't be enough. But like the vows I'd made the day she became my wife, I would remain by her side, even in death.

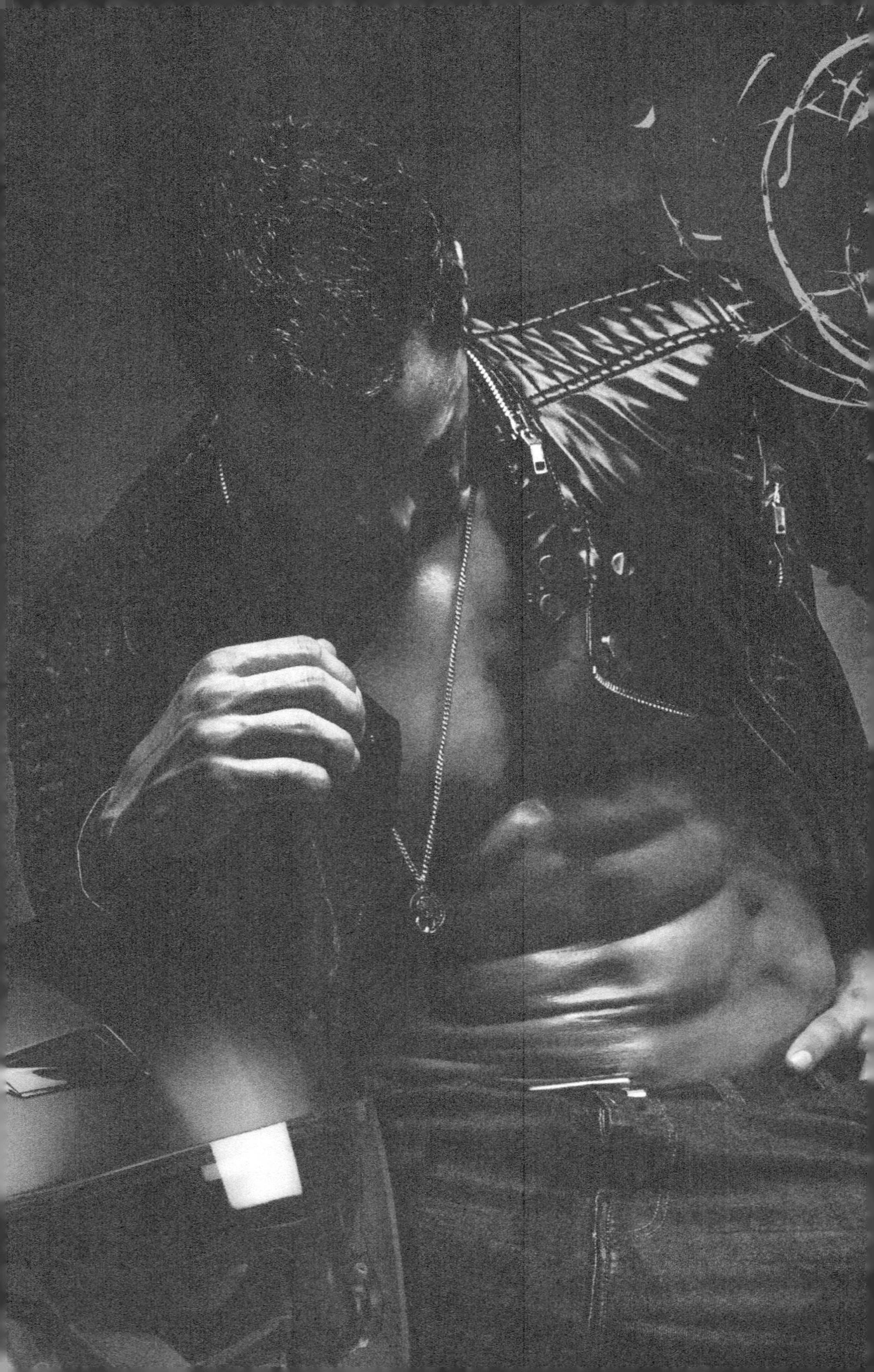

Chapter 40
Kai

One Month Later

"IT'S beautiful."

I circled my arms around her waist and kissed her neck.

"I think so, too," she said, placing her palette on the table and twisting around. "I have something else to show you."

"Yeah?" The way her bare breasts pressed against my chest made it hard for me to concentrate on anything she was saying. The times I'd come into her studio and left without bending her over a table or getting on my knees were very few and far between. The fact she was always naked made for easier access which led to many fun times and filthy fucking sex.

"You've been asking what I've been working on the times I've locked you out," she said, idly pretending to play with a button on my shirt. "Well, I'm finally satisfied with how it turned out. So, close your eyes."

Trusting her completely, I didn't hesitate to do what she asked. This secret project of hers was important, and that was all that mattered to me. As she slipped away, I tugged her back at the last second by her throat and kissed her. The little moan she released inside my mouth had my cock at full attention.

"Hold that thought," she whispered over my lips while also giving my dick a squeeze.

I heard her hurried footsteps moving to a far corner of the studio, then back at a slower pace now that her hands were occupied. There was more rustling, and things shifted and slid around until I almost couldn't take the waiting any longer.

"Don't you dare peek," she said, as if reading my thoughts, though I was sure the way I was tapping my thighs gave away my impatience. A grueling moment later, I finally heard, "Okay, open them!"

Blinking several times, I opened my eyes to a large canvas. Amalia was a brilliant artist, and the painting was stunning, as strange as it was seeing a portrait of my face staring back at me. She perfectly captured every detail, from the small scar below my left eyebrow to the stubble and facial hair.

"If I say it's beautiful, does that make me conceited?"

She laughed and threw her arms around me, rising to her toes and beckoning for a kiss. "You have every right to be."

I dipped my head, forehead resting on hers. "I would have posed for you. All you had to do was ask."

Laughing, she slowly traced my lips with her finger. "It wasn't necessary"—kiss—"because I've memorized"—kiss—"every piece of you, Kai." Tears had gathered in her lashes as her eyes locked onto mine. "I love you."

I thought I'd waited two months to hear her say those words, but as they fell from her lips and melted into my soul, filling every crevice, I realized I had waited my entire life for her.

Framing her face, I went in for another kiss, but she pulled away.

"What's wrong? That's not exactly the way I expected this moment to go."

She reached for some documents on the table I hadn't noticed. I assumed she'd placed them there while my eyes had been closed.

"I've thought a lot about this, and it just feels like the perfect time."

The black words against the stark white paper drew my immediate attention, sending cold chills through my body.

DECLARATION FOR DIVORCE DECREE

"Divorce?"

She nodded with a heavy breath. "Kai, I know what this looks like—"

"But you just said…" Amalia reached for my hand, but I stepped back as painful waves of rejection, hurt, and betrayal washed over me. "I don't understand."

"I married you for all the wrong reasons. My vows were disingenuous, and the sole purpose of our union was to retain this property, my family's name, and inheritance. Our love was built on a lie." She lifted her arms behind my neck once more, grounding me with her touch. "Kai, I don't care about any of those things anymore. None of it matters." When she kissed me, I instinctively closed my eyes and felt her smile against my lips. "It's you. It's always been you, even when I didn't know it. And I want to do things right. I love you. Look at me, baby."

I understood what she was saying, but I disagreed.

"No." I tore the document in half, then ripped it again for good measure.

"Kai!"

I hugged her fiercely. "What happened back there doesn't define who we are or what we mean to each other. Because without it, I wouldn't be here. I would have been condemned to walk the rest of my life, missing my other half. So I regret none of it. I don't want to live a single day in a world where you're not my wife."

Sliding my hands down her waist, I lifted her into my arms. "I want it all with you, *mi reina*. The dog, the house, the goddamn picket fence, and babies—lots of fucking babies."

"We're going to need to compromise on that last one," she said with a hearty laugh.

I kissed her slowly, drawing her tongue into my mouth and squeezing her body against mine.

"Kai," she whispered between kisses, "I'm going to ruin your shirt."

"Fuck, baby, do it, because there are two things I love about you."

"Mm, and what's that?"

"Your heart and your wet pussy."

Her smile was wide against my mouth, and I gripped her ass tighter, pushing her closer to me and reveling in the heat of her sweet little cunt.

"Let's go somewhere," she pleaded, fingers tugging at my hair.

"The only thing I want right now is to bury my face or my cock inside you."

Yanking harder, she pulled my mouth away from hers. "Well, then follow me."

Amalia shoved out of my arms and wriggled to the floor. I gazed at her beautiful curves and thought myself the luckiest son of a bitch.

"Where are we going?"

A sheer floral robe covered her body, though it did nothing to hide all the parts of her I needed to get my hands on and thus only made the ache in my pants stronger.

"Catch me."

And with those words, she took off through the doors and into the open air. Amalia was barefoot, but that didn't stop her from gunning it through the courtyard, her robe waving behind her as she ran.

"If any grounds crew sees you, just know their blood will be on your hands."

She looked back and laughed. "The blood on my hands is pretty thick already, Cain. What's a little more?"

"Amalia, wait!"

We crossed through an interior front gate that led into the driveway, and I caught her by the waist and spun her in the air, then carried her bridal style to where my bike was parked and set her down on the seat.

"Now, where's my prize?"

"Let me take you, but we have to hurry." She threw one leg over the side of the bike and revved the engine. "Hop on," she said.

"Sunset?" I asked, doing as I was told. My hands settled on her bare waist, and God, it took everything in me not to push her body forward and fuck her right there.

She blazed down the trail behind the estate, and I held her tighter with every burst of acceleration.

"Easy, vicious. No helmets." Without our link, I had to get close to her ear when I spoke. "Remember when I said that if you messed my seat, I'd make you clean it?"

Amalia nodded as I snaked my hand between her legs. "Don't kill us."

"I'll kill you if you don't start touching me."

I laughed and nipped at her ear as my fingers slid across her wet seam. "My wife, always so goddamn wet for me." The bike slightly jerked when I strummed her clit. "Focus, baby."

"Easy for you to say," she moaned, as I drew tight circles and tweaked a nipple between my fingers.

The usually smooth ride to the lake became jerky the harder I stroked. Her knuckles blanched against the handles, and soft moans fled her lips as she neared release.

"You think you can come and keep this bike steady?"

"Fuck…Kai, don't stop."

"Beg me."

"I hate you."

I chuckled into her ear, and she shattered, crying out my name.

"I fucking love you."

"I love you, too," she said between ragged breaths.

We reached the lake moments later, and Amalia turned in her seat and climbed over my lap.

"What do you think about selling this place?"

My cock was aching to break out of these goddamn pants, but I humored her. She was glowing and still coming down from an orgasm. How could I not?

"It's up to you. This is your home."

"There's nothing left for me here. My mother refuses to visit after Gio. Things with my girls just haven't been the same, you know that. And I want to start fresh—somewhere, anywhere but here. For him, for me." She touched my face and gifted me the sweetest smile. "For us."

There wasn't a damn thing I wouldn't do for this woman. My greatest joy in life was the privilege of waking up by her side. Even on the bad days, when her tears were relentless and her heart would shatter all over again, I was thankful to love her, pick up the pieces, and be there when she needed me most.

Isabel and Antonio loved their daughter, but were equally navigating their own grief and guilt over the circumstances surrounding Gio's death.

"I'll follow you anywhere. You're home for me."

"I'm about to sit on your cock, so relax with the sappy shit, okay?" She laughed, kissing the tip of my nose.

I gripped her hips, grinding her over my erection. "You're lucky I love you."

"I know. And that's why I have a surprise for you."

"I'm listening," I said, shoveling my pants down, relieved that I had decided to wear sweatpants.

"I bought another art studio."

"That's great." I kissed down the column of her neck.

"In downtown Philly."

Freezing mid-kiss, I peered up and she was beaming. "You what?"

"Life is short and unpredictable, Kai. I don't want you to have regrets like I do. I know you miss your brother and want to see your niece grow up. Milly misses her, too. And our kid will need someone to play with."

"What did you just say?" She must have seen the shock on my face or felt how loudly my heart thundered in my chest where she pressed her hand.

"I'm not pregnant, Kai. But I want to be someday."

"Fuck, yes. Let's do it!"

"Which one? Moving or having a baby?"

"All of it."

"Good, because I might have found a buyer."

"You've done all this *and* handed me divorce papers on the same day."

"Let me sit on your cock, and I'll tell you all about it."

I didn't waste time with a reply and gripped her hips, positioning myself at her wet entrance.

"On second thought, *mi reina*, just shut up and let me fuck you."

Amalia's laugh quieted as she let herself fall, sinking over me until I bottomed out, with a groan into her shoulder. Her feet couldn't touch the ground, which left her without leverage to bounce on my cock the way only she knew how, so I guided her hips, setting the rhythm.

It didn't matter where we laid down roots or what crazy curveball life threw our way. As long as she was my wife, I was home.

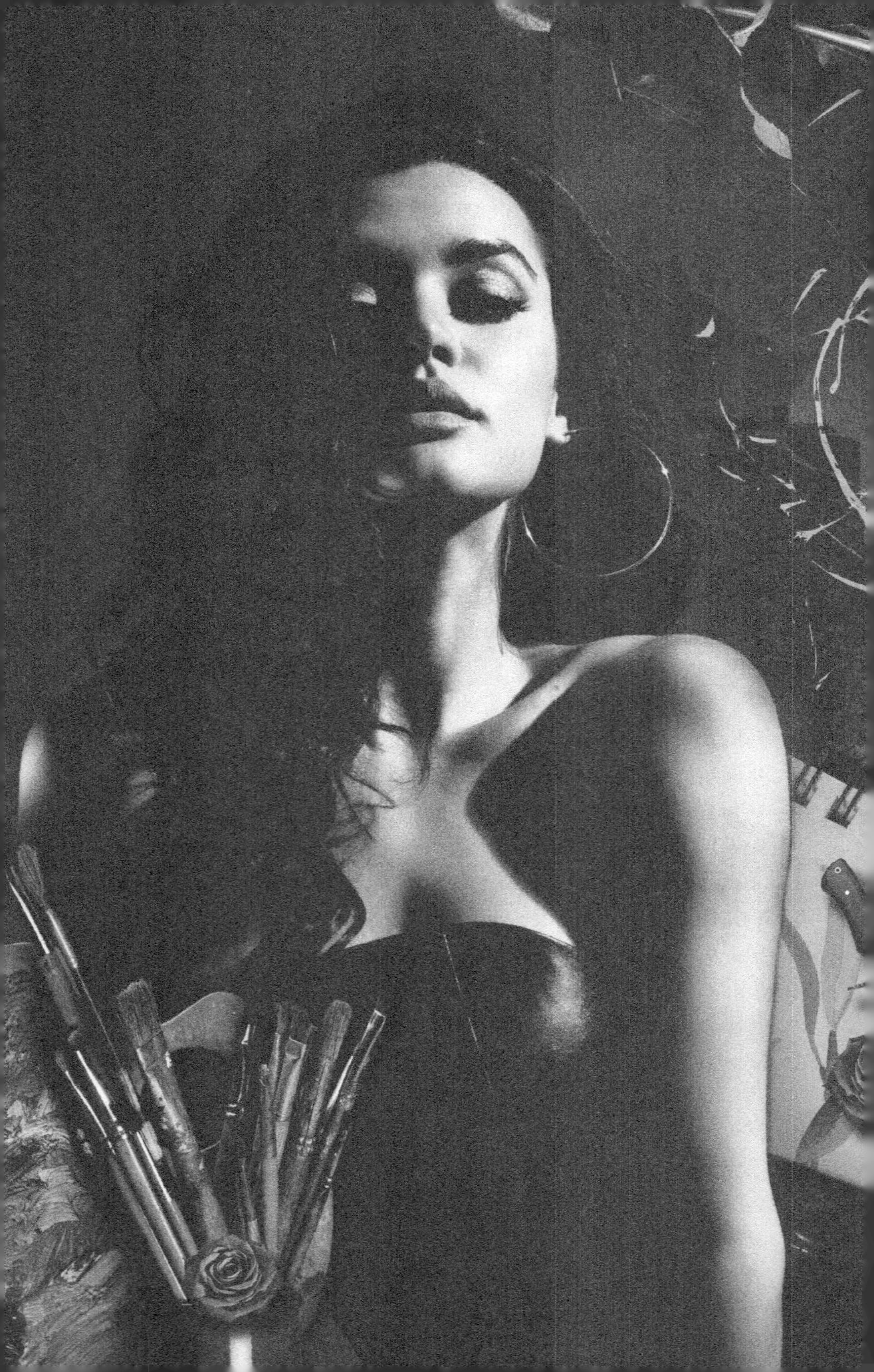

Epilogue
Amalia

Miami, FL

SUNSET would always hold a special place in my heart and memories. While nothing rivaled that hilltop and the views of the city below against the horizon, the world from this high-rise overlooking the marina was undoubtedly a close second.

I clung to the railing, my eyes shut tight, as the warm, salty city air caressed my face, carrying the bittersweet memories of Villa Dorada. The pain that accompanied those thoughts was soothed, if only for a moment, by the gentle touch of the wind. A sense of peace washed over me, signaling the end of a chapter in my life. The documents were signed, and Villa Dorada, with all its ghosts, belonged to someone else. In the six months since Gio's death and my severed ties with what was left of my girls, I'd experienced a whirlwind of emotions—healing, crying, and falling madly in love every single day.

Kai had this way of reading me, feeling my energy, and always being there when I needed him. As if I'd called out to him in my thoughts, there he was, with strong arms around me. I had always taken care of myself, but I had never felt so protected and loved in his embrace.

I looked up at his handsome face, and he leaned to kiss me.

"Ready to get back to our room?" he asked, holding me tighter.

"Yeah. We should get some rest. We've been traveling all day, and I still want to catch the sunrise and stick my feet in the sand before we head out."

"Sounds like a plan."

The moment the elevator doors closed, I was on him, arching up on the tips of my toes as he reached down and lifted me. I'd never get enough of being in his arms.

"I'm not that tired," I whispered, kissing along his jaw.

"I wasn't either, but I needed an excuse to get you back in our room as soon as possible."

I chuckled against the skin of his neck, inhaling his crisp, masculine scent, which made me want to taste him.

"No sense in beating around the bush, Cain. Take what you want when you want because you know I'm yours."

He used his thumb to caress the bridge of my nose and over my eyebrow. "Sometimes, even now, I wonder what I did right in this life to deserve you."

"You've done many things right, baby," I said, kissing his lips. "That thing you did with your tongue this morning. Perfect." He laughed. "The way you eat is unrivaled."

"I did kill that omelet this morning pretty fast, didn't I?"

I swatted him and joined his laughter. "Yeah, you sure did."

The metal doors slid open, and an older couple stood at the entrance, watching us with a mixture of surprise and unease. I kissed Kai one more time before he set me down, intertwined his fingers through mine, and led me out of the elevator.

As I passed the woman, I noticed her flushed cheeks but was a little taken aback by her smile of approval and the slight nod she offered as I walked by. I sent a wink her way and wished her a night of fun in my thoughts because everyone deserved explosive orgasms.

The moment the door closed, Kai lifted me over his shoulder and tossed me on the bed. I squealed as I fell and bounced twice on the soft mattress. Hauling me by my ankle toward the edge of the bed, he slid off my heels, kissing the tops of my feet.

"I always knew I'd have you kissing my feet someday," I said with a laugh.

"Baby, there isn't a place on your body I wouldn't taste or haven't tasted."

I rose to my knees and unbuttoned his shirt before shoving it off his shoulders and kissing his chest. "I love you, Kai," I whispered, ghosting my lips over the hard planes of his abdomen.

"I love you, *mi reina*." Kai reached for his holster, but I brought a hand over his and his gun.

He looked down at me curiously, and I grinned and ran my tongue up his rippled abs. Kai was so damn sexy, so delicious. I would eat off this man… And I had.

"What are you doing?" he asked, tilting my chin.

"You trust me?"

"Of course."

"Good," I said. Sliding the weapon from its holster, I engaged the safety and lay back on the bed. "Take off my thong, Kai."

Kai eyed me for a beat before groaning and biting his lip as he reached for the straps of my panties and slid them down my legs. Our eyes connected, and I dropped my thighs open.

"When we first met, if there was one thing I hated about you, it was how fucking wet you always made me." That put a cheeky smile on his face.

"Mmm," he groaned, opening me up wider, his eyes hungry. I knew that look so well. Kai would devour my pussy until I cried, and I loved every second of feeling on the verge of a sweet, sweet death by orgasm.

"If it's any consolation, you had me walking around with a goddamn hard-on every day."

"I noticed," I said, bringing the gun close to my lips, causing his eye to twitch slightly until I ran my tongue up the titanium barrel. "Thought we'd have a little fun."

"What did you…have in mind?" Kai knelt on the bed in front of me, hands smoothing up my inner thigh.

"Oh, you know…" I slid the barrel down the wet seam of my pussy, and watched as Kai's eyes widened.

"Oh, fuck, vicious."

He wrapped his hand over mine and guided my movements as the weapon slid against my clit over and over. My head fell back onto the mattress as pleasure swelled, and my soft moans filled the room.

"My wife getting fucked by my gun is one the sexiest things I've ever seen." He tugged the straps of my dress down and covered my nipple with his mouth, pushing me closer to release. "That's my fucking girl. Come for me, baby."

His words were all I needed to fall over the edge as I bit his shoulder and scraped my nails along the back of his neck. My poor husband sported new scars more often than not, but he never complained. He proudly wore my marks because he knew every part of him was mine.

"Fuck, Kai," I muttered, still trying to catch my breath.

"My turn." He took the weapon from my trembling hands and licked my cum off the barrel before tossing it on the floor and flipping me over. His teeth nipped at the back of my thigh, making me jolt. "Easy, vicious. Bring that ass up."

I looked over my shoulder and watched as he stroked his cock, his eyes so intent on my pussy, I nearly came at the sight. Of feeling so wanted and so beautiful.

"I stopped my pills yesterday." His smoky gaze snapped up to mine. "It doesn't mean that—"

Before I could finish my sentence, Kai's cock stretched me and pushed inside so deep it was almost painful. My mouth parted as he pulled out, slamming back into me before I could take a breath and sending my body forward. I gripped the sheets as he fucked me hard and fast.

"The vision of you pregnant with my child— Fuck, I love you," he growled into my ear, sweeping kisses down my back.

"*Más*," I begged, as his strokes slowed to an agonizing pace, driving me crazy. I reached down and found my swollen clit and cried out at the contact.

Kai tugged me back onto his lap, wrapping one hand around my throat, and with the other, he rolled my nipple between his fingers as I bounced on his cock.

"Listen to that, how goddamn wet you are. I bet you're dripping down my balls."

I raised a hand and tangled my fingers into his hair as he increased his rhythm. I was so close. My thighs trembled with every stroke against my clit. The tighter my pussy squeezed his cock, the tighter his hold around my throat.

"I want you to come all over my dick, and then I need you to clean me up."

Biting my lip, I let my head fall on his shoulder as the high from the lack of blood flow started to take over. "Can you do that, wife?" I gave my best attempt at a nod. "Good girl."

Kai knew I wasn't a fan of being called a fucking good girl. I'd make him pay for that.

Just as I was nearing passing out, he loosened his grip on my throat and reached down to guide the fingers on my clit, and it was all it took to break me. I cried out his name and clenched his cock as the waves of my orgasm rolled through my body.

While still panting for air, I turned around and took him into my mouth. He was right, my cum was all over his thighs and coating his balls, and I made damn sure to clean him up thoroughly.

"Oh, shit," he groaned, hands in my hair as I worked him deeper until tears filled my eyes.

Kai's cock swelled in my throat, and his body tensed. I knew he was close, but our baby-making sex could wait. I craved to taste him, working his cock until hot cum slid down my throat. His loud grunts and how he began to crumple filled me with pride…but he still owed me for that good girl slip.

"Shit…Amalia." The strain in his voice caused a chuckle to bubble up and vibrate against his already sensitive cock, causing him to fall back on his calves and grip my hair tighter. But I didn't let up. I sucked him down until he was writhing above me, my name like the sweetest song on his lips.

I looked up at his contorted features and popped his dick out of my mouth, satisfied I could make him squirm.

"That's a good boy," I said with a laugh.

"You're evil." He tugged me into his arms and fell back, taking me with him. "But so goddamn sexy."

I kissed his chest, then laid my head over his heart, closed my eyes, and let the rhythm soothe me. "You want to catch the sunrise on the beach?"

"Yes," I said, flicking my thumb over his nipple just to see it pebble. "Leni said Santino will meet us around 10 a.m."

Silas and Leni gifted us a private charter on one of Santino Leone's yachts and a two-week Mediterranean honeymoon. We told them it wasn't necessary, but Leni and I had gotten closer over the last several months, and she'd insisted. I knew it was her way of trying to ease my grief over Gio's loss. Even though Kai and I hadn't taken a honeymoon because of the tragic events following our wedding, I was surprisingly okay with that. Not only was every day a honeymoon next to this man who stole my heart, but I hadn't been ready until now.

We'd settled into our new home just fifteen minutes from Derek and Eva, which was convenient for Milly to visit as often as she wanted. She'd really taken to Eva and the baby. My parents were also set to arrive in a few days to keep her company as we were on better terms these days. We'd all mourned the loss of Gio in our own ways but were slowly coming back together as a family, and that was all I could hope for.

Kai's love for me was beautiful and unwavering. I knew that, and I believed him when he said he was happy by my side. But I also knew that reuniting with his brother and being an uncle was also a big source of his happiness. The way his eyes lit up with Vali melted my heart.

One day, I'd make him a father.

"I haven't seen Santino since I was in Greece, back when Leni lost her dad. But he's a good friend to them."

I sat up and straddled his abdomen, bracing myself since I was still slightly sensitive and slick with cum.

"I looked him up. He owns that gentlemen's club down by the marina. Illusion." Kai nodded, and I gauged his expression. "You want to take a stroll inside? Check out the place?"

Kai gripped the back of my neck, and he crushed me to his lips. "Not in the slightest." He kissed me. "You're it for me, Amalia. Forever. My vicious queen."

I laughed over his lips. "Good, because this was the perfect position to slit your throat, depending on your answer."

He barked a laugh, kissing me again. Softer this time.

"Talk to me?"

We grew quiet as the weight of his question settled over me. It was his way of keeping communication open, of letting me know he'd always be there for me when I needed him. The nightmares followed me to Philly, though they weren't as frequent. I would never get over my brother's murder and the image of him on that cold floor—It was one I wanted more than anything to purge.

"I'm safe, baby."

He didn't press, and I was thankful.

"Ready for tomorrow?" he asked after several moments of a soothing silence.

I reached for his hand and threaded my fingers through his, my eyes falling on the pale band of skin where his Ares ring had once been. Two weeks ago, Kai had walked through the door of our home, covered in blood and wounds. He paid his debt to The Six. Much like he'd done that day of Rocco's death, I took care of him, helped clean him up, and didn't ask questions because I knew he'd come to me when he was ready.

"Am I ready to spend the rest of my life with you? Absolutely."

Kai chuckled and held my hips, lifting me over his hard cock. "Again?" I asked, letting my body slide over him.

"I'll never get enough."

Kai raced down the highway on the red and black Ducati Superleggera he rented. Gloria was back in Philly. The itch to ride had gotten the best of him, and there we were, weaving in and out of traffic and soaking up the adrenaline. I held him tightly, his hand over mine, as we stopped at a red light.

"The marina is just two blocks from here," he said through the speaker of our helmets.

"So you're telling me I have time?"

Kai took off again. "Time for what?"

I said nothing and slid my hand over his thigh, and he tensed under my touch.

"Relax, baby. Let me make you feel good."

"Amalia—*fuck*..." he growled as I stroked him.

"My name sounds sexy on your lips when I have your cock in my hand."

"We're going to crash."

I chuckled and squeezed his shaft, causing him to jerk the bike.

"Then you better keep steady."

"I would if you didn't have my dick in your hand, and if I knew that once we got to where we're going, I could bend you over this goddamn bike and fuck you till you cry."

"You're no fun," I said, retreating my hand.

"Wait, wait, don't stop."

We shared a laugh and pulled into Santino's marina a few minutes later. Club Illusion was an impressive two-story building with blacked-out windows and sleek white concrete.

I shook out my hair and climbed off the bike as Kai followed. He signaled toward the entrance, where a well-dressed man was standing. He was handsome, and the tattoos on his hands, especially the ones branching out from beneath the neckline of his designer suit, screamed Italian mafia.

Kai took my hand and introduced me to Santino.

"There's about an hour left before The Mirage leaves port. Please, enjoy drinks and lunch on the beach or inside," he offered warmly.

"We'll soak in some sun and sand," I replied, and Kai nodded in agreement.

"Perfect. There's a private cabana just down the path. Look over the menu, and I'll have someone bring down your drinks."

The heat of the Miami sun was overwhelming, but the large, mounted fans and a slight mist made the experience relaxing.

"Kai, I need more sunblock." I held my hair up as he rubbed the lotion onto my shoulders. We heard footsteps approach, and my mouth watered with a desperate need to quench my thirst, even if it was with some fruity drink.

"Hey," a soft, feminine voice greeted from behind us. "I'm sorry it took so long. I'm filling in for…" Glass shattered against the cabana's wooden floorboards, and I whipped around, immediately confused by the stare-down and shocked expressions between Kai and the woman who'd brought us our drinks. She was beautiful. Long curly hair and the most intriguing eyes I'd ever seen. One brown, one blue. But something was wrong.

I touched Kai's arm, and the woman took off running the moment he spoke.

"Athena…"

Kai stood, intent on chasing after her, but I needed answers. Who was she? And more importantly, who was she to him?

"You know her?"

"She's my sister."

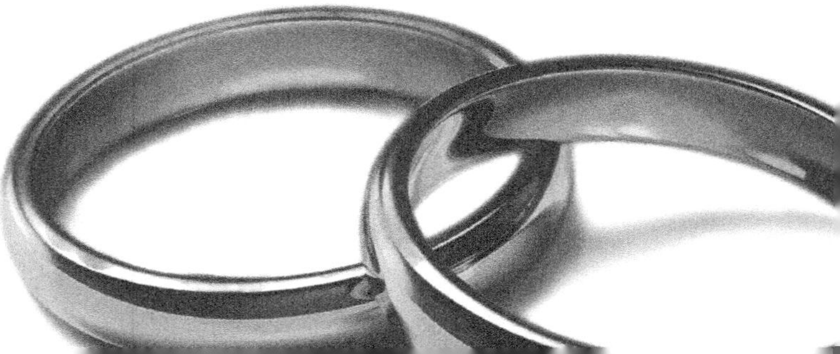

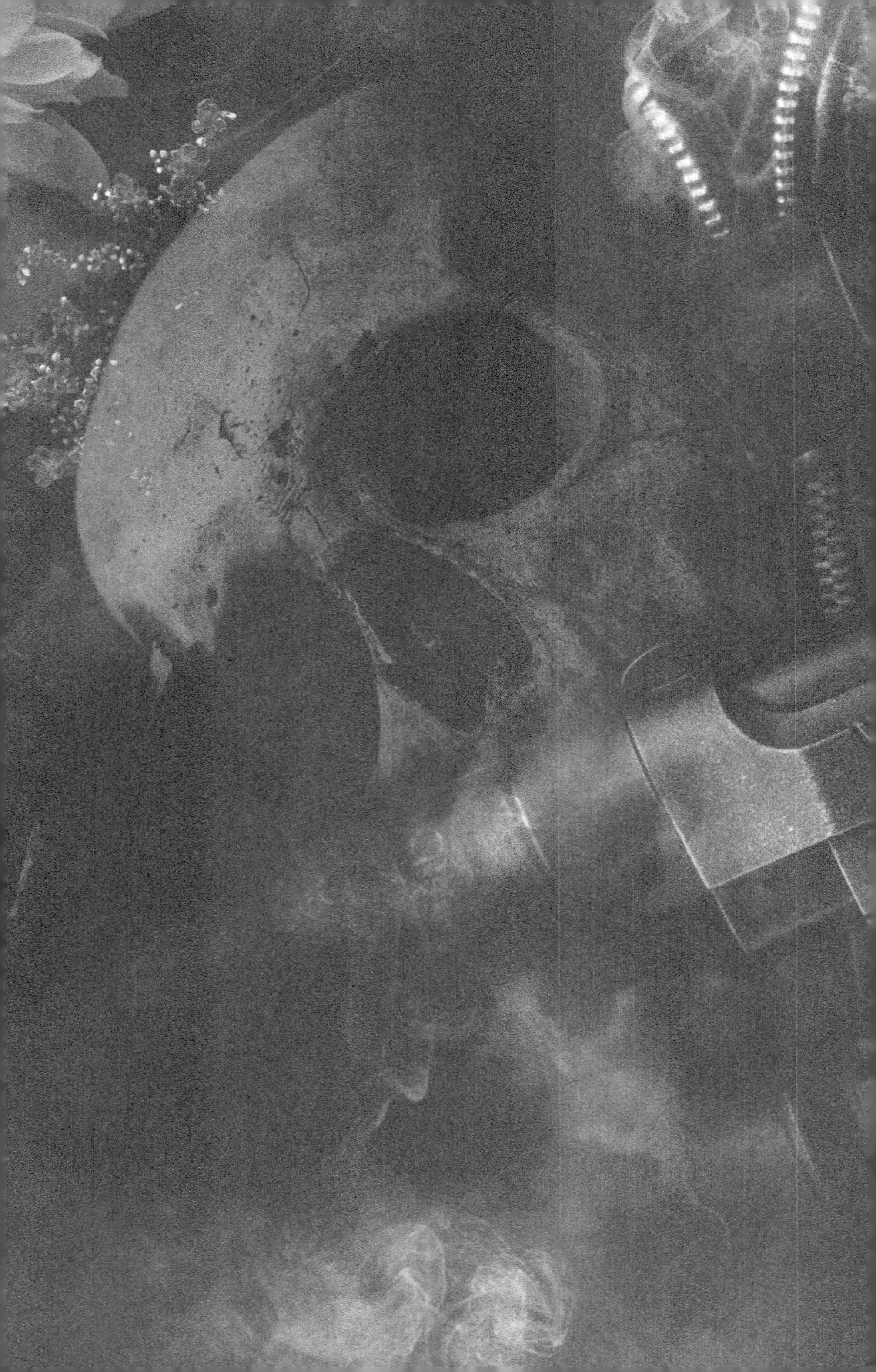

LIBERATED BY SIN
Book 4, the final installment of the Severed Signet series, is available for pre-order.
Fall 2024
https://mybook.to/6TiQmJ
I lived in secrecy for years, beneath the cover of shadows and red lights.

OTHER WORKS INCLUDE:

MIKHAIL PETROV: DARK MAFIA ROMANCE
Available for pre-order
Release date May 28, 2024
https://mybook.to/9wkJLU5
He's the heir to an empire. The world at his feet. Yet she's the one thing he can't have.

This novella is part of The Petrov Family anthology:
Nikolai Petrov by M.A. Cobb
Viktor by Darcy Embers
Lev Petrov by Harper-Lee Rose
Aleksei Petrov by M.L. Hargy
Roman by Luna Mason

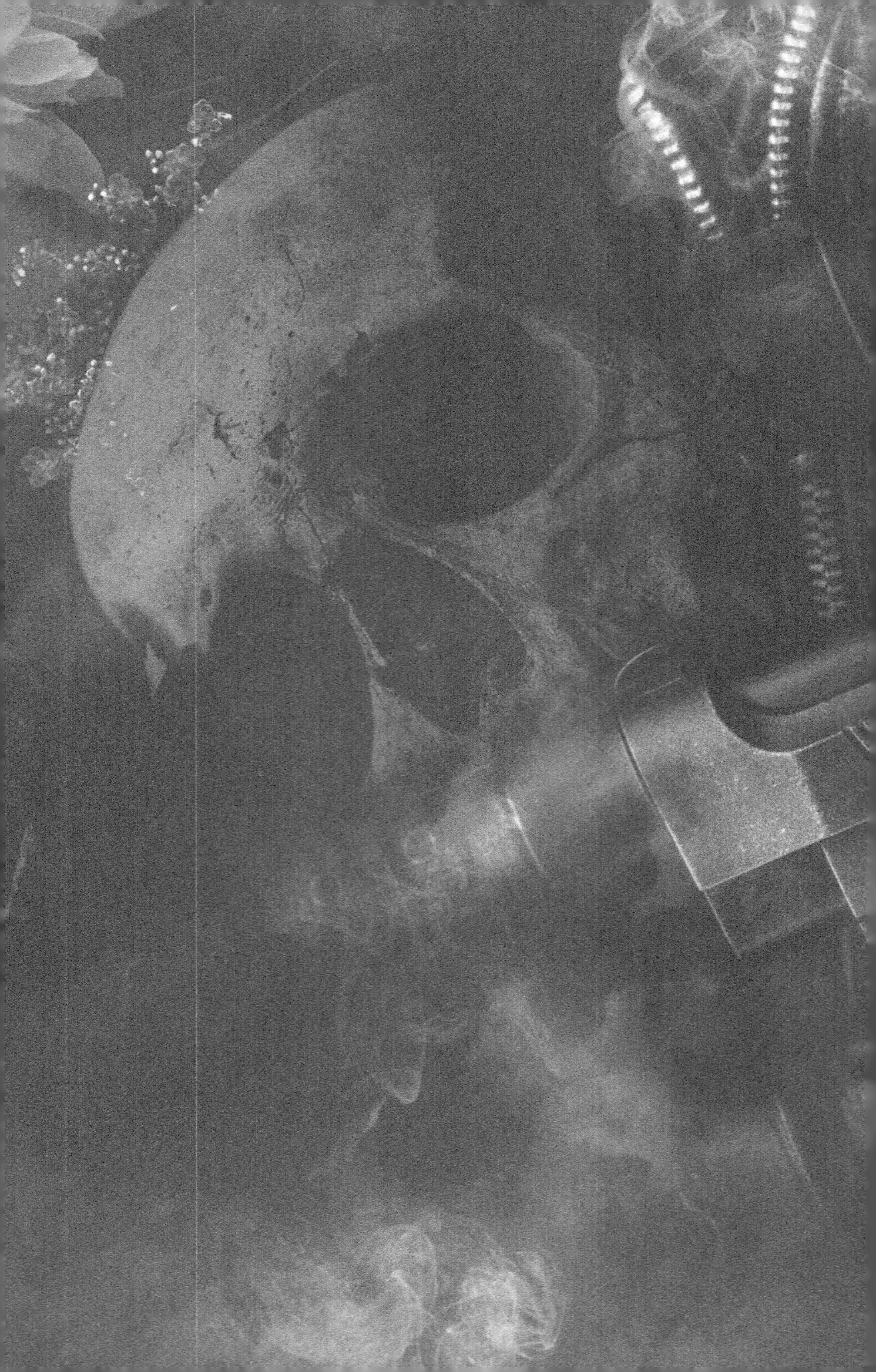

About The Author

ELLE MALDONADO

writes dark, contemporary romance. She lives in the U.S. with her husband and three kids and enjoys spending time with family, watching movies, and reading.

Subscribe to her newsletter for all upcoming releases, sneak peeks, giveaways, teasers, and extra scenes.
https://tr.ee/t5xCxlh6hc

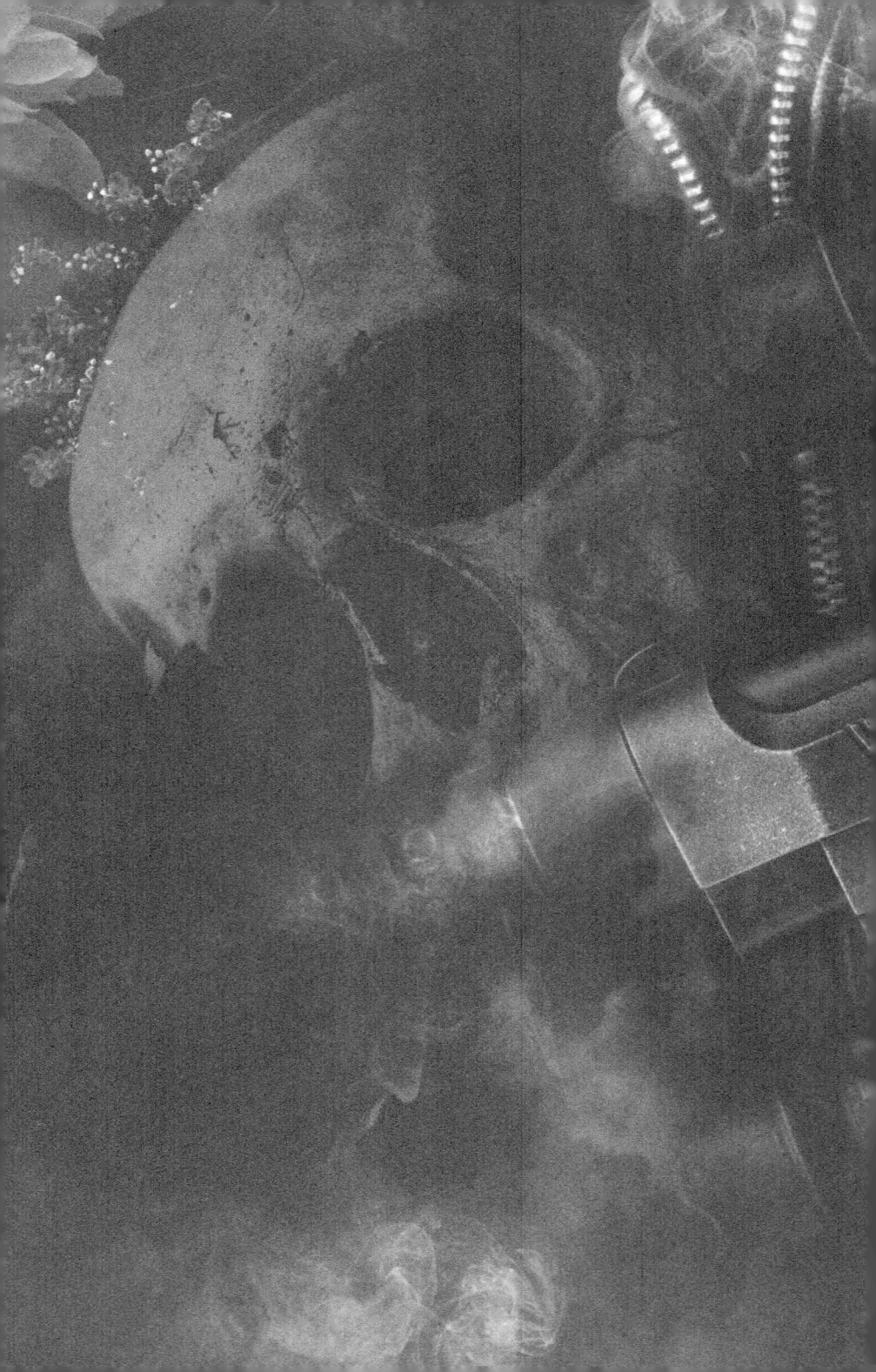

Acknowledgments

I almost can't believe this is my third book! Again, my husband and biggest supporter—I love you! Thank you for keeping the house in order and caring for our family while I was in my writing cave. And, of course, thank you for tackling those laundry baskets. You're the best.

To the beautiful friends I've made on this journey. Jan, Lucy, Melissa, I honestly don't know I would have made it this far without your support, our chats, and laughs. I am so incredibly thankful for you all and cannot wait to meet you!

Mackenzie, as always, thank you for helping shape this story and for your words of encouragement!

Isis, thank you for letting me slide into your messages and bother you with my questions. I hope you spotted those little details in this story!

Words will never be enough to express my gratitude to everyone who has given my series a chance and for all your love and support. Thank you from the bottom of my heart.

Printed in Great Britain
by Amazon